Isabelle Tchang

In My Town

C S FLINT

To Stuart with all
my thanks for his
previous help.

Claudette Flint

June 2019

To Carl, Kristian, Marianne and Louisa

Acknowledgements

I would like to thank David Barnes and Stuart Pooley for their help in solving some mysteries of the English grammar, Carl, my husband for his immense patience with my limited understanding of IT and, finally Philippe Bonnet and Alain Kermarrec for their photos for the covers.

" When you are not loved, you feel miserable.
When you don't love you die."

Philippe Val,
former director of the French magazine
Charlie Hebdo

ISABELLE TCHANG IN MY TOWN

Mum called me Sophie because the Countess of Segur's 'Sophie's Misfortunes' was the only book she read in her life. I was born on the French Riviera in 1944, me too, I landed in June. One of the most terrible years of the century, when a civilized country, starved by other civilized countries, became insane and turned into a serial killer. Some gathered to confront it; the others, terrified, took the side of the killers. I was lucky, Dad was a war hero and Mum, the hero's wife. They did everything to spare me but I was deprived of the luxuries.

1 Primary School

The cicadas are dead, it's my first day at school but I'm still wearing my summer clothes under my smock. We don't say 'primary school' yet, we call it the 'Community School'. As usual in our region, autumn is late. Some swallows have stayed behind and watermelons and nectarines are still on the market.

Mum is sad and worried, but I am delighted and dad can't stop laughing at my school grey overall, identical to the Armenian grocer's. Because of the war my parents were not sure I would have a place. This war killed so many people that we were short of men and short of teachers and the post war baby boom has filled the classrooms. My parents keep talking about it and sometimes in low voices. Thank God, dad is a War Invalid so that I too enjoy priority over other people.

We were thirty-eight in my class and the teacher applied a basic teaching technique. We all learn to read and write in nine months thanks to her strict discipline. We learn our letters on a slate. The teacher has promised that, if we are good, after Christmas we will have an exercise book, a pen with ink and a book like the seniors. Those three things become our obsession. I crave for them, more than for my first cigarette.

After the glorious first year, things start to go wrong. I enter the long dark tunnel of Arithmetic. I have no problem learning by heart about the areas and the perimeters. We know the times tables because that's our Morning Prayers. Then the teacher writes a moral quotation on the board like "Malicious gossip hurts, slander kills". This is the only one I remember.

Mum teaches me division and multiplication every Sunday, after mass. We sit in the sun lounge for just an hour because she has to prepare the lunch. What I never understand is the wording of the maths questions. Neither do my parents.

In the afternoon, while dad is asleep, we attack the decimals. On Saturdays, when I go to the Synagogue with my father to meet my grandparents, I play upstairs where the women and children gather while the men are praying downstairs.

*

Two years later, repeating my class brings me a brand-new feeling: despair.

A year will be wasted because I can't cope with fractions. I had no problem with halves or quarters but 'one fifth multiplied by three sixths' is beyond my grasp at the age of eight and a half. I shall have to wait until the lower Sixth to find a teacher who brings some light to bear but it will be too late, I became used to the darkness of Maths.

*

From the back of the class we look at the new girls coming in, younger than us, smiling and enthusiastic. There are six of us who have to repeat our year, mourning for our fellow pupils gone to the glory of the upper class. We feel all the more abandoned because the mistress is now only showing interest in the new ones. Despite putting our hands up to answer her questions -the same ones as last year- she ignores us. After a while we get tired of it, we no longer learn our lessons and boredom sets in.

The cinema becomes the subject of our conversations. We review films: 'The Knight of Castile' with Tyrone Power or the latest from Alan Ladd. My God, how handsome the Americans are! We read comics like Mickey's News that has just come out. Also L'Intrépide and Fillette, exciting and cultural children magazines. We swap pictures of film stars found in chewing-gum packets. A photo of Charlton Heston for one of Martine Carol.

From time to time we catch bits of the mistress's talk: "the subjunctive… the river Loire… La Fontaine… Vercingetorix...". I become dreamy and let my eyes rest on the beautiful mimosa tree of the villa across the road. I lose myself in its dazzling yellow against the blue sky, it's like an hypnotic soft sun.

The other subject of conversation is boys. Their school is attached to ours. No chance to meet them: they have a stonewall and a different timetable. Sometimes, the boldest ones hang around at the gate. I notice a tall, contemptuous-looking blond boy who makes me feel nervous. In order to meet him, I find a possible ally among the girls repeating the year with me. She is eleven, quite old. She is the wine merchant's daughter and a typical dunce but it doesn't affect her at all. She can't care less about school and even the brilliant pupils envy and fear her. Nicole Gasiglia wears New Look skirts with tight-fitting jumpers that highlight her magnificent bosom. She gives me a complex. Even with Mum's bra full of handkerchiefs, I can't rival her size. To cheer me up, Mum says her breasts will flop when mine grow. I keep an eye on them.

4

Gasiglia is relaxed with boys, she impresses the top girl of the class and shows a total indifference towards the teacher. All the girls who are repeating want to be her friend; she is somehow our model. I speak to her about the blond boy and she tells me he's called Eddy and his father is an American living in Washington. I fantasize.

I give her lots of movie stars' photos and liquorice rolls. The next day she informs me that she has talked to him. My heart skips a beat.

"He said he prefers girls with tits."

The bell tolls for the end of the break. To cheer me up, she informs me that I will get them the day I get my period. I don't understand so she refers me to my mother for an explanation. In the evening, Mum is annoyed but she consents to explain the 'thing'.

"Why didn't you tell me before?"

"Can't that brat mind her own business? I thought it was too early to tell you."

"Does it hurt?"

"Not always."

Right, now I have to keep an eye in my knickers as well!

Gasiglia has also a gang in our district but I don't belong to it. They are called the 'boy chasers'. They meet boys behind the children's library in the public garden of the Villa Thiole. Things are going on in the public toilets while I laugh helplessly as I read Tintin with Lambert my best friend.

In the evening while we listen to the radio series, the 'Famille Duraton', I write a hundred times 'I must listen to the teacher and must not behave like a clown.' When Miss is really upset she wants me to write my lines in all the tenses of the subjunctive. Most of the schoolteachers are the starchy product of their training colleges. Today we call them 'psycho-rigid'. A good teacher should be appreciated by the dunce as well as the bright ones. Once in my life I come across this phenomenon. It's the day when our schoolmistress is on sick leave for a varicose vein operation.

The supply teacher looks about twenty-five. Her lesson is a total upheaval. Her teaching technique is revolutionary. She asks the girls repeating their year to come and sit in the front. She says we have things to tell the others! Apart from Gasiglia who carries on reading "Nous-Deux," a photo romance magazine hidden on her lap, we all become very attentive. I never found the school more interesting than this term. Her song, 'Colchiques dans les Prés', becomes an unbearable nostalgic memory. She also tells us that the name of our school, 'Fuon Cauda' means 'warm fountain' in the local dialect.

My remarkable progress lasts only one term. When she leaves, the standard regime resumes to the great relief of the top girls.

A new girl arrives in the middle of the year. N'Guyen is Indo-Chinese (Vietnamese today). We always call each other by our surname in the school of the 'République'.

She is neither pretty nor plain and her Asian eyes are extremely lively with a permanent sparkle in them. Her mother comes to pick her up dressed in white satin trousers and a long blue silk tunic. N'Guyen is one year ahead of us and in one term she becomes top of the class, just like that. Lafarge has to go down to second place despite her parents' intervention. Lafarge is not too popular. We can't understand how she can always be top of the class since we have to explain the rules of a new game to her many times. However, once she has understood, she is better than us at it! She never laughs and is rather lonely. She spends her Thursdays [1] at home and refuses invitations for tea because of her homework!

N'Guyen is the 'Oriental mystery'. We never see her working and yet she's good in every subject. Foresi, always well informed by her parents who run a bakery, tells us she goes out every Thursday. She comes with her grandmother to buy a 'pain au chocolat' then they go to the Promenade des Anglais where N'Guyen loves roller-skating, even in winter.

When the term exams come round, there are only three girls who remain relaxed and unaffected: Gasiglia, N'Guyen and Paoli, the girl who always come bottom of the class. Paoli spends her time looking at her watch and a small calendar [2]. She always wishes us 'Bonne Fête' on the right day. She must know the 365 saints of the calendar by heart. She also informs us at what time the sun has risen and when it will set.

We notice she crosses four days every month but won't tell us why. There are four years between N'Guyen and Paoli.

I get a hundred lines because of N'Guyen but, this time, the punishment is nothing compared to my humiliation. The mistress is explaining the mystery of fractions once more, while the little Indo-Chinese girl is observing the sparrows in the playground. Suddenly

---

[1] Thursday was a day off in French schools
[2] French calendars show the name of a saint for everyday.

Madame Delacourt addresses N'Guyen, "You're not listening, repeat what I've just said," The girl repeats everything, the thirds and the quarters. The mistress feels humiliated. The girl carries on observing the sparrows.

"This girl is too clever," I say to Lambert.
At break time, I ask her how she did it.

"I just played a trick on her, I pretended I was not listening. Delacourt isn't very smart and I'm so bored!"

I can't believe it! The best pupil in the class doesn't like the teacher! My admiration is such that I want to imitate her. I pretend to be distracted but as I am at the back of the class, it takes her time to notice me. Soon my mind is captured by the little fights going on between the sparrows over breadcrumbs. They are sending the dead leaves flying. The bustle informs the pigeons of possible food and they start landing heavily… I cease listening. Miss pounces on me, knowing she could not fail; I can't repeat a word of what she said. A hundred lines. I would like to write "One can't pretend to be intelligent," a hundred times.

I wish I were N'Guyen's friend but she had none, or rather everybody is her friend.

In the schoolyard there are four high chestnut trees and some magnificent stone steps leading to the caretaker' lodge but he never uses this entrance so we turned the steps into theatre seats. I wonder how we manage to transmit our nursery rhymes, children dances and silly plays from generation to generation. We have a repertory of songs, stand-ups, dances and plays. There are two categories of plays: the adventures of a stupid boy called Toto and Charles Perrault's fairy tales. We also have a girl who can sing like Edith Piaf. As for me, I am the star of the farce. For the fairy tales we choose the prettiest girls and the star is Chantal Mercier, the sister of Michele Mercier who will later be a real star in the films series called 'Angelique, Marquise des Anges'. Chantal is neither kind nor wicked, neither intelligent nor stupid, just beautiful. She lets us admire her with a Mona Lisa's smile. Her long golden hair falls in waves down to her waist. It's so rare here, in the South.

We bring fabrics, tulle, hats, old evening dresses and we dress the heroine in an atmosphere of 'premiere'. Sometimes the first and second years leave their hopscotch to come and watch us, but when the teacher approaches, her presence breaks the spell and makes her realise she's not part of our world.

*

When an adult, I would come back to the school to vote and I would find everything a lot smaller than I remembered it. The wall between the boys' and the girls' school has been pulled down, outlandish buildings have replaced all the beautiful villas and concrete has pushed out the palm trees, mimosas and bougainvillea. The warm water fountain is now encased in a cement tomb.

2 Religion

Our church is not at all classical and doesn't really deserve the glorious name of Sainte Jeanne d'Arc. It consists of six giant hard-boiled eggs and a spike that holds them together. The whole thing in reinforced concrete to protect against earthquakes. Inside the spike hang the bells whose gloomy tolling sounds much the same for weddings as for funerals.

As for our synagogue, it is as gloomy as the bells of Sainte Jeanne d'Arc.

I can understand the success of the Catholic Church, which has an innate gift for marketing. In the one, the murals pay homage to the King of the Jews, while the statues of his family and disciples venerate him and the little sunlit stained-glass windows sing of his glory. In the other, there is nothing to see, and one is obliged to pray without distraction or encouragement.

On Tuesdays the school lets us out at eleven to allow us to go to catechism. We have to do three years of catechism before attending Holy Communion. Thursday, our day off, is taken up with the Brownies, the Children of Mary and the Youth Fellowship. I pester Mum to let me join the Guides but she will never give in. The woman from the dairy shop said to her: 'My nephew says the Guides are rather brazen. They go camping with the boys! Can you imagine!' Lambert and I greatly envy girls who go camping with boys. And no, we can't imagine.

In the first year we are taught the Gospel – that is, a Gospel revised and adapted for nine-year-old girls. We don't understand much of it, but we are not expected to understand it, just to learn it by heart. Jesus died to save us. Why, what from? No idea. What is certain is that the school and the catechism test our memory to the limit. Luckily mine is very good.

The second year we go through the Bible as told by Father Barin. He is great, he presents the Bible as a sort of spaghetti western. As soon as the gloomy bell strikes midday, he stops short and leaves us in suspense. 'Next episode on Tuesday!'

We discuss the Bible as if it was a film. Lambert wonders if the sea is really going to open up.

"Course it is, you don't think God's going to let Moses be killed – he's the main hero!"

"That's just it, you never can tell with God!"

"It makes me think of 'Tintin and the Incas.' He gets them to think he can command the sun, and there's an eclipse..."

"Oh yeah, I loved that! By the way, have you finished reading my 'Fillette' album?"

"Yes I have, I'll give it back this afternoon."

In our class, Cherguitte is different from the rest of us because she is the only one who doesn't go to catechism or to the eleven o'clock mass. At the time I am the only one in the class who knows that there is more than one religion, because dad is Jewish and mum Catholic. I go to synagogue on Saturdays and church on Sundays. I prefer the synagogue because the children can play on the first floor (where they'd put the organ in church) while my granny chats with her friends. The mothers and grandmothers show off their children. At the synagogue I always get the impression I am important and pretty. In church I always feel guilty of something. I am always being told to bow my head. Later, the nuns would require us to be docile and submissive as a successful form of communicating.

When I realize the Jews are attracting animosity, I start to feel guilty there as well. I have guilt in stereo!

I sometimes meet Cherguitte and her parents outside the synagogue. They even invite me to tea and we have a good time. One day the girls pester her to ask why she doesn't go to catechism or mass. She tells them she goes to mass at six in the morning. Wanting to get to the truth, I say it's because she goes to the synagogue. A silence falls. Nobody has ever heard that word. The next day, the girls have had an explanation from their parents. As Cherguitte's skin is suntanned by the Algerian sun, we dance round her chanting 'Dirty girl, dirty girl, Cherguitte's such a dirty girl...'. I didn't really understand the girls' reaction, but not wanting to get into trouble, I run with the wolves. Deep inside me, I'm not proud of this. And what's more, N'Guyen refuses to join in, which makes me feel even more uncomfortable. Lambert too does what the others are doing. I look at the mistress to see her reaction, hoping she'd intervene. She watches us impassively.

I stop being friendly with Cherguitte, because I am afraid of the others. I had succeeded in getting closer to N'Guyen, her mother smiled at me. But now they both avoid me. I have the vague feeling that I destroyed two friendships, but I make no effort to understand why.

The next time I go to the synagogue, the Rabbi comes up to me and asks me why Myriam is being bullied. Madame Cherguitte has spoken to him about it. I don't know what to say. Then he says something to me which will take me ten years to understand: 'Do you know that your mother's god is Jewish like your father himself?' I shall never forget these words because they are so puzzling. That's how great misunderstandings are born, live on and destroy.

A few years later, a Whit Sunday as sunny as usual, I go to attend the eleven o'clock mass. There is hardly anybody I know, now, in the church. Anyway, it looks as if there are less and less people at the Sunday masses and more and more tramps sitting on the steps. We start to call them 'homeless'.

Instead of staying down below, I take the narrow stairs up to the organ loft. The organist has known me when I was seven and used to play shop with his grandson. For two years he has taught me music without letting me touch the keyboard, so I have always considered the piano as a sacred instrument reserved for child prodigies like Roberto Benzi.

Monsieur Toesca is over eighty now and his feet have difficulty reaching some of the organ pedals. He gives me a smile and starts to play my favourite tune, Bach's 'Jesus, Joy of Man's Desiring'. The new senior priest has given him permission to play Protestant music. I put my missal on the parapet overlooking the nave. At the far end, high above the altar, rises the magnificent statue of Joan of Arc dressed as a soldier and holding the standard of the Kingdom of France. Her armour is sparkling, softened by the sky blue tunic with its fleur- de-lys pattern. The statue still has a few years to go before being removed and put in the crypt by a new priest. He will consider it inappropriate to have a woman dressed as a man and occupying a place above everything, even the Cross itself. And yet the church is dedicated to her; showing her in her glory was the least they could do.

Mum never misses mass. Even though she is pious, she has rebelled against the Church. She is less afraid of God than of Dad. In fact she is servile with Dad only, probably because he is her breadwinner and her boss. When Pope John XXIII decides that Catholic women married to Jewish men at the register office would no longer be excommunicated, she will turn down the offer: "Too late," she says, "I am not going to those plonkers for confession." She will keep her word without wondering whether it's going to upset God or not.

*

The summer holidays are not far off. We can already smell the perfume of the heavy bunches of wisteria that the school caretaker grows round his door, at the top of the stairs where we sit for our theatre plays.

Because of the heat, the mistress lets us sit outside in the playground, for needlework and drawing lessons. In June, the swifts chase each other with piercing little cries. It is not hot enough yet for the cicadas but the cherries and the nectarines are already on the market. Every society has a rite of passage. In ours, it is First Communion. The catechism exam is the only exam I pass without hard work.

"Who is Jesus Christ?"

"The Son of God."

"Very good, who is his mother?"

"The Holy Virgin."

"Yes and what is she also called?"

"......?"

The priest points toward a statue of the Virgin dressed in white with a blue sash.

"Ah, the Matriculate Conception."

"Immaculate."

"The Immaculate Conception."

Next comes confession, where as usual I have to invent a few minor sins because I can't think of any. Lambert wonders if Gasiglia says what she does with the boys in the lavatories at the library. I wonder if it is a sin. Later there is a little scandal at the parish holiday camp. Gasiglia is said to have 'compromised herself' with the priest. It turns out that nothing has actually happened but the priest goes to another parish.

The night before First Communion I can't get to sleep. I am terribly excited by my long white dress, the long bride-like veil and my first watch. Catholics know how to celebrate, to advertise events and impress people with lavish displays. Everywhere fat candles are blazing, the organ echoes like the thunder in the mountains, our songs to God's Glory rise up under the domes like fireworks and the scent of incense fills my nose with the fragrance from Heaven. A great silence follows, broken by the altar boy frenetically ringing the little bells to announce the Elevation.

Lambert gives me a nudge with her elbow and I follow her gaze. I can see Gasiglia dressed in a sumptuous meringue-like crinoline and an embroidered organdie bonnet in the Marie-Stuart style. She looks like a 19th Century's bride. I glance across at the boys, the most loutish ones resemble idiotic angels, their hair parted on one side, smarmed down with brilliantine and wearing their white knotted armbands instead of wings! I meet up with Lambert again at Vespers.

"If only you could see the two Communion cakes my godmother's had delivered! They're from Vogade Patisserie."

"Is she rich?"

"I think so, she's married to an American."

We stop talking because of the black disapproving look of a nun.

My relationship with God is direct and so to speak, business like. I never use intermediaries, having learnt at the synagogue to deal with Him without going through the saints. So I promise to perform all sort of good deeds in exchange for favours or small services. I have been greatly impressed by the agreement concluded between the Protestant future king of France, Henri IV and God: "If you let me win this battle, I will become a Catholic."

And he did. So one day I ask God for a favour I really want. At first I promise in exchange to convert my father to Christianity. The favour is not granted so I change tactics and promise to convert my mother to Judaism. God remains impassive, I conclude that He can't care less whether we are Jewish or Catholic.

Returning from Vespers, I am rather disappointed. Nearly all the guests and their children have left. The two cakes, a bible made of chocolate and a marzipan garden of roses, have been decimated like the floats at the 'Battle of Flowers' when the tourists are let loose upon them. But the worst thing is an argument between my parents.

I don't know how it started, I just notice my father was lonely during the celebration, as if ostracised. In the evening I hear him shout at Mum that he has picked her out of the gutter. Mum defends herself by saying that at least he knows she was pure but he says he didn't care. My aunt is furious because she has paid for the Communion party and that Mum has had to borrow my dress from my cousin. The cousin, who is poor, boasts about it in front of Dad. What's more, my paternal grandparents didn't come. Later I hear that when I was baptized, the priest asked Dad to wait outside the church because he didn't have the right religion. I am totally confused and to see my Mum crying makes me feel devastated. The merriest day of my life ends the saddest.

The next day I talk to Lambert.

"When they argue he keeps telling her that he married her without a dowry."

"My parents," replies Lambert, "never argue, in fact they never talk to each other. When he comes back from work, my father collapses in front of the radio and after eating he goes to bed."

"What does he do?"

"Railway worker. He has to get up at 5 in the morning."

"Did he marry your Mum without a dowry?"

"I don't know, neither of them has got money."

"When I grow up, I will work and won't marry so that I won't need to beg money from my husband."

"I prefer to marry a very rich man" says Lambert.

The next morning, it is the tradition to bring the teacher sugared almonds and religious images, all dressed in our Communion costume. In the playground we are surrounded by girls of the other classes and we give pictures and sweets to our best friends. Cherguitte keeps her distance and watches us with her large black eyes. I would like to give her some sugared almonds but I dare not in front of the others.

*

I am twenty when I go upstairs, next to the organ pipes, to attend the mass for the last time. Monsieur Toesca is not playing anymore. Last year, he collapsed onto the keyboard and the organ called for help, but it was too late.

Now, the music stops, it's the Elevation of the Host, and silence falls, broken by the frantic shaking of little bells indicating God descending into the church, accompanied by the Holy Spirit. Even so, if it's true, one ought to ... I don't know... I ought to feel something. A sign, an emotion, an impulse or at least a draught! No, there is nothing. If I have been Jewish like Dad, I would understand, but I was baptised and it doesn't have the slightest effect on me. When I think about it, I find that what Jesus says is not stupid, he understands a lot of stuff. As a man he is quite a genius but as a god, he is pretty useless. ... A dog comes into the church, sniffs at the font, and decides it isn't for him and leaves. I leave too. There can't be a God, one would feel his presence.

Philosophy and Bunuel's films will reinforce my decision. At the end of the day, the Philosophy teachers are right. Religion was invented by men to give a meaning to life and death whereas Philosophy is to explain that to be a human is to accept the Absurd and cope with it. I have just understood Nietzsche's little sentence: 'God is dead'. It isn't him who has died, it's my belief in him. To die you have first to live. Maybe it is a risk before sitting my final school exams, but lighting a candle won't make me pass. Amen.

3 Hatred

Poisseau is another 'personality' in the class. Her aggressiveness and nerve frighten us. She is the one who started the attacks on Cherguitte. One day she changes her marks in her report, and the mistress notices. We witness a terrible scene. Poisseau, not wanting to lose face in front of the class, defies her arrogantly, looking straight into her eyes. The mistress, exasperated at making no impression on her, tries to keep her composure in front of us. In the end she grabs Poisseau by the arm and drags her off to see the headmistress. Later, Poisseau has to keep the report pinned to her back and to walk round the schoolyard for the whole day. Everyone is entitled to watch the show: the seniors, the mothers, the boys, and the passers-by. I always have the impression that our punishments look like revenge. I think she's strong, as she doesn't shed a single tear. If it had been me, I would have fainted. Gasiglia says she won't be expelled because her father works in the police. She comes back the next morning as if nothing has happened but with a large bruise on the right hand side of her face. We steal glances at her, and the mistress avoids eye contact.

A few weeks pass. She has given up tormenting Cherguitte because of her lack of reaction, and we are wondering who's going to be her next victim. If Gasiglia enjoys a court, Poisseau runs a gang. Between them there is a balance of power, so they would never confront each other. Lambert says that Poisseau is afraid of Gasiglia's big brother. I think that with a father in the police, she wouldn't be afraid of anyone.

I am popular with my friends as the class clown. I make them laugh in plays and in class. I know that it annoys Poisseau when her gang crowds together on the stairs to see me act the fool. On the other hand, she can't care less about Lafarge's academic successes. For her, Lafarge is a worm but, strangely enough, N'Guyen intimidates her. I could make the whole class laugh at Poisseau's expense, but I never dared. The incident that's going to make me her new prey, however, is independent of my will.

Every year, the mistress makes us recite this poem to celebrate spring:

> Le temps a laissé son manteau
> De vent, de froidure et de pluie
> Et s'est vêtu de broderie
> De soleil luisant, clair et beau.[3]

[The season has cast off its coat / of wind, cold and rain /and dressed up in embroidery / of glistening sunshine, clear and beautiful.]

That weather report is accurate. In the South of France, when May arrives, coats, pullovers and woollen blankets are mothballed for the summer. The first swallows land on our roofs and, in the playground, the chestnut trees burst into flower.

To honour Spring, Madame Delacourt, our teacher, always gives us a drawing homework. We have to draw a wallpaper design for our bedroom. I trace a Donald and a

---

3 Written by Charles d'Orleans when prisoner of the English in 1415 after Agincourt.

Pluto from the Mickey Mouse magazine that has just come out. I show it to Lambert for her approval. She can find nothing better to do than to take the drawing and put it under Poisseau's nose. She looks at it and says with a shrug: 'It's traced.' I deny it. She asks for the opinion of the class. Everyone agrees. I deny it more strongly. So she gets up, comes towards me and hands me a pencil: "Prove it to us." The whole class turn to look at me. I'm hopeless at drawing. I can't even draw hearts of the right shape and size for a Mothers' Day card. No way out. Back to the wall. Panic.

Suddenly I am gripped by one of those fits of anger whose roots lie deep down in some paternal gene and which would save my face several times. Poisseau's smile of anticipated triumph has made me furious. I grab the pencil and the piece of paper and I reproduce the Pluto as accurately as the tracing. A flash of hatred glints blackly through her fringe of greasy hair. The whole class admire my drawing and Lambert keeps repeating to her: 'You see! You see!'

I am too astonished to understand and appreciate the situation. It is the first time in my life that I have drawn anything properly, and I didn't know I could. In the evening I try to do the Pluto again. It takes me half an hour and a lot of rubbing-out, and the result can't be as good.

I should have understood that with Poisseau it is better to lose. She starts by barging into everyone on the stairs and putting paid to one of our performances. The next day she pushes me violently when I am balancing on one foot in the middle of a game of hopscotch. I get up with my knee covered in blood and insult her. She calls her 'girls'. Some of them pull my right arm while the others pull my left. My shoulders start to hurt, I am unable to move and I think of that horrible picture in my History book where Ravaillac is dismembered by four horses pulling. I start to scream, horrified by the pain. A circle has formed but nobody intervenes, not even Lambert who is scared stiff. Hearing my screams, the mistress appears at the classroom door, and the girls let go of me.

I have neither a court nor a gang to protect me. The others avoid me for fear of upsetting Poisseau. Lambert speaks to me only in class. I begin to dread break time. I go and sit on the steps to watch the others perform. I can't join in the performances anymore because Poisseau will immediately sabotage them. And then, one day, she comes and sit on the steps to my right, with her friend Lorenzi on my left. They start pinching me and pulling my hair. I try to get up but they hang on to my smock and hold me back by my arms. While the others force me to stay sitting, Poisseau grips my face with one hand to stop me seeing and breathing. Her other hand tightens round my neck. I can't move anymore and I start to suffocate. Two girls sit on my legs. Unable to get any more air, I feel I am going to die.

Suddenly, I have another fit of anger like the one I had the day of the drawing but much stronger. While trying to free myself, I manage to get one of Poisseau's fingers between my teeth and I bite it with all my strength. I hear her give a scream. Other girls attack me to make me loosen my grip. I try to do this but can't. My jaws are locked tight and my teeth bite harder and harder into her finger. They twist my arms and pull my hair so hard that my skull is burning. The more it hurts, the tighter I bite. It's only when I feel the taste of blood that my jaws relax.

They crowd round to comfort Poisseau, but the tears that run down her cheeks are going to weaken her reputation. The matter goes to the mistress. She is horrified to see Poisseau's finger and threatens me with expulsion. I try to explain to her how I got to that point. She asks me to show her the marks of my injuries. There are none. Poisseau is taken to the infirmary and I go into detention that evening with a bad conduct mark. I sob at such injustice and at my inability to warn Mum of my delay. I notice that my violent sobs give me the hiccups and a bizarre spasm.

Poisseau will be bandaged up for a long time. I am warned that her father will be coming to the school gate. I reply that my grandmother will be there as well. Granny has such a reputation that the father never came and the incident is closed. Poisseau leaves me alone now and Mum, who is obsessed with germs, makes me rinse my mouth out several times with Synthol antiseptic.

Later, when I will be at the convent school, my anger and hatred will break out again. After weeks of bullying, jealous twins throw my beautiful leather-bound missal with gilded edges in the bin; it was a present from Granny for my First Communion. I find it soiled and torn. One of the twins is boasting about it, and, like lava from a volcano, my adrenaline erupts. I give the girl a terrific thump that sends her flying onto the 'prie-dieu'chair. I am still astonished that she never reported it to the nuns.

It isn't worth mentioning at Confession. After all, a thump is not in the list of sins

4 Sex

I go to the local cinema every Saturday night with my parents. Sometimes Lambert's parents join us. They don't have much money. Her father is a railway worker and her mother, a caretaker. She never goes to the Paris-Palace or the Rialto-Pathé because they are expensive cinemas showing the latest films. My parents decide to go exceptionally because my aunt has urged them to go to see The Greatest Show on Earth with Charlton Heston. Lambert and I are collecting his photos; we think he's the most handsome man in the world until we come across James Dean.

In our school everybody is talking about that film and some girls want to play scenes from it in our theatre. Lambert is on the verge of tears. The cinema is free for Dad because he has a War Invalid card and Mum pays half because she is his carer. They agree to invite Lambert. Mum can't help saying: "With the Child Benefit for six kids, they could afford to pay for once."

What we love about the American films is the happy ending and after the Pathé News there's always a cartoon of Merry Melodies or Tom and Jerry. With Italian and French Films, one has to endure a black and white documentary and the end of their films is always tragic.

I adore those large rooms with a mezzanine. When the lights come back for the interval, Lambert points at Gasiglia sitting in the fourth row, licking her 'Eskimo' iced chocolate.

"I had to go to her place to get my Spirou comics back. My brother told me off because she hasn't given them back yet. She says she doesn't read those silly things anymore."

"Oh what does she read then?"

"Photo romance magazines!"

"Just like my Gran!" "That's not all! While she was looking for my comics, I saw a magazine on the side table, with a woman without a bra on the cover!"

"Noooo!"

"I swear on my Mum's head! She said it was her brother's and she showed me the inside! It was disgusting, it was full of naked men and women doing things!"

"What things?"

"I can't tell you here."

"How old is her brother?"

"Eighteen."

"That's why she is so relaxed with boys!"

I turn to Mum and repeat what Lambert just said. Lambert turns red like a watermelon and whispers: "You're crazy to say that to your Mum!"

"No, look, she's laughing!"

"Gosh, she's modern! Mine would have given me a clout!"

My mother and my aunt had informed me about the making of babies a long time ago. However, the dirty stories circulating on the playground, and the naughty remarks I collect here and there lift up a veil on the possibilities of great complications and odd situations.

Those complications added to Gasiglia's behaviour bother me sometimes. On the one hand I despise her as a boy chaser; on the other hand I envy her and occasionally feel abnormal compared with her. I often wonder what's going on in the lavatories of the children's library in the public garden. One Thursday afternoon, I arrive early at the library and since there is almost nobody there, I pluck up my courage and go to have a pee in those infamous lavatories. The smell of urine is strong in the Turkish toilets. Inside the door, I discover dirty but informative graffiti. I decode these hieroglyphs with the same interest as Mariette and Champollion in Egypt: "Gasiglia 'as big teets," "Jean-Pierre touched zem," "Poisso 'as hairs," with suggestive drawings to illustrate the comments. I mention my discovery to Lambert during the sewing lesson. She's surprised that among all the girls' names found on the doors, Chantal's was not to be found. And yet she is the most beautiful girl in the school.

When nearly everybody has seen the film, we play scenes of The Greatest Show on the Earth in our little theatre at the bottom of the stairs. Chantal is away so I play the trapeze artist and another girl, a little masculine, plays Charlton Heston. She takes me in her arms, we close our eyes and she kisses me with her mouth closed. Then, for a few seconds I believe she is Charlton Heston and I feel my body going soft and a weird wave sweeping through me. The audience yell and boo. The rumour spreads that we kissed on the mouth.

A few days later, a girl tells me that girls have different sex organs. To prove her wrong, I show her mine. Immediately she informs the whole class. The scandal is cut short by the Easter holidays arriving just on time. However I get the reputation of a sex maniac and I discover that sex is taboo. Without Mum's common sense, I would believe myself to be abnormal.

5 Foreigners

The next term a tribe of seven new girls descends on the school with two brothers at the boys' school: the Delaware. They come from the North. They make an impression in the district. The mother has been appointed a high civil servant at the EDF[4] and the father stays at home to look after the children and do the housework. And yet, he looks like a Viking warrior with his blond hair cut like a brush and piercing blue eyes. The oddest thing is the way the girls are dressed. Whatever the season they all wear a short knitted loose romper suit with red and green stripes. In winter we feel cold for them. Their hairstyle too is bizarre. They attach a bunch of hair on top of their head with a woollen string. I think we are all too amazed and intrigued to make fun of them. They all turn out to be generally good pupils. Of course the local gossips have a field day.

"They come from the Belgian border."

"They got a whole floor for themselves!"

"It's him who does the housework and the cooking! How shameful!"

Mum would not mind having a shameful husband like him.

Marie-Louise, one of the girls, invited me home. Mum asks me questions. I reassure her that, their place is very clean. The father is a maternal warrior and the mother, a paternal lady. Is that what the North is like? Here, in the South we see it as a sinister region, black like their sky and their coal with Zola's miners or white with snow. In a

---

4   EDF: French Electricity Board.

word we see it in black and white! The young civil servants are sent up there and those near retirement are sent to us, except for the Corsicans who know how to stay in the South. I ask Mum to show me where the North is on the map of the Post Office calendar, she says that the North starts in Valence.

Granny, who comes down from her village in the mountains from time to time, makes a point of picking me up from school. The girls fear her because her eyes are saying, "Watch out or else…" She went through two wars almost on the front because it was out of the question to leave my grandfather alone for a minute.

When we get back home, she tells Mum that she has seen the Northern aliens.

"I wonder what kind of place they come from!"

For Gran, the people of Levens, the village across the valley, are foreigners. She speaks the local dialect, the 'Nissarte' banned in schools, but which will be taught at university decades later. Thanks to the dialect, she gets a good price at the market and with taxi drivers who operate two scales of prices.

However, one day, a taxi driver replies: "I don't speak Italian."

Mortified, she complains to Mum: "We are not chez nous anymore! The Pied-Noirs took over!"[5]

As for the Italians, they have been here a long time before the French but are considered as integrated foreigners. People have not forgiven their behaviour during the last war. Mum always criticizes the Italians crossing the border at night in the mountains near Gran's

_____

5   "Pied-Noirs": French expatriates from Algeria.

village. The catch phrase was: "They come bare footed, squeeze a whole family into a one-room flat, and eat only tomatoes". Yes but most of them became rich and they imported the pizza. For Mum, eating meat every day is a sign of success and upper class. Even though she's intelligent, she doesn't want to admit that the Italians immigrants coming to us ran away from Fascism, from poverty and the regular floods of the river Po.

The beautiful villas built by the Italians are to be pulled down and replaced by big blocks of concrete flats sold to the Pied-Noirs at non-stop rising prices. Half of the girls in my class have Italian names. They are the best bakers, the best delicatessens, the best builders, the best workers in general and, what's more, always smiling. If I don't like the Italians, it's to please my mother but I get on very well with them. I don't bother about the nationality of my friends but in our town, it's always the foreigners' fault. After the Italians, it will be the Pied-Noirs, then the Arabs.

6 Childhood

My end of term exams are never brilliant, just average with bad results in Maths. What makes my father mad with rage is not my marks but my poor behaviour. He wanted to have a boy, he has a girl, therefore, I should behave like a girl. On the other hand, Mum is worried about my marks but doesn't really care about my lack of discipline. She used to love learning but Gran took her out of school when she was twelve to keep her at home, be her maid and bring up her brothers and sisters in a lost village of the Alpes Maritimes. Her lack of education has given her a huge complex for life. She has always thought normal to be her parents' housemaid, then her husband's since she has no education. For her, it is out of the question that I would do the same.

I seem to have a tomboy tendency. When people ask me what I want to do later, I say I want to be the Captain of a warship like the USS Salem, an American destroyer that lies at anchor in the Bay of Villefranche.

"How funny your daughter is!"

When it is found out I love reading, I am given lots of books: 'Gulla the Girl on the Hill' and 'Heidi'. ' Little Lord Fauntleroy' and 'Alice in Wonderland' reveal to me the existence of a magic, romantic and mysterious England. Being the only child, 'Little Women' enchants me away. When Mum calls me for dinner, I am surprised to find myself in the drawing room. The books of Comtesse de Ségur and Tintin teach me more about morality than the Church. My aunt always sends me comics like Flash Gordon and Mandrake but I can't read them because they are in English. There is a book with pictures that fascinates me, one shows a boy flying around a clock tower but I can't read his adventures; all I understand is his name: Peter Pan. I find this frustration unbearable and I can't wait to learn this magic language.

I love fairy tales, they are addictive, I read them again and again. I read and see The Beauty and The Beast a dozen times and find the Beast more attractive than the Prince! All my life I will suffer of the lack of magic power, therefore, at night, before falling asleep, I live a different life, shaping it with my imagination. I find it more exciting to save the world than being saved by a prince. Maybe that's why I enjoy nightmares as well as dreams.

Some nightmares are triggered by stories about the war. I used to eavesdrop them: I am seven, my head deep in a too soft pillow and just before falling asleep, I can hear the beating of my temples or my pulse somewhere in my head. This beating turns into the sound of boots hitting the tarmac; I get up and, through the slats of the shutters, I see German soldiers on parade. They carry severed heads on planks and I dare not breathe in case they find me.

However there is an intriguing recurrent nightmare. Not knowing that children can have hallucinations, I believe that our villa is haunted. I still remember clearly these dwarf women whose faces are hidden by the hoods of their black capes. They stand around my bed and observe me in silence. I am holding my breath for so long that I nearly suffocate. I am sure that if they hear my breathing, they will take me down the corridor. It happened once. They were carrying me with their arms above their head and I was gliding horizontally in the air. At the end of the corridor, I felt an excruciating pain in the kidneys. Despite all this, I am not afraid of the dark, quite the opposite; I believe that darkness protects me. In fact I ask Mum to block the light under the door with a rag. One night, I pluck up my courage, I get up, open my parents' bedroom door and stand ready to call them. After a while, the dwarf women arrive, gliding on the parquet floor and take their place around my bed. I am so terrified that I can't call my parents nor move. Eventually they leave the room in a single file. The next morning, Mum asks me why is the door open. I jump! So I did see them when I was awake. I tell her everything. She says that I must have had indigestion but if it happens again, it will be sleep walking, therefore she will take me to the doctor. What I love about my mother is that her explanations are always down to earth, it's very re-assuring.

To cheer me up, Dad takes me to the cinema to see Bambi.

The Gestapo and Walt Disney share my imagination.

7 My Father, the Hero

Dad is a Jew and an atheist who eats ham and goes to the Synagogue once a year. He is macho, tyrannical and very courageous. He reads three books a month that Mum gets for him at the library. This is due to the way he has been brought up. Two strong scenes are engraved in my memory.

When Papa comes back at the end of WW2, I ask Mum what has happened to his leg. She says he lost it somewhere between Dunkirk and Bethune.

"But is someone going to bring it back?" I ask.

She explains that he had been shot and the leg had to be cut off to avoid gangrene.

"Is it going to grow again like a lizard's tail?"

"Your father is not a lizard! The government is going to give him an artificial leg."

It arrives by post. I hear my mother shouting "Darling, come quickly, your leg's arrived! You must sign the receipt."

Dad comes hopping along in the corridor, in such a hurry that he doesn't bother to use his crutches. We go to the lounge. Mum opens the enormous packet. The brown paper seems to make a terrific creaking noise. Then it emerges, superb and terrifying, made of shiny metal and dark leather, articulated at the knee and ankle. A pair of khaki braces is attached to the top of the leg. Cotton bonnets to wrap the stub of the leg and avoid friction are also in the box. It takes my father a month to get used to it. He suffers from bruises, pains and cramps but the stub hardens. Then he manages to control his walk. Soon one

33

would think he only has a slight limp. I think he's a softy because he complains about pain on the leg that is not there anymore!

Now he has a War Invalid card that gives him priority over everything and everyone. What I like best is jumping the queue.

One day he takes Mum and me to a new cinema in town. The rain is pouring down on an endless queue. As usual he walks up to the counter but doesn't not bother to show his card. People should guess, but they don't and start insulting him. I learn some interesting vocabulary. He says he's a war invalid and that he has fought for them. They laugh and shout rude words. Instead of showing his magic card, he puts his wallet back in his pocket, undoes his belt and unzips his fly revealing his camouflage braces attached to the leather bandage on top of the metallic thigh. The metal captures the bright light of the cinema and beams it back at the queue. The crowd go dead silent and paralysed after uttering an "Aaaaaaargh."

My mother and I pretend to be busy looking at the film stills displayed in the hall; we don't want to know him. In the dead silence, he fastens his trousers and shouts to us: "Are you coming?" and all the heads turn to us. For the first time in my life, I blush like a bougainvillea.

That leg will be the cause of another humiliation. A class friend, who comes to play at my house, discovers the leg in a dark corner. She got very scared. I explain to her what it is but she spreads the rumour that dad has a detachable leg and they start to call me Frankenstein's daughter. Fortunately, the teacher, for once, intervenes quickly and says that my dad is a war hero with the Legion d'Honneur. In fact people show him admiration so often that it has spoiled his character; that's why he doesn't bother to show his card on many occasions.

8 Summer

The song of the cicadas in the plane trees is even louder than the sound of the intense traffic. I can feel the heat of the overheated pavement through my espadrilles. And yet the fashion is for 'Spartan shoes' but my legs are too skinny to keep them laced up to the knees.

Summer is advertised in our market. It is the stereotype of a Provence market. Mum always buys me a huge slice of watermelon that I hold in a fig tree leaf. All morning the merchant is chanting "Dear ladies, have one slice for five francs". While Mum is looking for the best courgette flowers to make 'beignets' I don't like, I admire the shiny aubergines reflecting the light of the sun next to the multicoloured peppers. I can breathe in the scent of the white peaches and melons from Cavaillon. When she choose some greengages to make jam, her hand is surrounded by bees but they are docile and don't sting us. I remind her not to forget the Agen prunes for Dad because the Agar-Agar is not enough. Dad can't stand being constipated, it's the only thing in the world he is afraid of. He goes to the toilet at eight in the morning and if nothing happens by a quarter past eight, he takes plums and prunes on top of the Agar medicine. If that doesn't work, Mum has to phone the doctor. We know when he is successful because he sings 'O Sole Mio' while shaving. We also buy lavender honey from Puimoisson in the Basses Alpes and curdled ewe's milk, which I am crazy about. Since becoming an adult, I have never found that taste again, even in the most sophisticated yogurts.

14th July. For Bastille Day, Mum and I accompany Dad on the traditional visit to the War Memorial. Cut out of the rock and facing the sea, it receives the intense sadness of the trumpet playing the Last Post. Most of Dad's mates have, like him, a missing limb and a chest covered with medals to compensate. To compensate even more, they walk into the Old City where the narrow streets of cobblestones hold some coolness and sit at a café to savour a Pastis. At noon, we go to eat a Socca, the local oily chickpea pancake, and drink a Monaco beer.

I prefer the afternoon when we watch the pageant of the Nations. They are people dressed in the typical costume of their countries. The Swiss are throwing chocolates to children but even at ten-year-old one has enough dignity to refuse to fight with the other kids just for some chocolates. In the evening, Gran takes Grandpa and me to see the fireworks. We watch the colours exploding on top of the Colline du Chateau and the sparkles dropping into the dark sea.

The holidays really start the next day when I leave the town with my grandparents to stay in their village. The only way to stay on good terms with Gran is to never disappear from her sight and to inform her as soon as Grandpa will be out of sight in the vegetable garden. My grandmother had eight children and seven miscarriages in between. My mother was born in no-man's land, 50km from the Verdun front line where Grandpa was fighting in the trenches. Gran had rented a house there because she was afraid Grandpa would go to see the naughty women in Paris when on leave. As there was nobody else around, it was the Army's veterinary doctor who took the role of the midwife. After she gave birth to my mother, he treated

Gran for puerperal infection with the same medicine as he used for mares. It worked! Then she gave birth in Morocco and in Germany following my grandfather's postings. She survived all infections without antibiotics. She didn't know that her own body was producing more powerful antibiotics than the Roche Laboratory.

After a few kilometres along the Vésubie River on the 'route Napoleon', the coach stops outside a little café for lorry drivers, where we get off. I carry my bag, Gran two suitcases and a bag of food on top of her head. Grandpa doesn't carry anything but he gathers wood for the cooking. There is no gas at this altitude (800m). We always climb up the goats' path that is much shorter than the winding road. From time to time Gran has to stop to let Grandpa and me catch our breath. I love the perfume of thyme burnt by the sun and the heavy scent of pressed olives telling us we are arriving at the village. The cicada's concert is over and Gran starts the fire for the 'soupe au pistou'.

The village is the disgrace of the region: no running water, no gas, and the electricity arrives almost exhausted by its journey; it looks like a glow-worm in a bulb. And yet Gran must find it too dazzling for she has encased the lamp in a green scarf with wooden beads. Next to it, hangs a roll of flypaper she changes before eating. In the evening the neighbours come out with their chair to sit and chat in their patois while I remain hypnotised by the dance of the fireflies in the dark.

On Wednesday night, Gran doesn't go to bed, it is the 'water night'. There is a spring in the mountain providing the village with water. Every family has the right to six hours of water a week, partly collected in a tank and partly running down terrace to terrace round the olive trees and to their plots. However, it is necessary to move a rock to change the direction of the water. My grandparents' turn comes at three in the morning. It's out of question to let my grandfather go up there alone, in the middle of the night; he could meet a woman. At one o'clock Gran takes her torch and leaves under a starry sky. She waits until the cracked bell of the church chimes three to move the rock. A few seconds and, from my bed, I can hear the sound of the water gurgling down the mountainside in its channel, then the loud splash as it starts to fall into our tank.

Thursday is the day when the grocer's corrugated Citroen van heralds his arrival with the sound of hooters echoing round the valley. He's selling bread that takes away all the teeth of everyone in the village, dark chocolate more bitter than camomile tea, meat you had to cook for the whole day, rancid biscuits the town people don't buy and the rough Marseilles soap to wash clothes, body or hair.

The only entertainment on Sundays is the mass and the visit to the cemetery. Gran washes the tomb with a lavish splash of water, makes the marble shine and changes the flowers. I realised that Gran is not religious at all but she believes that the dead are not dead. She is happy that the dead have a panoramic view over the Alps and are protected from the direct sun by huge olive trees. This cemetery witnessed my first mortal sin that I always forget to confess. On one of the tombs, stood a lovely, polychrome porcelain cherub. It was too beautiful. When I was five, I stole it and hid it under my bed. A few days later it disappeared. I concluded that it had flown away.

At the entrance to the cemetery, one strange tomb was at ground level, with a rotten wooden cross. It was the tomb of a Polish Marshall's wife. Her body was found in

1946 by a boy of the village, on the riverbank, cut in bits in a bag. The 'Gendarmerie' told us that it was probably involved with spying but would not say any more than that. I never knew her of course but I often think of her. Then her tomb vanished to make space for another family who could afford marble and porcelain angels.

The trees are quiet. The cicadas are dead. The sky is still blue but the swallows and the swifts have gone. I am quiet, I'm going back to school.

9 The Little Winding Road

O f all the true stories the villagers keep telling at night, under the stars, before the advent of television, this one is my favourite because we all nearly died.

Gran's village has a couple of features in common with Hitler's Eagles' Nest. The village is on top of a mountain from which one can see the road winding up and the mountain is also in the Alps.

Though thirty miles from Nice, Gran's village was so insignificant that it was not even mentioned on any map of the region. Consequently the Germans ignored its existence and it was never occupied throughout the war. Just like Asterix's village was never occupied by the Romans. The Resistance guarded it as a real Heaven.

The village did not have a magic potion to protect it, just incredible luck and bushes that hid the beginning of the road. One of its inhabitants put the village at risk every day. His name was Henri. Henri fought in World War I and managed to survive it. On 11th November 1918, he celebrated the Victory with a bottle of Champagne followed by a bottle of Cote-du-Rhone. Since then, he had never stopped and was still celebrating on 8th May 1945. Only he could not remember which war had just ended. The village used to tremble when he zigzagged down the little winding road for a refill. If arrested by a German soldier, he could talk about the existence of the village. He did but nobody understood him.

I was two months old and there was such a shortage of milk in town that my parents decided to go to the village where milk was provided by a goat.

The village priest, Father Ranguin, was a saint. His cassock was washed once a year maybe and his beard was solid with food residue and yet he did not smell. He would give everything he needed for himself to his parishioners and answered any call for help, night or day. The village used to bring him food, each family taking turns. He kept a matchbox of Colorado beetles to feed his monstrous friend. I saw it when I was five. He called it and it jumped out of its hole, ran along its cobweb and leapt onto the table to share his meal. The first time in my life I saw a spider; it was enormous but I was not yet scared of them.

One gorgeous day, in spring 1945, the village had gathered to watch the men play pétanque under the lime trees. They were hoping or expecting the Allies to land in Juan-les-Pins or Cannes. But, there was no news. They were not sure what was going on in town as the radio reception was very bad and Radio London almost inaudible. The members of the Resistance had gone on a mysterious mission as usual. Father Ranguin had gone to town to try to find some sugar and soap for the village. It had been some time since someone came up from town. Henri was nowhere to be seen. Mum was worried about what could have happened to him. A few days ago, someone saw him fast asleep in the middle of the main road down in the valley. Dad tried to tell him it would be better if at least he slept where the road is lit by the moon. Henri said he couldn't sleep with the light on. We were happily cut off from the tragic world outside.

The sudden sound of an engine made people rush to the low stonewall overlooking the little winding road. Panic broke out when they saw German vehicles making their way to the village. Mum and Dad were the last to leave the square as Dad had one leg and two antique crutches. (He lost the other leg in Dunkirk). When the Germans reached the deserted village, they got out of their jeeps and armoured cars and went into every house. They looked very agitated. They ordered everybody to line up outside the church in three rows. A line of soldiers was put in front of them with a gun pointed at us. They said that if they found a single gun in any house, they would shoot the whole village. Someone whispered, "I bet Henri spoke". When three officers reached Marcel's house, Mum and the rest of the village thought, "That's it, it's the end". Marcel was a hunter and he fed the village with the produce of his hunt, sold cheaper than the black market. He had two rifles. Some minutes passed when you could have heard the priest's spider chewing her Colorado Beetle. Then suddenly the three officers ran out of the house. Some of the villagers started praying. One officer yelled an order to the soldiers in front of us. Mum shut her eyes and held me tight. But instead of shooting, the soldiers ran away and the whole lot fled at such speed they could have been expecting a ticking bomb.

Everybody stayed motionless, still frozen in terror. My father was the first one to move on his crutches. Then they all ran to Marcel's house. They found him pouring himself a glass of wine with a shaking hand, his wife sitting, looking very pale and his 4 year old kid in bed with a dirty face. Marcel should have been awarded the Legion d'Honneur but he never got it. He had saved the village by putting his two rifles in the bed with his daughter. He squashed berries on her face and convinced her not to say a word whatever happened. When the German officer asked what's wrong with the child, he said "Nothing serious, only the Scarlet Fever, you know," The three officers panicked immediately and they all ran away from this terribly contagious disease.

An hour later Henri turned up, as drunk as usual and boasted that he had scared the whole German Army. "You don't... don't believe me... I... I... saw them... they were scared of me...yes they were..."

Later they found out that the Allies landed in Juan-les-Pins and that the Germans had fled from Nice and had taken the Napoleon Route to the North. Then some of them had taken what they thought was a shortcut; in fact it was the little winding road going to the cul-de-sac village. A few days after this memorable fright, there was another alarm. Someone rushed to the square shouting, "They're back, they're back!" Everybody ran away as before but while my father was picking up his crutches he caught sight of a white star on a vehicle and shouted, "Come back! Come back you idiots! It's the Americans!" Father Ranguin had invited three GIs to the village. He was standing in the jeep, his filthy cassock shining gloriously in the sun of victory.

10 First Love Sickness

In August I go with my parents for a health-cure in Châtel-Guyon. in Auvergne. We take the 'Cévénol', a train that rivals the jet plane Concord for noise. The wagons jolt so violently that it's hard, when in the toilets, not to pee on the floor. You need a health-cure just to get over the journey.

The newspaper L'Aurore has organised a festival for children. They will make a recording for each candidate. The theatre is crowded. A twelve-year-old boy sings O Sole Mio with a tenor's voice. I can't sing so I recite a tragic poem by Victor Hugo. It's about his journey to his daughter's tomb in Honfleur to place some flowers. The parents in the audience writhe with laughter, the presenter bites his lip as he casts knowing glances to left and right. I am about to burst into tears when I get a standing ovation. I discover that I have an accent and that the southern accent is the most popular and the most hilarious one in the country, except in the South. I must have sounded like Shakespeare recited with a Geordie accent.

At home we have the sea and the mountains but here they have water kiosks and dead volcanoes. The park is full of gurgling springs, hot and cold, stinky and odourless, with ladies serving the waters. I carry Mum's glass in a wicker case. There is a children's park with a Punch and Judy show theatre in a wooden house. It's in this park that I meet him for the first time. He is helping his father to work the roundabout. He's twelve and has freckles. Unlike the boys at school, he doesn't frighten me. He never say rude words, doesn't roll his shoulders when walking and, to my great relief, he has no mates. I go every day for a ride on the roundabout and sometimes he lets me on for free. When he is inside, his father calls him: "André, here's your girlfriend from the South!"

One Sunday afternoon, André invites me to go with him to the Punch and Judy show but Dad has decided to go for a drive with some of his friends to Montaigut-en-Combraille. I am devastated. I convince Mum that it is important and that I have no means to let him know. She tells Dad that I have already been invited by a friend's parents. To my great dismay they have an argument about it. Eventually they go to Montaigut and I spend a wonderful afternoon. One of those rare moments that life gives you with a sordid avarice and then makes you pay for it.

We queue up and then he asks for two tickets, just like a grown-up would. We sit down on the wooden benches. He says that my blue dress is pretty. The little theatre is chock-a-block with kids, which forces us to sit close to each other. There are no adults, all the parents have left their children at the entrance and gone off again. The lights dim down, silence settles with the darkness. Three knocks on the floor, the little red curtain opens and the show begins. No technicolour, no stereo nor the special effects will ever bring me the same strong feeling again. No pop concert will ever have this atmosphere. Perhaps only its novelty can explain such an intense emotion. When the kids and we shout at top of our voices, André puts his arm round my waist and I can feel the warmth of his body. Then, I don't dare to shout with the other kids to warn Punch that the nasty character is behind him because I am not comfortable anymore sitting between these two chairs: childhood and adolescence.

The show finishes at four o'clock. We climb the hill overlooking the springs and we sit down on the grass, at the foot of the Calvary. We talk a lot without really listening to what we are saying and he kisses me on the corner of my lips. I do the same and I find his skin very soft for a boy. He walks me back to the hotel.

After that I see him when he's free and we walk hand in hand in the park.

He often takes me to see the 'water drinkers' playing tennis but tennis bores me stiff. It doesn't matter as long as we are together. I will learn more than once that not liking sport is a serious social handicap.

On 15th August, the Assumption of Mary Day, the park is crowded with tourists and patients. In the morning Mum and I have had to stand through Mass and now all the chairs and the benches in the park are taken. As I know that the roundabout and the children's park are closed, I drag my parents off to the tennis courts in the hope of seeing André.

Then I see her.

Blond and suntanned in her immaculate tennis skirt, leaning nonchalantly up against the wire netting of the court, with her racket lying at her feet. André is talking to her with his back turned to me. His hand is resting on the wire fence, close to her face. Mum understands as quickly as I do! "Don't make a face like that! There are plenty more fish!"

I feel lost, empty, I don't know what to do. Shall I retreat or let myself be seen? I show myself. He is very relaxed and introduces me to Patricia, eleven, ravishing and sporty.

I stop going to the park and we won't see each other anymore. I feel, at eleven, the first agonies of an adult-like love. It hurts a lot and keeps me awake at night. I don't feel like confiding in my doll anymore. How could she understand? I tuck her away in a shoebox for ever.

11 Slander

On the path in the park stands a poor old man selling lottery tickets. Dad always buys them regularly from him and they become friends. One day I hear the man talking to one of his customers, a member of the Rothschild family taking the waters. He is nodding his head and saying "You're right, the money all goes into the pot…" I don't know what demon got into me, but I have a wicked idea. I tell Dad that the lottery man said he didn't like the Jews. Dad stops buying his tickets. The old man asks my father for an explanation about his sudden coldness. He gets it full in the face and desperately tries to claim his innocence. From that moment I avoid the park. I want to tell Mum the truth but I am scared to disappoint her and to lose her trust. I think I can manage my conscience but my conscience refuses any compromise. At last I have a real sin to confess. I will go to several priests every Saturday before the Sunday Mass but they all get rid of me with ten Hail Marys and a couple of Pater Nosters for my absolution. On the Sunday I take Communion but on Monday the remorse is still there, burning. When I turn thirteen, I decide to write to the Bishop and I make an appointment. As I always collect the mail, I can intercept the letter before my parents.

The Bishop receives me with a cold and syrupy paternalism. His study looks sumptuous. Behind him hangs a full sized portrait of Christ with beautiful blow-dried fair hair, dressed in a long white tunic and a red toga over his shoulder. He is holding a heart dripping with blood.

I start to explain what brings me to him. He interrupts me almost immediately.

"How old are you my child?"

"Thirteen."

"Really? I thought you were seven or nine. Let's hear your confession."

He puts on his white stole like Granddad at the Synagogue and I kneel in a superb sculptured, wax smelling confessional. I tell him everything about my slander and the lottery man.

"Is that all?"

Bloody hell! What does he want? Isn't that enough? I was hoping he would be cross but he remains calm. I try to invent another one or two sins to satisfy him but still, it's not enough so he encourages me to make up some more.

"Do you go to Mass every Sunday?"

"Yes Father."

"Your Grace. You go alone?"

"Yes your Grace or with Mum."

"Not with your friends?"

"Yes, I do, sometimes."

"Do you have many friends?"

"Two or three."

"Are they nice?"

"Of course."

"Do you have male friends?"

"Yes, one."

"Aaah! Who's he? How old is he?"

"He's the sexton's grandson, he's eleven."

"Good, good, and what's your parish?"

"Sainte Jeanne d'Arc."

I wonder when he's coming back to the sin that is bothering me.

"What's his name?"

"Who?"

"Your male friend!"

"Jean-Marie."

"And you like playing with Jean-Marie?"

"Yes Your Grace, a lot."

"And what game do you play?"

"We like playing Monopoly."

"All right, but not always?"

"No… (I hesitate, I am afraid he finds me naff.)

"Go on, talk to me, you must say everything at confession."

"We play at being merchants. We make fruit and vegetables with Plasticine."

I can sense that he is annoyed. He sighs deeply. I wonder what Jean-Marie has to do with my sin of slander.

"Do you like Jean-Marie?"

"Yes, I do."

"Do you play Mummies and Daddies?

"Oh no, that's for babies!"

"Or nurses and doctors?"

"No, we prefer grocers."

Deep silence, I could hear an angel flapping his wings but it is only the heavy curtains in the draught.

"Would you like to marry him?"

"I never thought of that," I say laughing.

"One doesn't laugh in confession! Why exactly did you write to me?"

"But… I told you Your Grace, about my slander…"

"Nothing else. That's all?"

That's all? What is he thinking of? It's very serious!

"All right then, just say the Rosary for punishment."

Then he absolves me. I won't recite the stupid Rosary. I leave the Bishop's mansion with a long crack in my faith. The only thing that will sooth my acute remorse is, a few years later, reading the Stolen Ribbon where the great philosopher Jean-Jacques Rousseau wrongly accused the family's young maid.

12 Another World

The return to school is a disaster. Madame Delacourt has delayed her verdict. She calls all the girls on the register to announce which ones have passed, and which ones will repeat the year. I don't pass because I don't understand fractions. My despair is unbearable. I feel a fire burning at the bottom of my stomach. I stay two weeks in this class full of kids I don't know. In the playground, my old mates hardly talks to me. Not only have they passed into the upper year but also their classroom is on the first floor whereas I stay on the ground floor. I feel ill, I feel sick all the time, I can't eat. During lessons, I don't bother to open my books and the mistress ignores me completely.

As I am losing weight, my parents are looking for a private school and the doctor prescribes me vitamin B12.

That Sunday I am sitting with Mum, attending Mass. Just before the 'Ite Missa Est', we get up to leave when someone grabs my wrist. I see a nun with a transparently angry face. "The Mass is not over, mademoiselle," Who does she think she is? I shake her grip off and run across the church to catch up with Mum.

The appointment is for two o'clock. Meals at home always proceed in the same way. Mum eats at the corner of the table making sure that Dad has everything he needs. She pours his wine and peels his fruit. I have never heard him saying 'please' or 'thank you', therefore I do the same and she finds it normal. However she makes me say please and thank you to anybody else.

Dad misses his afternoon nap to be at the new school at two.

It's a cramped little building, a villa that must have been quite pretty but someone has done everything to make it look austere and severe. Inside and outside, everything is white or grey like the nuns, except the dark red floor tiles. Nearly all the nuns have a wax-like face crossed by blue veins. Occasionally their tight smile shows yellow teeth. God must have forbidden toothpaste. We are asked to wait in a tiny room. The heavy silence is abnormal for a school. I am thinking of Lambert, wondering if we will see each other again. It would have been wonderful to sit together on the first floor. I could have seen the top of the chestnut trees for a change, my other friends from our theatre and N'Guyen who had to get a special exemption because she is too young for the upper year. Here I am, at twelve, already thinking back to my childhood... There is a rustling of material in the corridor and a nun comes in to tell us that Mother Superior is expecting us. I seize Mum's hand. We enter a dark study and I realise that my future is as dark as that room; the Mother Superior is the nun who tried to stop me in the church and that I had shaken off. She has the eyes of a boa knowing it's going to have a nice meal. She manages to convince my parents that repeating my year is better for me. I feel sickly again. What's the point of coming here? My parents are not used to dealing with this kind of person. Mum is servile, Dad embarrassed, the nun wins and she scares me. She shakes hands with my parents, I hold out mine. She doesn't take it and says: "Well-behaved girls curtsey to a nun."

I don't. I don't know how to. I have seen it in swashbuckler films and I am afraid of looking ridiculous.

It is the very first time I am scared to go to school. I have butterflies in my stomach.

I even have difficulty in drinking my morning Banania chocolate. On the way I'm thinking of my old school. When I arrive, a nun rushes across to me to say that one is not allowed to come to school without ankle socks, it's not decent.

The playground is a small concrete square without trees but an unexpected bamboo screen covers the fence of the boys' school next door. To begin with, weeks pass almost normally.

Silence is compulsory most of the time.

Boredom is the main subject.

First incident: the rat. I love them. That morning, after the break, I ask the teacher for permission to go back to the playground to try to find the handkerchief I have lost.

I hear a screeching noise between the bamboo stems. It is a big rat with an open wound on its neck. I am devastated to see it in that state. I know that nobody will help me to catch it and tend to its wound. All I can do is to throw it some crumbs from my old 'pain au chocolat' . Scared by my gesture, it flees then comes back to eat the crumbs while keeping an eye on me. I go back to the class and ask permission to take the rat away with me in a box. The teacher looks at me horrified, as if I were the rat itself. She sends for Mother Superior. She takes me back to the playground to show her where I have seen the rat. I am about to point in the wrong direction when the rat re-appears probably expecting more crumbs. The Mother picks up a dead bamboo stem and starts to beat the rat to death with the hatred of the Inquisition. My heart starts beating terribly fast and my stomach twists but all I vomit is bile.

The next day, after the Morning Prayer, the Mother Superior declares in a preaching tone: "We have got rid of a harmful creature. I hope," she says looking at me, "that you won't be too disappointed," The whole class erupts with laughter. To ease my suffering I imagine the nun's head caught in a gigantic rattrap. She is suffocating slowly and puts her tongue out. Hatred is contagious.

"Really, mademoiselle, your tastes are unhealthy."

"But, Mother, rats are very intelligent and…"

"Yes, diabolical! And don't reply when I am talking!"

The rats are coming to devour her tongue and she can't even yell for her pain. At night, in my bed, I keep repeating this scenario but it doesn't bring me enough peace.

Granddad doesn't like them either but he has respect and admiration for them. I'm talking about the rats, not the nuns. One day, he hid and watched them to see how they had access to the barrel of olive oil. They managed to pull the cork and one dipped his tail in the oil and allowed another to lick it. They did it in turn. Mum had a quarrel with him because she suspected he hadn't thrown the oil away. That must be why she always squeezed half a lemon and poured a lot of vinegar in the salad dressing.

My classmates are very different from the ones at the State school. They lack spontaneity, they never speak openly and they express themselves by hinting at things that I don't always understand. When they address the nuns, they keep their heads down and show airs and graces.

Encouraged by the nuns, the girls watch each other and tell on each other for the 'love of God'. In my previous school, informers and their reporting are highly despised. Here, if a pupil is caught glancing at another's writing, some girls improvise a Committee of Eternal Salvation on the spot and denounce the sinner.

Sister Eustache is telling off Marie-Jo.

"Marie-José, your homework is full of smudges, I'm not correcting a mess like this."

I look at Marie-Jo, she is staring at the red hexagonal tiles of the floor. The nun continues to hurl abuse. Marie-Jo's head is bent down to 90°. I can't stand anymore of it.

"Sister, there was her brothers, they took her pencil case and…"

"What insolence! Be quiet and bow your head! And you should say 'there were or it was'. Didn't they teach you grammar at your state school?"

Then she sends me to stand in the corner for the rest of the day. Great humiliation. Later Marie-Jo kindly advises me to never look the nuns in the eye.

"Why?"

"It's rude and provocative."

"In my old school, it is the opposite, they say 'Look me in the eyes when I talk to you."

"Yes but that's the state school, here you're in the free school[6]."

"Free? That's the best one!"

I am denounced for bringing the wrong comics to school like Mickey and Tintin. Apparently these kids'

---

6   Free school (école libre) means private religious schools.

magazines are subversive. The nuns recommend Bernadette and Bayard, the height of boredom.

I am so bored that I have nothing better to do but observe my classmates.

A curious mixture in which, two devious twins, Chantal and Dominique, are the nuns' favourites and yet their parents are divorced but the father makes generous donations.

Marie-Jo's father is a pious Catholic grocer. Her mother is perpetually pregnant and she is expecting her eighth or ninth child but soon will be going to die of exhaustion. She is eventually found lying in the huge cellar of the grocery. She couldn't finished stacking the shelves with the rice and boxes of milk powder. Marie-Jo has a delicate constitution and divides her school year between a sanatorium in the mountains and the school. She tells me that she spends endless afternoons in deckchairs and I feel vaguely sorry to be in such good health.

Monique becomes my best friend. She doesn't belong to the committee of denunciation. She is frivolous and spontaneous. The nuns keep confiscating her bangles and making nasty remarks about her pretty clothes. Her father is the conductor of the orchestra that plays on the bandstand in the Albert 1st Gardens. She's living in the White Russians' district. I ask her if the black ones stay in Russia. Her mother explains to me that they are not black but red and the colour is not of their skin but of their political ideas.

Then there is Anne de Santinovich whose father runs the annual church fête and is called 'Monsieur le Consul' by the nuns. Mum discovers that he is a soap salesman now. Anne is not very smart and bad tempered.

Soon I realised that I am the only 'keeper of the secret of making babies'. My mother has explained almost everything to me a few years ago.

We are sharing the playground with 14-year-old senior girls. I overhear one of them saying that babies come out of the ears and another one laughing at her and saying she is wrong, it's out of the belly button. Santinovich, the daughter of the Consul selling soap, is somewhere in the middle of a family of seven kids, declares: "You're ridiculous! It's well known that babies are provided by the hospital."

I can't hold my tongue any longer.

"Honestly, have you never seen your Mum's belly growing bigger?"

"It's because she has to eat a lot to breastfeed."

"No, no! It's because of the baby in her belly!"

Everybody looks at me with horror. The one who mentioned the belly button was triumphant.

"See! I told you!"

"No, no, it doesn't get out that way, it comes out there, between the legs. Why don't you ask your Mum, since she's had seven children," I say to Santinovich.

She stands dumbfounded. The trouble is, she follows my advice. I don't know how things went on that evening at her home but I become the 'scandalmonger'. The next day Mum is asked to come to the Mother Superior's office for an interrogation and a sermon. Mum never knows how to handle an argument with people who have more education than her. She is told that her daughter is the black sheep who's corrupting her flock, I have lost my innocence, I know too much for my age. What's more I have put a model mother in a disgraceful situation and I have triggered a family drama. Later I find out that none of the kids knew the truth. It's a good job I haven't mentioned the father's role. Mum keeps apologising and tries to reassure the Mother about my intentions. But the nun insists and tells her that I have abnormal tastes like loving rats. Mum is completely lost. Once outside I explain about the rat. She laughs, relieved.

"What morons your classmates are!"

"And the nuns!"

"Don't mention it! It was the same in my days! Anyway, it's not your job to inform them on baby making; for God's sake, mind your own business and leave people in their ignorance! Telling the truth is looking for trouble."

13 The Media

There is one girl in my class who know about a thing that I don't: television. She talks a lot about 'Cousin Bibi' and other children's programmes but nobody can discuss them as she's the only one who has the television. The first time I see one, it's in a shop window. A crowd outside the shop, crushed against the window, attracts my attention. I manage to make my way through and I'm fascinated to see the Coronation of the Queen of England. I ask my parents to buy a set but it's too expensive for them and I am disappointed to find out that it's not the radio programmes that are visible on the screen but entirely different programmes.

Every evening and at lunchtime I listen to the radio with my parents. Some words keep coming round like 'Algeria'. Mum sighs: "First Germany, then Indo-China and now Algeria! There is no end to war," I have a vague idea about Indo-China because they always mention the Foreign Legion. In the magazine Paris-Match I can see lots of photos of a nurse called Genevieve Gallard in Dien-Bien-Phu, a sort of Florence Nightingale. My parents and their friends comment about the cruelty of these countries. Apparently the worst ones are the Japanese in Korea. My uncle came back weighing 35kg, amoebas included. He told the family that the Japanese lay prisoners on a bed of bamboo seeds that grow through their body in a few days and kill them slowly.

On one of our bookshelves stands a peculiar book. I don't understand the photos. They are showing black heaps shaped like bodies, lying on the ground. Some look 'undone' or 'spread out'. On the cover of the book there is the profile of a red eagle with a swastika and the title is 'Oradour-sur-Glane'. I ask Mum about the meaning of this book as I am just learning to read. She puts it back on the top shelf and says that one day I will understand it.

On my way to school I always pass a newsagent kiosk and I often catch sight of photos and the headlines. For a few weeks one event occupies the front page and my parents pay great attention to the news. A farmer, not far from our town, killed three English tourists who had dared to park their caravan on his land. It is the Dominici Affair. Gran says it's typical of the Italian peasants from up there. She knows what she's talking about. At night, her grandmother used to patrol her vineyard and the olive grove with an antique gun. She pretended it was for the foxes but would have shot anything moving. Today, the black and white magazine Detective is showing frightening photos and pictures. Dominici has finished off the girl with two bullets and she is the same age as me. I have just realised that one can be killed and even die at my age and not far from us!

I tend to read more or less everything I find. Thank God, all the magazines are not like Detective. Some are in colour. What I like, when Mum buys fish, is that they wrap the rockfish with 'Cinémonde' or 'Cinérevue'. They are full of movie stars in Technicolour. My favourite is James Dean, he's so different from the boys round here. To begin with he looks handsomely healthy. Very different from the French or Italian actors; he appears kind, strong and vulnerable. The French ones look ill or tormented.

14 Friendship

I can't live without friends and I have no problem making them. It exasperates the nuns who find friendship unhealthy. Monique is my best friend because we share the same fits of giggling; she's eleven, a year younger than me. Every Sunday afternoon we go to the cinema together. Monique is crazy about detective films, the 'films noirs' and she makes me stay to see them twice. So I had to see 'Les Diaboliques', 'Strangers on the Train', and 'The Night of the Hunter' twice. But I make her stay to see '20,000 Leagues Under the Sea' with Kirk Douglas, another attractive American; he made me cry in 'Spartacus'.

Shortly before Easter, the Mother Superior announces that we are going to see a very beautiful film. While we are drinking the milk generously given by the Prime Minister Mendes-France, she praises this film in a solemn tone. It is about a saint-like girl in Italy. Monique rolls her eyes. Of course it's not a detective film, but at least it's about the murder of a girl who tries to protect her purity from a nasty man, so he stabs her.

"If only Eddie Constantine was the detective!" Monique whispers. (Constantine is James Bond's ancestor). Once in the cinema, we sit together. When the film becomes frightening, we hold each other's hand. Suddenly a nun pounces on us, seizes Monique's arm and drags her to another seat. I am completely lost, the nun frightened me more than the film! What's the matter with her, what have we done? We were not even talking. Resentment is burning in my heart. I decide not to watch their stupid film and I force myself to stare at the ground until the end. The nun is livid at my resistance. Back at school, they say that I have a vicious disposition, and Monique and I are immediately separated in class and on the playground. They forbid us to play together at break time. Fortunately there is nothing they can do on Sunday afternoons. Two other girls in our class are in the same situation; it brings us all together. We fancy ourselves being the 'Three Musketeers' (who were four) and Mother Superior is Cardinal Richelieu. We make an oath: never to be part of the 'Committee of Denunciation'. On Sundays, after the Mass, we play together in my garden and enjoy it all the more because it's forbidden. They don't know either that sometimes Monique and I go together to blocks of flats to sell stamps in order to raise money in the fight against tuberculosis. They think we are going alone.

The Eleven-plus exam has been a nightmare for many generations. Mine is no exception. Rejection and separation are hanging above our heads. For the nuns, one of the main criteria is to separate the wheat from the chaff. To begin with, the Mother Superior tells Mum that with a limited intelligence like mine, the best thing for me is an apprenticeship. My mother is strongly opposed to this point of view. It's out of the question that I should finish up like her. So the nun advises her to put me in for Modern Maths stream because it's supposed to be easier than Latin. I am hopeless at Maths and love History and Literature. It is the beginning of a long road to Calvary where I have to carry a cross for much longer than Jesus. Monique, who's clever with Maths but dislikes Literature, is put in the Latin section. Her father intervenes energetically, so, eventually, she goes to Maths. My poor results prove the nun right: my intelligence is very limited, I will never understand Trigonometry or Geometry.

I find myself in the First Year with Monique, Santinovitch, the sneaky twins, Nadine who has television and two of the Musketeers, Huguette and Nicole.

English immediately fascinates me. I believe that one day I would be able to understand all the gorgeous books Auntie Andrea keeps sending to me from America: the little Indian Hiawatha, an adventurer called David Crockett, Peter Pan, etc… Alas! My first English book, written by Carpentier & Fialip, is second hand. It is damaged and in black and white with hardly any pictures. I just discover that Peter Pan's clock tower is called Big Ben and does exist in England. That text book is as dull as the teacher. We are so eager to learn and we are very proud to be able to say a few useful phrases like "This is a brick," and "My sister is not a boy". Mum too was very proud to say "My tailor is rich". She learnt it during the Liberation of our town in a book called La Méthode Assimil in order to communicate with the GI and ask them for cigarettes and butter.

I look at the last page of my textbook. There is an extract from a story. I don't understand any word but the name of Captain Scott keeps propping up. I am amazed because we are told that by the end of the year, we will be able to read and understand the last page. We'll never reach the end of the book, not even the middle but we know one hundred irregular verbs by heart.

Winter 1954 is the winter when the French Riviera and I discover snow for the first time. Mum comes to get me out of bed, she throws a coat over my pyjamas and leads me to the garden. I am breathless. I could not have imagined it would be so beautiful. The snow has transformed the palm trees into giant cauliflowers. The magnolia looks like a powder puff. Mum hopes that the pink oleander and the mimosa tree will resist the cold. She starts to throw snowballs at me but I don't appreciate the cold running down my neck. I can't wait to go to school. Unfortunately, the nuns are always keen to deprive us of fun. They have cleaned the whole place. There isn't a single snowflake left in the playground. At lunchtime, I invite the whole class to come to play in my garden. We have a field day but we make it late back to school. We run along the corridor and arrive with red cheeks, wet hair, happy, excited and noisy. We have to stay standing up in silence without moving for half an hour, then pray to ask God for forgiveness for our despicable behaviour. I am put on detention, accused of being conceited for showing off my garden, having a bad influence on my classmates and interrogated on what I have been doing exactly. Was I playing with all the girls or with one only? Were there any boys?

In the middle of winter, new girls arrive: Martine from Chad in Africa with a chameleon and a 'tribe' of six pretty blond and sporty sisters from Flanders. Martine is a little shy but makes friends thanks to her chameleon. The Lherminier sisters are open, forward and relaxed. The welcome is a bit cool because the girls are intimidated by the sisters' self-confidence. I am delighted to be the first one to talk to them. Then, of course, a nun pushes me away and orders me to leave them alone. She says that I'm preventing them from talking to the others. They play dodge ball but I am not allowed to join the game. Am I supposed to have a bad influence on them? The Mother

Superior tells Monique's Mum that I have a very bad influence on her daughter: I take her to see dirty films on Sundays.

The Lherminier family live in a pretty villa just outside the town, in the Parc Chambrun area. To my great surprise, they invite me for 'le goûter' at four. Their mother is amazingly young looking, informal and wearing trousers. Her six daughters look so much like her that I tell her she made the same model every time. She bursts out laughing.

"We told you, Mother," says the youngest one.

" I heard a lot about you. They say you are very natural and you have a hilarious Southern accent."

"It's true, Mother. The others are not funny and they have a sly look."

"Monique is not like that!" I say.

"Of course, she's certainly not like the others if she's your friend," Mme Lherminier says.

I am charmed by her manners and find it strange the girls would be so formal with their Mum and yet so close. There are lots of beautiful photos of the family with the father in different countries. Piles of books and National Geographic magazines strewn on the floor, here and there, and a guitar on an armchair. It's a distinguished untidiness. We play Monopoly with a version that has the street names of New York. I regret being the only daughter and they feel sorry for me.

It will take a long time for Martine from Chad to come out of her shell but then she'll become the fifth Musketeer. We have lots of fun in the playground despite the constant surveillance. One day Martine gives me a new ring binder full of sheets of blue paper.

"Here, it's for you. My parents and my uncle bought me the same one."

I'm moved and amazed, it's the first time that I have seen a ring binder with sky blue sheets. Usually they are black with white pages. I promise her to write nice and exciting stories for her. I catch sight of the Mother Superior watching us from the first floor. I feel vaguely guilty but can't see any reason for being punished. And yet, she comes downstairs, pulls the bell five minutes before the end of the break and her eyes follow us all the way to the classroom. When, at four o'clock, we are about to leave, the nun holds me by my sleeve and asks to see my new ring binder.

"Where does that come from?" she asks.

"Martine gave it to me."

"Why?"

"Because she's got two of them."

"This is a waste of paper. You don't need it. I confiscate it and I will give it to someone poor."

She'll say to Martine that I gave it to her for the poor. Martine thinks that I wanted to show off with her gift to the nuns; she's very disappointed. Even though I swear to her that the nun has confiscated it, she remains doubtful. I feel betrayed and my friendship violated. Back at home I cry my eyes out. Mum says she will buy me a better ring binder. She doesn't understand that I'm not crying for that but because Martine thinks that I have betrayed her.

I'm chatting with the Lherminier sisters in the playground and I tell them how much fun I had at the state school when we turned the caretaker's stair into a theatre. I make them laugh by showing them how I played the fool on the stage.

Suddenly Sister Charles rushes to us. Seeing my worried face, they look back. The nun seizes my arm and shouts at me in an exasperated tone.

"For God's sake will you stop, preventing the new girls from joining other groups! I've never seen anything like it!" Then to the Lherminiers," Go and play with other girls."

The sisters give her a cold look, move back a little and stand together.

A few days later, I hear that Sister Charles phoned Mme Lherminier to warn her that her daughters should avoid my bad influence and make an effort to play only with the other girls. She recommends the sly twins because they come from a good and pious family. Mme Lherminier thanks her for their advice and tells her not to worry about them because her daughters are mature and know what to do and what not to do. However she's grateful to them for showing a genuine interest in her daughters.

At the beginning of Spring, the Lherminier twins ask me to walk back home with them for a bit. I say I would do it the next day because I have to let my Mum know why I will be late, otherwise she would be very worried. They smile and say: "Ah, being a single daughter!" I tell Mum that they have more freedom than me. She replies, "When you are in a group of six, nothing bad can happen."

The next day the tragic accident is on the front page of the newspaper: 'Bus driver loses control of his vehicle, strikes two girls and crushes three of them against the door of a garage. The eight year old has died, the twins are in a coma and the other two have various fractures. They are all from the same family whose father is an international reporter on National Geographic and l'Aurore, etc…''

Mum can't swallow her coffee. I have shivers and feel sick. The nuns make us pray for Catherine who is in Heaven and the twins who are in the hospital. A girl in our class lives near the garage and kindly informs us that there is blood all over the place. The accident has taken place ten minutes after I left them.

When I know that the twins have come round, I want to go to the hospital but the Mother Superior forbids us visiting them because they need peace.

A few months later, the twins come back on crutches. I bring them sweets and tell them that I wanted to go to the hospital but the nuns told us it was not allowed. They smile and shrug their shoulders. To celebrate their return, the nuns take us to the chapel of St Dominic to attend a mass for Catherine's soul. The priest talks about God's will, He was doing her a favour to call her to Him. The twins, sitting next to me, don't pray and don't sign themselves. They just hold their crutches tight to their chests, keeping their heads up even during the Elevation. The nuns look at each other. Monique, behind me, whispers in my ear that the priest looks like Gary Cooper. A month later, the Lherminier sisters stop coming to school. I'll never see them again.

15 The Original Sin

As I can't be alone with Monique or Martine during break and I have lost the Lherminier girls, I am allowed to play dodge ball again. The game has already its star players. Among them, two Eurasian sisters. Their dad is from Brittany and their mum from Indo-China (not yet called Vietnam). I get on well with them but I have to hide it. I join a basketball club to see them more often. Despite my efforts, sports bore me stiff. I can't see the point of putting a ball in a stupid net. The only sports I could put up with are cycling or roller skating but Mum forbids them and wants me to do judo or swimming but I hate cold water and violent sports.

It is very difficult to play hide and seek because the playground is a concrete square without any trees except the bamboo hedge. I can play with Monique only if other girls join us. So we invite de Santinovitch to play hide and seek with us. We know she's not very smart. I suggest to Monique, "Let's hide in the lavatory. She'll spend the whole of break looking for us and we'll be able to chat in peace!"

Monique chortles and we lock ourselves in the tiny wooden loo with a painted glass door. Through a little hole in the paint we can see Santinovitch coming and going all over the place, disappearing in the bamboo hedge and looking so gormless that we cry with laughter. Then the bell rings but the hook on the door is stuck. When a nun passes our door we have to call her and explain the situation. She rushes to the Mother Superior.

I have an idea. I detach the chain, pass it under the hook and pull it up over my shoulder. Unfortunately, the thin chain cuts into my skin so I take off my skirt, fold it into four to make a protective pad and slip it between the chain and my shoulder. Feeling no more pain, I pull it hard and the hook gives way. I open the door with my skirt in my hand. Mother Superior is standing in front of us with a black, icy gaze. Monique stays ten minutes in her office; I am wondering what they can be talking about. Then it's my turn, and the painstaking and incomprehensible interrogation takes a whole hour. She draws the curtains at the window and directs the light from her side lamp straight to my face. She keeps repeating the same questions over and over. "What were you doing in the lavatory? Why weren't you wearing your skirt? What was Monique doing with you?" And I, I am thinking, "Who is this woman with no breasts, no hair, no make-up, no toothpaste?" Behind her a crucifix was nailed on the wall. Nailed twice. In her office there are no colours, no noises, no scents. I am sweating, my eyes hurt. I break down in tears and ask for Mum.

That drives her mad. "Every time you commit a sin, you ask for your Mother! Don't you know that God comes before your Mother?" That piece of news gives me a shock and suddenly I find God to be not very nice. I stop crying.

She sends for Mum to inform her that I am a black sheep possessed by vice. When we get home, I explain it all to Mum and ask her what I have done wrong. Mum tries to explain the Mother Superior's suspicions.

"But I was not with a boy, I was with Monique!"

Mum says not to worry, that it's them who are the dirty black sheep.

A few weeks later, I am in deep muddy water again. The sly twins' mother found a fantastic masseur, a PE teacher called monsieur Moreau. He comes twice a week to her house, in the morning when the girls left for school. Monique and I are very impressed by this luxury. Mum says she's no fool…

Chantal, one of the twins, manages to convince the nuns that Mr Moreau would be a very good teacher for us. He's an excellent athlete who runs the gymnasium of the town. He's at least forty with greying hair at the temples. He rules his pupils with an iron hand and gets good results in the regional competitions. Mum encourages me to develop my sparrow-like muscles. Every Thursday morning for a month I go to be trained on the parallel bars and the beam. One Thursday, Mr Moreau tells us that we need to have a medical examination to see if we are fit for the bars and the beam. It happens in the changing room, which is dusty and badly lit by two fanlights filtering a dark grey light. It's cluttered with clothes and shoes and two long wooden benches that leave just enough space to move. When it's my turn, I'm a bit surprised that there is no doctor and no nurse and Mr Moreau locks the door behind me. He asks me to undress so I took off my cotton vest and shorts. He starts to feel me all over, talking all the time as if to tame a mad dog. I feel more and more uneasy and become eager to get out of there. He is a masseur so it must be normal but I don't like it and yet the other girls haven't said anything. He keeps on repeating that I always have to smile in life, that when you smile the body relaxes and you feel more confident. I make an effort to smile, hoping that perhaps he would let me go sooner. Instead of that, he pulls the elastic of my knickers and looked inside them to see if my glands are swollen. He thinks I need a massage but his hands are going too far and I jump to one side.

"Ah, that's typical of girls, always afraid they're going to be hurt! You know that next week you'll start to do the splits on the beam and you don't want to break those bones (he puts his fingers on) so you must train those little bones of yours to come apart without breaking."

I say yes and I hurriedly get dressed. Before unlocking the door he kisses me on the lips and wishes me good luck. I join the others on the parallel bars. They look at me with intense curiosity, I avoid their eyes and get on with my exercises but my arms and legs seem weak and shaky. I can't even talk to Monique. The idea of coming back the following week fills me with deep anxiety: I can't, I can't....

I just declare to Mum that I don't want to go back to the gym. First she thinks I am being lazy.

"Do you remember what you said about Mother Superior's suspicion about me and Monique in the toilets? Well... he put his hand in my knickers and then he kissed me."

Mum is horrified and asks me a lot of questions. First she doesn't want to say anything to Dad, he would go and knock him down. For once, I feel very proud of my father. Eventually she takes me to the doctor to get a certificate to exempt me from the gym. The doctor doesn't react as Dad would. He says to Mum that she has chosen the wisest solution by avoiding scandal.

The nuns tell me off, calling me a spoilt brat and they force me to go to the gym and watch the other girls. I feel trapped. Mum thinks I could go since I am not doing the exercises.

With a heavy heart, I pluck up my courage to take the bus to the Place Masséna. I am dying to get off at every stop: first was Prisunic where Mum always gets off, then the Nain Bleu, the wonderful and unaffordable toyshop, now the Marquise de Sévigné with its fairy like and very expensive chocolate boxes, the Société Générale, the bank that will be robbed one day by the famous Spaggiari and finally, the Place Masséna.

I get off and join the group waiting for me. We wait for Mr Moreau to pick us up with his van. I wonder whether I have made a mistake...maybe he didn't have bad intentions. The sly twins laugh at my worried look and ask what what's the matter with me. As I am facing the plaque commemorating the Martyrs of the Resistance, I reply that I am thinking of the two men hanged by the Germans outside the Galleries Lafayette. Suddenly one of the girls shouts: "Here's Mr Moreau's van!" and they pick up their bags. Then I am stricken by panic and run away. I say to Mum that even if I am making a mistake, I don't want to go back. I am so relieved when Mum lets me settle down in my armchair, in the sun, and read a comic with a bar of Kolher chocolate; pity we can't afford The Marquise de Sévigné chocolates. Feeling secure is bliss.

The next day at school, I have to face the music. The sly twins have told everyone about my sudden flight. No girls ask any question. The nuns say it was typical of spoilt children. A few years later, Mum'll find out that Mr Moreau had been appointed to the South of France from Lille to avoid a paedophile scandal. The Ministry of

Education carried on appointing those people somewhere else so that they keep renewing their 'stock'.

Sometimes, on Sunday morning, to 'please Jesus', our school sells books of stamps to help fight tuberculosis. The state schools do it too, regardless of Jesus. So we have to go into blocks of flats to try to sell as many as possible. The nuns give me more books than the others to punish me for avoiding the gym. They don't know that I am going with Monique and that it's fun to be together. She takes me to her area where the people are more affluent. For the first time I discover the Russian Church. So pretty with its turquoise dome that it looks like a Walt Disney building. Two hours later we are left with two books of stamps to sell. We are in a superb building Art Nouveau style, on the top floor. We ring at the door of a flat. A sullen-looking, elderly man opens the door. We give him the usual sales talk about children in the sanatorium. His face cheers up and he asks us to come in and sit in his drawing room unlike any I have ever seen. It's gold and red and has mirrors everywhere. There is a tiger carpet on the floor. "Like in films," murmurs Monique. She's sitting in a deep armchair and her feet don't touch the parquet floor. I am sitting on the edge.

"Well, then, ladies, explain to me again what those books of stamps are for exactly."

While I am speaking, he stares at Monique's feet; she's wearing spotless white ankle socks and white sandals. My green espadrilles are a bit dirty. On the ceiling there is a painting of a naked woman riding a flying bull. He is so absorbed by Monique's feet that he doesn't listen to a word of what I say. I insist and say louder: "They are one hundred francs the book."

"Sorry? Ah yes, the tuberculosis! ...All right then, I'll have two books. Won't you have a little drink before you go? Please come with me Mademoiselle," he says to Monique, "you can help me to carry the glasses."

Monique is delighted, we sold our last books of stamps and she is impressed by the cinema décor. She follows him to the kitchen, at the end of the corridor. I try to tell her that it's nearly lunch time and that we should go but a door is closed behind them, then another door. I wait for long minutes in a total silence and go to the window to admire the turquoise dome of the Russian church sparkling in the sun.

Next to it, on the tennis court of the Parc Imperial, two young women are playing tennis. Apart from two pigeons cooing, the rumble of the streets doesn't reach me and in this oppressing silence, Mum's voice echoes in my head.

"Stay together, don't go inside, especially if it is a man alone…"

My heart skips a beat. I don't even hear them talking. I ought to go to the kitchen. Suddenly I hear stifled screams, a rush of feet and the door at the end of the corridor opens and Monique come running out with a look of panic.

"Where's the front door?"

"There! What's the matter?"

Monique throws herself at the door to open it but it's locked and the bolt is too high. I have to jump up to reach it. Monique's frantic behaviour scares me. I manage to open the door but I just remember I have left the two books of stamps in the drawing room. I hesitate and I shout to Monique.

"Wait for me, we forgot the stamps."

"Never mind, go downstairs."

I must get them back or we will have to pay for them. I go back and I find myself facing the old man in a dressing gown with the same sullen looking as before. My knees go weak but I find the strength to seize the books.

"Don't you want the money? Your friend is a bit mad!"

I charge downstairs, Monique is waiting for me two floors down.

"If I had to wait one more minute, I'd have ringed the bell at a door."

"What happened?"

"He's like… M. Moreau… one is enough!"

"What? You too, you…?"

"I don't want to talk about it."

I am disappointed, I thought friends did not have any secrets from each other. It's true that I didn't say anything either. Monique leaves the school at the end of term; her dad has been appointed in the South West.

*

Before Easter, Dominican missionaries come to visit our school. The first thing they offer is to hear our confession. In our church, it's dark and you can't even see the priest's head behind the wooden lattice. Here, in the school, the nuns have improvised a confessional, in a sunny room, with a normal chair for the missionary and a prie-Dieu for us. We are forced to go. It's out of the question to confess anything. I didn't do anything wrong and suddenly I don't believe anymore in that sacrament. It feels like a trick or a trap, even more so in the sunlight. I kneel down, cross myself, and recite the Confiteor. Then I start to reel off my standard list of insipid sins.

"Is that all?" he asks in a disappointed tone.

"Yes, Father."

"I'm sure you're forgetting a few. Let me help you my child. Did you ever have temptations?

"Er... yes."

"Which ones."

"...To copy my homework or to say bad things about people."

"Ah! Who for instance?"

"Don't know,... wicked girls."

"And what about boys?"

"I don't know any."

"And grown-ups?"

"Ah yes! One day I lied about an old man who was selling lottery tickets; I said he was speaking evil about the Jews and it was not true!"

"Alright, alright that's not really serious. Aren't there other people who did bad things to you or by whom you may have been hurt?"

"No, no, only the man selling lottery tickets and..."

"I know, I know. And you know that the Devil has a thousand ways to tempt pure hearts and to turn them into perverted hearts.

I wonder if I ought to confess the clout I gave to one the sly twins, but since she didn't complain about it!... I stop listening when he embarks on a speech about temptation. It will soon be lunchtime, my knees are getting sore on the hard plaited straw and I have to get to the newsagent before twelve to get 'L'Intrépide', my favourite comic. I get away with the usual number of Pater Nosters and Ave Marias. I'll recite them before falling asleep; it's more effective than counting sheep.

16 Improvement of Status

Hurrah! I am changing school! Dad and the nuns wanted me to get the necessary School Certificate to get an apprenticeship but Mum is determined: "Never! Over my dead body!" Her dream was to study and become independent, she had never been allowed to make it. I will make it instead. She would like me to be at least a schoolteacher: paid holiday, sick leave, retirement pension, job security, maybe accommodation and certainly Independence! I quite like that but, above all, the idea of a whole class under my control and my power is quite grandiose. Also I could do so much better than all the teachers in the world! Nobody will repeat their class and I will help the dunces and sit them on the front row. I will never tell the parents that their child is stupid, I will never humiliate a pupil and never give them a zero mark. I will take them on trips and to see good films.

Financial independence is Mum's obsession; she is not even allowed to have a chequebook of her own. "You don't want to have to ask a man for money to buy a pair of stockings." She nearly never buys something for herself. She wears her sister's clothes or makes her own dresses. My aunt Andrea sends her parcels from America but she has to alter some clothes as the fashion over there is far from ours. I wonder why all Aunt Andrea's parcels smell of cinnamon! Sometimes I dream that we both would go to America but she says she doesn't have enough education to leave my father. Therefore, her dream becomes mine; I'll have diplomas or degrees, then I'll be rich and I will take her away with me. That's my motivation to go to school.

My new school is rather friendly. It is a two-storey white building with large windows and a spacious playground full of pink oleanders and bougainvillea. It looks like a private hospital. Nuns again! The Order of Charity. They seem to be more open-minded. They have an avant-garde chapel with the sun flooding in and Picasso-like stained glass windows. These nuns follow the changes of the Vatican; the priest faces us to say mass and the space between the altar and the worshippers is considerably narrower. The same for the theatre: no more space between the stage and the audience. The mystery and the holiness have vanished from the Church and the Theatre. They have been vulgarized.

The inauguration of the chapel causes a certain disturbance in the area. It's the first time the priest is facing the congregation and using more French than Latin.

In the playground I make acquaintance with my future fellows. We are all rejects from the state system, apart from some very catholic families who just despise the state school. The merciless selection in the state schools keeps filling the private education.

At ten, the mass starts. Chance puts me in the front row with some other second-form girls. The girl standing next to me looks sulky and has a ponytail. I feel a little uncomfortable at being so close to the altar. There isn't even a dais or a step to raise it in height. I look at Sulky-Face, she smiles a little. I nudge her with my elbow and point at the priest's flat Charlie Chaplin feet with huge black shoes. She chuckles and the priest looks up and casts us a black glance. We realise straightaway that we are so close that he wouldn't miss a thing, thus creating the perfect climate for a fit of giggles. For a while we avoid looking at each other and keep staring at what's happening at the altar. His gestures, which used to be hidden, are now taking place under our very noses and we find them ridiculous. He cuts the host in two, puts half of it into his mouth and chews it as if it were a 'pan bagna[7]'. Our elbows touch. Then he pours the wine and swallows it greedily with a gurgling sound and a smack of his tongue. Our elbows press hard and I let out a chuckle. This time he chooses to ignore us and unfolding a white cloth, he begins to wipe the chalice and gives it a final polish. I lean over her and whisper, "He's doing the washing up," She collapses in a huge silent laugh. I can see her ponytail trembling and her shoulders shaking with tiny spasms. Laughing like yawning is contagious and I implode in silence when I see the priest shaking the cloth, folding it and ironing it with his hand. We're both aware that it's out of question to cause a scandal the first day in a new school. We have to put up with the delicious torture to stifle the terrible laugh that is trying its hardest to explode. We don't know where to look any more and the slightest thing would lead to an explosion. We put our face in our hands as if in deep prayer. I don't know how we manage to hold out until the "Ite missa est," the dismissal.

Here, I'm not the black sheep anymore, quite the opposite. I am the only one to still wear ankle socks; all the other girls wear nylon stockings. For the nuns, the ankle socks are the last bastion of innocence. At home, I try putting on the nylons but the seam at the back divided my legs and makes them look skinnier.

---

[7] Salade niçoise in a sandwich, a local specialty

However here too, they need a black sheep but it won't be me. Mum calls it a scapegoat. For once, she's told that her daughter is intelligent … but she must be careful of bad company! She is referring to girls who wear makeup in town and are too mature!

My giggling companion in the chapel is called Roseline. Unlike Monique, she's not spontaneous and cheerful. She already has a best friend but the nuns separated them quickly as usual, so we have to share the same desk. The second form contains a strange cross-section of girls from twelve to fourteen but none of them are really nasty. Among them I meet Paoli again, one of the girls repeating her year with me at the state school. She hasn't changed, she is still a dunce. I wonder how a girl with such a beautiful handwriting can be such a poor pupil. She has a wide range of pens and magnificent fountain pens. She writes headings and titles in Gothic or Art Nouveau in our exercise books. Her books are works of art; her dictations seem to be printed and she decorates her work with artistic friezes. But her beautiful presentation is ruined by the teacher's red pen because her dictations are full of mistakes, her essays off the subject and her Maths wrong.

I don't know if the situation is the same with boys but, in a girls' class, there's always a large gap between the mature girls and the babyish ones, regardless of their age. Nicole is more mature than me but we become friends because we have to sit together for a while. We laugh a lot together and we share the same taste for gherkins, hot baguettes and cakes, specially the cream puffs called "Religieuse," (Nun!) I think she's rich because her parents bought her a leather overcoat, the first PVC school bag and, to the permanent disapproval of the nuns, a sky-blue moped. And yet she lives in a very small and dark flat with no bathroom, just a basin. Her friend, next door, Josiane, a twenty year old, has a Vespa scooter. Together we roll down the Cimiez deserted avenues, the residential suburb and I discover that my town has Roman arena. At the top of one avenue, stands the Regina, a sumptuous white stone building with bay windows and slate domes. Mum says that it was the Hotel where Queen Victoria used to spend winter holidays because Buckingham Palace was too cold. When Gran was sixteen, she was ironing the Queen's knickers there and Her Majesty sent her butler with a jar of Piccalilli to thank her for not burning them.

However, here too, there is a Committee of Denunciation. The chief informer is called Annie Millet. During written tests her eyes are sweeping the class. Roseline, next to me is correcting her dictation with a blue pen instead of the red one. I warn her: "Look out, the light house is looking at you". She drops her blue pen on her knees, picks up her handkerchief and blows her nose assiduously. When Millet's eyes turn away, she thanks me with a smile.

Roseline goes to real parties with boys. It's her friend who knows a girl in the fourth form who takes them. That fourth year girl, Marilene, is the nuns' 'bête noire'. She is beautiful, blond, sexy and buxom, as Mum would say. The priest who comes to teach us Religious Instruction says that it's because 'the Marilene' looks like a Rubens painting that the boys come to wait for her, hanging about in clusters at the school gate, at the end of the lessons. His smile is more Rabelaisian than dirty.

On 18th February, the nuns celebrate the Day of Saint
Bernadette and organise a show after mass. They are
looking for a girl who will play the role of the Immaculate
Conception, when the Virgin Mary appeared to Sainte
Bernadette in a white robe and a blue sash. We all want the
part. Sister St Andrew and the priest are auditioning the
candidates. We have to recite a stupid speech discussing of
the purity of the river Gave water, pure like her heart,
etc... Just as stupidly, I think I should get the part because
the Virgin Mary was Jewish like Dad and I look like Anne
Frank. Out of the whole school, it's Marilene who gets the
part. The priest chose her for her beauty and the nuns
because she doesn't have a Southern accent.

The next day, Nicole and I are rolling down the
avenue on her moped and, as we pass the Roman arena, we
see Marilene, on a bench, in a boy's arms with their lips
sealed. Nicole shouts to me "The purity of the Gave!" We
laugh but we envy her more for that than for her
interpretation of the Immaculate Conception.

17 Distortion of the Body

My periods appear on a sunny Sunday afternoon without any warning. At the age of fifteen, it's about time. My parents are relieved and I am delighted because I believe I have become a woman within a minute. I was dreading the pain. I have seen Nicole writhing in pain. She puts a hot iron on her tummy and doesn't feel the burn for a while because her pain is so acute. She showed me the large blister she got once and we laughed about it! I don't feel any pain and my body is not transforming at all. I don't put any weight on despite Mum's gnocchi in the 'pistou' sauce and Gran's polenta. I keep growing up with the same weight. My chest shows only two pink warts and I've got three spots and some hairs on my face. Most of the girls in my class display an uplifting bosom and some of them develop large hips. My body is an alien. We soon find out about our shortcomings as the boys shout at us "Hey Big Arse," or "Look, she's got an arse like the Place Masséna!" I am told I have a very cute arse but, because of two teeth pushing forward, a big nose, my black curly hair and my eyebrows joining, I am called Dracula's daughter or Louis XIV. Mum can't see my imperfections and thinks I have the same eyebrows as Elizabeth Taylor. The fashion icon is Brigitte Bardot. She succeeds to Martine Carole. The Dictatorship of Fashion is far worse than the Dictatorship of the Proletariat. Adolescence is the age when you most need to have an engaging appearance and for me it's the age when nature denies me this advantage. With birds, the male or the female is magnificent to attract its partner. I am as ugly as the female of the peacock but that female can't care less because she knows she is meant for the beautiful peacock. I don't have a peacock I am meant for. How can I rectify my plumage? In my town the demography is seven girls to one boy. That explains the multiplication of beauty salons, hairdressers and lovely clothes boutiques with sexy lingerie.

On Sundays, most of my friends go out in groups with the local boys. I stay at home with Mum, read a lot and fill gaps with sleep. Roseline says that if I want to go to a party, I must wear stockings and heels, not ankle socks and flat shoes. Mum buys me my first suspender belt and the Dimanche stockings.

Nicole no longer takes me on her moped to roll down the streets around the Parc Valrose.

A certain Monsieur Patino, 'the king of copper,' has just given his chateau and its park to the town to become a university with a Faculty of Sciences.

Also Nicole prefers to go out with Josiane, her neighbour. They go to Villefranche on her Vespa to meet the American sailors of the Sixth Fleet. They say they are so different from the local boys. They show a charming politeness and would hold the chair for you to sit down. The first time this happened to Josiane, she hung hard onto her chair, thinking he was going to play a joke on her by pulling it away.

They were offered tea with small triangular cotton-like sandwiches with strange stuff called peanut butter.

"They even pay for your drinks," says Nicole.

"Don't they ask anything in exchange?" I ask.

"No, I wonder what they expect!" says Josiane.

I would love to go to Villefranche but Josiane says I am too young and at any rate, there is no room for three on a Vespa.

Roseline doesn't like to go to the beach alone and her best friend has gone on holiday with her parents. She decides to go with a boy she knows from her clique but it's out of question to tell her Mum. I am the ideal alibi. She rings me to say she will pick me up with him but tells her mother she's with me only. Mum is aware and doesn't mind.

When I open the door, Roseline is standing with a dark, handsome sixteen year old boy. His name is Rodolphe. I make them wait in the hall and he stares at the ceiling. Our ceilings are painted by a fake Michelangelo.

"Are you ready?" asks Roseline.

"Yes… no, er… wait a minute, I'll go and get my bag."

Mum is not worried about the boy, she's worried about the sea.

"Don't go swimming out of your depth! Remember that the sea bed drops 2000 metres after a few steps."

"Don't worry, I am not going to swim at all."

I take a towel and throw away my ridiculous frilly swimming costume. It is out of question to show off my skinny and suntanned body with wet hair like a dead weeping willow. In women's magazines, the top models' measurements are less than mine and yet their bodies are bigger than mine, proving that magazines lie. For years I'll carry my body like a cross. So, I pretend to have forgotten my swimming costume and Rodolphe, who thinks it clever to show off his knowledge of female hormones, asks me if it is the wrong time of the month.

18 Politics and Culture

As we are walking up the Avenue de la Victoire, the handsome Rodolphe meets a friend. After a brief introduction, they become engaged in a hermetic conversation. It's about being for or against the independence of Algeria and the FLN[8]. Then they carry on with the films of the Cannes Festival and Marilyn Monroe's latest film, The River of no Return.

Roseline and I haven't got a clue what they are talking about. We are so relieved that they don't ask us our opinion. Back at home, I ask Mum. She rolls her eyes.

"Is that all those little brats think of talking about? Who do they think they are?"

"All right, but what does it mean?"

"It's about that nasty business in Algeria."

"What about it?"

"It's a kind of war… because Algeria is a French department but also a colony. They are set up by the Communists. When you don't fight on your territory, it is not a war, it is politics.
The Arabs and the Pied-Noirs are fighting because… Ask your father, he reads the papers!"

I begin to realise that there is another world above mine where a lot of events are happening beyond my grasp. On the kiosks, we can read the bold lines of the papers with words I don't understand: devaluation, bomb scare, terrorists, insurrections…

---

8   FLN: Front de Liberation National. Algerian terrorist movement of the period.

"Dad, what's an insurrection?"

"A kind of revolution."

"In Algeria?"

"No. In Hungary."

"Why?"

"Because they don't like the Russians."

"Why?"

"It's too complicated for you, mind your own business, I'm reading my paper."

I try another time.

"What's the opposite of Communists?"

"Fascists."

"Are we fascists?"

"Certainly not!"

"What are we?"

"…Nothing."

That's what I thought.

*

Summer is back, I'm chatting about the holidays with Nicole and Roseline, while we are waiting in the queue at the dispensary for our Polio vaccination. There has been an outbreak. Luckily, it is no longer an injection in the tummy but a lump of sugar soaked in a solution. Roseline will go to her grand-parents in Italy as usual, Nicole to Annecy. I'll have to go to Châtel-Guyon again but this time for a 21-day water cure because Mum caught a bacterial infection last time we went there. It must be a way to bring the tourists back.

It's not the Châtel of my childhood anymore. I don't find the park interesting and when I see André again I think "How awful he looks!" He too has spots and hairs on the face and a horrible downy moustache. I am so bored that Mum takes me to the Library where I am advised to read a saga about a woman called Brigitte. The heroin is very pious and married to a very pious husband, then they have a lot of little catholic children. It is even more sugary than the Comtesse de Ségur's books. I read them all hoping something terrible would happen. I ask Mum to buy me a few comics like Tintin and Spirou; they are much more fun.

In the dining room of the hotel, we meet a very distinguished, middle-aged lady and Mum and she become friends. One day she offers me two Claudine books by Colette. Mum says that she heard Colette's books were 'sulphurous', meaning they smell of Hell fire. The lady puts her mind at rest: "The spring waters smell of sulphur too and yet they cure," Mum laughs and now I can read anything I want to.

I am so happy she has a friend. Madame Hennequin explains to her how she caught amoebic dysentery in Indo-China when she went to take her dying son away. Dad doesn't like her; he thinks she has a superior air. As for her, she doesn't revere his war hero status. She invites Mum to have tea in town but Dad doesn't let her go. I'm livid and even more cross with my mother for giving way to my father's tyranny.

"One day you will understand," she says for the hundredth time, "family must come before friends."

"I shall never lose a friend for a man!"

In the hotel there are photo-romance magazines lying everywhere. I have contempt for them, it's always the same story: a woman giving up everything to gain a husband's love. In these stories, women are rarely studying or would never become independent. Sometimes the magazine would tell the story of famous couples like Marie-Antoinette and Axel Fersen or Antony and Cleopatra. When Madame Hennequin lends me a book called David Copperfield, I keep crying to the end of the book. There again, I swear to myself that a man will never force me to do what I don't want to do. Madame Hennequin smiles and says: "You will need to have diplomas or qualifications to be free…" Mum told her that when she was a child she found a book called 'Sophie's Misfortunes' by the Countess of Segur. She loved the book but before she finished it, my grandmother threw it in the bin saying that reading was for idle people.

*

During the exams term Gran met Chantal Mercier's grandmother at St Rita's Church in the Old City of Nice. Saint Rita is the most popular saint in the South of France and Italy. She gets hundreds of candles a week, a lot more than Saint Theresa or the Virgin Mary. In fact she is the Saint of Impossible and Desperate Cases. Gran is burning a candle for my school exams and Chantal's Gran for Chantal's sister, Jocelyne, who's trying to enter the highly competitive entrance exam for the Ballet of the Marquis de Cuevas. Once more Saint Rita shows her efficiency. I pass my exam and Jocelyne fails hers but gets the main part in the very successful film, "Angelique, Marquise des Anges." Then her name becomes Michèle Mercier.

The Church gets alarmed by all St Rita's successes. They decide to change the name of the Church, it becomes 'Notre-Dame' and they put Saint Rita in a dark corner. Priests are conscious of social class among saints and make sure it is respected. But Saint Rita's dark corner is still illuminated with more candles than anybody else's.

19 The Rock and Roll Years

The nuns don't realize that Elvis Presley has replaced Tino Rossi and that James Dean is an 'idol' who makes us fantasize. They are too busy fighting back Brigitte Bardot's influence.

"Mum, I must have a Gingham dress like Brigitte Bardot!"

"Still bothered by Vichy!" Mum says referring to the Occupation[9].

In a fabric shop, we meet Lambert. I hardly recognize her. Her peroxide hair is tightened in an enormous bun like a wedding cake. We are so excited that we both speak at the same time. She's learning secretarial skills at Pigier's. She wants to work as soon as possible and earn enough money to buy herself an Austin Mini and dresses. Her brother is preparing for the Maths Baccalaureate and he takes her to parties! I am so impressed! She asks me if I have a telephone and writes down my number. I thought she'll forget me but the next Sunday she invites me to a party in the afternoon, a real one with boys! When I arrive, I am more nervous than for an exam. I can hear the music through the door: Only You-ou-ou-ou-ou, The Everly Brothers, Paul Anka... I pluck up my courage, take a deep breath and ring the bell while they're playing 'All I Have To Do Is Dream, Dream, Dream...' I ring again and the door opens releasing a torrent of music: Elvis is yelling, he's divine. Lambert lets me in. All the boys are wearing suede jackets and a ties, all

---

9   Gingham material is called Vichy fabric in French.

95

the girls a lampshade skirts and a twin sets bought at the Vintimiglia market just on the other side of the Italian border. She takes my handbag to put it in a cupboard. I don't know what to do with my hands so I accept a cigarette to look cool but don't smoke it. My first cigarette was a Gauloise Bleue without a filter from Dad's packet. After the second puff, I thought "Never again," Since then I have been pretending.

A boy passes and looks at me.

"Dear me, we're getting girls from the primary school now!"

"Ignore him." says Lambert.

"I don't know how to rock and roll!"

"Never mind, dance the slow foxtrots! I'll ask my brother to teach you rock-and-roll."

A skinny short boy with ironic eyes invites me to dance. I have the impression that he is doing me a favour. I can't refuse, he would think I'm stuck up. Here we are, him trying to hold me tight against his body and trembling and me, remaining distant and as stiff as a broomstick. When I meet Lambert's eyes, I roll mine up. She laughs and goes to change the record.

"Come on, my brother is going to show you how to dance rock and roll."

Jean-Jacques is patient and very kind. By the third single, I'd loosen up. It takes me ages to understand when to spin round and, when he pushes me away, I learn to step back without running. But I must stop clinging to him for fear of falling over. Then the smooch music comes back and the little skinny boy too. All of a sudden, half way through Jack Scot's My True Love, he kisses me like a savage! Yuck! Yuck! Yuck! It's worse than swallowing an oyster. I think I'd better to pretend to enjoy it otherwise he would call me frigid. Back at home, I go straight to the bathroom and rinse my mouth with Listerine. Lambert says he's from Corsica and fancies himself as Casanova.

The 'Second Year', just before the Baccalaureate years, is a cushy time, there's no exam. New girls arrive at our school, rejected by the lycée, -the state grammar school,- as usual. They immediately form a clan. They are all daughters of lawyers, doctors and businessmen well known in town and yet they are not interested in studying despite their parents' pressure. We are impressed by their expensive clothes; it drives the nuns feverish and they keep sending them out with sand paper to remove their nail varnish. They colonize smart Cafés such as Le Masséna where all the boys from the Felix Faure lycée are spending their money on Espressos.

The nuns put one of the new girls next to me. Her name is Luce. I have a discreet peek at her work and I realise that there's no risk I'd copy off her.

One morning, I take the opportunity of a free period to write the essay we have to hand in in the afternoon. Luce is looking at herself in a vanity mirror, exchanging knowing smiles with her mates then sucking her Parker pen. I'm half way through my essay when a better idea strikes my mind. I cross out all my work and start again. She jogs my elbow and asks me why am I throwing away my text. When I tell her I've just had another idea, she asks me if she could have my text. Amazed and flattered, I warn her that it isn't very good. She can't care less, she just wants something done! I quickly and carelessly finish off the text and give it to her. She copies it out word for word. When the teacher gives us back our work, she has fourteen out of twenty and me twelve. Very proud of her mark, she doesn't say thank you and ignores me.

Roseline and I envy Luce riding a Vespa with a good-looking guy. I would exchange my ability in writing essays for this Vespa and its driver. Esau's mess of pottage!

Roseline and I are forming a good tandem pair. I write the introduction and the conclusion of her essays and she gives me the theorems for the Geometry problems. As soon as the nuns realise we have become good friends, they separate us and this is why Luce is sitting next to me.

While we are rock and rolling, the bomb attacks increase in cafés in Paris and in Algeria. I wonder how plastic can be made into bomb. At home, an event is going to have the effect of a bomb. My aunt Andrea from America manages to convince Dad to buy a TV set. She arrives, one day, with a record player, Louis Armstrong and Elsa Fitzgerald's LP records and her uncontrollable twins. She says they need the TV to keep calm. As a result, Dad won't do his striptease in the cinema queue anymore, besides, he doesn't feel like going out anymore. Mum is delighted. I play with my little cousins. They are eight and have been brought up in the American way: no limits, no complexes and even giving their opinion. Mum says to her sister: "Your kids are badly brought up and unruly," Auntie replies: "Your daughter is inhibited and full of inferiority complexes."

Dad loves watching the Westerns on the Monte-Carlo channel, Mum and I love a series called 'Rocambole' but only when Dad allows us. The twins think that French television is crap. I am twice their age and yet I enjoy playing with them, they are fun and mature. Ralph can sing Louis Armstrong's songs!

One Thursday, I am passing the Massena Café with Auntie Andrea and I point out to her the clan of girls in my class, sitting on the terrace.

"Do you want to sit with them?"

"No, no, we're not friends."

"Did you fall out with them?"

"No… it's a question of… of status. Their parents are doctors, lawyers…"

"And that is why you don't talk to them?"

"They don't talk to me."

"What a country! I thought the war had ended all that! In the US, we're not communists but the doctor addresses you by your first name, like a friend! Come on, let's sit with them."

"No, no, no, for God's sake no!"

"How can you have such complexes? You should go and see a psychologist."

"I'm not mad!"

"Psychologists are not just for mad people! They help anyone! What a country!"

"It's not just that. They are womanlier than me. They think I'm a baby."

"Of course, if you behave like a baby!"

"No, no, you don't understand anything. They sleep with boys, I don't."

"Ah?… And what are they like in class?"

"Useless. They have other fish to fry."

"Have you got a boyfriend?"

"No, I'm not exactly a pin-up. Besides, if you don't sleep with them, boys only keep you for three days."

"Well, yes, er…if you slept with them they would keep you two more days."

"Months."

"In any case don't do anything without a condom."

Auntie Andrea always calls a spade a spade.

Dad has full control of the TV. To watch Sylvie Vartan or the Beatles, I have to go to a friend's. Before, I was kept informed by the Pathé News at the cinema. Now I only hear bits of news on the radio. The headlines of the papers talk about serious troubles in Lebanon. A girl in our class is crying because she has just left Lebanon. We ask the Geography teacher where Lebanon is. She replies that it's not in the syllabus. Exit Lebanon.

On Sunday there is a party, a 'boum'. I'll buy the new Bill Haley record.

20 Death

Oone night when I am in the middle of a deep sleep, the telephone rings. Who's the idiot ringing up at three in the morning? I can hear Mum's voice talking to Dad. Then she comes in my room.

"Are you asleep?"

"Not now, who was that on the phone?"

"The Red Cross. There's been a terrible disaster at Fréjus. The dam has burst and the whole town has been submerged. They are calling for first-aid workers. I'm getting dressed."

"Can I come with you? I've got the first-aid certificate too."

"It's not a job for you and your Dad needs someone to prepare his breakfast."

I blow my top. I go to tell Dad that those people are about to die. To my great surprise, he agrees and Mum looks annoyed. For the first time I suspect my mother of using my father to have a better control of me.

We put on our boiler suits and boots. She makes a flask of coffee and takes a packet of crackers.

A convoy of ambulances, vans and cars starts up in the night. There is no motorway yet, so we have to follow the contours of the Esterel Massif. During the journey, we revise artificial respiration, mouth-to-mouth resuscitation and other rescue aids. When we arrived, the Police searchlights light up a scene like a Hieronymus Bosch's picture. Some of us vomit, I can't. My coffee and the crackers have turned into concrete in my stomach. We stand there, in the icy air and water with arms dangling. In fact we wonder what to do. In accidents simulated for training, the sun was shining, we had a lot of fun with fake fractures and we made great efforts to perform an artistic bandaging. The funniest was mouth-to-mouth resuscitation and it had even led to a marriage!

Here, in front of us, now, there is a sort of hill of sticky grey mud from which emerge bodies, arms, legs, and pieces of furniture. Everywhere little streams of water are still running. A fireman shakes us into life. He's dragging a body by one of its arms.

"Dead ones here, living ones over there," he yells. I've never seen a dead person before in my life. My parents have always kept me away when a death happened in the family.

I pull my first body out of the mud. I ask myself how to know whether they are dead or alive. I don't dare to look at the body I am dragging then I force myself to. She's a woman, with staring eyes and my hand is so cold that I can't feel hers. I pull her across to the 'pile' and I go back to the mud hill like a robot. I try to think of something else, something nice. I start daydreaming about myself as a ballerina at the opera, I'm dancing the Sleeping Beauty and a mysterious man is watching me in the audience… Someone shouts, "Where are the living ones?" Was it really over for those bodies? The survivors are between the sea and the Roman arenas. The arenas are so strong that they resisted the tumbling waters and divided them into two torrents with much less violence. The dam was called Malpasset (bad passage) because the Romans found the ground dangerous and never built on it. Some American helicopters arrive at dawn. I don't get any opportunity to save a life. In a way, I am relieved I don't have to do mouth-to-mouth resuscitation. I feel as if my mind was wrapped in a film isolating me from any emotion. I don't feel anything and I keep pulling bodies out of the mud in a mechanical way. Eventually I faint and come round in a moving van. I sleep for two days during which, helpers are still dragging bodies out of mud and water. I would need pills to forget those images. How do the survivors of the concentration camps manage to sleep? They don't says Mum.

Quite often, Dad would tell his mates how his platoon had surrounded a group of German soldiers who were so young that they hesitated to shoot them. The officer galvanised them as if before an important football match and gave them tots of rum. Then they shot them all but when they saw how young those soldiers were –some had acne- a few cried. The officer said "Cheer up, I got you off the Court Martial" It was one of Dad's recurring bad dreams.

21 Going Back to the State System

The newspapers and radio are talking about civil war in Algeria but they call it the 'Algerian Events', the word 'war' is taboo. People complain that they can't find wine from Mostaganem anymore.

However, for me the worst event is that the nuns want me to repeat my class because of my lack of maturity. They consent to offer me another chance: an examination in September. I am waiting for Roseline to come back from Italy to start studying. She has to repeat her year because of her spelling. In the meantime, I am going to the beach with Lambert. Her brother has just passed the Baccalaureate in Maths. He wants to be a teacher but he has already been called up for Military Service. His family are worried sick because he may be sent to Algeria.

At every party that summer we can hear 'The Green Leaves of Summer', and 'A train is Whistling'. In all the transistors radios Sheila shouts that 'School is Over' and Françoise Hardy is crying about being lonely when all the boys and the girls of her age are walking hand in hand. All the posters and adverts for swim suits show a girl in a bikini surrounded by boys. And yet, on our beach, it is the opposite: an ordinary boy surrounded by gorgeous girls in bikinis.

I am going up to my grandparents' in the mountains to drown my loneliness in more loneliness. I'll have siestas under the olive trees with the cicadas and comic books. I envy Granddad playing 'pétanque'; he doesn't have to worry about his future. I wonder if the trenches of 1914 were more terrifying than being thrown into the unknown…

The rich girls of the 'clan' who have to repeat their year are leaving to go to private colleges specializing in swotting to pass the Baccalaureate; those 'boîtes à Bac' are far too expensive for my parents. In the meantime, they go to Saint-Tropez or in Brittany whereas I am moping about in a dump in the Alps, at Grandma's.

At the end of August, as I am desperately trying to solve some insipid equations, I see Gran in the distance, rushing down the olive tree terraces and waving a letter in her hand like a white flag. Gran's joints are so elastic that her bones must be made of rubber!

"You have been accepted in 'Première' (Lower Sixth) at the lycée in September!"

What is she on about? The grammar school! I can't believe it! Without any exam! How can it be possible? Mum must have bribed an MP… no, she's far too shy. Dad? As the daughter of a War Invalid? I can't wait, I must go back down.

Explanation: the new headmistress of the lycée is a 'Pied-Noir'[10] and her school is under threat of being turned into a smaller school without a Sixth Form. To keep its status of grammar school, she must have a maximum of pupils entering the Baccalaureate years. It is a miracle (Thank you Saint Rita) I am going back to the state school. No more nuns, no more cliques! I rush to write to Roseline who's dying with impatience to leave her own dump but on the other side, in the Italian Alps.

---

10 Pied-Noir: Black-Feet, nickname given to the French from Algeria referring to the first people going with black shoes.

*

First day of term. It's a bit less hot. The bus stops in Place Garibaldi. I notice a superb patisserie called Cappa, whose cakes will cheer us up in dark hours. My heart is racing. It is the first time I've ever set foot in a grammar school. I hope there are no cliques here. I enter the playground. Funny, it's got chestnut trees, just like my first primary school! I feel like kissing them! I watch the girls. They look nice and are not dressed in the latest fashion. They know each other and observe us with curiosity. I feel awkward in my Sunday best. At last, Roseline arrives just before the Deputy Head appears with lists. She starts with the Upper Sixth. When it's our year's turn, we hold each other's hands tightly. There are four Lower Sixth years. We have little chance of being together. I even worry about being on the list at all. Suddenly I hear my name then hers. Hurrah! We are in the same class. We are even allowed to sit together!

The atmosphere of the lycée is so different. Everybody swots. A below-average mark can cause a drama. Roseline and I quickly realise that, to be accepted, we will have to work like mad. Thank God we are over with prayers and religious stuff. We won't hear ever again that He died for us. Anyway God is banned in state schools. We don't realise immediately that we are almost the only ones not to be from a Communist family. They all know we come from the private sector and therefore we are under observation. Here there is a distinct relationship between teachers and girls. It's as if they know why they are there.

Most of them are preparing for the very high standard competitive entrance exam for Teacher Training College as well as the Baccalaureate. The teacher's diploma is cherished by working class girls' families because it secures a job with paid holidays, paid sick leave and a retirement pension. It's ideal for women's independence. Whether we have the vocation for teaching or not is hardly considered. This way of thinking coincides exactly with Mum's dream. Strangely enough I had the impression that Dad's dream was very much like the nuns': women in the kitchen.

One day, during the reading of Moliere's "The Miser," when Harpagon exclaims, "She is the star of the stars..." the French teacher interrupts the monologue and asks "How could you describe Harpagon at that point?" I just shout, "He's star-struck." After a second of surprise, the girls burst out laughing and the teacher smiles. On that day I am accepted. I am so happy to hear myself called by my surname once again. It is virile and fraternal. Roseline, who has never known that tradition, finds it vulgar.

The lycée is ideally placed from a geographical point of view. At a stone's throw from the sea, opposite a bistro, next to the best cake shop in town and a military barracks where the 'Chasseurs Alpins', the Mountain Infantry, will protect us from the 'blouson noirs', the local teddy boys.

I come through the first term's exams respectably but I have never worked so hard in my life. The level is so much higher than in the nuns' school. Other girls are arriving from private colleges and one of them is from the clique. She regards herself as a swan among ducks. She won't stay very long.

Deschannel, the top of the class, is not conceited and is even popular. She too is preparing the competitive exam to enter the Teacher Training College. In the school, I've found my niche as the clown of my class, and it suits me.

During a break Deschannel tells me that "Dangerous Liaisons" is on and that she will be going to see the film on Sunday afternoon.

"Aren't you revising for the History paper on Monday?"

"Done it. I'll look at my notes on Sunday evening."

I spend the weekend on it. One hour of revision for three hours daydreaming. In our school we are entitled to be thick but we are not allowed to show it. To make up for the deficiencies of my moderate intelligence, I make extensive use of my memory. I learn by heart the Laws of Descartes, the formulas in Chemistry and the formulas of the sines and cosines, but people must not expect me to understand them as well. I am not very fond of the French teacher, - she is from Grenoble in the north and she reminds me of the nuns' mindset. The fact that she makes us learn by heart long extracts from the great classics such as Racine or Molière doesn't bother me. But the fact that she uses me to make the class laugh without my permission exasperates me. I suffer from a strong southern accent that might be the equivalent of a Geordie accent in England. So she finds nothing better to do than asking me to recite Phaedra's Despair with the Marseille accent. She says it relaxes her at the end of the day when she feels tired! What kills me with laughter is Cermino. Quite short with a high bun on top of her head and with red chubby apple-cheeks she performs the tragic Phaedra, in the Sarah Bernardt over-dramatic style. The teacher is entranced and the class is shaking with hidden giggles. Thanks to the two of us, the girls enjoy some happy moments. However, I am proud when Deschannel confesses that she nearly wets her

pants when listening to my Phaedra. It must sound like
Steptoe reciting Hamlet.

22 Boys

The area round our school becomes rough when night falls. A crowd of Teddy-boys gather at the gate to try to pick us up with no romantic feelings at all. Rumour has it that the pop singer Dick Rivers used to be with them. Crossing the Place Garibaldi without getting our bottoms pinched is like an assault course. Fortunately, the Mountain Infantry next door sometimes rescues us and we leave the battlefield with the dignity of offended queens.

Roseline and I don't fancy neither soldiers nor hooligans. We prefer trendy boys with Vespa scooters.

Both of us are living in the northern part of town called Borriglione. We always take the longest way to go back home because the Boulevard Jean-Jaures, the Place Masséna and the Avenue de la Victoire are lit as bright as day and the shops line up their wonderful windows. While we are walking up the avenue de la Victoire, we often encounter a young man as handsome as an American actor. Always alone, walking nonchalantly down the avenue. As soon as we catch sight of him, we nudge each other and try to look at him with indifference but Roseline can't hold a little nervous and stupid giggle. One day, he gives us a kind smile. We freeze. We don't have any illusions about our physical appearance. Roseline is fat with a flat nose and I am skinny with spots. That smile makes us fantasize for days. From now on, we look out for him. We meet him outside Prisunic, the department store he will mention in one of his books one day. His smile is just kind, we never see him trying to pick up girls and he never mocks us like the other boys. We talk about him to the whole class and

Cermino decides to walk with us. She comes, she sees him and she is convinced. I don't fall in love with him because, for me, he is from another planet. Not a hooligan, not a trendy boy, no Vespa, dressed in a classic way, but so handsome. We don't know yet that his name is Jean-Marie Le Clezio and that one day he will get the Nobel Prize for Literature. He'll never know that he will more or less destroy Roseline's life.

*

I wonder why Roseline and I persist in going dancing to parties because we are always the wallflowers.

"Monique gave me a tip to attract boys but it doesn't work," I say to Roseline.

"Oh yes? What's that? In any case she doesn't need it."

"She says that she sits down and looks depressed and immediately a boy comes to ask her what her problem is."

"Did you try?"

"Yeah. Nobody came and a boy asked Lambert if I often pulled that face!"

"Don't be such an idiot! Her tip works for pretty girls like her, not for us! We have to be smiling."

"I know. I've lots of male friends because I make them laugh but no one would think of asking me out."

"I can't even find male friends because I am not funny and I can't even dance the rock and roll."

"You should try to lose weight and change your hair style. Why don't you do the gym?"

"Because I can't wear shorts with my fat legs."

"I do and I'm knock-kneed."

"Yeah! But you can climb a rope and you can swim."

"So what? A boy isn't going to ask me for a dance because I can climb a rope."

Overcome by uncontrollable giggles, we get two hours detention from the teacher.

*

One Sunday, going to the cinema to see Exodus, we come across Nicole. She left the nuns' school after her Brevet exam, the GCSE, to attend a secretarial college. Now she is working in a bank and earning money!

"Are you enjoying it?" asks Roseline.

"You bet, I'm working with men, not boys and I'm going to take my driving test."

"And Josiane?"

"She's going to get engaged to an American sailor of the Sixth Fleet. He's with the 'Military Police'. He's got money, he showed us photos of his house and swimming pool!"

"She must be very happy!"

"You bet! When she is over there, I'll go to see her."

"And her family?"

"She's thrilled to be moving out. She's a bit upset because she can't introduce her parents to the guy. Her father's always drunk, her mother's incredibly stupid and they don't speak English."

Nicole is radiant. Her long fair hair is arranged in a skilful disorder, false eyelashes casting a shadow like a blind. She walks away on her stilettos.

"I think I prefer to stay at school," I say to Roseline.

"Me too, but if the blond boy in the avenue asked me to go to China with him, I would give up everything!"

"Really? No, I don't think I would. The Baccalaureate first."

23 The Pieds-Noirs

The Red Cross calls Mum again. The war is over. We lost Algeria. Thousands of repatriates are arriving on board two full boats. She has to go to the port. These people are French settlers, colonialists who are leaving Algeria. During the last few weeks, at the baker, the hairdresser, the market, and on the radio I hear this frightening little phrase: "The suitcase or the coffin." Three thousand people who chose the suitcase have landed in our town and have to be accommodated immediately. Lots are put in boarding schools. The younger ones regret leaving behind their flats, their houses, their cars and their furniture. The older ones are upset to leave behind their loved ones in the cemetery. Later, all of them will be longing for the beauty of Algeria, the easy life and… serious girls.

One morning, two new girls arrive from "over there," in our class: Suzanne Perez and Françoise Lévêque. There are in their twenties when joining our school. In Algeria they could be teachers or have all sorts of jobs without the Baccalaureate, but not in France.

The government allows them and even encourages them to resume their studies. Suzanne is cute, plump and suntanned. She looks like a Spanish dancer with her black hair parted down the middle and rolled up into a large bun on the nape. I sense she is ill at ease, especially with the teachers. I suggest that we go and introduce ourselves but Roseline is not enthusiastic.

"Did you see how arrogant she looks? Like a girl from the Masséna clique!"

The other girl, Lévêque, has immediately been given the nickname 'Seen-it-all'. She has a ravaged face, speaks very little and disappears during break. She comes to school in a 2 CV given by her uncle and has an old-fashioned leather school satchel that is coming unstitched.

Perez is the stereotype of the Pied-Noir with a strong accent. I wonder if the French teacher is going to ask her to recite Phaedra. She also has the habit of giving us back our essays with sarcastic comments and by starting from the top to increase and enjoy the suspense.

"Mademoiselle Perez, nine out of twenty, your essay is mediocre."

"The topic too Madame."

Gotcha! I exulted.

"Mademoiselle, kindly note that I make the comments in this class and that I shall inform the Headmistress of your insolence."

Perez smiles. Madame Montfort is not a headmistress like the others. She is a Mother to her pupils and she is a Pied-Noir too. Lévêque, who often forgets her homework, gets Saturday afternoon detention quite frequently. She never goes and spends long sessions in the Head's office. The staff rolls their eyes and misses the old headmistress who has supported them whatever.

Perez is alone, leaning up against a pillar in the covered yard, and Lévêque has disappeared into the toilets as usual. I buy two brioches from the caretaker and I beckon Roseline to follow me. I go up to Suzanne Perez.

"You're looking frozen!" I say to her with a smile.

"It's so humid too!"

"The Castle hill blots out the sun."

"Where's the castle?"

"It's been gone for a long time. In 1543, Catherine Ségurane, name of our lycée, pushed the Saracens back from one of the towers…"

"…Now it's the Saracens who push us back…" she cuts in.

"…There is a beautiful view of the sea from up there. You'll see when the Gym teacher comes back, we go up there… Don't you want my other brioche? It's still warm and I got too many!"

"Thanks a lot, I'll pay you back in class."

"Don't be silly, it's my welcome gift!"

"That's nice of you. What's your name?"

"Sophie and this is Roseline but here we call each other by our surname."

"Roseline is a pretty name."

"It's not my real name. My parents called me Marie-Rose like the product to kill lice."

"Oh crumbs!" She bursts out laughing for the first time since she's been here.

We ask her what she thinks of our class.

"I find the girls a bit youngish, even babyish, but that's normal."

"And the teachers?"

"They certainly let you know they've got a PhD. You can tell more by their arrogance than by their knowledge."

"Yeah, but not all of them."

"And you, you're from here?"

"Yep! Roseline and I were born here, in Nice."

The bell calls us back. Roseline finishes her third brioche and Lévêque joins us in the row with a whiff of tobacco.

*

One Sunday, Roseline and I are queuing to see Ben-Hur. I am crazy about Charlton Heston, he's quite different from Le Clezio. Heston has something wild that a woman would love to tame. I just catch sight of Perez at the end of the queue. I wave to her to join us.

"Are you on your own?"

"My parents prefer a cat nap!"

"I would never dare to go to the cinema on my own," says Roseline.

"What are you afraid of?" asks Perez.

"Dunno."

I am swept off my feet by the film. I perspire in the arena with the lions, I shiver with fear when I see the giant blades fixed to the wheels of the Roman chariots, I am overwhelmed when Ben-Hur hears a man talking to the crowd "Verily, verily I say unto you…" Jesus at the cinema is altogether different from the glamorous, bland or bleeding Jesus of Religious Education. There, Hollywood makes him alive. It's quite an anti-climax to find the 20th Century's pavement again. We walk to the Café de Paris to have an espresso. Some of the cliques are there but we manage to ignore them. I ask Perez if she's the one who chose our school.

"No, the other grammar schools were too hard to get into. Calmette grammar demanded a school record."

"Don't you have one?"

"The Fellaghas[11] didn't allow us the time to go to the Education Board."

"Ah…. And Lévêque… do you know what's the matter with her?"

---

11 Fellagha: fighters for the Independence of Algeria.

"Big problems."

"You don't want to tell us? We could help her maybe…"

"Well… Don't tell anyone, it would finish her off."

"You have our word of honour."

"Her twin sister died of leukaemia and her father was shot by the Arabs on the way to the boat. She and her mother had to take the boat without burying her father."

We were horrified.

"I thought… in any war they let people bury their dead!"

"It's not exactly a war… It's like a revolution….you can't understand."

I think she can't understand it herself. She starts crying.

Roseline's mother is not impressed, "Those people! They're all pretending to be martyrs so as to milk the government! Because of them the price of flats has soared like mad!" Mum, who was there with the Red Cross when they arrived, is more tolerant. I can't make up my mind, I always agree with the last person to have spoken. Both Perez and Lévêque have convinced me they are right. Deschannel, whose father works at the Patriote, a local communist paper, says that France should have left Algeria long ago, that colonies belong to another century like slavery. But Perez says that Algeria was not a colony but a French department and that we are doing more harm to the Arabs by leaving. Lévêque tells us that in Algeria, France did, in one century, what forty-three kings and five republics have not achieved in some French provinces. Deschannel says that the Arabs didn't see the advantages of it until 1947, if then! And she quotes Albert Camus: "For

the moment the Arab empire doesn't exist historically –
except in Colonel Nasser's writing- but it could be achieved
through world upheavals which means that World War 3
would not be far off."

I like Perez and Lévêque a lot and I admire
Deschannel a lot. They never talk to each other. I start to
read Camus.

*

A few weeks later, as we enter the playground, a
surprise awaits us. Two young men are standing there with
an attaché-case. Perez and Lévêque are speaking to them.
We join a group of classmates. Deschannel calls out to me.

"Have you seen?"

"Who're they?"

"Guess!"

"Too young to be teachers, too old to be at school."

"Brilliant deduction!"

"Pieds-Noirs?"

"Yep! And they're entering the Upper Sixth."

"Can't be, we're a girls school."

"Not anymore! All the schools are full to bursting,
Félix Faure and Parc Imperial have become mixed."

"And Calmette?"

"You're joking! A fascist lycée! You have to be
whiter than white…"

"Of course, it's rather difficult for a Pied-Noir!"

My remark causes an outburst of shrill laughter. The
two men frown. Perez reassures them.

"Don't worry, it's only Sophie."

24 Teachers

Even with a PhD, some teachers can be useless. Being civil servants, whatever they do wrong they can't lose their job. The worst ones are at the University but in our lycée, most of the teachers are decent. At that time, the whole school is in a state of effervescence: we are going to be mixed! The teachers find it more difficult to maintain order and the tutors[12] are not happy, they have to work on Saturday afternoon because of the increasing number of detentions.

Our PE teacher is close to retirement and often away. It takes thirty minutes to walk up the winding road to Castle Hill and twenty to come back down again.

Then twenty minutes to get undressed and dressed again. So there are forty minutes left for the gym out of two hours.

Some girls miss gym three times a month because of their periods, others forget their shorts and when it's raining, it's cancelled. What is going to happen for the boys? No problems, they can get out of it since they have to do their PM instead; it's a preparation for Military Service.

Our Physics teacher is from another century. Steeped in religion with a son who's a monk at a 'Trappist' Monastery, she never smiles and doesn't need to enforce discipline. As soon as we enter her class or her laboratory, we go as silent as Carmelites.

---

12 Tutors: students working in schools in charge of discipline and admin.

She generates an Inquisition-like terror. Small, stocky, with grey curly hair pulled back in a tiny bun tied at the nape; she opens her mouth only to explain Physics or Chemistry. She never makes any remarks on our homework, we have a mark on our copy and that's all. If we have an outrageous hairstyle, too high stilettos or too tight skirts, she remains stony-faced.

Physically, she reminds me of Golda Meir, Israel's Prime Minister. One day, as we are going into her classroom, she is sitting at her desk, presenting her backlit left profile to us. Then when facing her, we notice that the right side of her face is grotesquely swollen, probably by a dental abscess. Nobody says anything. We don't dare look at each other in order to hold back our giggles until the next lesson. I don't know if it's because of the pain but on that day she makes an historical exception; she gives Lévêque her copy back and says: "Mademoiselle Lévêque, if you have any difficulties with Chemistry, come and see me and I'll give you some help."

At break time we all rush over to Lévêque.

"Do you realise it's the first time she has spoken to a girl? Will you ask her for help? You'll tell us about it, won't you?"

For the first time too, Lévêque gives a pale smile.

During the Geography lesson, Roseline being away, I sit down next to Lévêque. As I am not particularly enthusiastic about the port of Rotterdam traffic, I strike up a conversation. I know the boys are Pieds-Noirs like her.

"In which Upper Sixth are the boys?"

"Science and Maths."

"Oh dear, they're going to have your new pal!"

"She's the only teacher who's said anything nice to me."

"You know them?"

"They're also expatriates."

"Do you live far from the school?"

"No, by the harbour."

"Did you have problems finding accommodation?"

"No, friends of my parents left to teach in the West Indies and let us have their flat."

I am about to say she's lucky but stop in time. I find out that the boys are resuming their studies to postpone Military Service. They used to work but they have only their Brevet (GCSE). Jean-Claude, the oldest, is 22 but dresses like a 40 year old. He is quite attractive but looks at the others with disdain.

The other one, Pierre, 20 year old, can't look at a girl without assessing her. He's going to be busy with six hundred girls. A girl from the Science Sixth forms tells us that their teacher (the terrible Golda Meir) wrote the name of the boys in her register as if they were ordinary new pupils and ignored them during the whole lesson.

However, a new girl is going to set her a challenge. She comes from a private school in Paris. She is tall, blonde, sweet-looking with beautiful blue baby eyes asking, "Where am I?" Marie-France Guillaume is the first unintelligent girl to enter the grammar school. She isn't aware of it and therefore doesn't try to hide it by working harder. The day before the History Term Exam, the whole class reckon that the Austro-Hungarian Compromise will be the question. We kindly mention it to the boys and to Guillaume. Bingo, the question comes as predicted. During the exam, I nudge Roseline and point towards

Guillaume. She has been sitting there for two hours, sucking her pen and then she hands in a blank copy. The teacher, totally confused, asks her."

"Don't you want to write your name?"

In French literature, when the teacher requests her opinion, she's unable to answer. Annoyed, she asks her: "Do you read books sometimes?"

"Yes Madam."

"What do you read?"

"Guy des Cars[13]."

The class collapse. And yet, we have all read one book by des Cars otherwise we would not have laughed. After all, it's a beginning. I'm delighted not to be the French teacher's laughing stock any more.

During a test in Chemistry with Golda Meir, Guillaume dares to take the book out and opens it on her lap. The laboratory tables are so basic that there's nothing to hide the book. Everybody can see what she's up to. We are terrified for her. The silence is such that we can hear her turning the pages. The teacher doesn't make a move and looks elsewhere.

At the end of the test, she asks Deschannel to collect the copies. No one reports her, -we are not at the convent. Next day, Golda Meir gives back the copies with no comments as usual. When Guillaume gets her test back she turns to her neighbour and whispers: "I've got zero! That's not fair, I wrote two pages on copper."

"If I were you, I'd shut up."

She puts her hand up. We hold our breath.

"Mademoiselle Guillaume?"

---

13 Guy des Cars is the equivalent of Barbara Cartland in France.

"Madame, why did you give me a zero? I wrote two pages!"

"Yes, on copper. It wasn't the question. We are not doing that metal until next week."

25 Men

Lambert and her brother are giving a party, a 'boum'. Roseline and I are invited and Suzanne Perez will bring two blokes from the upper Sixth. Roseline fancies Jean-Claude. She rushes to the hairdresser to get a super Brigitte Bardot bun. It's like a tiered wedding cake on which the lacquer shines like caramel. I go to have my hair straightened. I have to endure two hours of ammonia smell but my fringe is still waving like an astrakhan sheep. It has nothing to do with Brigitte Bardot's lovely wisps popping out around the face. I just look like Louis XIV. The girls have to beg me to go to the party. When we arrived, Perez introduces Jean-Claude and Pierre to us. The small flat is chock-a-block. Lambert's brother gives me a peck and has to yell louder than the music.

'How's that Maths coming along, then?"

I introduce him to Perez.

"Suzanne, this is Jean-Jacques, -Einstein, he helps me with my Maths."

"Pleased to meet you, my problem's with Physics."

"I can solve any problem!"

Then he invites her to dance to Johnny Hallyday's amorous song 'Retiens la Nuit', i.e "Don't let the night go". I go over to Roseline who's holding a cigarette and a glass to look the part.

"Where's Jean-Claude?"

"Over there, on the arm of the chair. He's smoking and isn't asking anyone to dance."

Suddenly, Pierre interrupts us, he takes my arm and drags me on the floor for a dance, without asking. I can't believe it!

"Suzanne talks a lot about you."

"Does she? …"

"She says you were the first one to talk to her. The others were rather stuck up."

"They are shy with newcomers and you are all older than us."

He is not holding me tight and we carry on dancing to Italian pop songs, 'Una Lacrima sul Viso', 'Volare'…

"Doesn't your friend Jean-Claude dance?"

"It's not his thing,.. Why, do you want to dance with him?"

"No, no, but I think Roseline would like to."

End of the Italian songs, beginning of Bill Haley's crazy rock. Pierre says that rock and roll is not his thing. A bit boring, that bloke!

In the evening, at the bus stop, I chat with Suzanne.

"You're in luck to be rated by Jean-Jacques, he's nice and clever."

"He's a kid!"

"Only three years younger!'

"I prefer older men."

"Berks!"

She shrugs her shoulders with a smile. Roseline has a face as long as a fiddle.

"What's the matter?" asks Suzanne.

"Jean-Claude. He didn't make a move during the whole afternoon. All he did was smoke and change the records."

"He's not feeling comfortable, you should understand, everybody is much younger than him, especially mentally. In Algeria, he watched tragic events happening, then over here, he sees the young people interested in Johnny Hallyday and Sylvie Vartan's romance. And girls like Cermino who make a scene if they can't find a nail polish matching their lipstick. Also he can't bear the school discipline. It's very hard for him after street fighting with the OAS[14]."

I don't dare ask her what the OAS was.

When Suzanne gets off at her bus stop, Roseline says to me.

"Listen, Pierre seems to like you, why don't you go out with him, it'd help me get closer to Jean-Claude!"

"I'm flattered that he asked me for a dance but that guy doesn't mean a thing to me."

"Make an effort… at any rate long enough for me to become friendly with Jean-Claude."

"We'll see, there's no hurry. Did you know he fought with the OAS?"

"What's that?"

"I was going to ask you. Aren't they terrorists or something?"

"Dunno. Let's go to Etam tomorrow, they're selling Chanel skirts at a bargain price"

*

At last our class too is becoming mixed! From the last boat, four boys and two girls arrived. One of which,

---

14 OAS: Organisation de l'Armée Secrète: people against the independence of Algeria.

Joelle, is a ravishing false blonde. The two girls go to the Upper Sixth and the boys come into our class. Since the arrival of the Pieds-Noirs, we talk a lot about politics at the lycée. It looks as if there are already disagreements between them.

All of them would have preferred to stay over there but not for the same reasons. Roseline and I are curious to ask them what the difference is between French Algeria and Algerian Algeria but they are so excitable about that question that we never dare.

The lycée has been agog for three days now because the film star Robert Hossein is shooting a film on our Place Garibaldi. We desert Madame Susanne's bistro to see the actor. What a disappointment! He's a short man with hairy ears, and a face covered with thick make-up. His conversation with the cameraman is instructive: "…Which girl would you like to shag?" Joelle makes an impression on him. She quickly realises it. She starts simpering and smiling around. Roseline comments, "Who does she think she is? Brigitte Bardot?" Then later, people saw Joelle coming out of his hotel.

A more important event breaks the routine for the second time since the arrival of the Pieds-Noirs. Our PE teacher is on sick leave for, at least, two months. All that the Education Board can find to replace her with is a military instructor who's training parachutists.

The first male teacher in the lycée! Therese Gali, slightly worried, asks how long that man is going to stay.

Gali hates Gym and sports. She holds the record for the number of periods in one month. She's going to find it difficult to explain to a soldier that she can't do the Gym because of her period, for the third time this month, the register showing her absences. I explain the situation to Lévêque who bursts out laughing, then suddenly starts to cry.

"What's the matter? What did I say?"

"No, no, it's not you…it's the first time I've laughed, I didn't think I could again…"

I don't know what to say, I put my arm round her shoulders. The Deputy-head arrives and yells - it's her way of speaking.

"Lévêque, you don't have to do Gym."

"Come and do Gym with us, it's better than staying behind on your own." I say.

The next day, we gather in the playground with our sport bags. The instructor, all kitted out, arrives with the Deputy head. He's built like a rugby player.

"Ladies, may I introduce your new PE teacher, Monsieur Scortesi."

Roseline whispers in my ear.

"With a teacher like him, I'm not going to miss a single lesson,"

Monsieur Scortesi displays an engaging smile.

"Ladies, you have five minutes to change."

"Sir, we always change up there."

"Not with me, go to your class and get changed. Hurry, we leave in five minutes. If you're late, ten push-ups!" and he takes his stopwatch out.

We rush like mad to our class, change and run to the gate where he's standing with the Register.

"Off we go, at a jog, breathe in… breathe out."

Gali starts to be seriously worried.

"He's not going to make us run up there, is he?"

We reach the first bend, already breathless.

"Hey, lasses, where are you going?"

"We follow the road, Sir."

"Roads are for cars, we go this way!"

Nobody moves because nobody understands. His finger is pointing at the hill, the trees and the bushes.

"We're taking the shortcuts, the goat tracks…"

Gali is on the verge of a nervous breakdown.

"I knew he was a nutcase. I shouldn't have come! I'm sick of this circus. Tomorrow I'll go to the doctor and get a medical certificate!"

We are all thinking the same, but in the meantime, we are climbing on all fours, trying to go round the nettle bushes and hanging onto roots. I can see Gali, far behind us. When we reach the top, we're encouraging her with screams and laughter. As soon as she manages to get there, with a scarlet face and breathless, the teacher blows his whistle and we have to go again in a mad run to keep up with him. The final whistle gives us a break to breathe as we are all panting.

From the top of the hill, there's a panoramic view of the Bay of Angels. In the distance, above the airport, veils of mist are being torn apart by the breeze and the Mediterranean Sea is glittering peacefully in the sun. Just below us, the Old City draws its red roofs tightly together and, in the middle, the multi-coloured dome of the Italian church pops up.

Nice is on the last step of the Alps' giant stairs, then the next one plunges two thousand metres under the sea. Lévêque is looking towards the airport.

"Beautiful, isn't it?"

"You haven't seen the Bay of Algiers."

The whistle blows and we go on again. Push-ups, scissors jumps, high jumps, exercises, the lot. Gali is half dead.

That's it. It's over. The end of the lesson! But the mad man goes crazy and makes us climb down the hill by crawling across the brambles. We arrive in the playground, dirty, scratched, exhausted. Monsieur Scortesi is holding Gali by the waist and she is hanging onto his chest on the verge of fainting. The headmistress sees us from her study and rushes downstairs.

"Monsieur Scortesi, what have you done to my girls?"

"Nothing Madame, a good shower and they'll be fine."

"We don't have showers in the lycée!"

The next day, stiffness makes every move painful and Gali is away. She won't ask for a medical certificate and won't miss a single lesson until the return of our old PE teacher. And then, her periods will come back three times a month as usual.

*

The general atmosphere of the school is changing considerably. Fashion is taking on an outrageous importance. One has to wear excessively pointed shoes, a suede jacket, a pleated Chanel skirt, and backcombed hair with so much lacquer that it looks like snail slime. Deschannel says it's no longer the Dictatorship of the Proletariat but the Dictatorship of the Fashion. If the competitive exam to enter the Teacher Training College and the Baccalaureate remain the top target, the conquest of the male is number two. I always wonder where, all these perfume samples circulating in school, come from, all of a sudden.

Princess d'Albret or Calèche d'Hermès are favourites but difficult to find. After lessons we always meet at Madame Suzanne's, very different from the posh Masséna café. We wear out the sturdy table football, the 'babyfoot' game. 'Chez Laurette' will become a nostalgic song reminding us of the very happy hours spent at Madame Suzanne's bistro.

The boys are so excited to find themselves in a girls' school, they can't get over it. Some of them were at a Jesuit or a Marist College in Algeria. However it does help those who are traumatised by the independence war. The Pieds-Noirs suffer from a 'chagrin d'amour,' love sickness for the land of Algeria. The girls are the first ones to recover and they quite quickly turn the page. The boys find it slightly more difficult not to maintain their way of life. They find the girls from France too emancipated. Coeducation is a new situation for them and the effect is not what one would expect. The boys find it difficult to concentrate, especially those who come from the Jesuit Colleges. As for us, girls, we swot even more than before to show them that we can do as well as them. We think that's part of our strategy to conquer. Deschannel goes from an average mark of 15 out of 20 to 18 and yet she does nothing to come closer to the boys. She always seems to look at them with pity. Gali is making great progress in Gym, Cermino knows all Racine by heart. Roseline and I manage to maintain our standard above average. Not in Chemistry for me. I can't accept that an acid plus a base can give salt and water. Therefore our Mediterranean is made of acid and base? Crazy. Roseline rolls her eyes.

Apart from Algeria, little reaches us from the external world apart from the regular appearance of the Yeti in the Himalayas and the flying saucers renamed UFOs.

We're looking forward to the Easter holidays. The teachers make us work like dogs: term exams, mock exams, tests, one after the other! The boys find it hard to follow and make fun of us because we work. Some of them think they are above it, so they give up and often meet at Madame Suzanne's to play cards. Deschannel joins them, as she has already done her work. Marie-Jeanne Deschannel is always ahead in her work, she's not a top-of-the class like the others, she's also intelligent in life. Roseline, Gali, Cermino and I sometimes meet the boys there for a short session of table football.

One day the buses are on strike. Usually we come back on foot but this time we are exhausted by two hours of Gym with Scortesi, two tests in Science and finishing at six. Lévêque offers to take us back in her 2CV. At the traffic lights, I catch sight of our handsome blond going down the avenue with his typical nonchalant walk.

"Look, look!" I say to Françoise, "He's the bloke we told you about!"

"Him? I know him!"

"I can't believe it!" Roseline screamed.

"He lives in my block of flats, on the floor below."

"Do you talk to him?"

"No, he's not talkative but he has exchanged a few words with my mother."

"What does he do? What's his name?" Roseline asked.

"He's a student at the Faculty of Letters and on his letter box, you can read J. M. Leclézio."

"Don't you find him awesome?"

"Er…I think he looks barmy. I prefer dark handsome men."

"And she's the one who lives in his building! What luck," sighs Roseline.

"If I were lucky, I would still live in our flat in Oran."

I give Roseline a black look but she shrugs her shoulders.

26 Parties

The basement of our villa is quite spacious so I get permission to have a party. I get on well with all the girls in the class and yet some of the hard workers won't come. Deschannel comes with Lorrain, her best friend. Suzanne thinks that it's just as well because the hard-working girls are really too young. When there's a party in my town, it's quickly circulated by boys going from café to café on a Vespa or a moped and the party gets fifty guests instead of twenty.

"Did you invite Nicole?" asks Roseline.

"Yeah but she says she prefers mature men!"

Lambert and her brother Jean-Jacques come. He's in charge of the records and his sister of the drinks. Roseline tries to filter the guests at the door. As for me, I stay in my bedroom to do my homework. The party is for my mates. I usually get bored being the wallflower and I don't want people noticing it. At about three o'clock, Roseline comes upstairs and knocks on my door. She wants me to see the transformation of Lévêque. She is superb even if the makeup makes her look older. At four, Roseline comes back all excited.

"Guess who has just arrived? The clique from the Masséna!"

"The girls from the nuns'?"

"Yesssss!"

"What a cheek! Just think, we cross over the street to avoid their mockery!"

"They don't know they're at your place. They came along with well groomed guys."

"What shall we do?"

"Come down, don't leave me alone. We can pretend we are guests. Also Pierre asked where you were. Make an effort, be nice to him. He's with Jean-Claude who's got his long face."

"I thought you were crazy about Leclézio."

"Yeah, but it would be easier with Alain Delon."

I go downstairs. They are all there. The girls look down at me and say some words to the boys who start laughing loudly. Jean-Jacques puts the Everly Brothers records on. To look busy, I pour myself a glass of Pschitt Orange. One of the girls approaches me.

"You came alone?"

"No, with my friends."

"Is that the bloke who's giving the party?" she says, pointing at Jean-Jacques.

"Dunno, think so."

"Bloody nice house he's got, there's enough space for plenty more people."

She goes up to the ground floor and unashamedly uses our telephone to call a friend and asks him to bring all his friends from his college.

"Let them come," Roseline advises me, "We might meet new people."

They arrive looking self-satisfied, with their American cigarettes and the arrogance of 'daddy's boys'. They are noisy, play their own records and make nasty remarks. Jean-Jacques asks them to smoke outside because the oil tank for the central heating is in the room next door.

"Bloody hell! There isn't a clean glass anywhere and now we can't even smoke!"

Lorrain watches them with lenient curiosity. Deschannel shows an almost aggressive contempt and Gali looks at them with pity. Jean-Claude is speaking with Suzanne and Lévêque is on guard. A boy and a girl are arguing above the record player and the needle skates across the surface of a Ray Charles single. Mum appears to warn me that there are cigarette stubs smouldering on the ground around the oil tank. On seeing her, one of the boys exclaims "Hullo, that's all we needed, the old fogies have arrived."

I feel so inferior compared to them that I don't know what to do. They are more at home in my house than I am. Perez, Lévêque and a few girls of my class come to tell me that they are going to leave. "Those girls are taking away the only male friends we know!" Suddenly one of the boys calls Cermino an ugly cow. Everybody hears him, some laugh loudly. Cermino freezes and turns red; poor little humiliated Phaedra, standing there with her old-fashioned skirt and her Brigitte Bardot bun shaking slightly on top of her head. At that moment I feel a sudden and sound rage overwhelming me, drowning all my fears and complexes. I switch off the record player and I shout to the Masséna clique to shove off. One of their girls bursts out laughing.

"It's not your home!"

"Wrong, it is my house, you stupid little goose! You and your friends, get the hell out of here."

"If we go, we'll take everybody with us to another party."

"Great, go ahead and don't forget your stuff."

I pick up a pile of their records and throw them at her feet. The whole group goes away but the rest stay behind. Lévêque comes to me.

"My God, I don't recognize you!"

"Me neither! My heart is beating like mad! I'd never have believed they would go so easily!"

"You didn't see your face!" Roseline says.

The others are staring at me as if they are seeing me for the first time.

Jean-Jacques switches the record player back on again and quickly chooses 'Anyone Who has an Heart', a romantic Petula Clarke song and invites Suzanne to dance. I am about to go back to my bedroom when Pierre invites me to dance. He hasn't seen anything, he was in the lavatory. I hesitate for a second then I catch Roseline's begging eyes. Eventually everybody is dancing, even Roseline with Jean-Claude. I can hear Lévêque laughing, she is dancing with a Corsican friend who imitates the old-fashioned crooner Tino Rossi.

And now Pierre starts to hold me tight. I decide to give way to help Roseline but I also have a desperate need to have a boyfriend. He plays the war hero and tells me that he was in the street with the generals during the Algiers Putsch[15] on 13th May and that he was nearly killed. And I, poor idiot, melt like snow on a dirty boiler.

---

15 A failed coup d'état to overthrow French President de Gaulle.

27 Virginity

Suzanne Perez gave me the address of a beautician. Because the demography of our town shows a ratio of seven girls to one boy, the number of beauty parlours tends to exceed the number of bakeries. Roseline goes first to test their makeup. The beautician is an artist. She transforms her olive foundation into apricot and manages to thin her puffed cheeks thanks to clever shadows. The address of her salon goes round the school.

I believe that, going out with Pierre, will give me self-confidence. At the end of the lessons, I wait for him at the gate; I am keen to show off I am his girl. When I want to take his hand, he takes it away quickly and in the street, he walks a respectable distance from me. I get the idea he's ashamed of me so I rush to the beauty salon and ask the beautician to remove my blackheads and my hairs.

With a kind smile she replies that there's going to be a lot of work. Plucking my eyebrows takes her half an hour and she says that my nose looks like a grate because of the big blackheads.

Pierre doesn't seem to notice the change. Mum finds my thin eyebrows ridiculous but my classmates think it's a vast improvement. One says that now the beautician has removed the gutter, she can see I have beautiful green eyes.

One Saturday, Pierre invites Roseline, Jean-Claude and me to go to his place to have a drink. Roseline bunks her lessons to go back to the beauty parlour. I would have but Mum wouldn't give me the money. In the bus taking us to Pierre's, we are very nervous.

"It's not a party…"

"I know, I'm a bit worried."

"Me too. What's your perfume?"

"A sample of Balanciaga."

We arrive outside a baroque style block of flats. It's on the third floor but we don't take the lift because it's an enormous creaking machine. The silence is oppressive when we ring the doorbell. Pierre opens in shirtsleeves, smoking a pipe! Jean-Claude stands in the drawing room, holding a glass. Roseline and I sit on the sofa next to each other. Jean-Claude is bitter because he will have to leave the lycée. He's no longer allowed to defer military service. He doesn't like the lycée but hates the Army. He can't bear the docility of the swotting girls who think only about exams. "You don't need diplomas to get married." He's tried several times to stir things up in class but nobody has ever joined in and he has found himself being the only one playing the fool or the rebel. Roseline and I pretend to side with him.

Then he looks at me and said: "So I heard you're the agitator in your class?"

"Sort of. Just crossing swords with the French teacher."

"The worst are the supervisors[16] They are my age and they give me orders in front of everybody!"

"It's their job and they are students. Maurel's got a Degree in Law…"

Maurel is everything Roseline and I want to be. Nearly as beautiful as the Italian star Sophia Loren, she has

---

[16] Supervisors are paid students in charge of discipline and admin work.

curves and a brain. She's confident enough to feel above the clique of the Masséna. Once, I have to stay two hours with her as she's supervising detention. We start to talk, as there is nobody else. I tell her how much I admire and envy her. She smiles and says that life was not that easy for her and that her beauty can be a handicap. Law students don't take female students seriously, especially if they are good looking. She envies another female student who left after two years to become the film star Marie-France Pisier. I am dumbfounded when she tells me that she is going out with a seventeen-year-old boy! She says he's more mature than any student and above all, he's not a 'macho'. It is the first time I hear this word.

Someone touches my shoulder.

"What are you thinking about, you've gone silent!"

"I was thinking about Maurel."

"That bird is not impressive but she thinks she is Marilyn Monroe," Jean-Claude exclaims.

Pierre puts on a record of romantic music to establish a more intimate contact. He draws the curtains. Nobody is fooled by the scenario but we pretend to dance. Jean-Claude is already getting excited kissing Roseline and I can see his hands slide in under her blouse in search of the fastener of her bra. Doesn't he know that Velcro has just been invented? Obviously not, so he drags Roseline to the bedroom to study this new system. Pierre is using the same tactic and I am worried stiff that he's going to discover my breasts are only big enough to fill half the bra. He too drags me to his bedroom and makes no comments when passing his hands under my bra. After a moment, I stop the action.

"What's wrong?"

"Nothing but it's almost six and we must get back."

"Your Mum's waiting?"

"I just prefer not to go any further."

"Why are you afraid? Is it the first time?"

"Yes, and I don't want to get pregnant."

"But I can pull out beforehand."

"Too risky!"

We hear the sound of a door.

"You see, Roseline wants to leave too."

I adjust my clothing and we leave the room. Jean-Claude is smoking and looking out of the window. Roseline is ready to leave with her coat done up, her bag slung over her shoulder, her mouth slightly red with irritation and a lock of hair undone. Our eyes meet. We take the lift that creaks and shakes. Once outside we take a deep breath of fresh air.

"Well?"

"Well?"

We laugh.

"How did it go? Tell me first."

"I don't think he'll see me again," Roseline declares.

"You don't seem that disappointed!"

"I dunno... I don't understand... kissing and cuddling is pleasant! Why do we have to move quickly to dirty things! And he called me a teaser as well!"

"He just wanted to go to bed with you."

"Not quite. I can understand that even if I would not have done it. No, it's not that. He unbuttoned his flies and got his thing out. I hadn't even noticed until he took my hand and put it on it! I took it away immediately. He did it again and tried to keep my hand there. When he understood that I didn't want to touch it, he said "Are you frigid, or what?" I didn't reply so he put his trousers back on, looked at his watch and lit a cigarette.

"Did he ask you when you were going to see each other again?"

"You must be joking! Not a word! And you?"

"Oh the usual thing, he tried and I didn't want to and yet I would have liked to! But, just by thinking I could become pregnant, I panicked."

"Yeah…I wonder how such an ugly thing can give so much pleasure. His was even uglier than the one of the statue on the Place Massena!"

We crack up together.

*

It's Easter. Resurrection for some, slow death for others. The palm trees give their hearts for weaving artistic branches. My heart feels 'woven' and I'm watching the candles burning. Who to pray to? No saint is a specialist in my problems, not even St Rita. The Virgin Mary would not have a clue. Maybe God, after all he's supposed to be a specialist in everything…

I start my revision by doing ten minutes' actual work for every two hours of daydreaming. If only I could grab hold of my mind with both hands and tie it to that chair! I keep playing scenarios in my head.

I go back to Pierre another Saturday. Jean-Claude is there with a girl from the Philosophy Upper Sixth. She's a little curly-haired blonde with an angelic face, hiding her wings under a grey, shabby duffle coat. This time, no scenario, no drink and no music. We disappear straight into the bedrooms. I know it's the D-Day. I also know that I will never confess that to any priest. While Pierre is putting his condom on, I notice there's a crack in the ceiling that looks like the river Rhone on the map of France. I close my eyes because I was told it would be divine or atrocious. It is neither. I am still waiting for the effect, but he has already finished. He is lying next to me with a hard face. I give him a cuddle and snuggle up to him. He pushes me away and says "You're taking me for a fool….Don't look innocent! I must be the third or fourth boy to whom you offered your so-called virginity!"

"Are you mad?"

"And you're frigid as well!"

Frigid? Quite possibly because I didn't feel anything. But I was a virgin and I am expecting a passionate gratitude for that gift! I go to cry on Roseline's shoulder. She's perplexed. She says I am the only one in our class not to have painful periods and to have had them so late. That's all I need! I am abnormal! I tell Roseline that virginity ought to be removed at birth, just as they take out children's tonsils. She bursts out laughing. That doesn't help me. Why didn't I bleed? Why didn't I feel anything?

*

Leaning over my Mallet-Isaac book of History, I am reading the chapter on the 1830 Revolution for the tenth time. My mind keeps running away and asking questions that have nothing to do with Thiers or the removal of the guns, which I can't care less about. I also lose interest in the television in favour of the telephone. I call him sometimes, just to hear his voice. And yet, I feel it's not really love, it is not lust either but I don't know what it is. My mistake is believing in showing servility, submission, resignation and in consenting to sacrifices in order to be loved. I'm not going down to Hell as the nuns would say, but to the sewage.

Roseline wants to know everything about Joelle, the girl who replaces her. I don't have very much to say. I see her, sometimes, when I go to Pierre's. We don't have the time to talk, we come here only for one thing. Pierre never talks to me in the school playground and Jean-Claude does the same with Joelle. I lose the little appetite I had and Roseline gets hungrier than ever. She keeps a baguette in her school bag. As the bread is still warm and her father makes it exquisitely, I eat some, sitting with her on the bench in the covered playground. The girls are teasing us; they say that with a bottle of wine we would look like tramps. I think that's not a bad idea and I try wine. Fortunately, like the first cigarette, the first sip without water makes me sick.

Sharing that fresh bread brings us a kind of comfort and relief. At lunchtime I am not hungry anymore and Mum pulls her hair out. I lose weight and Roseline gains more.

At the beginning of May, Cermino decides to have a party to provide a break in revision. Her flat is not large enough so her parents restrict the number of invitations and don't want unknown guests. For once, I'm looking forward to coming with a boyfriend. I should have known better. Pierre arrives late afternoon with a girl from the Maths Upper Sixth. He dances and flirts with her then they leave an hour later. Some girls know I'm going out with him. It is total humiliation. As from that day, I can't swallow anything and one morning, I pass out in the corridor. In the sick bay where I come round, the Biology teacher puts a cushion under my head.

"Ah Mademoiselle Lefranc! You gave us a fright! You're not overworked, are you?"

"No…"

"Did you have breakfast this morning?"

"No, I can't swallow anything."

"It's got something to do with a boy, hasn't it."

"How do you know?"

"Mixed schools aren't a good idea. You must have a kind of anorexia."

"What's that?"

"When girls refuse to eat because they're obsessed with their weight."

"But I want to put on weight! Only I'm not hungry, I feel sick."

"Oh dear! You didn't make that big mistake, did you?"

"No, no."

"I hope you're not ruining your future for nothing!"

Until the next lesson, she tries to convince me that the most important thing in the world is my Baccalaureate and that to be able to pass it, one needs an iron constitution.

"You will see that girls with a high education don't find boys that important anymore."

I agree but…

Back at home, I ask Mum to let me sleep and not to force me to eat. I sleep two days. Then I half wake up, floating in a semi consciousness. The image of Pierre appears suddenly but I remain indifferent. Great, I don't care, I've got over it! I'll go to the cake shop, then to the library to revise my English texts. I dare not move fearing that if I move the bottle, I would stir up the lees. And that's exactly what's happening. I get up and wait for the phone to ring.

28 Isabelle Tchang

I've decided to commit suicide after the Baccalaureate.

"Sophie! You're really out of your mind!" exclaims Lambert rolling her eyes.

"Precisely. I don't know any more how to get rid of this ridiculous fixation!"

"Why after the Baccalaureate?"

"I don't want to have spent the whole year working for nothing."

Lambert sipped her espresso and sighed.

"My brother too is desperate because of Suzanne."

"She plays hard to get?"

"Not at all. She doesn't want him, that's all. She doesn't mind being good friends so Jean-Jacques accepts seeing her as a good friend to keep her. Can you imagine the state he is in!"

"Still, it's easier for a boy, he can take his mind off her by chasing other girls."

"He doesn't want to chase other girls, he wants her. Mind you, he's reacting more positively than you, he wants to impress her by passing his exams with distinction and going to uni."

Talking with girlfriends is remarkably soothing. I pay for my coffee and we part. On my way home I call in at Prisunic to buy a few provisions for Mum. I am third in the queue and yet I have been waiting for half an hour. I emerge from my languid thoughts and look towards the till. A middle-aged woman is leaning across the checkout assistant with an exasperated look and violently hitting the keys on her till. I hear her exclaim: "She hasn't got the first idea! You'd be better off planting cabbages, my girl."

The people in front of me are blocking my view of the future cabbage-grower, so I fall back into my icky daydreams. I am going round in circles between Pierre's bedroom, where pleasure is absent, and the school ground where he looks away from me. Perhaps I ought to light a candle to Saint Rita… no, I'd burn two to God himself. I'm not asking Him for Pierre's love, I am asking Him for his death or to change me… Oh good, it's my turn. The young exasperated woman is now beside herself.

"How can anyone be so thick?"

She calls me to witness.

"I've been telling her for an hour how to type in the code, then the price, press this button and push this lever to open the drawer, then…"

She drones on, unstoppable. I look at the checkout girl. She looks like an alley cat. She's wearing a navy blue and white dress and is bending over the till, sniffing.

"Look, it's so easy, I've shown her ten times! I wonder where they got her from!"

She humiliates her in front of everybody. I suddenly come out of my daydream.

"I think it's complicated and you're too fast! I couldn't remember a word! Let her write notes."

"Whatever next! I've got other things to do! Now Tchang," she says to the girl, "finish with that customer and off to the warehouse!"

Tchang, the alley cat, gives me the change with trembling hands and we exchange a brief look of connivance. I am reluctant to leave but people behind me are getting impatient.

In the evening, I talk about the incident with my parents and eat all my 'pistou' pasta and ham without realizing it. Mum can't believe I ate all my meal…

Jean-Claude has gone off to Military Service. The first heat wave arrives in mid June. We all make the fatal mistake of trying to do our revision on the beach. We compare our arms to see how tanned we are. Lévêque doesn't want to stay in the sun, she wants to stay as white as Algiers[17]. Only the French from Algeria laugh at that joke. Sitting on the terrace of the Madame Suzanne's bistro, Lévêque asks me how far we have got with our revision.

"I find it almost impossible to concentrate."

"You're still seeing Pierre?"

"Yes."

Silence. I am sipping my Vichy-fraise. I ask her.

"Do you know him well?"

"Better than you."

"Why do you say that?"

"Listen Sophie, don't be cross with me but he's not an interesting guy."

"I know, I can't get off the hook."

"I can help you. He tried to go out with two girls in Upper Sixth, they turned him down…That's not enough? All right, he's been boasting about having lived off a little Arab streetwalker in Algeria. What's more, rumour has it that he and his family are claiming from the government money they never lost. That gives a bad reputation to settlers like us who really have lost everything."

"How do you know all this?"

---

17 Algiers is nicknamed the White City because of its white houses.

"Jean-Claude."

"But he's his best friend!"

"Jean-Claude needed to use Pierre's flat…For Gods sake, you're not going to cry for that guy. Why don't you get angry like you did at your party?… Listen, let's do the revision together. Come on Saturday, we'll revise Geography."

I look down, under the weight of my stupidity.

"I see. It's the day you see him? OK, come on Sunday but honestly…."

In books and in religion, love works miracles through making sacrifices. We are studying Alfred de Vigny. In an extract of his romantic poems, he talks about Eloa, a young woman who has managed to make Satan fall in love with her. I identify with her but I am forgetting that Satan is a very intelligent and a very handsome archangel with a strong personality. I may have Eloa's qualities but Pierre has none of Satan's. I go to his place and throw myself in his arms. He says he's a bit busy today but he would like to try something new. He talks about sodomising. I never heard of the word. He explains. I am horrified of that invention of his. He says it's been known for centuries. I am sure that Eloa would not have accepted this indignity. I pick up my bag and walk towards the door. He catches me up and insists, and starts to sing the praises of the act. I feel my heart draining away, getting rid of a heavy weight. It hurts like pressing pus out of a boil but it is such a great relief. I leave, feeling so light that I don't bother to take the lift.

Sitting at the evening meal, I can't swallow anything. Mum is furious. I tell her it's over with Pierre.

"It's about time! Tomorrow I'll get a box of B12 vitamins, you're all skin and bone."

I ring Lévêque to say I can come and revise on Saturday. She congratulates me.

29 The Baccalaureate

The Baccalaureate is an exam that locks your mind in a cage. Then you have to study and pass it to be able to leave the cage.

It is the last Saturday before the exams. We have been on study leave for a week now. Lévêque comes to my place and we are working in the shade of the magnolia tree. I ring Deschannel to ask her a tip on Geometry. Her mother tells us that she's gone to the beach. I can't understand how she manages.

"She always had more brain than heart' Lévêque says. "That's luck!"

Mum brings us a bottle of Orangina and while we are quenching our thirst, Lévêque announces the news. Jean-Claude has deserted! He intends to go to South America but nobody knows where he is.

On Sunday I go to Lambert's. Her brother Jean-Jacques is helping me with Algebra: curves going from minus infinity to plus infinity take the shape of a corkscrew in my graph. If only I could have done Latin! Lambert brings us pomegranate juice on the rocks.

"I'm so happy I left school after the 'Brevet[18]', I earn money and I don't have a papier maché face."

"It's not only studying that affects health," I say.

"Still with Pierre?"

"No, precisely."

"So your problem is that it's ended, and Jean-Jacques's is that it hasn't started!"

---

18 Brevet is the equivalent of GCSE.

"Annie, give it a rest, will you," Jean-Jacques says.

Lambert leaves the room, shrugging her shoulders. It's the first time I've heard her first name!

"You know that Suzanne prefers older men, don't you."

"Yeah, the whole world knows. But she hasn't got anybody!"

"She's very worried about the Bac, she won't find another job if she fails it and she can't repeat it at her age!"

"At the end of the day, we're all are victims of the Algerian war."

What a pity we are not in love with each other! We are getting on so well together and he's good looking too.

I leave at about six. It's still 34° and the theorems are sizzling in my head. I make a little detour by the beach to wet my legs and arms. Most of the tourists have left the pebbles. Those who stay have peeling and inflamed or blistered skin. They can never have enough sun even if it hurts. I take my espadrilles off and walk into the sea, holding my dress up. I splash water over my neck and arms. I would like so much to get further into the water and swim even with my dress on. It must be so nice, quiet and cool under there.

The poor Little Mermaid would have been better off staying where she was and I, would love so much to join her. Yeah… but Mum would get worried and tomorrow is the first day of the Baccalaureate. I pull myself out of this lovely submarine coolness, pick up my books and climb the stone steps leading to the Promenade des Anglais.

I notice a girl dressed in dark clothes, sitting on the parapet with her arms folded round her knees. She is so slim that she reminds me of the Inca mummy in Tintin's book, The Seven Crystal Balls. I walk past her then I remember where I saw her and retrace my steps.

"Excuse me, aren't you the girl sitting at the till in Prisunic with that witch?"

She looks at me surprised. She must be Eurasian. She reminds me of France Nuyen who acted in the Little World of Suzie Wong with William Holden.

"Is she still a pain in the neck?" I ask.

"No, now I work in the store house but the whole staff think I must be retarded."

"What idiots!... Aren't you too hot with your long sleeves and stockings?"

"No, I'm fine…The boat over there, do you know where it's heading to?"

"It's the ferry to Corsica."

Our eyes linger on the boat as it moves towards the horizon.

"Are you a student?" she asks looking at my books."

"Not yet, I'm revising for the Baccalaureate, it's tomorrow and I've just been to a friend to get some help with Maths. A zero would disqualify candidates."

"I loved Maths but spending months on simple equations put me right off."

"Oh, you did Algebra?"

"Yeah, I'm not all that thick, Algebra was easier than the till at Prisunic. I was expelled at the end of the fourth form," she said with a pale smile.

"Why? Which lycée were you at?"

"Calmette… I wasn't doing any work at the end and they wanted me to repeat my year."

"I'm not surprised! Calmette is for an elite. Couldn't your parents put you in a private school?"

"The standard of study is too low and it's too expensive."

"What's your name?"

"Isabelle Tchang, and you?"

"Sophie Lefranc."

Funny, I can't get away from Tintin's adventures, now it's the Blue Lotus[19]

"Can I see your Algebra book…"

I look at my watch, I must go but she's absorbed in my book as if it were a Captain Haddock's adventure.

"I have to go but we could have a coffee together after the exams. Will you ring me?"

"I haven't got a telephone but I finish work at six."

"Ah, and where is the 'stage' door?"

"You can wait for me outside the main entrance."

*

Mum waits until I finished eating to tell me that Pierre rang. It's too late to ruin my appetite but I immediately feel sick. Mum is furious. She's fed up with him and says it's a pity that the Arabs haven't shot that thug. I feel the same. I'm dying to phone him but instead I call Lévêque.

"Hallo, Françoise? It's me."

"So, old thing, finished your revision?"

"I don't know anymore. It's too much. Especially History and Biology!"

"Don't panic, we'll make it. How will you get to the Parc Imperial lycée?"

"I'll get a taxi with Roseline."

---

19 Blue Lotus, a Tintin's adventure in which he meets Tchang who will become his best friend.

"Walk to the station and I'll pick you up in my 2 CV."

Eight in the morning is nice and cool before the heat wave. From the window of her car, I look at the passers-by and envy them. They don't have a Baccalaureate to take and neither do they have a jerk they can't get out of their mind. Françoise points at a magnificent bougainvillea with flowers falling like little flames from a balcony.

"It was everywhere in Algeria."

Roseline doesn't notice anything, she is checking her pencil case for the tenth time. When we get there, the problem is to find the right floor, the right class and the right desk. This lycée is immense. It used to be the holiday residence of the Russian tsars in the old days. The teachers are sullen and if a late candidate panics finding his way among all those corridors, he will be told off on top of that. Teachers are always telling us that one day we will pay for our laziness, negligence, and our indiscipline; but will they pay for their lack of compassion, their arrogance and their abuse of power?

All of a sudden I am alone. Roseline has to go to another classroom. I put my ID card on the desk. While we are waiting for the question papers, the invigilator gives us our rough paper; to avoid cheating, that paper is a different colour for each candidate. Then we are given the question papers. We have to write our name on the top corner, fold it and stick it down to make it anonymous. This is French Literature. I am greatly relieved when I see the three questions. I choose the one on Montaigne. During the three hours, I am not thinking of anything else but my essay on Montaigne and I enjoy it.

The last day of the exams is Biology. Roseline and I have skipped a lot of chapters. While the papers are handed out, I am aware of having an empty head and damp hands. It's two o'clock and the classroom has been sun drenched for hours despite the blinds and the draught. Everybody takes their shoes off to cool their feet on the tiles. I notice that those who have already got the questions have a gloomy face. My heart starts to beat faster. We have to choose one of the three questions. Then I read the first one: skipped it. Second question: vague idea. Third question, I hold back a cry: "The oral tract of insects!" I revised it last night and we did it as a term exam. I know it by heart! I ask for extra papers for the graphics. A desperate girl behind me whispers, "Can you let me look at your graphics?" I am so happy that I spread my papers over my table so she can have a look. At the end of the three hours, I run to the palm tree where my classmates are waiting. They are gesticulating and roaring with laughter.

Deschannel says we must be the only class to choose that subject. Lots of girls are crying because it was the last chapter of the book and some teachers haven't bothered to go over it.

We walk to the Café La Buffa to celebrate. It has been a long time since I felt so happy and so light-hearted. The friendship and the laughter of friends are a marvellous soothing cream! We tease Gali who passed her Gym test with success. Suzanne tells us how lucky she was to take the English oral test with a Pied-Noir examiner.

The heat and the excitement of the day keep me awake that night, so I start to read an extraordinary novel: 'The 25th Hour' by Virgil Gheorghiu. At four o'clock in the morning, when the freshness of dawn enters my room, I have read the last page of this story where men and women manage to overcome despair and transcend absurdity in World War II.

*

Mum has made a superb but simple dress for me. The same one as the pop singer Sylvie Vartan but I know I won't be the belle of the ball[20]. None of the girls in my class want to go to the ball! Roseline and Lévêque agree to come with me but they don't want to stay long. Against Lévêque's advice, I ring Pierre. Yes, his exam went well. He got some tips on Physics. Françoise who's listening, looks disgusted. I ask him if he is going to the ball. No, it isn't his cup of tea. How about summer? He'll go to Corsica. And then? To university to study Law and then join the Police. Françoise restrains herself from laughing. Why the Police? Because it's the best job for breaking the law and still be covered. Françoise pretends to collapse on her chair. I tell him I am going to the Ball with Roseline and Françoise Lévêque.

"Really? You managed to corrupt Françoise?"

She gives me a black look. We have no more to say to each other, so I hang up.

"Let's go to the cinema, they are showing A Bout de Souffle[21] and Bonjour Tristesse."

"I've seen Bonjour Tristesse."

"That's obvious," says Françoise, "lets go to A Bout de Souffle and then we'll go to the ball."

---

20 'La plus belle pour aller danser': pop singer Sylvie Vartan's hit song.

21 Breathless - a film by Jean-Luc Godard.

Looking back on it, I wonder why Françoise is so patient with me.

Jean Seberg is so beautiful and so natural in this Godard film! If I were like her, the world would be mine and yet she would later commit suicide for reasons as trivial as mine.

We arrive at the Ball and I see Pierre dancing cheek to cheek with a vulgar-looking and luscious little brunette. As usual, in this kind of situation, my body produces a poison that spreads quickly in my blood and makes me feel sick. We sit at a table. Roseline is annoyed to see me in that state. Nobody invites us for a dance, there are too many girls as usual.

I didn't know yet that, in my town, the demography is seven females for one male. At this Ball, it looks as if there is one boy for fifteen girls. After a while Françoise gets up.

"Come on, girls, I'm taking you home, this is no place for us."

Roseline agrees and I consent to get away from this ultimate humiliation. We finish the evening in a little café on the port. The jukebox interrupts our conversation and we listen religiously to this song:

> Imagine there's no heaven
> It's easy if you try
> No hell below us
> Above us only sky
> Imagine all the people
> Living for today…

I don't understand everything but the music is so beautiful and we imagine that Lennon is dreaming of another world just as we are.

Another ordeal is waiting for us: the posting of the results. No, I refuse to fight to reach the Wailing Wall. I stay at home and I will look at the results in the newspaper list of names tomorrow morning. The telephone remains quiet, that's a bad sign, nobody dares to call me to say I failed. The next morning, when I wake up, I am paying attention to all the sounds of the house. Dad is in the bathroom singing O Sole Mio. Mum is making a bit of a racket in the kitchen; she always has too much physical strength to handle objects carefully. The scent of coffee reaches me, it must be seven. I can hear her taking the keys and going out. She's going to get the bread and the newspaper. After several long minutes she's back and talking to Dad: "All the croissants were already gone, I had to get brioches instead." Then a whisper…

A long silence. My mouth is dry. She comes into my room and puts the tray on a chair. If she is bringing breakfast to me, it's to cheer me up. She opens the blinds making an effort not to bang them. Then she gives the paper to me, it's opened at the page of the results. I don't know where to look. She points to a column: "There, your name is there! Brioches and coffee in bed to celebrate!"

I collapse on the pillow. Apparently, our region has the best results, twenty five per cent success!

It is an intense and unique moment of happiness. I look at the other names. The whole class has passed except Marie-France Guillaume. We have even better results than the Calmette lycée! Our headmistress must be on cloud nine. Deschannel and Jean-Jacques passed with Mention (Honours). Pierre has to retake it in September.

The heat wave and the cicadas settle down. The anti-climax is brutal, all of a sudden, I have nothing to do. I could go to the beach but Roseline has already gone to Italy to her grandparent's. Lévêque is going to Paris, to her cousins'. Lambert is working. Suzanne has found a job looking after kids in a holiday camp. I am reading lots of books and having long afternoon naps. When asleep, I don't think, I heal. I often dream I am flying above valleys and hills, the wind blowing in my hair, my arms stretched out like wings. One morning, Mum asks me to go to Prisunic and suddenly I remember Isabelle Tchang. I go to see her at the exit of the store. She's surprised to see me and gives me a pale smile.

"I came for a bit of shopping and I thought of you…"

"That's nice. So how did the Baccalaureate go?"

"I passed."

"Great! Congratulations!"

"Thanks. Shall we have a coffee?"

"Yes but iced!"

"Good idea!"

I feel a bit silly. I really must hate going on the beach alone to have come and picked up an unknown girl at her work. We sit on the terrace and she chooses a place in the shade. She doesn't like the sun very much. I'm not surprised since she is wearing long sleeves and stockings; she must be boiling. I can see minute drops of perspiration glistening on her forehead. I take a surreptitious look at her. She is pretty. It's a pity she wears that wretched plait covered in black velvet on her head. It looks terribly dated. I see a photo romance magazine popping out of her bag.

"Do you read those?" I ask with a superior tone.

"Yes, I'll lend it to you if you like. There's a super serialized photo romance in it, look."

She showed me the page: Anna Karenina.

"I know the story, it's a Tolstoy novel."

"Is it? I love it."

Had she been a girl from my class, I would have laughed at her. In our school we consider that reading this type of magazines is for silly young girls or grannies. Most of us read classic literature or fashionable books like Camus, Sartre, or de Beauvoir.

"You ought to read the real Anna Karenina, the original is a lot better. I've got all Tolstoy's books at home but I've only read that one for the moment. I'm going to start War and Peace soon."

"I thought it was a story invented by the magazine."

"Certainly not. I can lend it to you but it's longer and more complicated than that."

"All the better, because I find the story good but a bit too simple. They don't say much about the characters and then I have to wait a week to read more of it. There was also a good story before that one, the Lady of the Camellias, do you know it?"

"Of course, everybody knows it…"

We are interrupted by Joelle passing by. I wave to her.

"Will you sit down for a minute?"

Joelle is ravishing, blonder than ever, suntanned and wearing white trousers and a short and red T-shirt showing her slim waist. I can't blame Jean-Claude who preferred her to Roseline. We speak about the Baccalaureate. Our lycée has excelled itself. The Segurane lycée's proletariat beat the Calmette lycée's bourgeoisie. I remember that our

History teacher has told us that the dream of a democracy was to bring the proletariat to the level of the stupidity of the bourgeoisie. I'm not sure that I understand her. Joelle says that the results of the exam were published the same day as the Independence of Algeria. Our region, the Alpes Maritimes, did the best with 25% success.

"By the way, did you hear the news?"

"What news?"

"Pierre is getting married."

"Really?"

"Didn't you know?"

"No. Is the girl pregnant?"

"I don't think so. They're getting married in August and the girl's father is buying them a small flat in town."

"What about his Law course?"

"He'll do it alright. His fiancée works as a secretary... Oh dear, it's getting late, I've got to go."

The sick feeling resumes. If only Lethe existed, I'd drink its water until I had forgotten my existence.

"Is she a girl from your class? asks Isabelle, I get the feeling she didn't give you good news."

"No, she was in Upper Sixth. The bloke she's talking about is getting married. He was my boyfriend."

"Oh... Maybe you've had a narrow escape."

"Quite possibly."

"Will we still go to the beach on Sunday?"

"Yes, of course."

"I have to tell you something... I have a skin condition, that's why I wear long sleeves and stockings... I have eczema and people find it disgusting."

I find my own problem so much more important than hers that I'm not at all put off. I suggest a part of the beach where very few people go. She agrees to meet there.

As soon as I got home, I ring Lambert to tell her the news.

"You're not going to do something foolish?" she enquires.

"No, now I've passed the Baccalaureate, I can't commit suicide. I just can't do that to my Mum!"

"Excellent! My brother's looking better as well. Listen, tomorrow evening I'm taking both of you down into the Old Town to have a 'socca'[22].

---

22 "Socca": A local speciality, a pancake made with olive oil and chickpeas flour.

30 The Americans

The next Sunday, I meet Isabelle at the War Memorial that overlooks the beach. It's a huge, white monument, Greco-Martian style, built directly into the rock. I am really coming here for her sake because I hate this beach called Rauba Capeù (where the wind steals your hat). It is made of gigantic cubes of stone in a line along the edge of the seaside. The sea pours in between the blocks with a frothy gurgling. Smaller rocks form a staircase to reach the burning surface. To go into the sea, you have to do a tightrope walk, then slip cautiously from a rock into the water, then you are out of your depth immediately. A few metres further, the bay plunges two thousands metres down. It's the last step of the Alps.

I remember vaguely that Isabelle mentioned eczema to me but I am not prepared for the sight! While she's taking off her clothes with infinite precaution, I can see scabs and scales appearing; where there aren't any, the skin is raw and inflamed. She has them on her forearms and her ankles. It's pretty revolting and I put my clothes as far as possible from hers. If I tell Mum, she will force me to take a bath with bleach! She has always refused to swim in the sea because the sewage pipes of the town are a bit too short and some of the 'stuff' comes back floating toward the edge. They say that salt is a natural disinfectant. One day they will extend the pipe!

I put Anna Karenina in her basket and ask her if she has seen a doctor.

"Yes, he said it's common."

"Don't you put a bandage on?"

"I tried but it starts oozing."

"Sea water should be good for you, salt is a disinfectant."

I hold back a look of disgust. I suddenly think of that story by Flaubert in which a man agrees to lie down beside a leper to give him some warmth and the leper turns out to be Jesus in person! Even if he believed that he was the Son of God, it is not the kind of thing to do to humans. I could not touch Isabelle even if she were the Virgin Mary. I swim far away from her for fear that one of her scabs might brush against me. When I think of the fuss I made for a minute spot on my face!

Isabelle is lost in reading Anna Karenina when a group of young foreigners begin climbing the south face of the cube next to us. They are speaking and laughing loudly with the American accent of Donald Duck. Most of the girls proudly wear a brace that is quite different from ours. Each of their teeth is circled with metallic wire. Ours is one wire running across the teeth. The boys wear long Bermuda shorts. None of the girls wears a bikini. They are bold enough to dive into the water despite the rocks. The adults in charge stay on the stone cubes and one of them keeps an eye on the group with his binoculars. Girls and boys come out of the water and chase each other from one cube to the next.

"Can't they see the stone is slippery when you are wet?" I say to Isabelle.

When the girls realise, it's too late. One girl slips down between two cubes and screams loudly. They all rush to the edge and lean over. We run as well to see if we can help. All of them are shouting her name "Debbie! Debbie!" I manage to see her. Her arms and legs have been badly grazed against the stones and three quarter of her body is in the water. Every time the sea drains out, a wave returns brutally splashing against her face and diluting her blood. One of the boys tries to reach her but the space narrows down and he can't manage. In the meantime Debbie faints and her head lolls to one side. A few hysterical girls start to scream again. I try to gather all my English vocabulary. Unfortunately, all I can remember are snatches of poems and set phrases designed for textual analysis. I make the lamentable discovery of six years of useless English. I approach an adult in charge and say, like a sort of French Tarzan speaking to the civilized, "Me call 18 for police and ambulance," He understands. I have the pleasure of being looked upon as the Saviour. Quickly I cross the road in my bikini and rush into a restaurant. What a relief to be able to express myself.

Isabelle is keeping out of things, holding her clothes against her body. The girls try to cheer up and encourage Debbie but her head is still lolling to avoid the splashing of the waves.

The ambulance arrives and the first-aid worker checks her spine before hoisting her up. Off she goes with two adults of the group. One of them puts his hand on my shoulder and thanks me. A long light brown lock of hair falls across his forehead, a hint of badly shaved beard glints on his cheeks. My God! He's handsome and looks kind.

They are a group of young Americans on a study leave in Europe and they are staying in the lycée of the Parc Imperial.

The next day, the accident is in the paper and I receive a big bouquet of roses with a card signed William Jackson, John Cassidy and the group. They have names straight out of Westerns! I am invited to an evening with them. Mum never lets me go out on my own in the evening. I ring the lycée and find out that they will come to pick me up at seven. I pounce on the telephone to call Lambert to tell her all about it and to express my despair about my horrible frizzy hair and my poor English. She informed me that the Galeries Lafayette store has just got a new iron to straighten hair called Babyliss. Mum agrees to buy me the magic instrument. For the first time, I won't look like a sheep. I beg her for more money to go to the beautician. She reshapes my huge gutter-like eyebrows into elegant arches, reduces and hides my black heads with a discreet makeup. I can hardly recognise myself: I am almost pretty. I just need a hammer to hit my two front teeth to stop them sticking out. I put on a white cotton dress that emphasises my suntan and conceals my thinness. I ought to eat more… I don't have any more perfume samples…

Someone rings at the garden gate. I run to open it. They are standing there. I thought they would dress for the evening party but they are wearing old jeans cut at the knees and a 'Peace and Love' T-shirt. I look in the street for the car but instead, they came with their coach and their driver.

I spend the evening on cloud nine. All want to try out their French. I despair at my lack of vocabulary for a simple conversation. I ask them if they know John Steinbeck or Ernest Hemingway but they laugh and they say that America is too big to know everyone. Their teacher tells me they were very shocked that in Rome, the Italians pinched their bottoms during the Pope's blessing at the Vatican. They also ask what my father did and if he was earning a lot of money. A fourteen-year-old girl plays La Vie en Rose for me on the piano, then William and John take their guitars and accompany the whole group singing rock, pop and folk. It's a good job I can dance the Rock because, apart from passing the Baccalaureate, I don't have any talent. I can't sing nor play an instrument. The oral tracts of the insect or the Austro-Hungarian Compromise are only useful for exams. I would sell my soul to sit at the piano and sing Hugues Auffray[23].

Shortly before midnight, the teachers and their couriers bring fruit tarts and cakes. They find the French cakes extraordinary. William apologizes for the tepid Coca-Cola. He complains about the fridge of the lycée being too small. Pam, a guide who can speak French come to sit next to John and me. They say that Debbie only has superficial injuries but she is in a lot of pain and the hospital is too hot. Why don't we have air-conditioning? I don't even know what it is. And why don't they give her painkillers? I say that, perhaps, she's not in too much pain. They are horrified. I am horrified too when they complain that Kennedy forces them to take the same bus as the blacks. I thought it's because the blacks are not going in the same direction as them! I've no idea of the rules of segregation

John and William come from Kansas City and they think I'm funny because I thought it was in Texas.

At the end of the evening, John takes me back in the coach. We are sitting together at the back, both of us making the effort to speak the language of the other. From time to time, he pushes his hair back by running his fingers through it. His smile is bright and candid. I feel relaxed

_____

23 Hugues Auffray: French folk singer.

170

and he makes me feel interesting. I'm going to be their guide for their next countryside excursion and to Saint Jean-Cap-Ferrat. They will be still there for 14th July and I tell him not to miss the celebration. I learn they call it Bastille Day and it is a few days after their Independence Day. It was not in the Baccalaureate syllabus or maybe I missed it.

31 Bastille Day

Their touring schedule is crazy. They want to see the maximum number of things in the minimum of time. The coach goes on the 'Grand Corniche', a road with many bends that goes to Monaco. The driver can't stop turning round to admire a fourteen-year-old American girl, a mini Jane Fonda with turquoise eyes. In France, we haven't yet heard about contact lenses that can change the colour of your eyes.

They are disappointed they can't see Grace Kelly. They thought she could have come on to her balcony like the Pope at the Vatican. Two girls from Philadelphia throw a tantrum and demand to see Grace! The driver tries to park the coach outside the Hotel de Paris but only clean cars can park there. One is not allowed to break the harmony of the place. One of the teachers gets thrown out of the Casino because she wants to take a photo of the ceiling; another one because she is not well dressed enough. The Oceanographic Museum, the ice creams and the sodas are too expensive for them. We leave Monaco slightly disappointed and in a bad mood. Fortunately, the Villa Ephrussi of the Rothschilds in Saint Jean-Cap-Ferrat, brings some serenity back. They are all excited to be able to see some of the furniture belonging to Queen Marie-Antoinette and the garden overlooking the sea gives us a refreshing breeze after the sauna session in the coach.

After the visit to the Villa, I show John and William the Somerset Maugham's mansion house, at the end of the Peninsula and just opposite us the Villa of Monsieur Grand Marnier. It is too late to go to Vallauris. All the better, I hate its pottery and the girls would have demanded to see Picasso on the balcony of his villa.

I'm making great progress in English but I never go out without my pocket dictionary.

I have always preferred Bastille Day to Christmas. First of all, because it is warmer and also I don't feel obliged to be happy at any cost. There is no pressure. In fact, we celebrate the end of oppression. During the pageant, I push the girls in front of me so that they can take plenty of photos. They have a very advanced camera. It takes a photo and then the photo comes out of the camera; it's a bit wet but the colour picture appears when drying. I envy them a lot, not so much for their gadgets but for their natural confidence, detachment and lack of any hang-ups. When we go shopping, they try a few clothes and shoes and leave saying it's too expensive! In France we would rather die than mention the price. We say we're going to think about it. They have never seen a bidet and William asks Pam if the tap was to flush the toilet. As for John, he's amused and shocked to be solicited by a prostitute on the Place Grimaldi whereas for me, they are part of the décor.

The Bastille Day Ball takes place in the Albert Premier public garden. The fireworks are set off from the Castle Hill where we did our Gym. I'm thinking of Gali climbing the Hill. Isabelle joins me and together we are waiting for the coach by the bandstand. Isabelle is a bit tense and I am nervous. I notice she wears high heeled espadrilles but no stockings. She wants to let her eczema be in the open air but she has covered her arms with a long sleeved blouse. They arrive. We look at each other with a smile and we take a deep breath.

Dancing rock and roll is OK but an accordion waltz is not my cup of tea. I would have the same grace as the hippopotamus in the film Fantasia. It makes John laugh, he says he dances like the crocodiles in the same film. The slow, cheek-to-cheek dances are the best moments. I see Isabelle dancing with William, her braid of black hair lightly touches his chin. From time to time they look at each other. They make me think of the couple in West Side Story but they don't know each other's language.

John is so gentle to dance with. He doesn't smell of vulgar after shave lotion but a very light scent of cinnamon comes from his clothes, like Auntie's Andrea's parcels. He is tender without holding me tight like a sex maniac. I don't have to fight him off, I feel relaxed and moved. He puts the back of my hand against his cheek and I think of Jean-Claude who put Roseline's hand on his willy! The Latin lover…

The American girls are dancing a wild rock and roll with some local rough boys in sleeveless T-shirts, or black leather bomber jackets. The teachers are keeping an eye on them. They all have flat shoes, only French girls wear stilettos. At midnight we walk to the beach to watch the fireworks. On the black surface of the sea, trimmed with a white edge, the little lights of fishing boats are dancing in the distance like fireflies. When the 'string of pearls' goes dark, it's the signal for the show to begin, and John puts his arm around my waist. The first rocket bursting makes me jump and makes John laugh. The whole of the Castle hill lights up in a wide range of colours and the smoke looks like a multi-coloured mist shrouding the trees and the bushes. When a huge cascade of white fire descends on

Rauba Capeù, Pam says it looks like the Niagara Falls. John asks me if I have ever seen them.

"Yes, in the film Niagara, with Marilyn Monroe."

After the fireworks, we stay on the beach. The heat releases its grasp and the girls take a few steps into the sea, holding their dresses up. John and William get undressed and keep their boxer shorts on to swim an Olympic crawl. I take my skirt off but I keep my Moroccan blouse. I don't want anybody to see my padded bra. The water is warm, it's the first time I've been swimming at night. I can't say whether I am swimming in the sea or in the sky, they have the same colour, the same temperature, the same little lights in the distance. I am floating on my back. I even forget I'm wetting my hair. The soothing freshness, the restful darkness, the silence letting some distant laughter go through fill me with a senseless serenity...floating...I hear my name then a splashing sound.

"Sophie! Are you crazy?"

John is next to me, his dark blond hair shining against the dark water like a ghost. Why does he look so worried?

"Come back!"

Suddenly I see the shore in the far distance. Oh my God, how did I get so far? How am I going to get back? I start to panic.

"Come on, I aide vous!"

I swim too fast and too jerkily then I get breathless. I have to stop to get my breath back. John tries to encourage me to calm me down but I don't understand what he says. I feel as if the water has thickened and I don't seem to go forward, as in a bad dream. Then William's head is approaching. With the two of them I might make it.

"Take it easy! Take it easy!"

What does that mean? They show me how to swim more efficiently. I close my eyes, I don't want to see the shore. After long minutes I hear them laugh. We've got there and I am still swimming conscientiously while they are walking out. I collapse on the pebbles. Isabelle still looks very worried.

"What got into you? Suddenly we couldn't see you anymore! We called you but you didn't answer."

"I don't know, I didn't realise, I found myself out there without meaning to swim out so far."

"Must be the currents."

"Yes but you don't realise at night."

"I'm so sorry," I say to the two boys. Then I ask Pam to tell them how grateful I am.

"Is that true what John said? He said he found you asleep," Pam asks.

"No, I wasn't asleep, I was dreaming."

"It's the same."

Some girls are laughing loudly and chasing one another on the beach. Pam and the staff find it difficult to control them. "They're drunk," says Isabelle. I can't believe it, they drank wine from the bottle. Suddenly, three men in suits come towards to us. They introduce themselves to the staff. Pam doesn't find it easy to understand them. I ask them what's the matter. Greatly relieved to be able to speak French they say they were plain-clothes policemen and ask questions about the group. I tell them they are a group of young American students on a tour of Europe. They want to see their passports.

"Ah no, that's not possible, I told them not to bring them. They are in a safe, at the lycée."

"What's wrong with the girls? They hid something as soon as they saw us."

"Yeah, they are a bit drunk. They're hiding some red wine bottles."

"Wine? You must be joking! I bet it's drugs."

"Not at all, in the US, it's more difficult for them to get Côte du Rhône than drugs."

They ask for proof and I show them a bag with a bottle of Côte-du-Rhône. They leave, shaking their heads.

"You exaggerated," says Pam, "we're not all drug addicts!"

"Really? So what are all those pills you are taking?"

"Vitamins!"

"And Jacky?"

"Pills for travel sickness. The blue ones are to spoil my appetite, the white ones are for sleeping, that's all!"

To go back home, I share a taxi with Isabelle. She's quite silent.

"They'll leave in three days," I say.

"I know. Did you enjoy the evening?"

"The best evening of my life, and you?"

"Me too. In three days, it will be over for ever."

"How do you find John?"

"Unique… I felt…unusual feelings."

"Me too."

"Three more days. Edith Piaf sings that life gives you a lot to take it all back later."

She slams the door of the taxi outside a building with closed shutters and a copper plate I can't read from the distance.

Two days later, the group invites me to see Rudolf Nureyev dancing the Sleeping Beauty at the Roman arena in the town. As we are early, I take the opportunity to show them the magnificent building of the Regina Hotel where Queen Victoria used to spend her winters. It was there that my grandmother was working when she was sixteen as one of the ironing girls. She had a special mission: to iron the Queen's knickers without burning the lace. Gran had a thermostat in her head and knew when to take the iron away from the open fire.

For the sake of Rudolf Nureyev and Tchaikovsky, the town council has asked the airport to divert the planes flying above the Arena. During the interval, Pam takes the girls to see Nureyev. I don't bother to go with them knowing that he is not going to receive them; it's like when they wanted to see Grace Kelly. After waiting a long time, I look at my watch and I realise that the performance is ten minutes late. It's a good job since the girls are late as well. Eventually they arrive with glorious smiles. They have met him and had a chat together. He told them he has a flat in New-York not far from Pam's. He simply delayed the show to finish the conversation. I must learn that the impossible can be possible.

32 Love, love, love

Yes, well, I know, everything has been said about it except our own experience.

The village of Saint Paul-de-Vence is delightful, medieval, artistic, intellectual, snobbish and expensive. Vallauris is a lovely village with horrible pottery and Picasso won't appear on his balcony. Therefore, I take them to the village of Breil-sur-Roya, deep in the French countryside[24].

Whether Catholic or not, we all attend Sunday mass in the open air. Isabelle is radiant. We go to eat in a nice little local restaurant. The managers are a charming couple who have not been seen Americans since the Liberation. They can't do enough to please us. In front of us, the lavender fields wave up to the feet of the mountains where the olive trees are climbing in terraces cut in the mountainsides.

They go through the ravioli, ratatouille, melon and can't believe they are allowed to drink the local rosé going with the meal. At one o'clock, the cicadas catch their breath and we can hear the insects buzzing. The soporific effect of the heat, the wine and the digestion in process make a siesta a must.

Away from the others, I lie down with John against a plane tree. He holds me against him and I can hear his stomach. We laugh and I tell him it's the melon. He loves my eyes. If the mini Jane Fonda of the group has turquoise contact lenses, I have false eye-lashes the beautician put on artistically one by one. He looks at me in a way no one has

---

24 La France profonde.

done before. I brush back his lock of hair, everything about him is luminous. On his chin, the golden hint of a badly shaved beard glistens. He starts kissing me so gently that we don't have time to realise we have reached the violence of a sudden and mutual desire. And then he freezes, breaks away, looks at me and says that if I don't want to go any further, he'd rather stop. I am dying to carry on but I don't want to break the enchantment by trying to explain by gestures that I don't want to become pregnant if he hasn't got a condom. Biology ignores romantic feelings. He lowers his head, his lock falls back and we wait for our senses to cool down.

I ask him what he will do when back in the States. He says he has finished university. He would like to be a lawyer for the poor but he is going to join the Marines for a year or two. He's looking for a different experience of life. If he's going to Vietnam, he can maybe help the victims of Communism to free themselves from its grip. I wish Deschannel and the girls of my class could hear him.

In the evening, we are all gathered in the Church Hall. William plays the piano, John the guitar. Ray Charles's 'What Did I Say' meets with frantic applause. The girls sing Bob Dylan. Thank God the priest knows some Hugues Aufray's French folk songs but played on an old harmonium they are not very impressive. Then John and William perform a sketch imitating Laurel and Hardy. We all collapse with laughter and Isabelle is wiping her mascara. It's already time to go back.

In the coach, Pam tells me that their sketch is not improvised, they have already performed it for their graduation day. In France, we don't have any ceremony, neither for the Baccalaureate nor for a Degree. The French

Revolution abolished everything that looked like glorifying the elite, thus depriving generations of nice memories!

I ask Pam what are they going to do when they got back.

"First of all, we'll spend four days in Paris, four in London, then back to New-York."

"Do you all live in New-York?"

"No, only me! Their parents will come from other states to pick them up."

"That's must cost a lot."

"No, domestic flights aren't at all expensive, it's like taking the bus!"

"Why are William and John the only males in the group?"

"To allow them to see a bit of Europe before going to Vietnam."

I look at Isabelle who is resting her head on William's shoulder. Three girls approach William laughing and talking to him. He takes Isabelle on his lap and the three girls undertake to change her hairstyle. They remove the velvet ribbon and her hair rolled down like a dark cascade. They twist a heavy bun on her nape and put some flowers they had picked up in the fields. She loses her antiquated look and appears magnificent.

While we are waiting for our taxi at the coach station, I ask Isabelle if William has made any remarks about her eczema.

"He says that in America, they would already have cured me."

"Of course!"

"He said it must be psychological."

"That's typically American… You know they are leaving tomorrow… for ever."

"Yes."

"I'll go to the station to say goodbye to him. You will be working, won't you?"

"I'll take half the day off. Nothing will stop me from going to the station, not even my Madame Léger!"

In the taxi that takes us back, Isabelle doesn't hear me talking. She's light years away. I don't dare to interrupt her reverie. What would we do if the mind could not escape?

At the station we take platform tickets. The American girls give us postcards of their states with touching messages. John drags me into an empty compartment and holds out a little paper bag to me with a Dior perfume bottle. He apologizes for not wrapping it in nice paper. I should be happy but I feel desperate. We cling tightly to each other. I am thinking of Faust selling his soul to the Devil and I have just understood him. I put two twigs of lavender I found in my pocket in his hand and then, a noisy flock of July holidaymakers invades the carriage. It's over. I go back on the platform. I see Debbie waving her bandaged arm out of the window. Isabelle puts her arm under mine and we leave the station slowly backwards, our eyes fixed on the last carriage.

"You're going back to Prisunic?"

She nods her head. She tries to twist her hair into a bun again but it's collapsing to one side. She's wearing small gold earrings.

"Are those a gift from William?"

"Yes."

Tears are rolling down her cheeks. How does she manage to cry or laugh in silence? I'm not feeling anything, I am numbed,… empty.

"It's the first time in my life that I have been happy…" She blows her nose. "Do you have other Tolstoy books to lend me?"

"Yeah, well, they are not going to cheer you up."

"But it makes me stronger!"

"I must try then."

"You don't need to, you've got a family."

33 Going Back to School

The summer is drawing to an end. The station and the airport are crowded and the roads are blocked by traffic jams. Even the new motorway can't manage to relieve the National 7. The big wave of noisy and happy tourists is retiring. It is replaced by another wave, a quieter one: retired people and older foreigners who don't choose the same season or the same holidays as us. Why do they look for the sun so desperately? I know they also come for Matisse, Picasso, the Old City and the food. Why is Onassis's yacht casting its anchor off Monte-Carlo? I often go out with Isabelle. She must be ashamed of her family because she never asks me to visit her at her home. I hold it against her to hide a part of her life from me. Either we are friends or we aren't. Her eczema starts to fade away a little, especially around her ankles. I suggest she dresses in the Indo-Chinese clothes. Some wear it in the streets. It's large long satin trousers with a tunic buttoned on the side. I think the air would circulate better but Prisunic won't have it. Still we go to buy them in an oriental boutique.

Soon we are going back to the lycée and I go to Prisunic to buy school stationery with Mum since she's the one with the money. However I go on my own to sell and buy my schoolbooks. One afternoon, Isabelle is sitting on my bed and, for the hundredth time we are listening to Petula Clark's hit record, 'Chariot'. We rarely speak of other subjects than John and William. She's browsing my new schoolbooks. I'm proudly looking at my books of Philosophy by Cuvillier and another one by Greek philosophers. The yellow Trigonometry book is the ugliest and the most frightening thing I've come across.

"Is it difficult to take the second part of the Baccalaureate?" Isabelle asks.

"If you have a good memory, you learn the books by heart. That's three quarters of the exams. But if you have more than five spelling mistakes in French, you've had it!"

"Those books are beautiful!"

"Ah them! They are Lagarde and Michard's French Literature."

"What are they, those papers you're throwing away?"

"Last year's courses and homework."

"Can I have them?"

"My Maths is terrible, all wrong!"

"I don't mind… your Biology exercise book looks interesting."

"Yeah, I'm not bad at drawing."

She has just finished reading Madame Bovary that I have lent her. She finds her sublime.

"I don't, I found her to be an idiot. She destroyed her life by making her dreams her master (I had read it somewhere)."

"I don't agree with you. She realized she made a mistake, that there were other possible lives and she tried to live them. She failed because in her time it was not possible… If the Bac was only a question of memory I could pass it. I have a very good memory, I learnt reading on my own because I didn't go to school until late."

"Your parents didn't help you?"

"No."

Each time I mention her family, her face goes blank.

185

My classmates come back from holidays, the telephone rings non-stop and Dad is cross non-stop too. I am the only one to use the phone. My parents have no friends and the telephone is only used to call the doctor.

Roseline comes back from Italy, sick of having to spend her holidays with her Mum and Dad. Especially her mother who watches her every move, haunted by the fear of her daughter getting pregnant by looking at a boy. Suzanne, dashing and suntanned, was more Carmencita than ever. She is delighted by her time at the summer camp at the Moulinet in the Alps. The supervisors were nice and the same age as her. The director works at the Education Board and, as she got a good report, she expects to get a local post as schoolmistress in the region after the Baccalaureate. Lévêque keeps me an hour on the phone to tell me about her Parisian holidays. It's the first time she has seen the Eiffel Tower and her cousins. Lambert calls me a dead loss when I ring her, so I have to promise to tell her all about John. It's strange, all I can manage is a banal account about the handsome American boy on Bastille Day. It is not at all what Isabelle and I experienced. Perhaps I can't find the right words.

The day we go back to school is both a pleasure and a pain. Deschannel goes to Maths, Gali to Science, Roseline wanted to do Science but comes to Philosophy to join us: Lévêque, Cermino, Perez and me. Most of our last year class goes to Maths or Science. Gali joins our group in the playground.

"This year, I've got myself permanently excused from PE thanks to our doctor."

"You didn't! We thought you loved it now!"

"Real gym, yes, but I can't stand starting up again on those idiotic exercises on this year's syllabus. With all the work we're going to have, I am not going to play the fool on top of the Castle Hill."

"Even if the teacher is replaced by a certain army instructor."

"In that case, I'll think it over."

After a good laugh we change subject.

"I heard we're going to have eight hours of Philosophy a week with a handicapped teacher."

"In Science we have her only three hours a week."

"In Maths we're going to have a super Philo[25] teacher!"

"Why can't we have him?"

"Because he's got a Master only and she has a PhD."

"We wouldn't care if the Master one is better."

"Some parents have pulled strings to send their daughter to go to the Calmette Lycée."

"What's wrong with our teacher then?"

"I heard she keeps nodding off during lessons and her voice is inaudible."

"That's rotten to give us that bloody teacher for eight hours a week!"

This last remark comes from Marcel, one of the four new boys in our class. He is the darkly handsome type with big muscles (Raf Vallonne in The Bridge). Marcel soon becomes popular as he is very relaxed with girls, treating them as mates. But, to his great dismay, he is short and the girls tend to treat him as a teddy bear. The whole

---

25 In France, even if you choose to do Maths, you have to do
    Philosophy as well, but less.

year round, he'll wear the same suede jacket, taking care not to get it dirty.

Each of the four boys has his own distinct, almost stereotyped personality.

Gerard Manfredi will be an inexhaustible source of giggles. Blessed are those who make others laugh, for their lives will have been most useful. He's very tall and lean, with slightly greasy, wavy and dark hair, an eagle's profile in opposition to his character and huge tentacle-like hands. The piano is his passion, but his parents' is his Baccalaureate. He is gentle, almost effeminate in manners. When worried, he rolls bulging eyes and makes us collapse in laughter. He is obviously happy among the girls and seems to be bored by the boys.

A girl repeating her year informs us that Mademoiselle Goujon, the Philosophy teacher, is a member of the Communist Party.

"Bloody hell!" said Marcel, "If they are all like her in the Party, I'm not surprised the Patriote [26] packed up."

"During the war, she was deported because of being a Communist and she did two years in a concentration camp. That's why she's always sleepy."

"Why doesn't she retire? So that she would be able to hibernate!"

"Fat chance! I know it! My father is a War Invalid, like her, and they have rights and priorities over us," I say.

"That's going to be fun!"

"At the Felix Faure Lycée, there is a Maths teacher a bit like that," says Gerard, "from time to time he asked us to leave the classroom and to wait in the corridor. It was

---

[26] Was a Communist newspaper

to change the dressings on his feet. He was tortured by the Germans."

"But that's almost twenty years ago!"

"Yeah but the wounds hadn't healed properly."

"You saw them?"

"No. The boys drove him mad because he was walking like a duck. One day the Deputy head told us that he had the soles of his feet burnt because he wouldn't talk. If he had told us before they would have left him alone. I'm glad I didn't do it."

"Why did you leave Felix Faure? You got expelled?"

"Nearly. They couldn't stand it when I missed lessons because of my piano practices."

"What dickheads!" exclaimed Marcel.

Deadly silence greeted the fatal word, never heard in a girl's school.

Lessons have started. Strangely enough we are now calling each other by our first names. Roseline is sitting next to me and Gerard next to Gisele who's repeating her year.

"The lycée would be great if we didn't have the bloody exams," I say, imitating Marcel.

Roseline starts her first fit of giggles of the year.

We've just had two hours of Philosophy with Mademoiselle Goujon and our morale is low. She teaches her course in a tense silence so that we can hear what she's saying. We are trying desperately to understand what we manage to hear.

She seems to suffer as well. She stands up, propped against her desk, with her hand clinging on to the corner as if to stop plunging into sleep. Sometimes the flow slows down and she begins to swing backwards but a desperate and miraculous bit of energy brings her back forward.

The bell shakes her then she pounces on her Gauloise cigarettes and walks heavily out of the classroom, staring straight ahead of her.

We are panicking. We will never be able to pass our exam, so we decide to go and talk to the headmistress. She shows empathy but says that there's nothing she can do about it. Once only, her course will be interesting: the day the Inspector sits in our class. The effort she made leaves her white with fatigue. The Inspector leaves the class saying:

"You are so lucky, children, that your elders' experience should provide you with such fine teachers."

34 Cruising Speed

We ask Gisele, the little ginger girl who's repeating her year, how she manages to put up with another year of Philosophy with Mlle Goujon. In the end, there weren't many failures. In fact, what happened was that the students quickly understood the situation and decided to study Philosophy from their books during the lessons. Gisele explains to us that the Cuvillier book is a very good book. At the end of each chapter, there is a list of recommended readings.

"You choose one or two of them, you go to the Dubouchage Central Library and you make a summary of the ideas of those books for the others and the others do the same for you."

"Bloody hell, think of the bloody work we'll have to do!" says Marcel.

"Do you have another solution?"

Thus, we start our studying with the first volume: 'Thought as the Condition of Cognisance and Action' It is a good job we have Freud and Charcot to have a laugh, because Bergson never made us laugh despite his Essay on Laughter .

On page 231 of our book there's a schizophrenic patient's drawing we find pretty and original, it shows wheat growing on a beach in the sunset. Well, it is not what we think! Dr Vinchon declared it to be an insane man's watercolour. Poor doctor, he has never visited the Fondation Maeght[27] in Vence!

---

27 Avant-garde art gallery.

Another drawing is circulating in our class showing Marcel fishing the 'goujon' (gudgeon) while reading a philosophy book.

It is naïve, but in the context of a class that is enduring eight hours of droning a week, it has a comical effect. The whole class collapses in silent hilarity but Marcel can't control himself and bursts into shrill laughter, awaking the teacher. Aghast, she looks at Marcel as if she's seeing him for the first time. Covered in confusion, he explains that it's the schizophrenic's drawing in the book that's making him laugh.

"Monsieur," she says, "you ought to pay more attention in class, I haven't got to that point yet."

We are very proud to realise we are two chapters ahead of her.

A month later, Isabelle rings me. Damn! I've forgotten her. I explain the situation to her and how the homework now comes crashing down on us with hellish regularity. It is Stakhanovism after two summer months of idleness. Isabelle buys second-hand text books for the first part of the Baccalaureate. She loves looking at them, browsing through them and reading some pages just as Granddad used to. Granddad and Isabelle are the only people I know who enjoy looking at school books.

One Saturday, I meet her at Madame Suzanne's bistro. She brings me my last year Geometry homework and explains to me that I went wrong because I had chosen the wrong theorem.

"Of course! I didn't even understand the question!"
"How did you manage to pass your exam?"

"I told you, I've got a good memory so I made up with good marks in History, Geography, Biology, French, English…"

"That's all?"

"What do you mean, 'that's all'? That is a vast amount of work! Try and you'll see."

"I wouldn't mind but I would need someone to give me homework and to mark it."

"Last year, there was a girl from Cambodia who had to go back home in the middle of the year. She took her exam by doing a correspondence course with a lycée near Paris.

It's called the CNTE[28] in Vanves. It's free but you must have a good reason…like having a family to support or being seriously ill, or…"

"That won't be a problem."

"Really?"

"I've got a… rather unusual family situation."

I wait for more but it's not coming.

"Listen Isabelle, I thought we were good friends enough to…"

"To tell you all my secrets? What about you, do you tell me all yours?"

"I haven't got any!"

"Sure?"

"Of course I'm sure! If your father were in prison, I would not inform the whole school! Don't you trust me?"

"Yes, I do…. But it's worse than that… I don't have a family, I come from the DDASS."

---

28 CNTE Centre National de Télé Enseignement (Teaching by mail and TV).

"The dass? What's that?"

"Social Service Homes."

"Orphanage?"

"That's what they called it in the nineteenth century."

I suddenly look at her as if she was coming from Mars. Last time I heard of it was in a book called Oliver Twist.

"I'm not afraid that you'll tell the whole lycée, I'm afraid you will find me less interesting now."

"Less interesting?"

"I mean… not good enough?"

"Not good enough?"

"Not from the same milieu as you?"

"My milieu?"

"Stop repeating what I say! You know what I mean!"

"I don't! Not at all!"

I've just learnt that I belong to a milieu, me!

"On the contrary, you are even more interesting! You are what the Deputy Head calls 'a social case'!"

"Precisely! That's what I don't want to be! I want to be normal!"

"I never said you're abnormal."

"Yes, you did. You called me 'social case'. As soon as you say you are from the DDASS, people look at you with sympathy and pity as if you were ill or handicapped and people overlook all your mistakes because they are expecting them."

"I thought people would be stricter with you."

"No. You get plenty of pity, people feel sorry for you but when it's about simple affection or sheer friendship, people give you the cold shoulder. Besides when we get someone genuinely interested and attached, we are immediately separated."

"Oh you too!"

"What do you mean 'you too'?"

"When I was at the convent school, the nuns would separate us if we became good friends."

"At our place, if we got attached to our foster family, we were taken away."

"That's insane!"

"Outside the Home, you can't have friends because you can't invite your friends back."

"If you didn't tell them the truth, they couldn't understand."

"Is that what you believe? If I told the truth, the parents didn't want "that sort" in their home."

"Not my mother!"

"Tell her what I am."

"I will, besides, she's a member of the Red Cross."

"You'll see."

I'm outraged.

"It's not because you're in a Home that you must believe everybody is against you."

"You've got more in common with your school friends than with me."

"Of course, I live with them! I had a schoolmate with whom I'm not friendly anymore because she left to work in a bank and for her, now, I'm a baby. The difference is "There," I say, putting my finger on my temple. I don't do Philosophy for nothing.

"That's exactly what I meant." Isabelle says.

The CNTE didn't raise any objection.

That very evening, I try the experiment light-heartedly and tell Mum that Isabelle comes from the Social Services.

"Honestly, you pick up anything, can't you stick to your friends? You wait, you won't be able to get rid of her."

I gasp, I repress a wild desire to burst into tears. Then I am taken aback by Dad's reaction.

"Don't exaggerate," he says to Mum, "I had some mates in the Foreign Legion who came from the Social Services and they were the best soldiers and the best friends I ever came across."

"It's well known that the Foreign Legion picks up anything."

Dad gets cross, they argue, I feel ill. Later in the evening I tell Mum that Isabelle had predicted her response word for word and I had not. Realising that Isabelle has shaken the blind trust I have in her, she'll detest her from now on, but as discretely as possible. Isabelle never asked me if I had told my Mum. She spares me lying.

The term passes too quickly. After the Christmas mock exams, we go to the cinema to see 'Is Paris Burning?' with Roseline and Françoise. We leave the cinema devastated. The handsome Anthony Perkins is quickly shot in the streets of Paris after enjoying a visit to a French bistro. The liberation of Paris was sweet and very sour. Then we go to a Café where Isabelle joins us. Some girls from Science arrive and sit down with us. We tell them what happened during the four hours of the Philosophy writing test. The teacher fell asleep on her desk. We kept quiet so as not to wake her up. Half of the class was cribbing from their books under the desk. I'd finished writing the introduction and the conclusion of the Roseline's essay. (She made the drawings of the ox's eye dissection for me.)

"Didn't she wake up?"

"Yes, she did once, when Gerard dropped his book on the floor, she jumped! She looked round, then she resumed her sleep."

The whole café resounds with our laughter.

"The best one is about the brioches. In break, I took everyone's money and made a list of how many brioches people wanted. Marcel, of course, wanted three pains au chocolat. I went out on tiptoe. The caretaker didn't ask any questions, he was too happy to sell thirty brioches in one go. The biggest risk was meeting the 'Chief' on the stairs with my arms full but I got back to the classroom alright, handed out the brioches the pains au chocolat and the change, then we went on with the rest of the exam."

I get a hysterical laughter but just a smile from Isabelle, then everybody leaves and I ask Isabelle for her phone number in case there is a party on Sunday.

"I'd rather you find me a friend who's good at Chemistry, there're one or two things I can't quite understand because I can't do the experiments."

"You should have said it before, the girls who have just left are from Science."

"How do you manage?" Roseline asks.

"I'm OK. History and Geography are easy, just learning them by heart."

"I'll ask Deschannel," I say.

"Who's she?"

"The Maths and Science expert, she beats the boys! She should be called Poincaré[29]"

---

29 Poincarré and Deschannel were both Presidents of the Republic but Poincarré was also a famous mathematician.

Deschannel agrees. After all, she's for the 'Cause of the People'. They meet between midday and two at Madame Suzanne.

There is an attractive boy at the Café who's showing some interest in Marie-Jeanne Deschannel but she can't care less.

She is always with her best friend Claire Lorrain. They are both 'Bolsheviks' as Marcel puts it but Claire is more feminine and sentimental whereas Marie-Jeanne has the male militant's rigour.

"Marie-Jeanne could be pretty if she was not wearing the stereotypical working class' odd get-up," Marcel adds, "she seems to be afraid to look bourgeois."

The Philosophy teacher wears the same style. As for Roseline, Lambert and I, we are obsessed with fashion. We are an increasing number like that in the lycée, since the arrival of the boys. We exchange addresses of shoe shops and hairdressers. Roseline and Susini, whose fathers are respectively a baker and a lawyer, have enough money to compete. Only, Roseline's Mum doesn't always agree to buy certain garments. She refuses point blank to buy those too sexy thigh boots. Susini wears them with an air of triumph. Roseline manages to obtain the little padded Chanel handbag but it's a copy bought over the Italian border, in the Vintimiglia market. As for me, I'm very lucky. Mum has magic fingers and can reproduce a new Dior suit.

I stop Deschannel at the school gate. (I can't manage to call her Marie-Jeanne.)

"How are you getting on with Isabelle?"

"Very well. She's not stupid. She understands quickly. It's funny we're almost neighbours. I live in the street of the Eva Peron Home.

I am flabbergasted! She has told her immediately that she's from the Social Services! Suddenly, I see Roseline on the other side of the street, waving in a frantic manner while holding a newspaper. I leave Deschannel and cross the street.

"What's the matter, have you won the Lottery?"

"No, you idiot! Look!"

I avidly read the article she points to. It takes me a short time to realise that the girl who has taken her own life by putting her head in a gas oven is Josiane, the one who was going to marry her rich American sailor-boy from the Sixth Fleet. Her dream must have sunk straight to the bottom.

"I can't believe it!"

"We thought she was gone, married and happy."

"With a swimming pool!"

"We must ask Nicole."

"I don't see her often. She's always in her Austin Mini. She lets her arm hang out of the door to show off her diamond engagement ring."

"If you read the end of the article, it says that her parents said she was suffering from depression."

A few days later, a very brief news item in the paper stated that the autopsy has revealed she was pregnant. The destroyer USS Des Moines is not anchored in the Bay of Villefranche anymore, the American base has closed down.

"Do you really believe that people don't go to Heaven if they have committed suicide?"

"I find it grotesque that the Church decides…we should ask the Philo teacher what she thinks!"

It's getting near the Christmas holiday. We are walking back home, approaching Prisunic and it's six o'clock in the evening. The weather is humid and cold but the lights of the department stores have warmed up the atmosphere. In the falling night, the wet pavement is lit like an artificial rainbow. Roseline and I are walking up the Avenue de la Victoire, arm in arm. We are dawdling along, window-shopping. Suddenly she tights my arm.

"Look who's coming our way…"

"Where?"

"There! But don't make it so obvious for God sake!"

"You're telling me to look…ah, it's him!"

Le Clezio is walking down the avenue with his typical nonchalance. Roseline advises me to pretend to be doing nothing. I burst out laughing.

"We don't need to pretend!"

We pass him, he smiles nicely at us and Roseline goes into a trance.

"You saw it, you saw it, he smiled at us. We must go back to Françoise to do our revision. If we meet him on the stairs, he will have to say hello to us!"

"Roseline, please, stop. You know he smiles at everybody! What are we to him?"

"Precisely, we don't know him!"

"No need to. Alain Delon too, I don't know him and I don't like him."

"And yet, you loved Pierre and you were dead wrong!"

It is the first time I hear his name since July. I immediately feel a light familiar sickness. It must be the

Pavlov's reflex the other way round: Pavlov's dog felt hungry when he heard the bell, I feel sickly when I hear that name.

"I was wrong because I thought I could change him but I always knew what he was worth. The proof is, I would never have married him."

"So why were you so infatuated then?"

"If only I knew! We can never talk about those things with the adults. It's a good job we have friends but we all have the same experience of life."

"Yeah. At least you can talk to your Mum."

"Yes, but there are limits."

"With my Mum," Roseline continues, "a woman is either a spinster, a whore or a married woman."

"Mine says that education is to avoid all the cases you've just mentioned. You'll see, one day, we'll be the new women, the Independent Women! Ah here is Isabelle, see you tomorrow."

We go to sit at a café. Isabelle says that Marie-Jeanne has explained the Chemistry experiments and the Geometry of space to her.

"You call her Marie-Jeanne now!"

"I'm not in the lycée and she gave me her first name, I'm not going to call her Deschannel! Did you know she lives in my street and she knows about the Eva Peron Hostel?"

"That's right and you told her immediately you were from the Social Services! Why do you laugh?"

"Because it's the first time someone has been jealous of me!"

"Not at all, only it took you two months to tell me."

"Yeah but she lives in my street...Did you notice my eczema has almost gone!"

She rolled up her sleeves and I could see almost normal skin. Still dry and peeling a little but nearly smooth.

"That's fantastic and your ankles are cleared. You see, the fresh air did it now you have stopped wearing stockings. Before I forget, I brought you a super book but a bit depressing." I give her 'The Diary of Anne Frank'. I tell her what it's about in a few words. She has never heard of Hitler because he is only in the Upper Sixth syllabus and nobody has ever mentioned the second World War to her. Because of the American films she thought there was a war just between the Americans and the Germans!

"I've just finished reading this year's History book. Did you know that Indo-China was also called Annam?" Isabelle asks.

"Er, ...I think so."

"Haven't you read it?"

"I did but I can't remember. You don't remember everything, do you?" I ask Isabelle.

"Yes, I think I do. It's very interesting. Do you remember the Ku-Klux-Klan?"

"Oh that, everybody has heard of them! And how are you doing in French?"

"Finding it difficult. Your essays are superb!"

"I've got a few years training."

"I lack vocabulary. I would say: '...right in the middle of Romanticism' but you wrote: '"...in the midst of the Romantic Movement.'"

"You ought to read critics, they give you phrases like that. I'll take you to the central library on the boulevard

Dubouchage. I have to go there for my next essay in Philosophy.

Behind the central library, there is a small public garden usually full of mums, babies, pigeons, sparrows and dogs. The garden is empty at lunchtime. All around, open windows let out the scent of olive oil cooking and the sound of pots and pans. It's the time when the whole town stuff themselves and when cars jump red lights. I am too early. I sit down on a bench, put my textbooks next to me and start to read my Philosophy book. I can hear an old song about the Pyrenees Mountains 'singing under the Spanish wind'. Pictures emerge in my mind, I am in a romper-suit and, at that moment, I remember the words of the song. I start to sing them in a low voice when suddenly an operatic voice sings them next to me. He's a tramp.

"You can't concentrate on your clever book, can you?"

"It's because that song reminds me of things."

"Ha, ha! You must have been in your nappies and I was a gentleman then."

He picked up one of my textbooks.

"Oh dear, you poor little thing! What are you meant to make of the Positivism of Auguste Comte, I ask you?"

"I must say I find it difficult to understand!"

"What about your teacher? Isn't he meant to explain things?"

"She's ill."

"Bloody typical of teachers! Paid to stay in bed."

"No, no, she's not in bed!"

I explained the situation.

"Bloody war. I'll explain that old sod's positivism to you. Go on, take your pen."

For twenty minutes, he explained it in clear terms and without a single swearword.

"You got it now?"

"Yes. Were you a Philo teacher?"

"Me? Ha! Ha! Certainly not!"

"Pity, you could have replaced her."

"You're a sweet girl. The war screwed me up too but I'm not making anyone else pay for it."

"I don't know how to thank you."

"You've done it, girl, you've done it. Bye."

When I tell my classmates, they want to track down the tramp and ask him to give us paid lessons. We never found him.

When I tell Mum she gets cross and says again not to speak to strangers! Then she adds that people coming out of concentration camps never really recovered.

"But what could have been done to them?"

"Ah that…"

I don't really learn about it at school. In my History book, the camps are mentioned in five lines as if a detail. I will have to wait until going to the university cinema to see Alain Resnais's Night and Fog. Its simple and naked horror with no story attached to it has never been challenged by any horror films. "The Killing Fields", on Cambodia, will make the same impression on me, thus joining two extreme regimes, totally opposed and with identical and extreme consequences.

If only the teacher could stop droning on and tell us about her experience in the camps. Besides, nobody talks about them. Instead, she goes on mechanically, staring straight ahead of her at nothing, with her hand clenched over the corner of her desk to prevent herself falling asleep.

If I didn't mention the fourth boy in our class, it's because we only see him during lessons. His name is Jean-Michel de la Tour. With a name like that, he should have gone to the Stanislas College but he is probably a skint aristocrat. What intrigues us however is that he arrives at school every morning by taxi. As he lives in Tourette, a little village just outside our town, we quickly nicknamed him 'de la Tourette'. He can't care less. He has refined features giving him an aristocratic look, he talks as they do in the Comedie Française[30] and his classy style impresses Cermino. He is excellent in Philosophy and one day, mademoiselle Goujon reads us an extract of his essay as an example of reflection and expression for us to follow. It sounds like Nietzche, we don't understand anything, so we are full of admiration. Some girls start to quiver for him. He reminds me of this old granny's song that goes: "…he was waiting for his carriage, he was waiting for his maid, Yvonne…"

I like him very much but I know I am not for him so I make him a good classmate of mine. Another one. Gisele, the girl who is repeating her year is mad about him. She told it only to me. She doesn't mix much with the others; she's too eccentric for them and older. They tend to laugh at her ginger curly hair. We exchange recipes to get straight hair but I always admire its colour: an incredible bright orange. Gisele dresses with the out-dated elegance of Coco Chanel in the 50's. She comes to school with gloves on. De la Tour and Gisele are always sitting side by side; they chat and giggle. The whole class suspects that they go out together but I know it isn't the case. I ask

---

30 'Comédie Française' is like The Globe Theatre in London.

Gisele: "What is he waiting for? You are such a nice couple!"

"The right opportunity. His manners are so refined. He's not like Marcel who puts his hand on your buttocks."

"What opportunity?"

"A party or the New Year's celebration."

"That's an idea! I might find someone too."

*

The Christmas Holidays go as usual: presents, Midnight mass, grandparents, Dad sulking, the golden turkey and the nap. Mum doesn't want me to invite Isabelle. At the end of the day she has more fun at her Home than I do. She says that at the boys' Home it is never merry because they seem to find it harder than the girls to spend Christmas without parents. When you are not happy, you suffer even more at Christmas.

For the 31st December, Marcel organises a party at his place. His parents prepared a fondue[31] before going to skiing. Deschannel doesn't come and yet, Claire Lorrain, her best friend is there. Gisele is there, of course, in a very smart dress from another era. To everybody's surprise, de la Tour arrives with a beautiful girl, blonde and unknown, at least 20 years old. He dances with all the girls at the party except her. Petula Clarke is singing one of her best romantic hits, 'Anyone Who has a Heart' and Gisele is dancing with de la Tour, her eyes closed. Isabelle asks why he bothered to bring this girl.

"To show her off I suppose."

---

31 Fondue: Melting cheese and dunking pieces of bread in it. A speciality from Savoy.

Marcel attempts to get off with Isabelle. He calls her Lotus Flower. He thinks her Indo-Chinese tunic is incredibly exotic and erotic. But Isabelle keeps her distance, which makes him say, "Bloody hell, she's the Inscrutable Orient!" Marcel lives in the Ariane district, a hill in the suburb and we get there thanks to Françoise's 2CV. Roseline is grumbling because her enormous chignon is crushed by the canvas roof of the car. On the way back, her chignon is like a jellyfish on top of her head. Between two dances, de la Tour brings me a drink and asks me if I've seen the new Buñuel's film 'The Exterminating Angel.' Stupidly I say yes and that I found it as obscure as 'La Dolce Vita.' Not only am I a wallflower but I have to put up with metaphysical analysis of the two films. To my great relief, Gerard interrupts him and de la Tour latches on to Roseline to discuss 'Last Year in Marienbad!'

Gerard is fascinating at the piano. His huge hands are literally flying over the keyboard. We thought he would only play classical music but he shows us all his talent in jazz and rock; he is almost handsome.

I tell Suzanne I'm surprised to see Claire without Deschannel. She says she came for Alain, a playboy going to the ski resorts who is in Maths. Deschannel is a mother to Claire and she usually keeps an eye on her. Tonight she could not make it.

"But this is not her business," I say to Suzanne.

"Well, they have plans together. They'll go to Uni and train to be teachers but Deschannel is afraid Alain will distract her from their plan. She says he's a bourgeois with the gift of the gab and Claire is too pretty to manage her beauty on her own."

"Manage her beauty? Where does she get those expressions from?"

"Politics."

After midnight, de la Tour picks up his 'possession' who's flirting in a corner and they leave. As they don't live in town, he tells us they are staying in the Hotel Plaza for the night. Nothing has happened between Gisele and him. They danced only once. Gisele left and didn't come with us to town for breakfast. The tradition is to have an onion soup but I prefer a croissant and an espresso.

What will the New Year be like? I am third in Philosophy and de la Tour is first.

35 Males and Pains

Gisele returns to the lycée one month later, much thinner. She says she had angina. Now she is sitting alone at the back of the class. She doesn't wear her gloves anymore. Sometimes she reads the magazine Marie-Claire during the Philosophy lessons. She avoids me and I don't dare to speak of de la Tour.

After the February half term and its everlasting Carnival that gives us two more days off, the boys come back from skiing with sun tanned faces. There has always been snow in our Alps but it's only now that fashion popularises this sport. The little mountain villages that used to hibernate in winter are experiencing a second revolution after the television: the invasion of the Sunday skiers. As mothers don't let their daughters go, we listen to the stories of their exploits with envy and admiration. Alain has the reputation of being the best. He shows off and complains that the pistes are too easy for him and he has to go off piste to match his skill. Claire laps up everything he says and Marie-Jeanne is livid. She should not worry too much; he can have all the girls he wants, and Claire is only an appetizer for him.

We undergo our eight hours of droning a week with our books on our laps. When giving back our work, the teacher tells me not to eat chocolate roll when writing my essays because it leaves crumbs. I reply that I found cigarette ash in my copy. She is amused but her smile is sad. I immediately feel remorse for my impertinence. Our essays are well corrected. She combs through them and writes long comments we can hardly decipher. Sometimes

the line of her red biro wavers and slides down to the
bottom of the page.

*

Maths lesson: Gerard is standing at the black board.
We settle comfortably into our seats, the show is about to
start. The Maths teacher is an old spinster, built like a
rugby player with a high-pitched voice and she is not used
to having boys in her class. She gives Gerard a quadratic
equation, which he has no idea about. For him, unknowns
remained unknown whether it is x or y. His bulbous eyes
signal desperate SOS messages in our direction. He has
one hand spread out on the blackboard, while his other one
tries to write what Marcel is whispering to him. He grips
the chalk so hard that it breaks in two. He bends down to
pick up the broken bit, leaving the moist imprint of his
huge hand on the board. I shout: "Looks like the tracks of
the yeti!" The class collapses with laughter. The teacher
looks in my direction but she isn't sure it's me. In the end
she gets angry with Gerard and throws the sponge at him.
He reacts by protecting his face with part of his shapeless
cardigan. I shout: "Go on, pass me the sponge…" words
of a silly popular song. This time she sees me and sends
me out of the room, sustained by a wave of laughter.

It's out of the question to take root in the corridor. If
the Chief-Sup sees me, I'll get four hours detention on
Saturday. I go down to the toilets on the first floor to wait
for the end of the lesson, and I find Claire bent over a
wash-basin, gripping it with both hands.

"Claire! What's the matter? You're so pale!"

"It's OK. It will go."

"Do you want me to call Matron?"

"No, no, don't! What are you doing here?"

"I've been thrown out by Filippini, and you…? Oh, are you going to be sick?"

"No,…It's…my period."

"Oh I see! Don't you want to lie down in the sick bay?"

"No, no!"

Her voice is hardly audible. Her hair, wet with perspiration, is sticking to her forehead. I am really lucky to have painless periods!

"Can you help me to sit down on the toilet?"

She puts one arm around my shoulder and hangs on the basin with the other. She makes a step forward and a trickle of blood runs down her legs.

"Hurry up, she whispers."

"Claire, you can't stay like that, I must call a doctor!"

She regains some strength.

"No, please, no, I'll explain…"

I help her to sit on the toilet. She points at the washing stand. I can see a sports bag. I step out and get it for her. She opens it without looking, her head leaning backward on the cistern pipe. I help her and find several sanitary towels.

"Sophie…"

"Yes?"

"Take one to get rid of the blood on the floor, do you mind?"

Yes, I do mind but I begin panicking and do whatever she asks.

"Lock the door."

"Claire, it's not normal to lose blood like that! Why don't you want a doctor?"

"I must get changed again, pass me three pads."

"Three? Do you always lose that much?"

"No, I'll explain,…after…"

She drops the blood-saturated pads in the bag and I hand the new ones to her.

"Your pants are soaked, have you got any clean ones?"

"No, I only thought of the pads!"

"You want mine?"

She looks at me with a perplex and sick look.

"I put them on this morning, there're still clean."

"Oh I don't care about that, I… I'm just surprised, thanks. Could you call Marie-Jeanne at the end of the lesson?"

"I'll try."

Claire is top in Sciences, Marie-Jeanne is top in Maths, and they are also brilliant at the other subjects. Marie-Jeanne Deschannel is also a member of the Communist Party like a lot of girls in this lycée, and most of the teachers. Except the Headmistress and the terrible Deputy head, the 'Chief-Sup, who are right-wing. However, if it doesn't cause the expected antagonism, it is because they share the same purpose: for women, education is the only ladder to independence, therefore power.

Marie-Jeanne and Claire have made a pact: to enter the competition for the very selective Teachers College together, "L'Ecole Normale Supérieure," The grant is equivalent to a salary.

I give her my underpants. We line them with the clean pads. From time to time her blood gushes into the toilet. When a stronger pain takes hold of her, she grips my arm tight as if she's going to drown. I wonder if she is going to die but one doesn't die from having heavy periods. When the pain goes, she resumes her normal breathing.

"OK?"

"Yes but it will come back."

The end of the lesson bell shrills, startling us.

"Sophie, swear to me that you will keep the secret."

"What secret? Yes, I swear it."

"I am bleeding because last night I had an abortion and the woman warned me that I could have haemorrhage and intense pains, she said that I ought to stay lying down but I couldn't stay home… my parents don't know.."

"Christ! You were pregnant!"

She nods yes.

"Alain?"

Yes again.

"Does he know about it?"

"He gave me the woman's address and some money. Please, now, hurry to get Marie-Jeanne. Close the door, I'll wait for you."

I run up the stairs and go into Marie-Jeanne's class. Two teachers are chatting; the one who's leaving and the one who's arriving.

"Please, Madame, can I ask Marie-Jeanne if she's got my book?"

They are so involved in the conversation that they both say yes. I throw myself on Marie-Jeanne and explain the situation. Then I leave her flabbergasted and run to my lesson. Fortunately, the History teacher likes me.

"Madame, please, can I go to the toilet, I had an accident and I have to get changed."

"Typical of you! Always disorganised! Have you got everything you need?"

"No, I'm going to ask Matron!"

She rolls her eyes and I run downstairs. I knock on the door.

"Claire, it's me!"

The lock clicks and the door opens. Marie-Jeanne is wiping Claire's legs with toilet paper. I close the door behind me and lock it. With three of us, it's rather tight.

"Hasn't it stopped yet?" I ask.

"I'm not sure, replies Marie-Jeanne, the foetus must have dropped by now."

"How do you know?" I ask, horrified.

"It's the expulsion of the foetus that triggers the haemorrhage."

"Don't you think that a doctor…"

"A doctor? And then a scandal, the woman arrested, Claire banned from the Teachers College competition forever and then, prison! Her future broken, ruined because of that bloody bastard!"

First time I hear her swear.

"He gave her the address of the woman and some money."

"How kind of him! Better if he'd put on a johnny, that bastard! And his father is a doctor!"

"Alain's father? A doctor?"

"Yes pal! And he's loaded, he goes skiing every weekend!"

I put my finger on my mouth to tell Marie-Jeanne to be quiet. Two girls have just come in. They are talking, have a pee and carry on their conversation while washing their hands. Suddenly the Deputy Head barges through the door with the grace of a cowboy swaggering into a saloon and shouts at the girls: "Why are you still here, in the middle of the lesson? Out! Two hours detention on Saturday."

We are holding our breath. She is checking all the doors, one by one. She arrives at ours which is locked. I'm petrified. She shouts: "Who's there?"

"Claire Lorrain, Madame."

"Are you taking root?"

"Could I go to the sick bay in a moment, it's about my periods."

"Are you all right? Do you need help?"

"No, thanks, Madame, I'm used to it."

"All right, I'll send Matron to the sick bay but don't stay here for ever!"

Phew! She's gone. I tell Claire that she should have gone to the Sixth Form girls at the Calmette lycée for money; they have a secret fund for this problem.

"Never in a million years!" exclaims Marie-Jeanne. "I would never ask those rich bourgeois girls for help. I hate that school. They only take the cream and everyone else has to go to private schools for the rich or the technical college for the poor.

"Marie-Jeanne," Claire implores, "it's not the time for politics, I'm bleeding again."

We help her to get changed once more and Marie-Jeanne has to give her pants. I almost giggle when I see she is wearing Petit Bateau children's pants. We manage to reach the sick bay. She lies down and takes the pills the "angel-maker[32]" has given her. We don't know what they are. Eventually, matron calls a taxi and Marie-Jeanne goes

---

32 'Angel-maker' was the nickname given to the women practising abortion illegally in France.

with her. I tell Marie-Jeanne about the weekend in London where the English offer a package of an abortion plus a guided visit of the City; the same price as a proper abortion here. She says that Alain wouldn't pay for that.

The next morning, I run to Marie-Jeanne and ask her how Claire is.

"I don't know, her Mum says she spent a quiet night but she still doesn't suspect anything about it. I don't know what to do, it could be fatal!

I see her crying for the first time.

"Stop crying, the capitalist is coming this way," I say when I see Alain approaching us.

He takes his sunglasses off and, a little embarrassed, he asks: "Is Claire all right?"

"She's not that well actually. We're not sure. But you can tell your Dad that his grandson had a second-class funeral in the school toilet."

He freezes. I have to repeat it. Marie-Jeanne chuckles.

While going upstairs, Marie-Jeanne Deschannel says that I deserve to be a member of the Communist Party. For my parents, that would be as bad as an abortion.

*

A few weeks later, after the Philosophy course, the three of us are sitting in a patisserie. Claire gets more coffee, more colour in her cheeks, more weight and more joie de vivre. She invited us to Cappa's, on Place Garibaldi, the best patisserie in town, to thank us. Marie-Jeanne comments on the last lesson: "To explain God's indifference, they say that He lets us have free will to master our destiny…(long speech)… religion is the opium of the people who have empty heads. God is us, Humanity…You are not listening to me!"

"Marie-Jeanne, it's not the time to talk about religion, try this chocolate éclair," says Claire with her mouth full.

"And the praline cream of this Paris-Brest[33]!" I add. "It tastes better than your Karl Marx's stuff!"

The Baccalaureate and Spring are getting close. In our town, this season is hardly noticed. The palm trees and the olive trees remain the same. The city of flowers hasn't got any except in the Flower Market. The change is visible in the shop windows exhibiting new bikinis, markets displaying the colourful fruit and vegetables of the season and the patisserie selling ice creams.

When the swifts arrive with their shrill screams, we'll know it's the season for revision. Long after the exams, the swifts will still trigger anxiety like the Pavlov's reflex. Claire swallows her last piece of cake and lets us know she has a secret to tell us but we have to swear not to tell anyone. A juicy gossip.

"The taxi who took me back the day of my…haemorrhage is the same one as the one who takes de la Tour. In fact, his name is Delatour in one word and the taxi driver is his father!"

"Noooooo!" Deschannel and I shouted.

"Yesssss."

"Perhaps we should tell Gisele," I say.

"It's despicable to be ashamed of one's father," Deschannel says.

"You don't understand people, Marie-Jeanne," says Claire, "when Alain told me his father is a doctor, I told

---

33 Paris-Brest :a classic cake of French patisserie.

him that mine is an engineer even if, in fact, he is an office clerk for the EDF and yet I'm not ashamed of my father!"

"Yes, you are! That's the proof! This bloke is vile! He even contaminated you with his bourgeois attitude!"

"Here we go again! Don't start again Marie-Jeanne, it's over now!"

"So it's true, you don't see him anymore?" I ask Claire in surprise.

"That business has cured me and Marie-Jeanne threatened to tell my father everything if I see him again!'

"True friendship is nice," I say

A pigeon lands on Garibaldi's head, the sky is pure, and we enjoy a fleeting moment of happiness…

36 Adolescence: it makes or breaks

The swallows have arrived and Isabelle's eczema has gone. Thinking of the Chatel-Guyon's spring waters, I've advised her to wash it with mineral water. I don't know if it's the water or something else, but it has gone. When we go to buy Indo-Chinese clothes, Isabelle becomes friends with the shop lady. She buys some products at a reduced price for her at Prisunic and the woman teaches her Indo-Chinese. I don't see the point of it but she enjoys it. As for me, I'm trying to improve my English by going to the American Club, the USO but I dislike the sugary attitude of the Mormons. They groom their students and I am not used to that behaviour from a teacher!

I help Isabelle with her writing.

"Isabelle, you must improve your French when you write an essay. You must not write in the same way as you speak. Learn by heart some phrases from reviews, critics and analysis...Are you listening to me? What's the matter?"

"I have something to tell you."

"Oh no, don't tell me you want to give up everything!"

"No, it's good news."

"Ah?"

"William wrote to me."

"Really? Fantastic! To the Hostel?"

"Yes, for him it's just an address."

"So?"

"He's thinking of me. He's in the Army and he says that John lost your address and asked William to write to me to ask for it."

I was speechless but she adds: "I don't know if he wrote for me or just to ask your address."

"Nothing forces them to keep contact, you know. He wrote for both of us."

"Do you think we'll see them again?"

"I don't know… I prefer not to think of the future. It's so frightening not to know what will become of me in life."

"I'd love to go to America one day."

"It's so complicated. We haven't any money. It costs a fortune for a passport and a ticket and then my parents will never let me go."

"I haven't got that problem. For the money, I could find a job as a waitress or a cleaner on a liner."

"Go then and when you are settled, you call me. By then I may be independent."

To keep the dream going on, we go to see a marvellous American film: The Magnificent Seven. Since then I have been haunted by the music of the film. I love those new cowboys: vulnerable, strong, violent and kind. And the music makes me feel like flying away…

The heat wave and the cicadas are back but a bit earlier than usual this year and they are there during the whole revision period and to the end of the exams. It's so hard not to abandon the exciting study of the earthworm's digestive system to go and dive into the coolness of a glittering sea. I am feeling very tired. Do we have to study the earthworm's digestion to have a future? Roseline calls me to revise Biology with her at Françoise Lévêque's.

Françoise's block of flats is facing the port. The reflection of the sun on the sea is burning hot and blinding. It's a typical red building with windows decorated with white sculptures and blue shutters. In the hall, the large black and white paving stones remain cool. Roseline, blind as a bat, stick her nose up against the letterboxes to read the names.

"Look! Look! His name is on this box: J. M. Leclezio. He lives on the first floor and Françoise on the second."

We climb the slate stairs. Roseline stops in front of his door and stares at it.

"We're going to look pretty stupid if he opens it."

"I'd be so lucky."

She questions Françoise on the man's habits but she knows very little. He never throws parties and never makes a noise. She thinks that a woman is living with him but she's not sure. He sometimes meets Françoise's Mum on the stairs and has a chat. He said he was a student at the Faculty of Letters. Roseline finds it very hard to concentrate on her revision. She is looking at the arrival of the Gallus in the port.

"I know what you're thinking about! Instead of boring yourself to death with Mendel's Laws, you'd like to take that boat and spend the day alone with him under the pines of the Lerins Islands.[34]"

In the end we leave. Françoise has started to show some annoyance. When we get out, Roseline asks me to wait for a minute and goes back into the building.

What's she up to? I bet she is writing a letter to him. Suddenly I see him crossing the road. Jesus! It's too late to

---

[34] Island off Cannes where the Iron Mask was kept.

warn her. After all, it might not be a bad idea if they come face to face. He enters the building. I wait, idly wondering what happens to all these dogs' pooh on the pavement? Waiting… I must look for her. I go up to the first floor. I see her sitting on the doormat, her head against the door. Her eyes wide, looking at nothing. She frightens me. I shake her by the shoulder.

"Roseline! Come on, don't stay there."

I am surprised to see her getting up, docile, and coming downstairs like a sleepwalker. Once outside her despair breaks out. People look at her. I drag her down to the port where there are benches facing the boats.

"He sent you packing?"

She shakes her head to say no.

"Honestly Rosie, you don't even know him! He could be a cretin or a bastard."

She doesn't seem to hear me. I have never seen her crying like that. Usually, we only have giggles.

"You're reacting like those crazy girls who sleep on the pavement, outside the Beatles'hotel."

I wait twenty minutes for that storm to go away, without finding the words to help. For a second I consider going and ringing his doorbell but he would think we are two hysterical cases. Together we are watching the sun turning pink and slumping between the masts of the boats. I envy that toddler in his pushchair. When she's calmer, we go and take the bus.

"What's eating you? You hardly talk about him. Is it serious?"

"What do you want me to say? Besides you're always stuck with Deschannel or that Isabelle."

"It's because I'm helping her to pass her Bac. She has no one, no family, we've got parents…"

"You don't understand… I saw him coming, I climbed some steps to watch him without being seen. He went into his flat. I just about caught sight of an unmade bed and then he closed the door. I heard a female voice. I thought I would die."

"If you love him so much, you ought to…"

"No, no, it's not that… it's…he represents a world that is not accessible, a life that I would like to have and that I will never have because… because…"

"Because we're not Jackie Kennedy nor Marie Curie!"

"That's right. We are nothing."

"But wait! You don't know what the future has in store for us!"

"You must be joking! Do you remember all they said at the Careers Office? There's nothing for you, except the Post Office. What's more, with my look, what kind of boy would want me? When he closed the door, I understood that my destiny was an insipid existence, worse than my mother's. For him, I am a worm."

"Maybe he too is a worm."

"Yeah! A handsome worm not like me."

I don't know what to say to that; she gets me down all of a sudden by making me glimpse the possible future of a life at the counter of the Post Office, married to Pierre. But I quickly pull myself together again. I don't despair for long.

"We will go to university, we will earn money, we will go to a beauty parlour, you will go on a diet and do some sport and then… we might leave this town."

"That will take ages. We're going to go from acne to wrinkles… I don't want to go to the North."

"We don't care about the sun! It's better to have everything except the sun rather than the sun and nothing else."

Roseline has had fever for three days. The doctor can't make up his mind between a bilious attack or stomach pains. A little dieting and a pack of vitamin B12 pills are just the thing to cure you of this terrible sickness known as adolescence.

I envy Deschannel. Thanks to her political convictions, she's sure to possess the world or, at least, to be able to change it and to have a place in the new one. As for me, having got rid of the weight of faith, I feel less docile.

I visit Isabelle at her Hostel. She has a small comfortable bedroom, almost tidy. On the walls, tourist posters are advertising the beauty of Tibet and the Grand Canyon and between them a large picture of a TWA plane. On a table, I can see her work corrected by the CNTE. She has reasonable marks but for someone coming from the fourth form and who has read only magazines for four years, it is quite remarkable. Her main problem is her lack of vocabulary. She says that she only learnt to speak when she was five and went to school. For a long time the teachers mistook her for someone mentally handicapped. She didn't talk because her parents or the people who looked after her never talked to her. She hates essays. She finds it senseless to follow the structure of writing an introduction, a main part with thesis and anti-thesis, then a conclusion. I advise her to write according to the teachers' opinions.

"Articles in the newspapers are not written like that!"

"You read the papers?"

"Yes, Marie-Jeanne advised me to."

"Ah yeah, the Communist newspapers!"

"No, no, all the papers. She lent them to me."

"I'm surprised she reads other newspapers."

"She said one must be aware of other people's opinions."

The month of June is the most beautiful month of the year. I always eat lots of cherries and vine peaches and Mum forces me to eat courgette flower fritters that I disliked. All the woollies disappear into the cupboard with mothballs, for four months. Revision and the race of the swifts in the sky accelerate. I skip quite a few chapters in Philosophy to concentrate on Chemistry and Trigonometry. Gran brings down some figs and wild strawberries from the village to cheer me up.

I can hear radios playing Dalida's songs. I put on a Petula Clarke's record, Anyone Who Had a Heart and Chariot… that's it…I am dancing cheek to cheek with John at the Bac Ball… I am wearing a Courrèges dress and my hair is straight and cut square as in Elle… I can't concentrate any longer. I leave my books and go out to buy an ice cream.

In the street a persistent hoot attracts my attention. It is Joelle, the girl who was in Philo last year in Pierre's class. She is in a convertible Caravelle. She double-parks and invites me to come on board for five minutes. She asks me for news about the lycée. I told her about the boys in my class. She laughs. She's reading Psychology at the University of Aix. Her blond hair is cut very short in the

Twiggy style. I tell her that I find her superb. She asks me if I remember Pierre. I lose my smile immediately.

"Of course, you know I went out with him a whole year."

"Really? He said you were just friends."

"Yeah, he wanted all the girls to know he was available and I wanted all the girls to know he wasn't!"

"Crumbs! You're still with him?"

"No, no, it's been over for some time now. I even wondered how I could…"

"That's true! You're cute, what did you see in that guy? He sweet-talked me once but I sent him packing. By the way are you aware about him?"

"Aware of what?"

"Pierre, he got married because the girl was pregnant. The girl's father bought them a nice bed-sit near the sea. He was supposed to carry on his studies at the Faculty of Law and she would carry on working as a secretary after she gave birth. So they went to Venice on honeymoon. Once there, the girl had a miscarriage at the hotel. What do you think he did? He left her there and went back to France. The girl's mother had to go quickly to Venice to take care of her. The father was furious and kicked him out of the bedsit! They divorced, he stopped his studies and is working in insurance."

"How do you know all that?" I gasp.

"I met him on the beach. He just told me everything to show me that he was available! What a joke! Him! Stupid, penniless and ugly! You had a narrow escape!" she says laughing.

"I'm mad at myself."

"Don't say that! You've learnt a lesson and you're luckier than that poor girl! What did you find attractive about him?"

"Ten boys for eight hundred girls in the lycée! I was flattered he chose me I suppose."

"Flattered! But, Sophie, you were too good for him!"

I let my ice cream run down during the conversation. Joelle gives me a tissue. We exchange addresses and we promise to see each other again but we'll never do. From an early age I have been losing so many friends on the way. They seem to disappear into a black hole.

This year we don't go to the Baccalaureate Ball. It's still the same thing: a hundred girls for a dozen boys. In July, cinemas show old films and there is nothing as good to cheer you up as a Fernandel comedy like a Don Camillo. It's the story of a priest always fighting with Peppone, the communist mayor of an Italian village. And Peppone makes me think of Deschannel.

On the day of the results we go down in groups to read the lists posted at the lycée Felix Faure. From the crowd congregating in front of the lists, shouts of joy and screams of despair are soaring. Pushed about by all the people who want to take my space, I look for my name. I go beyond the letter L and I am not there. With a beating heart, I start again reading the list of L names but I'm still not there. My future is not obstructed, it simply doesn't exist anymore! I feel what Roseline felt when she saw LeClezio's door closing. Suddenly, I hear her voice.

"Sophie, Sophie, look, I got it, I passed! Look: Conti, Marie-Rose!

In fact, the whole class has passed except me. In Maths, Alain and half the boys failed but all the girls passed.

Claire Lorrain and Marie-Jeanne Deschannel passed with Merit and they passed the test to go into Teacher Training College. Delatour passed with Merit. Gerard is wild with joy because now he has passed the Baccalaureate, his parents will let him study the piano. Marcel can enter the college to train as a PE teacher. Isabelle can retake the oral in September. I let everybody go to the Café to celebrate and I go to wait for Isabelle outside her store.

"You can retake the oral in September," I inform her.

"Phew, at least I got that! And you?"

"Not even retaking."

"Oh my God! What are you going to do?"

"Everybody is asking me the same question. Everybody passed except me!"

"How did you manage it?"

"I must have messed up the Philosophy essay and in Physics I didn't even understand the question."

That night, I don't sleep at all. If the despair caused by Pierre ruined my appetite, the despair caused by the Bac ruins my sleep. My parents don't say anything. Mum staggers under the blow and Dad shrugs his shoulders. I phone Lambert who advises me to give up studies. "They only give you an ulcer," she says. Suddenly I am hit by a terrible fit of nostalgia about last summer. I'm thinking of John. I am missing him and I write him a ten page letter. I cry a lot because of the throbbing pain caused by the terrible question: 'What am I going to do now?" I am enduring it night and day.

Roseline is going to Marseilles to study Pharmacy, Lévêque finds a job as a ground hostess at the Orly airport near Paris. Suzanne gets her dream job as schoolmistress in Beaulieu. Gerard will enter the 'Conservatoire de

Musique' in Paris. Delatour will go to the Faculty of Law and Cermino to study English in Aix but she will prepare for the competition exam to enter the Comédie Française. She wants to interpret the great classics roles.

"I know I don't have the physical appearance to play the tragic and romantic heroines but I can start by playing the maids in Moliere," she says to us.

Isabelle encourages her. They both think I should try again. Isabelle offers to get me a job in Prisunic and to prepare the Bac together with the CNTE.

"You would do anything to leave your job, don't try to send me there!"

On the radio, they say that Marilyn Monroe has committed suicide. Roseline used to say she had everything!

I go back to Gran's for the summer. The mountains suit my pain better. The sea has a cheerful aspect I can't stand anymore. The mountains are serious companions who protect you from society and prevent noises from reaching you. There, one doesn't hear the sound of civilization, only the little bells of the goats, the cicadas, some scarce birds and the rustle of the olive trees in the breeze.

In September, I go with Isabelle to the corridors of the Lycée Calmette to support her. I advise her to wear her Indo-Chinese tunic; it charms men and moves women. She comes out of the class.

"How did it go?"

"I don't know, I had a mad man in French."

She doesn't have time to tell me, she has to go to History. I ask the other candidates who had that mad man. They all talk together. He's a Philosophy teacher from

Menton and he had to replace the French teacher at short notice. He is a tall black man and his name is Monsieur Blanche. He addresses the candidates sharply by saying: "What bothers you? My colour or my smell?" The candidates are immediately destabilised.

"When he saw your friend arriving with her Indo-Chinese tunic, he said 'What's that? Do I dress like a Zulu?'"

"Oh my God and it's my fault!"

"Wait," she said "Maybe you're not a Zulu but I am Indo-Chinese' and then he went on with his catch phrase: ' What bothers you? My colour..." etc. And your friend said: 'No sir, you are bothered by my clothes and my colour."

"She's finished!"

"Not at all, a boy exclaims, she's too cute! I would not mind drawing her portrait!"

"You can draw?"

"Yes and if I pass the Bac, I will go to the Beaux-Arts in Paris."

Patrick, the future Rembrandt, passes his exam, so does Isabelle. He draws two charcoal portraits of Isabelle; one of which will be sent to William.

37 Lolita

With a heavy heart, I get ready to go back to school again to repeat the year. I am lonely in the playground. The new boys are much younger with acne and the girls, of the same age, giggle stupidly all the time. I have some hope when I find out that our Philosophy teacher has gone and is replaced by a dynamic man, in his forties: Monsieur Dumalle. Alas, I am down in the dumps again after his very first lesson! His Philosophy lesson flies very high and he makes peremptory statements that annoy me. He's terribly dogmatic and when I take the liberty to argue, he says it's not intelligent to repeat what the teacher said last year. Doesn't he know that the teacher, last year, said precisely nothing? Rumour has it that he is a royalist and he mentioned the 'Action Française[35]' a few times. My essays come back with the worst marks in the class, whereas I had the second place in Philosophy last year.

Three weeks after the beginning of the term, a new girl arrives. She is sixteen and the spitting image of Carole Baker in "Lolita," She has two passports, French and American. She sits next to me and fills in her form. I have a peep.

Name: St John-Wiltman.

First name: Vivian.

Father occupation: Reporter.

Mother occupation: secretary at the USA Consulate.

The Philosophy teacher is very impressed and he always looks at her like a dog discovering a raw steak after

---

35 'Action Française' was an extreme-right organisation.

years of Doggimeat. She is aware of this and exploits it with extraordinary maturity. We smile at each other. At break time she stays with me.

"Dumalle doesn't seem to like you very much."

"Probably because I am the oldest in the class... On the other hand he seems to like you very much."

"Yeah, another bloody idiot you can see coming a mile off. The day I meet a real man! That'll be D-Day!"

I am speechless. We become close friends. Her, sixteen, me, nineteen. The Philosophy lessons bore us; me because I don't understand them, Vivian because she understands them. We occupy ourselves by writing short satirical poems. She tells me with a disarming simplicity how she passed the first part of the Baccalaureate by cheating and not working.

She comes to lessons with some rough paper and a pencil. She never has a book or a file and drags around a large and worn out satchel.

"Why do you carry such a big satchel for a few sheets of paper?"

"It's my shopping bag to buy food. My mother doesn't always come back home so I have to cook my own food and sometimes hers."

She shows me a steak and some carrots she has just bought. I am horrified, sorry and touched. Mum would consider me a martyr if I had to make my own sandwich. One day I tell her of my pathetic affair with Pierre. Then she is the one to be horrified, sorry and full of pity for me.

"How could you?" she says.

Our lives are so different that we can't stop talking during the lessons and we get a few detentions. Thus, one day she tells me that last summer she got plenty of pocket money by working as a stripper in a London nightclub.

One Thursday, I hear someone calling my name from the terrace of a café. I turn round but don't see anyone I know. A sort of movie star is waving her arm. It's Vivian. She's wearing a blond wig, sunglasses and a skin-tight dress with plunging neckline. I am transfixed. She bursts out laughing.

"Come on, sit down a minute," All the men passing turn round and look at her, but she doesn't seem to see them at all.

"Do you like my wig?"

"You bet! You look like Veronica Lake."

"Who's she?"

"An American movie star. Didn't you see My Wife is a Witch?

"I never go to the cinema."

"Do you do your own makeup?"

"Are you shocked?"

"No, I'm impressed."

"That's kind of you."

The next day, I see her again at the lycée with her old satchel, her hackneyed shoes, her felt cardigan and her faded cotton dress. Without make-up, her face is somewhat touching. I tell her that she reminds me of Lolita, especially when she looks sad.

"I have been told that several times. Who's Lolita?" asks Vivian.

"If you never go to the cinema, you can't know of her but you must read Nabokov's book; the story takes place in America."

"I've only read two or three books in my life. How do you know so many things?"

It's strange but I feel stupid with all my culture.

"It's because I love reading and my parents used to take me to the cinema regularly."

"You're lucky, my parents are always on the move. I remember reading a book at the boarding school, called 'Little Women'."

"Ah, I know it, in French it's called The Four Daughters of Dr Marsh by Louise Alcott."

"How do you know that?"

"It's a popular book in France and I found out the English title in the English Texts we had to prepare for the oral of the Baccalaureate."

"Ah yes! I never prepared them! I spoke English better than the examiner!"

One day, in December, someone rings at the door at five in the morning. Mum comes up to wake me up to say that Vivian is at the door.

"At this time of the night?"

"You said it! I don't know where she's come from but she looks exhausted and she's carrying her shoes in her hand. If you could see the state of her feet!"

"It's all right, I'll come down."

"Listen, be careful now, I don't want any trouble with the family or the school. What is she up to at sixteen, alone in the street, at five in the morning, in an evening dress? Where is her mother?

"Mum, don't overdo it, I'll go and see."

Vivian is standing pale and shivering at the door, almost blue under the light of the hall. Her torn stockings show her dirty and sore feet. She is holding her wig and her bag under her arm.

"Come in quick, you're going to catch your death. What's happened to you?"

"Can I wash my feet?"

She takes off her black stockings and I run some warm water in the bidet. She sits on a stool and dips her feet with her eyes closed. She's wearing a superb black lace dress. She says she has come from 'La Siesta', a nightclub on the sea front, near Antibes.

"But it's 20 kilometres away!"

"I got a lift to the airport."

"You didn't walk from the airport on stilettos, did you? It's five kilometres away! Your Mum must be so worried!"

"No way! She's not home and besides she couldn't care less."

"What about your Dad?"

"I expect he's busy filming some war or other."

"Why didn't you take a taxi?"

"I didn't have any money. It's nearer to come to your house than going back to Beausoleil."

"You go dancing during the week?"

"Yeah. I was meeting friends. I enjoyed myself but on the way back, then I had trouble with a bloke in the car… in the end they got rid of me at the airport."

I can't find out any more from her. I lend her a pair of my felt pyjamas, she finds them hilarious.

"You sleep with those on?"

The next morning, we let her sleep and when I come back from the lycée at twelve, Mum says she ate a whole baguette for breakfast and Dad found her charming. She has to wear some of my clothes to go to school in the afternoon. On the way, she tells me she used to earn a lot of money in London, by being an escort; she was accompanying gentlemen to posh dinners.

"Vivian, isn't that prostitution?"

"It could be but as I am a minor, the clients behaved. It was just to accompany them."

Sometimes she falls into a sort of deep sadness, I try to distract her but one day the Philosophy teacher orders me to shut up. I whisper to Vivian:" Deliver us from Evil," [36] She bursts out laughing loudly. Furious, Dumalle shouts at me: "Here we are, the oldest corrupting the youngest!"

Vivian laughs even more but the remark hits me like a slap in the face. That slap has the beneficial effect of a kick up in the backside. It wakes me up. I go to see Isabelle in her Hostel to tell her that I can't stand the school any longer and I hate the Philosophy teacher.

"Is that because he is Extreme Right?" she asks smiling.

"No, because he's extremely wrong! He reminds me too much of the nuns. I've made up my mind, I'll go to England as an au-pair and I'll study for the Bac with the CNTE."

"You're leaving me?"

"How about coming with me?"

"You're on!"

"The most difficult thing is going to tell my parents."

"I haven't got that problem."

I climb down the stairs of the lycée slowly, telling myself that it is the last time ever. Each step evokes a

---

36 Pun: in the French Pater Noster prayer, it says: 'délivrez-nous du mal' (Dumalle is the name of the teacher).

giggle, a fit of despair, a new meeting, some secrets, friendship, joy, suffering and a crowd of faces. I am touched by Vivian's remark: "I'm going to be so pissed off without you."

She'll write to me to say that Dumalle expressed his relief to see that she's no longer under my negative influence.

"What a pathetic bloke," she writes, "he really deserves to be taken for a ride! It's quite flattering for you that he thinks you're the black sheep; assuming I'm an innocent little girl is too much! I'll show him who's innocent," I quickly write back to ask her not to do anything foolish but my letter brings no reply.

38 Albion

We dare and we do it. Pangbourne is a large village near Oxford. We are lucky with our host families, they are rather nice. What a pity we can't understand the television, the English was so different from our school English! Their programmes look a lot more interesting than the French ones. They have lots of original series. One is about a pretty witch who moves her nose to work magic. Another one is about two men in the rag trade in White Chapel, Steptoe and Son. They are hilarious even if we don't understand a word of what they say. Isabelle loves 'The Munsters', a series about a particular family: the mother is a witch, the father a Frankenstein monster and the son a mini Dracula. I realize how dull our French TV is. I am also moved to hear Marilyn Monroe and Charlton Heston's real voices for the first time.

Once the housework is done and the kids at school, Isabelle, who is in the same village as me, comes to join me and we work on our homework sent by the CNTE. She chose Maths and I stuck to Philosophy.

The natives are difficult to meet and get friendly with. The majority of them commute. In these days, there are no cafés and in the pubs we find boredom as thick as the smoke of their cigarettes; what's more men are separated from women! The Thames is grey, the swans white and the sky often black. Out of respect or discretion, the English southerners ignore you. One Saturday we go to spend the day in London. All the dummies in the clothes shop windows are the effigy of Twiggy. We get chatted up by Italian students in Carnaby Street. They have just come back from a crowd of people gathered around a psychedelic Rolls Royce, painted with some patterns inspired by LSD. We think the gathering is for the car but in fact, it's for a bloke sitting on its roof. He is black, dressed like a hippy with a bandana and a guitar. He is signing long play records.

"Look," shout the Italians, "it's him!"

"Who's him?" I ask.

"Jimmy Hendrix!"

"Never heard of him, have you Isabelle?"

"Never."

After a brief visit to the British Council where we meet only Pakistani men with an incomprehensible accent, we decide to leave them and go to the cinema. We leave the cinema choked by the smoke but the usherette won't open the door until the end of the national anthem. When we return to Paddington station, it is a disaster: no more trains after eleven. We have to spend the night on a bench in the station like tramps! We think our families will be dying of anxiety and that we are going to be told off. Nothing of the kind. They find the whole thing very funny and an interesting experience. Mum would have called the police straight away.

In the evening classes, again, we meet only foreigners like us, especially girls. Next time I'll choose a town with no less than three hundred thousand inhabitants. At the cafeteria of the college we gather in a French group as we all have the same problem: how to meet British people? I declare that I am going to chat up some English blokes. A French girl from Lyons says: "I don't go in for that sort of thing!"

"Nor me but you have to make the best of things! I'm not making any progress and all I'm learning is the vocabulary of housework!"

"You don't need a boy for that, a girl will do."

"I don't chat up girls, it's not my kind of thing."

"The British Council…" a German girl interrupts.

"Ah non! They are all sorts except English people."

"Fabrizzia is going out with an American guy," someone says.

Everybody shouts: "How did she manage?"

"She went to the bar of the American base."

Isabelle and I look at each other.

"Did you know there was a US base near here?"

"No idea, we've got to ask the Italian girls."

*

I am sitting on my bed writing Isabelle's Philosophy essay and she is sitting on the carpet doing my Maths.

"Listen, Isabelle, to this sentence I've just composed: 'Regret is remorse for negative actions, while remorse is regret for positive actions'."

"Not bad! Have a look at your parabola. You went wrong between minus infinity and plus infinity, that's why your parabola looks like a corkscrew!"

"I know, I always get lost in infinity. Thanks… Listen, I have a genius idea."

She smiles, which is rare. Strangely enough, I can't have with her the giggles I had with the girls at the lycée. Isabelle is like a tower surrounded by a crown of grey clouds and sometimes a pale ray of sunlight pierces through.

"I need serious Maths lessons and you also need help. Let's look for a student, male or female."

"That's not stupid!"

I am looking at the rain quenching the permanent thirst of the lawn.

"I'm nostalgic for the lycée. It's so quiet here with nobody in the streets, it's like being in a cemetery."

"I think it's beautiful here like Paradise!"

"That's right, everybody's dead. I'd like to be at Madame Suzanne's and have a laugh with my class mates."

"I understand but I'm not nostalgic for Prisunic. Too much light, too much agitation, too stressful! And at the hostel, we had the roaring of the lorries on their way to Italy during the whole night"

"Wasn't it cosy?"

"Yeah, in a way, but there was always a crisis. Before, I used to imagine the future with fear and anxiety but now I imagine it with interest, concern… and hope."

"Didn't you ever have giggles at school?"

"Never. I was bored to death."

"That's funny, Vivian too. But you were not always in a hostel, didn't they put you in a nice foster family?"

"Yes, when I was six. I was placed with a single lady in Beaulieu. She was wonderful, she spoiled me a lot. She always took me with her to the beach, on walks, to the cinema and even to the library…then the Social Services took me away because they were afraid I had become attached to her."

"I can't believe it."

"Yes, it's true and afterwards they put me in a family where I felt like a piece of furniture that was in their way. When I made a mistake, they locked me on the balcony at night and even in winter. In the end, I was allowed to stay in the hostel where the chef and his wife took me under their wings. Thanks to them, I had the impression of having a family."

"Fantastic! Did you send them a card?"

"No, I don't want to get attached any more."

"But that's stupid, you want to keep in contact with kind people!"

"I'll see."

We go to Oxford which is not far and we walk on the lawn of Corpus Christi. The colleges are separated from the outside world by high stonewalls. There you can leave your bike unlocked anywhere. From time to time, a low gothic door allows us to catch sight of a figure in a black gown, gliding between bushes of wild flowers, on a perfect green carpet. Some students are coming and going but we are not allowed to go in.

"How do they know we are not students?"

"Forget it, it's not our world," Isabelle says.

"Maybe we don't look clever enough!"

I see a girl getting off her bike. I go to her and explain that we are French and we are looking for a Math students for tuitions. She smiles and asks me to repeat slowly. She says she loves our accent and asks us to follow her. We march through the gothic door without the porter noticing anything. The sounds of the city stop there. The buildings of rectangular yellow stone are from another era and lean against each other. We walk in a fairy tale garden. As we pass a minute gothic window, the sound of a violin reaches us. That music is as mesmerizing as the song of the mermaids. Without stopping, our guide tells us that it's the music of The Lark Ascending, her favourite piece. She seems to walk quicker and quicker, then we arrive at a wooden door. I can't help thinking of Alice's white rabbit. We have to lower our heads to get into a small library. She asks us to sit down and to wait five minutes, and she takes a spiral staircase. The silence is such that we could have heard the specks of dust dancing in the pale ray of sunlight.

My idea works. James is a third year student in Maths.

He is as ugly as sin but so friendly and so full of beans that after a short while we don't notice his appearance anymore. He adores France because he has spent all the summers of his childhood in the Dordogne. The English think that this region looks very much like an English county: it's green, peaceful, full of rivers and very few people; the worst scenario for me who loves crowded beaches, thirty degrees, the sea in the front, the mountains behind and bougainvillea everywhere. James comes from Yorkshire and he says that the English from the North are not as cold as the ones from the South.

Little by little, we make acquaintance with other students. We go with them to pleasant pubs. Like the young American girls, they all practise a sport or an art. Isabelle and I cannot do anything. James even teaches us to ride a bike, so we buy second hand bikes.

One day, Isabelle catches sight of my camera on a shelf in my room. She looks at it from every angle.

"Hey! I never saw you taking photos," she says with surprise

"That camera is too sophisticated for me."

"Have you got the instructions?"

"Yeah, but it sounds like Chinese to me."

"Can I try it?"

"If it works, you can keep it. I'll buy a camera for children where you press on a button and that's it!"

"It's a beautiful camera," she says holding it like the sacred Host.

"That's why I bought it. There's a thing for the light, one for distance, one for the storm and lots of unknown gadgets."

Isabelle throws herself into the book of instructions while I read about the book of History relating the victories of Rommel in the desert. For once the Germans are winning, it makes a change from the war films. An hour later Isabelle makes me jump. She shouts: "That's it! It works!"

She plants herself in front of the window, and takes her first photo. Then she turns round and without warning me, she sends the flash right into my eyes.

"Ouch! You found the flash!"

"Yes, it's the gadget you called the 'storm'. The zigzag is the flash."

She hasn't realised it yet, but she has just discovered her passion. I envy her. I can't think of anything that would enthuse me to that extent. I've never been able to understand groupies who spend the night on the pavement outside a hotel or at the airport to see the object of their passion or Deschannel happily sacrificing her life for the sake of the Party. The passion I least understand is the one felt for God by a pretty, intelligent and talented girl who shuts herself away in a convent with the Carmelites; it was the case of Mireille Perrier who was a gorgeous ballet dancer. As far as religion is concerned, I suspect that somehow, somewhere, there is an imposture. If God doesn't exist, Mireille Perrier won't even be able to say "Crumbs, I was wrong! I wasted my life."

James is full of admiration for a failed photo. It is an autumn landscape in the grounds of Magdalen College. He says it looks like a painting by the Impressionists. He sends Isabelle to join a class to learn to develop your own photos. I thought you have to do optical studies for that! Without James, we would have had sad and boring times and yet he keeps saying we are the sunshine of his life. Our relationship is not ambiguous, he's like a brother. At a party when everybody is drunk, we ask him if he has a girlfriend. He says there isn't a chance with his face! Still some girls are interested in him because he has such a pleasant personality full of humour and intelligence but he avoids them. Isabelle and I decide to improve his appearance. He is wearing yellow glasses on a pale face with long, scattered blond hair. We made him buy glasses with a black frame like Michael Caine's. We convince him not to wear a mauve jumper; the dark ones suit him better but he refuses to abandon his orange and grey striped trousers. What doesn't help him is that in England, whatever you wear, nobody pays any attention.

There is, in Oxford an ageless woman who spends all day walking round the town centre. She has a child-like face but with wrinkles, and her hair is tight in a ponytail with a black satin bow. She wears clothes that used to be smart but today are worn out. Her bag is an attaché-case where she puts everything, including food. She speaks to everybody in the streets and in the shops. She's well-known and they call her Suzy. She's not begging for money but for attention. She could have been Miss Havisham in Dickens' Great Expectations. Her English is sometimes posh, sometimes vulgar. She walks past the perfume department saying 'goodbye' a dozen times and all the sales assistants kindly reply goodbye to her. We are eating scones at Browns' when she comes in. I expect her to be thrown out since she only comes in to speak to the customers. Everybody smiles at her and she embarks on a long meaningless speech and leaves. Sometimes she waits outside the station to say hello to the passengers arriving or leaving and everyone is polite to her.

"Is she a nut-case?"

"No," says James, "She's eccentric."

Another person intrigues me: the lady at the counter in the cinema. She is obese with a skull slightly out of shape. It would be easy to think she is retarded but she is not at all, and I never saw someone so fast with her maths. The cinema doesn't need a calculator or a machine, she is just as fast. In France, to work at the till, one has to be pretty, young and with good qualifications. As for the 'eccentric people', they are laughed at or rejected. Here, that friendly tolerance will never cease to surprise me.

Shortly before Christmas, Isabelle receives a letter that makes her very agitated.

"A letter from William," she says looking panicky, "He's coming!"

"What? Here? To see you?"

"Yes,…No, to the American base where Fabrizzia picked up her boyfriend."

"What for?"

"To test helicopters…"

"He doesn't say if John…"

"No…"

"Still I am very happy for you, that's great news… what's wrong?"

She looks dejected suddenly and her hands are trembling.

"Don't know…It's too much…all of a sudden…I thought I would spend my life between Prisunic and the Hostel. Now I am scared to lose everything and to find myself back at the warehouse."

"If you pass the Baccalaureate, you would be above Madame Leger!"

I've just caught myself speaking like my mother!

It wasn't a good idea to cycle to the military base.

That evening, I am doing baby-sitting for Isabelle and James comes to watch the TV with me and, like old parents, we wonder how this meeting will turn out. James finds it unwise to cycle such a long distance at night. He thinks that if William was a gentleman, he would come to get her. More practical, I think she is going to soil her nice trousers. The next morning, Isabelle calls me while I'm preparing the kids' cereals.

"So? Did you see him?"

"No, it started raining. The bottom of my trousers got muddy and I was sweating. I left a message with the guard and went back. There is one bus in the morning and one in the evening."

"Did you leave your phone number?"

"I forgot!"

"Isabelle, ask Mrs Stevens to phone the base. Explain to her."

"I knew it was too good to be true."

"Don't start! Do as I said, she'll help you!"

It works so well that William sends a taxi. I rush to the Stevens to see Isabelle in her new Mary Quant mini dress from Peter Robinson.

"I can't believe it, your eczema has completely gone. That's lucky!"

"It must be the climate! But I have to put on some cream because of the hard water."

"I know! Did you see inside the kettle? It looks like the cave of Saint Cézaire!"

"Are you going out tonight?"

"Yeah, with James and his mates. There is a new group coming to sing at Magdalen College. James thinks they are great. They have a stupid name: The Who.

Isolated by the decibels of the concert, I am thinking of Isabelle who must be having such a romantic evening. I start to fantasize and I replace William by John. I am the one with the Mary Quant mini skirt. In London you can follow the fashion with little money. He's amazed at my eyes with the Twiggy make-up,… he takes me in his arms and… suddenly a thick silence brings me to reality. The concert stops, a man takes the microphone to announce that President Kennedy has been murdered. He invites us to go next door to see the news played over and over again. We are all hypnotized by Jackie Kennedy's picture in a pink suit, leaning over her husband. The cameraman and the newsreader are showing lots of pictures but always come back to that one. Mum had made the same Chanel pink suit for me!

Isabelle will tell me that she stayed only one hour. She had to leave because the base was in a state of alarm. One hour of intense happiness is better than nothing. If it had been Roseline, I would have all the details of their meeting, but Isabelle remains silent and dreamy.

I get a letter from Roseline the next morning enclosing a cutting from the newspaper. It says that J M Leclézio got the Renaudot Prize for his first book, The Trial. So, our handsome unknown man is a writer. Roseline writes: "I knew he was exceptional, and besides, I didn't understand what his book was about!"

39 New Start

We feel a twinge of sorrow as we see the white cliffs of Dover disappearing behind us.

Will I see them again one day? I already feel nostalgia for this place of total freedom of expression, this incredible tolerance for others, where the craziest dream is considered as a possibility and where madness is called eccentricity. I don't know why I already miss the tea, the rain and the language.

Back in France we find out that two French girls, the Goitschel sisters, have become world ski champions, that the Beatles make the girls hysterical and that a magic pill allows women to enjoy the pleasures of the flesh without paying for the sin; yet we will have to find another excuse to say no to the boys. However, the invention of the tights is going to make 'things' more difficult. If it's embarrassing for boys to buy condoms, it's even more embarrassing for us to buy the pill. The chemist asks for an identity card in front of everybody.

A new designer has become the toast of the country: André Courrèges. It's a good job Mum is a skilled dressmaker, she copies him to perfection. I can wear his famous white cotton piqué dress for a tenth of the price.

Everything is starting again: the heat, the swifts' cry and the revision. Beyond the white cliffs, the wind is cool and the crows' cry doesn't tell me to revise.

We both pass the Baccalaureate and we are in a daze. A sudden void succeeds the intense work, the fatigue, the anxiety and the excitement. We fill it by going to the beach. I read Marcel Pagnol's childhood memories and Isabelle,

the Lord of the Rings that I lent to her. I bought it because
the author is a professor in Oxford, just like the author of
Alice in Wonderland. What I don't like with the fairy tales
is that I get so immersed that I find it very hard to come
back to reality. Fairy tales, unlike pills, start with bitterness
and end with sweetness. What makes me suffer most in
life is the lack of magic powers.

Isabelle would like to study Oriental Languages but
she doesn't want to go to Paris. I enrol at the Faculty of
Letters. The premises are called the Elysées Palace, a
pretentious name for a crumbling building. The area is full
of smart expensive shops and prostitutes. The First year of
uni is choc-a-block with 'tourist' students. The lecturers are
arrogant, blasé, union members a bit aggressive and the
secretaries, young and cantankerous.

As usual, the Careers office is totally useless and
unable to help Isabelle: Science is not for girls,
Photography makes them roll their eyes so, in the end they
offer her the good old Post Office.

"Isabelle, isn't there something you would like to do?"
"Yes, photography but they laughed!"
"Teaching?"
"No openings."
"Scientific research?"
"No openings for girls."
"Nursing?"
"No openings. Only the Post Office."
"We should have asked the Careers Office in England.
Let's phone James to have an idea."

James will spend an hour at the Career Office, where
he's given a ton of brochures and leads to pursue. But of
course it is for England. He advises Isabelle to find a

photographic laboratory and to ask to be a trainee or do work experience. We follow his advice and Isabelle starts to work in a newspaper photo laboratory as a cleaner. She quickly picks up the habit of attentively observing people working. She shows a great interest in their skills and they find it amusing to answer her questions. They give her little jobs to do in the lab and she eventually does more and more. After nearly a year, she works in the lab as a part-time supply employee. As for me, I am bored stiff at the university but I force myself to stay. The lecturers are rattling out their course. Fortunately, the Students' Union gives us duplicated lecture notes. Finding the literature books is an assault course. The library has so few and they are all out all the time. It takes ages for a bookshop to get them. Again, James saves me by sending some to me. The lecturers get out of their towers to throw their course at us and disappear again. We have to fight to be on the front row, the only place where one can hear and catch the meaning of the foreign language. Also, it is known that you have to be seen as often as possible by the lecturers so that they can remember at least your face. It is also known that we have to repeat in our essays what the lecturers say in their teaching. It is the proof that we attended their lectures.

Isabelle carries on her private tuitions with the old lady in the oriental shop. The lady turns out to be a better teacher than our lecturers.

Isabelle has just received a letter from William. She is waiting for me, outside the Faculty of Letters and takes the letter out of her bag. I can see the stamp of the US Army in Vietnam. That's the new name given to Indo-China. She shows me a photo where William is standing in front of a huge helicopter with double propellers. Neither Isabelle nor I really understand what the Americans are doing over there but now, this is the only news we are watching or listening to.

A letter from John has arrived from Florida.

This mail reawakens feelings asleep in resignation. John has become an image that I would cherish with no hope, like the photo of James Dean in 'Rebel Without a Cause'. My mind plays the same scenario a hundred times, while waiting at the bus stop or before falling asleep: he arrives at the airport and I throw myself into his arms. It is so realistic that it triggers a physical reaction in my body, like my heart beating faster or jelly legs.

John is taking a holiday in Florida after training for the Marines and before going to Vietnam. Pity I lost sight of Deschannel, as she would have been able to describe the whole political situation to me. I ask Dad but he says it's too complicated for me. Mum says that it's typical of men to fight each other and that I'd better tidy up my bedroom. For Mum, domestic problems are more important than war or politics. In his letter John says he keeps the Breil lavender twigs and if he comes back, we would live in the South of England so that we could land in Normandy from time to time… Doesn't he know that lavender doesn't grow in Normandy?

Isabelle regularly listens to the news and informs me that the Americans are very unpopular because they are using a weed killer called napalm. What kind of war is that where one has to kill plants as well?

Isabelle is taking a lot of photos. She leaves at five in the morning and goes to the Old City or to the seaside with her camera. She gets a snapshot of the little rubbish wagon colliding with a tiny Italian car called Icetta. This car, shaped like an egg, has no door, it is the whole front that opens. The newspaper buys the photo from her to publish it. It's the only happy event of the month.

Shortly before Christmas, William sends her a gadget that's still very rare here! It's a tape-recording machine with a magnetic tape where he recorded his voice and the sound of the helicopter. She listens to it, over and over again in the deserted and dark laboratory. Suddenly a man, who is working with her, tries to steal this magic moment from her for his own pleasure. He came in silently and jumped on her to rape her. In the battle the tape was destroyed and Isabelle managed to run out and takes refuge in an office. The man arrived behind her, laughing and calling her a teaser. The men in the office chose to pretend to believe him and smile. Now, when she has to go to the lab, she locks herself in. She doesn't make an official complaint because she wants to keep her job.

*

One Monday, I attend the inauguration of the student restaurant of the new Faculté des Lettres with Isabelle and Roseline. It looks like a glass pagoda with 180 degrees view over the sea. As she is not a student Isabelle is not allowed to eat in this restaurant but the student who checks the card and tickets at the entrance is a Corsican friend of mine so she can go in.

Roseline is in the second year of Pharmacy at Marseilles and she comes to spend three days with us during a fit of the blues. She collects temporary lovers with a royal indifference. She finds them all insipid and immature. She sleeps with them because she feels like it but for conversation, she much prefers a female friend. She says that the ideal man would be a homosexual who would sleep with girls! I think she idealises too much. She needs to fall really in love with a man and to accept him as he is, but she has a mental block there.

"I'm getting a bad reputation because I sleep with boys and then I dump them. Usually, that's a boy's attitude, you see!"

"I do! Do you remember the scandal of Brigitte Bardot's film 'And God Created the Woman'?"

"Yeah, exactly, except that I'm unforgivable because I'm far from being as beautiful as her."

"Typical! What about your lectures, how are they?"

"The female ones are much better, they are more conscientious but also fussy."

"That's funny! Me too. One of the rare teachers to be stimulating is the one teaching us about Shakespeare. She has a passion for his characters. Because she's young, some blokes try to chat her up but she's not interested so they spread the rumour she's a lesbian or she's frigid…"

Isabelle gets up and go to take some photos in the restaurant.

"Is she OK with her job?"

"Yeah, apart from the fact she nearly got raped."

I tell her the story.

"I can't even imagine what she can do about it, she's got no proof, no witnesses!" Roseline said.

"The others didn't say anything, some even chuckled. At least, she's got William."

"Great! The man of her life is in Vietnam! And you?"

"Me? Nobody. John's going over there too."

"I'm through with boys," Roseline says, "My only sincere lover now is Money. At least, it doesn't disappoint you. I could get a lot more but I don't like risks."

"What risks?"

"LSD, heroin, I have easy access to those substances in my studies."

"Jesus! I know LSD, it was popular in Oxford but I never wanted to touch it, I was too afraid. Did you try?"

"Yes but I asked someone to attach me to the bed beforehand."

"You're mad! You could have been abused!"

"They were friends I trusted. I found the experiment useless. I'm not interested in changing the world for a few minutes and then going back to square one. For that, we have the cinema. It's not worth bothering my precious brain with stupid hallucinations."

The Mediterranean winter sun is flooding the restaurant and turning it into a greenhouse. We look at Isabelle taking her snapshots.

"I'm glad she's got William, I'm worried she'll come across a bad guy."

"She's mature enough to know the difference!"

"I didn't."

"Yeah but you've learnt your lesson now. By the way, have you heard from him?"

"Didn't I tell you about his disastrous marriage?"

"Oh yes!"

We both burst out laughing. Isabelle comes back to sit with us. While we are finishing our 'îles flottantes' a student approaches us. She's wearing jeans, a denim jacket and no makeup. It's usually the uniform of a communist or a hippy but I would be inclined to communist because of her surly face. She gives us flyers inviting people to a demo against the Americans in Vietnam and she demands money for the poor people martyred by the Imperialists. Roseline rolls her eyes, Isabelle examines her camera with a sudden interest and I am annoyed at myself for not understanding the situation in Southeast Asia. I shrug my shoulders so she raises her voice.

"What? Don't you care that an innocent population is being massacred?"

Unable to argue and sentimentally linked to the Americans, I ask her to clear off because we are not interested. She flies into a rage and calls us bloody little 'bourgeoises', only thinking of the latest fashion. We are staring at the real Marxist-Leninist at work.

The students start to bang their plates with their forks and knives to cover her voice. The girl withdraws ranting. I envy those who have political convictions. Even if I have some, I am not able to defend them.

The season of examinations comes back once more with the swifts and their cries.
Lots of students have forgotten or didn't know that being registered at the university doesn't mean being registered for the exams: panic is followed by the first wave of student eliminations.

Also, we all know that in Literature, one question out of three won't be in the syllabus; we don't know why but we have to deal with it because it's out of the question to question the system. In France, they try to find out what the students don't know. In England they want to find out what the students know, that's why their papers have lots of questions, and lots of choice. The worst thing is the oral exam: I get Monsieur Leséjour, the 'exterminator-examiner'.

He has the reputation of reading his newspaper during the exam. I enter his class on jelly legs. He is sitting down reading Le Monde. With a nod of his chin, he shows me a heap of little pieces of paper folded in four where the questions are written. I am supposed to pick one at random. I do and get Jane Austen.

After the ten minutes of preparation, he calls me. I start the analysis of Fanny in Mansfield Park. He is reading his paper and turns the pages, then he looks at his watch and asks me if I have finished because my time is up. I stammer two sentences to conclude, get up and leave.

"You shouldn't have come suntanned," a girl tells me, "it makes a poor impression!"

I have no idea how I passed that exam, maybe because he didn't listen to me! Roseline too passes hers. We decide to go to the cinema to see Polanski's 'Rosemary's Baby' to forget it all. I thought we would have a laugh as in the 'Dance with the Vampires'. We leave the cinema confused and stunned. The cinema is changing. I thought that only Jean-Luc Godard breaks the rules but we've discovered François Truffaut whose characters seem to improvise all the time.

We go to the café La Buffa to have our espresso and Isabelle shows me a letter she's just received from William. He is back in the US, on sick leave. I can see she's not feeling comfortable. I try to cheer her up but she remains silent. Roseline and I look at each other.

"Is there something else? Why do you look so strange?"

"I'm going to him."

"What? Because of a fever?"

"No, I want to leave France for good."

"You're going to get married?"

"No, I'll leave with a tourist visa then I'll look for a job…"

"But you've got a job here. One day, you'll be a press photographer."

"No, I will have to sleep with someone here to get that job. I thought it would be different from Prisunic."

"Don't tell me you had to sleep with a bloke for that job!"

"No, no, I didn't, but when the men realised you are a single girl, they never stop chasing you and harassing you. The colleague from the lab was the last straw."

"You're right," Roseline says.

"Did you tell the people at the hostel?"

"Yes, they told me to be cautious."

"If John asks me to leave, I couldn't. I haven't got any money and I couldn't dump my parents like that!"

"William is going to send me an air ticket and some money. And you know I haven't got a parent problem."

"I envy you."

"Me too," says Roseline.

"It's the first time anyone's envied me!"

I suddenly remember that Vivian's dad is a war reporter and an American. I decide to try to find him or Vivian. I ring the US Consulate but her mother doesn't work there anymore. Eventually I find Dominique's number, a girl in Vivian's class. Dominique is delighted to hear from me. She begins to tell to me the whole scandal in the lycée. Vivian and the Philosophy teacher have had a brief liaison. I sit down, Dominique carries on: "…it didn't prevent her from passing her Bac without a stroke of work! The scandal happened because Vivian was a minor but the head mistress managed to cover it up by the skin of her teeth…."

"I bet he dumped her after sleeping with her!"

"You got it all wrong! She dumped him immediately and didn't give him a second chance! She gave him a glimpse of Paradise, then slammed the door. He was so ill that his wife came to the lycée. The headmistress asked Vivian not to come back to school and to do the last term at home. The scandal wasn't revealed because her parents were persuaded not to complain to the police for abduction of a minor. She led him by the nose, I daresay, to remain decent; she giggles. One day he was waiting for her in his little Renault, when he saw her passing in a superb Consular car with a chauffeur. She was sitting in the back with a mature man who had his arm round her shoulders. In a word, she married the Ambassador of Venezuela."

I am full of admiration for her quiet and destructive power. Dumalle was transferred to another school in another town; summer was not long enough to cure his depression.

The dreadful thing about summer is suddenly having time to think. There's no longer a timetable and syllabus to keep you going. I should not have told Roseline about Vivian, it depresses her.

"Why her and not me?" she says, "I'll never be able to meet a handsome diplomat in a bakery."

"Why not, they also buy bread…"

"Yeah but I'm less appetizing than a pain au chocolat!"

"Roseline, you're getting a sense of humour now!"

"How can a man like Leclezio look at me? I have no artistic talent, no personality, no charm. All I can do is mix and provide medicines."

"Look, if you are so keen on him, go to his place and speak to him. What have you got to lose?"

"That's right! I shall offer him the latest antibiotics and the new suppositories!"

We are in stitches. Then my laughter changes to tears, I don't know why. It must be the prospect of two months of summer on my desert island. Roseline shakes me and tells me off, it's her way to cheering me up. It does me good, like a cold shower after sunburn.

"How about going to Italy together?"

Our parents are opposed to the idea unless we can find a chaperone. Roseline finds one. She unearths a university friend in Marseilles called Laurent. He has just passed a PhD in Physics and Chemistry, he looks very attractive and is homosexual. Homosexuality is like death, it hits the best. With him, our parents are not worried. He'll enjoy that role.

"So I have to keep an eye on my two little chicks!" he says with a dazzling smile. He likes the idea because we are like a 'cover' for him. He has very good taste and advises us on our makeup and dresses. He says my legs are too skinny to wear shorts! In the streets of Florence, we meet girls from the hotel so he puts his arm round our waists or holds our hand to keep them at bay. It's not convenient for us because that way, he keeps the boys we want to attract at bay too! Laurent has a crazy success with both sexes. He attracts superb boys and we can't attract a single one. All we want is a boyfriend or a flirt to go for a stroll on the Ponte Vecchio or to throw coins in the fountains of

Rome as in the film Roman Holidays. But we don't look like Audrey Hepburn and the only boys we attract like flies, are fourteen or fifteen-year-old Italian urchins.

One evening, Roseline meets a young good-looking Austrian man on the banks of Lake Garda. They don't speak each other's language. We don't understand what he is studying but he is to join the UN in September. She leaves us and goes to spend the night with him. Laurent and I make a mental note of their hotel, just in case. Then we walk back to our hotel, lost in our thoughts. The next morning, very early, she comes back transfigured. That moment of euphoria over, Roseline will be overcome by a deep fit of nostalgia. She keeps repeating how well he treated her. When she woke up the next morning, she thought she had found her soul mate. He was the first one ever to make her feel remarkable! She had glimpsed a possibility of happiness, a door was open, it was possible, they got on so well. But at the crack of dawn, she had to leave, he had to go back somewhere and he softly closed the door behind her. She went to sit on a bench, on the edge of the lake and, for an hour, she listened to the lapping of the little boats moored on the bank…. How deep is the water?

Once back home, I have to kill the month of August. I receive a letter Isabelle sent me from America. She did it! She sounds happy and asks me to send her all the photos I can find in a box at the hostel. She has had her visa extended.

*

Roseline's Mum rings me to ask what did we do in Italy that makes Roseline so tired. Also, she has refused to eat for three days, even her favourite pasta. I say that she drove a lot but apart from that, we didn't do anything special. I don't dare to ask her if Roseline has nausea. A few days later she calls me back in a panic. Roseline has been taken to the Saint Roch hospital. She has been found in a coma on a bench at the port. I stay in the hospital with her mother for the whole night, in an overheated corridor leading to the Intensive Care unit. From time to time I go out to breathe the fresh air, but Madame Conti doesn't want to leave her chair. She is fanning herself with her identity card. Her white blouse remains starched and spotless until midnight. Past this time, as in Cinderella, it starts to look like a rag. Her plump fingers remain clenched on her bag and her grey bun is collapsing a bit.

She keeps asking me questions about what has happened in Italy. Knowing that Roseline never tells her anything, I don't mention the episode of the handsome Austrian. At the end, I tell her that if her daughter is so depressed, it's precisely because nothing has happened in Italy. She looks at me uncomprehendingly, then looks down as if further questions would be superfluous. For her, the main thing is that nothing has happened, the rest she can cope with. I ask her where monsieur Conti is. She replies that, as with Roseline's birth, he prefers to wait for the news while baking the bread.

I never like the dawn. In books, dawn has something fateful about it. Mum says that babies often cry in the evenings because twilight makes them anxious. I'm sure she's muddling things up; I find the twilight delightful.

Eventually, a man in a white overall appears in the corridor. He's the doctor. Quickly I think: "Oh dear, the doctor in person. Roseline is the only child, she should not have done that to her parents! Worrying them stiff by living a crazy life is one thing but to offer your death to those who offered life, is insulting... as when you return a present!"

The doctor says that pumping out Roseline's stomach has worked. Madame Conti flinches a little and the doctor helps her back on her seat.

"Can I see my daughter now?"

"Not yet. Her first words were to say she didn't want to see anybody."

"So... What do I do?"

"Madame Conti, come with me, let us have a coffee. She needs rest and so do you."

Roseline took too many sleeping tablets, which she can get without prescription and free of charge at the university lab. She took them outside Le Clezio's door and then she realised she had forgotten to put makeup on! She dragged herself off to the harbour where she collapsed with the image of black masts dancing against the painful light of the sun fixed in her eyes.

40 University

This summer again, I manage to kill the month of August by reading and swimming in the sea. I even buy a diving mask. I don't know why I feel so nice under the water. Is it being weightless? The silence? The temperature? I would stay hours but when I come out, my body trembles for long minutes despite the strong sun. If only we were amphibious! I would prefer to swim with the fish than to fly with the birds.

For the first time in years, I start knitting, I haven't forgotten how to. It is soothing and I let my imagination go wild. I am creating fancy jumpers inspired by the hippy era.

Roseline helps her parents at the bakery before going back to Marseilles. Isabelle is about to come back. I haven't heard from her for a long time and I was beginning to worry. Then she wrote to say she has great news to tell me. I suspect she's going to marry William. I go to meet her at the airport. If people want to be cheered up by looking at a happy crowd, they should go to an airport to the Arrivals and watch. However, I would not take Roseline there, I think it would be cruel.

I don't immediately recognise Isabelle. She is wearing a pale green linen suit with a white organdie collar, wide sun glasses and high heels. She has a new camera slung across her shoulder and is carrying a Hermes handbag. I stand there flabbergasted. She smiles.

"You look so wonderful!" I cry.

"Look at this camera," she says taking it out of its case, "isn't wonderful?"

"Crikey, is that a space telescope?"

We kissed.

"Gosh, you're wearing perfume!"

"Chanel No 5."

"Ah, I never liked it on me."

"It was Marilyn Monroe's perfume."

"Well, look where it got her."

"William loves it."

"Ah, that's a good reason."

Her arrival at the Hostel causes a sensation. Everybody makes a comment.

"When's the wedding, then?", "Will you introduce us to a rich American too?" Etc…

She shrugs her shoulders.

"That's all they think about! He's not rich, he just has a good income."

I look at her hands, no rings. She closes the door of her bedroom and sits on the bed. She looks round the room.

"They've lent it to me for a few days. I don't remember this room being so small."

"You're not going to stay here, are you?"

"No, that's the news I was telling you about."

"Ah. You're going to move over there?"

She hesitates a second.

"Listen, a big American magazine likes some of my photos. William paid for me to have an advanced course of photography and a magazine wants to send me to Vietnam as a freelance photographer. They found it exciting that the fiancée of a soldier would go there as well."

"Ah, so you're getting married!"

"Well, not really. And he's not exactly a soldier, but a helicopter engineer. The magazine's idea. And in the States, you have to be engaged, a fiancée, to be proper."

I find it difficult to accept the news. I am reacting like my mother. For me, it had been out of the question to study in Paris and Isabelle is going to be a reporter in Vietnam.

I try to convince her that she's going to a country at war, that she's risking death and torture. She argues that she would see William more often instead of waiting for him in France. Besides, she felt like 'a dead fish' in Prisunic. And since she's Eurasian, she would go unnoticed. What's more she would be able to practise the language. I ask if the Viet-Cong wouldn't make her miss Madame Léger.

"I wonder…" she smiles. "For once I am happy not to have family ties."

My face gives me away.

"It's not the same with you, you're my best friend and if you lose me, you'll find others…"

I thought friendship bonding was as strong as family's. So, like all the schoolmates, she is going to disappear into my past. I find it difficult to breathe in that tiny room and I get up.

"Where are you going?"

"I'm going back, it's seven, my Mum's waiting."

"Ring her, we're going to eat together. Let's have a socca in the Old City."

"No, it's too late, she will already have cooked the meal by now."

"So when do I see you again?"

"I'll ring you."

Isabelle leaves in November, when the Viet-Cong mortars are attacking Saigon. She is sent to Hué where William is waiting for her. I pounce on a map and look for Saigon and Hué. I don't find it straight away because I thought Indo-China was on the "left" of India! I should not have skipped this region in the Geography lessons. In the university restaurant, a student tells me that there are four hundred thousand men there and President Johnson is reluctant to send more soldiers because of the public opinion. The hippies are turning the people against the war.

"That's weird, they think like the Communists," I say to Gerard, a university mate.

"Never!" he says, "They're useless! They want to destroy taboos, conventional wisdom, so as to replace them by LSD, flowers, songs of love and peace."

"Maybe so but they don't kill anybody."

"What do you know about it? Destroying the foundation of a society leads to civil war or deprivation. What we need is a cultural revolution like the Chinese have."

"Really? I thought we did it in 1789."

As usual, I tend to be convinced by the last one who talked. I can't manage to construct an opinion of mine and to defend it. They all have convincing arguments. It's like Suzanne the Pied-Noir and Deschannel the Communist, both were right!

When I tell Mum that Isabelle has been sent to Vietnam by an American magazine to take photos, she declares: "That's what I thought! She's a little schemer, an adventuress."

"If she was such a schemer, she'd have chosen something other than a war to go and photograph!'

"You'll see, she'll make it and end up seducing some general! Look at your friend Vivian, a little hussy who got up to God knows what at night, at the age of sixteen! She managed to get her claws into an ambassador! And the decent little girls are left to vegetate!"

I wonder if she is saying this for her or for me. And yet, I consider myself lucky to meet such interesting characters as Vivian and Isabelle.

Lessons have started again. We aren't cheerful. The books are more interesting than the lessons. Half of the students don't come back this year, therefore we have more space in the amphitheatre. Two classmates from last year, more intelligent than me and harder working, failed their end of year exams. They decide to answer the call from the Consulate of Australia. They are desperately short of women over there, whereas at home, a plethora of girls are living in our town. The Education Board is talking about a majority of female students too. The two girls take lots of baggage and leave their parents in tears. One of them rapidly will become the headmistress of a primary school, the other will marry the director of a bank and resume her studies. They practice sports, receive lots of guests. They don't vegetate anymore but they suffer from separation and the clash of culture.

The month of November is sad like a Monday. There are still tourists left behind but also natives swimming in a sea warmer in than out. Isabelle has left for the USA to catch a B52 that will take her to Paradise on the path to Hell. Lambert is not available any longer, she has a steady boyfriend. Friends fall and disappear like the autumn leaves but I get a new one, Marilène. She is vegetating with me on the benches of the amphitheatre and she buys my first knitted jumper. We talk about boys. I tell her about John who left to save the world with the Marine Corps because society bores him. He was offered opportunities to make money but he wanted something else. To get killed won't be better.

"Isn't there anything other than money and death?" I ask her.

"Yes," she says, "knitting."

We burst out laughing. We completely forgot that the Dean of the University is lecturing us on Shakespeare's The Tempest. He gives us a black Jupiter like look from the top of his pulpit. For the practical work in English Literature, we are divided into four groups of a dozen students. In my group, we are cursed with an appalling teacher but rewarded with a brilliant and mature student, about thirty: a Pied-Noir with a very strong accent. He works as a waiter at our café, La Buffa, where the English writer William Boyd will go. Joseph looks older than his age, in fact he is older than the teacher. Slightly bald, with a bit of stomach over his belt and round glasses, he's always in a good mood, without any hang-ups and totally relaxed. He's the only male in our class so he should not feel very comfortable, he says: "Bloody hell! What luck! I am the only rooster among pretty hens."

As a contrast, our literature teacher is the exact opposite of Joseph, physically and mentally. Monsieur Charente is young, pale, and weedy with a mop of hair in the style of Beethoven, as if an invisible wind was blowing it backward. There is a dispassionate air about him as if he were in a waiting room. We've never had teaching like that before. He comes into class with a worn-out paperback of Great Expectations in his pocket and no notes. Joseph

favours him with a "Goode afterrnoon, Sirr". The teacher
gives him a tight-lipped smile and asks us which page we
are on. Then he crosses his hands under his chin, props his
elbows firmly on his desk and looks impassively at the
people who are with him in the 'waiting-room'. The first
time, there is a prolonged silence, leading to uneasiness.
The teacher looks at us and we look at him with our pens
poised, ready to note down his every word. However,
nothing comes out. Even Joseph is disconcerted. In the
end, Charente heaves a heart-rending sigh and resigns
himself to saying: "Since you've read the book, tell me what
you think of chapters one and two."

These precious words are half of the course he will
teach us that year. Unable to stand this embarrassing
silence, I open fire with a basic commentary. So much so
that we end up by discussing the beginning of the novel
between ourselves.

Charente and Joseph are watching us. Then Joseph
contradicts me but some girls agree with me: the discussion
becomes animated. Three weeks later, Charente asks us to
discuss in English; that was the second half of his course.
Until then we had exciting debates with Joseph without any
intervention from the teacher. Things go wrong when
Joseph tries his English. He is like a comedian performing
a stand-up.

The whole class is in stitches and Charente has a smile
full of pity. Joseph flies into a rage.

"Why do you laugh? It's true, that woman (Miss
Havisham) is a nutcase. You don't keep a wedding cake for
thirty years on a banqueting table because your fiancé
dumped you the day of your marriage! She is
schizophrenic, that's all! Besides, she could do that because

it was an English cake! With a French one she could never have!"

Even if Charente doesn't flinch, we can sense he is enduring it. And yet, without any fuss, Joseph is doing the teacher's job quite well. He's joking but he also makes very deep comments. One can see that he has lived far more than Charente had. Joseph often doesn't agree with us and we have hot debates. He has male chauvinist opinions and confronted by him, we become 'suffragettes'. It is obvious that he enjoys our angst. When Charente is late we hardly notice it. In any case his presence is superfluous. His function is to give us the title of the essays and to correct them but above all to inform us of the end of the lesson. I wonder what we would do without Joseph. We accept and endure this teacher because he's not nasty and doesn't make any humiliating remarks; we just tolerate him. However, he loses the whole of whatever credit he has left when he tells Joseph, a month before the exam, that if he wants to give himself a chance of passing, he'd better go and see a speech therapist or change his subject.

Not only does he never teach us, but, not once in the whole year, does he bother to correct our accent.

Much later we find out that monsieur Charente was preparing his PhD and he had other fish to fry than delivering lessons to students of an intellectual level far too low for him.

He has the same behaviour with all the other groups he is teaching but the others don't have Joseph to save them. We must fear these teachers so much to accept them without complaining. Will someone one day dare tell them that this isn't teaching? Or will they carry on until retirement, molly-coddled by their fat and secure civil service salaries, regardless of the quality and quantity of their work? Their attitude will be challenged in 1968. That year some truths will come out like this lecturer earning £900 per month for three hours teaching a week. He will be betrayed by a colleague who wanted to get rid of some leftist students molesting him. "Look at Forget's salary slip in his pigeon hole, he does fewer hours than me!" They quickly find the proof!

Isabelle has gone for a month now and not a single letter. I ring up the Hostel. They haven't heard from her. Having no family and being over eighteen, she can disappear or be killed; the Social Service isn't concerned anymore and no one would be informed apart from her employer. I am shocked. Then, shortly before Christmas, the postman delivers a parcel. I see the Vietnam stamps and post marks from the US Army. I also recognise Isabelle's handwriting. It's a Simon and Garfunkel album, Christmas in Vietnam, with the sound of gunfire and a soldier's voice in the background.

She has sent me this record because I love "Hello Darkness, my old friend, I come to see you again…" The Sound of Silence is not a song, it's a chant for all those who go through an endless tunnel. On the back of the sleeve, Isabelle has written: "On behalf of John," There is also a page torn from an American newspaper with photos of rice fields and helicopters. The article mentions Marines sent into demilitarised zones with impossible names: Khesanh, Dong Ha, Camp Carroll… and suddenly I see a hand-drawn arrow pointing towards the words: Ph. I. Tchang. All excited, I show Mum Isabelle's name.

"Look, look! They published Isabelle's photos!"
She glances at it and shrugs.

"Do you think that's a place for a girl!"

"It's less risky than the photo laboratory! In any case you wouldn't let me go!"

"Of course not!"

"So to have a life, it's better not to have a family!"

"It's better to have nothing to lose. My God, are you reproaching me not having given you up to the Social Service!"

"Not at all. I wonder why you hold it against her!"

"Nothing but I can just see that it's always the riffraff who gets the luck!"

"Mum! How can you speak like that? What's the matter with you? She has never been riffraff! She even passed her Bac on her own!"

"You bet! Thanks to you!"

"So?"

"Alright, it's your business. If you don't mind being used… It's always the same people who get the luck. For me, everybody took great care to make sure I didn't get any education: my parents, the school, the social legislation, my husband!"

From that moment on I avoid mentioning Isabelle's name forever.

Whenever I see a plane, I wonder if it's going to England or to Vietnam. I carry on going to uni to be able to present my mother with the bit of paper they call a Degree. A piece of paper written and crossed off by the hand of a cantankerous secretary who finds it difficult to follow the multiple changes of the syllabus. No stirring award ceremony like in England. The lecturers are becoming more and more casual. By fear of having their sacred aura removed on the one hand, and by putting the largest gap possible between the student and the teacher on the other hand, a storm is bound to break. If I had to spend another year with Charente, I think I would become violent. Instead of reforming teacher's ways of thinking, they reformed syllabuses.

Today is my last exam: the Literature Oral. Since we could not rely on Charente, we worked like mad and learnt by heart books of novel analysis. I know through and through Graham Green's The Heart of the Matter and everything about the author who is living in Antibes! I know all about Coleridge and Elisabeth Gaskell too. I still turn up at the oral ill at ease mentally, for the irrelevant question remains the sword of Damocles in our university.

I sit down in front of a Professor I don't know. I open one of the little pieces of paper and bingo, I get The Heart of the Matter! I take a deep breath but before I open my mouth, the examiner points his finger to the cover of the Penguin book and asks me: "Who painted this?"

Dumbfounded, I look at a modern painting showing a poor creature with a head shaped like an electric bulb with a black mouth wide open. He's holding his head with both hands on the background of a grey sky with bleeding clouds. I've always found this picture horrible.

Why on earth does he ask me that stupid question? Who knows who drew that front cover? I look at him with the eyes of a cow going to the abattoir. He is annoyed. I would prefer him to read the newspaper like Leséjour.

"Have you ever heard of a painter called Edward Munch?"
I nod to say no.

"This is his most famous painting! 'The Scream', mademoiselle! We want to get a Degree but we don't have any cultural knowledge at all! That's today's students for you! Right, go on, give me your speech on Graham Greene!"

Frozen in terror, I can't manage to utter a word. I feel like that poor bloke screaming. Me too I want to scream "Don't you want me to also talk about the quality of the paper?" But my screams remain quiet like monsieur Munch's portrait. Failing my final for that fills me with hatred forever. During the May 1968 riots, the following year, this professor will make sure to show himself on the side of the students! Mum tries to cheer me up by telling me that the world has not changed. During the Liberation, many Collaborators became Resistants. I suppose hatred must be a necessary ingredient for the maturity of the adolescent.

Another summer ruined by the prospect of retaking this exam in September! I decide to devote myself to knitting. The jumper I sold to Marilène has a lot of success. I make more and I mix wool with ribbons and lace. They are so successful that Mum has to help me.

"I'll help you only if you agree to retake your exam in September."

"If I have that painting maniac again, I'll throw the book in his face and go to Australia."

"It would be more intelligent to study all the covers of your books."

I am more like Dad, servility is not my weapon. She shouts from the kitchen: "Don't ruin four years of study for a question of pride. If he wants to know who painted the covers, get informed beforehand, that's all."

"It's not like that you'll change people's way of thinking!"

"It's not your job. Let those who have nothing to lose, do it!"

"Those people have finished their study, they don't give a toss anymore!"

"In life, one has to choose: either you get yourself qualifications and a decent job or you try to change the world."

Before making this dramatic choice, I go out for a breather and to visit Marilène.

Her mother opens the door of a superb apartment filled with trinkets and furniture. The telephone, on a wrought iron console, has been covered with pink velvet. She is dressed up and made up as for a grand dinner and her jewellery jingled when she moves. She doesn't so much look at me as scan me, immediately detecting a speck on my Swedish clogs.

Marilène takes me into her room where I am struck by the number of pictures on the walls. They have no frames and the paintings remind me of Dali, Magritte and Chirico, but nothing by Munch.

"Wow! Where did you find all these paintings?"

She laughs.

"I painted them."

"I can't believe you!"

She shows me her signature: M. Innocenti. I am speechless with admiration.

"Do you sell them?"

"Not often, they are not jumpers!"

"A hundred times better!"

Her paintings are classical scenes with surrealistic details. For example, a forest under water with fish swimming between oak trees and a sea anemone waving next to mushrooms.

"Do you have exhibitions?"

"I don't have enough paintings."

"What are you waiting for?"

"It's difficult. My mother doesn't want me to stain the furniture or the carpet."

"Cover the furniture or paint in the garage!"

"That's not possible. She doesn't want to move a single trinket and my father needs the garage for his car."

"With a talent like yours, how can your Mum…"

She puts a finger on her mouth and glances nervously towards the door.

"Let's have a coffee at the Provence."

While we are walking I say to her that if I had her talent, my Mum would move heaven and earth to find a gallery.

"Yeah, but how would you know it's worth it? My parents think it's just a hobby."

"Try to find professional people to give you their opinion. I'm sure it's worth it."

"Thanks. I don't mind not being famous but I would like to be able to paint."

"Find a job and move out."

"I can't, my mother would have a nervous breakdown. When the uni sent me to England, she got so depressed that I had to come back for every holiday and phone every week."

"What if you get married?"

"I will have to live in the neighbourhood."

I came to relax but now I am more frustrated than ever.

The cafés are crowded. People with sunglasses and flip-flops are coming back from the beach and it is the time when the tourists go for a drink. I'd rather talk clothing and fashion. Just before we sit down, someone waves to us. It's Joseph sitting at a table with a Cappuccino and a packet of Gauloises. We sit with him and I already feel more relaxed. We order two iced coffees.

"Hello buttercups! My congrats Innocenti, you're a graduate now! Not like us," he says with a knowing glance in my direction.

"Please, Joseph, don't twist the knife in the wound!"

"Poor lass! Everybody is talking about this asshole!"

"Edward Munch?"

"No! Your bloody examiner!"

"Ha! Aren't you working today?"

"Yeah but I finished at 2 today."

"So what are you going to do next year?"

"I'll go back to Algeria in a month."

"What? Are you crazy? What about your Degree?"

"Don't make me laugh! I have half a degree, that's enough over there. I worked two years in a hotel in London. I can speak French, English, Arabic and a bit of Spanish. I feel out of place here. I like the Arabs and they like me."

"But they got rid of you."

"Force of circumstance. In war and revolutions, there's no time for details. I've got pals there, I kept in contact, I know where to go. I know enough to help them out. At least they respect me, here they treat me like shit."

"Joseph! What are you talking about? Without you, we would have had a disastrous year. We all used your ideas, the ones in our debates. The other groups were envious."

"Yeah… you're sweet but did you notice Charente's contempt, that man!..."

"He should be the last one to despise you, you did his work!" exclaims Marilène.

"Most of the people are like that on the French Riviera. Look at the blokes from the Faculty of Law, they parade around the place in their little cars, with their little cliques, their parties, their cafés, their posh birds…"

"What about Louvier in Psychology isn't he a mate of yours?"

"You must be joking! Louvier stuck to me, hoping I would join the Communist Party! Because I wear jeans and grubby clothes to lectures he thought I could be easily one of them. I didn't realise what he was up to immediately, the swine! He played the scenario of friendship, you know what I mean?"

"You know we all like you," I say to cheer him up.

"Yeah, I know, I haven't too many problems with girls, although… with my movie star physique and my great wealth, not many of them want to marry me!"

There is a slight embarrassment there. We have always looked at him as a brother, but it never occurred to us that he might also be a husband or a lover. He adds: "It'll be easier to marry an Arab girl but educated and docile."

"Educated an docile hardly ever go together."

"With Arab women, they can do."

"But Joseph, once a woman is educated, obedience is questionable!"

"Ha! Ha! Come back and see me in ten years and we'll talk about it again! I'll act as an enlightened authority."

"What about the other Arabs?"

"They will change with Socialism."

"May Allah hear you!"

"Oh no, better not," guffawed Joseph.

We say goodbye with two huge pecks, feeling that I will never see him again.

41 May 68

We are always happy to see the month of May coming. Between the strikes and religious holidays, there are few working days left. It is as if The Church and the Unions were in competition.

In the Lycée Estienne d'Orves where I am working now as a tutor[37], I get on well with my colleagues. We have good fun between twelve and two, at the canteen. The teachers eat together as the elite of the school and the headmistress eats alone like the Sun King.

The chef of the refectory is a pal and when he makes his gorgeous sauerkraut, he lets us know so we can bring beer. His assistant is a Pied-Noir, as handsome as a Greek god but his feet smell miles away. Once a term he makes such a tasty couscous that the pupils never leave a scrap. The First Year say he must have washed his feet in the stock.

I am fond of the little First Years. They are spontaneous, cheerful, never nasty but often a pain in the neck. In my class, among the eleven year old kids, there are thirteen and fourteen year old boys who pretend to chat up the tutors to show the young girls of the class that they are not kids any more. I allow them some verbal familiarities because I know how hard and humiliating it can be to be two years behind and find yourself with younger kids. Nothing changes; they are repeating their

---

[37] A tutor is a teacher's assistant for admin and discipline

year for trivial reasons. Cadabra, a fourteen year old, the dunce of the class, is the tutors' pet.

I find it incredible that such a bright and mature kid can be a dunce. At break time he has a chat with the tutors on duty. During the detention hours, he is learning to play poker with the male tutors. Roger, one of them, works with me on the same floor and he's preparing for a Degree in Law. On Sundays, he is a guide at the Rothschild Museum in Saint Jean-Cap-Ferrat and he's becoming an expert in antiques. I go to see him once, while he's doing his guided tour and I am becoming enthusiastic about all the different styles of furniture.

I manage to convince my parents to buy a Louis XVI style dining-room to replace the horrible one from the 40's and the Formica from the 50's. But Dad doesn't want to part with the Formica bar and Mum's fond of the plaster trinkets I won in the church fairs. Roger says it's the same with his parents. They keep a fake marble table with imitation Knoll chairs and he's sure, that during the night, the Henri II dresser must be crying to be mixed with them!

As we are leaving winter behind us, everybody seems on edge. Roger says that his friend from the Faculty of Letters is spending his time in meetings in the Students' Union.

In the newspaper, they talk about the Faculty of Nanterre, near Paris, and also about Poland where the workers are on strike to support the students. This news excites two communist female tutors. They think I sympathise with them because I bought a record by Jean Ferrat, a Communist poet and singer. They are talking about an account in a paper of the handsome Cohn-Bendit, one of the anarchist leaders of the 1968 Movement, calling out to a Minister opening the swimming pool of the university. He tells him that his book on youth is worthless and that he should allow male students go into the female students' hall of residence. The Minister replies that if he has sexual problems, he should jump into the swimming pool. The two Communist tutors have no sense of humour. They even bought Mao Tse Tung badges. To tease them even more, Roger tells the girls that in Czechoslovakia, the young men are wearing a medal with an effigy of the Emperor François-Joseph. We also lose our sense of humour when we have to do their work because they are going more and more often to union meetings as if they were preparing a 'coup d'état'.

The day of the murder of Martin Luther King, in May 68, the two girls are so affected that they take sick leave. As for us we have to mourn him by working twice as hard.

On the French Riviera, May 68 starts with great enthusiasm but finishes on the beach with banners transformed into beach towels. I thought the world was going to be changed but I am disappointed to admit that sea, sex and sun take over. A student teacher demands that married couples ought to be appointed to the same region at least. Me too, I find it cruel and absurd to appoint the husband to Brittany and the wife to Corsica. It would be a big change for teachers but instead we are given a room to smoke in the university… All day long the Communist students are pestering us with The Cultural Revolution in China and the two tutors make me buy a copy of Mao's Little Red Book. I browse through it and I discover recommendations that we have been applying in France since the 1789 Revolution.

To please one of my colleagues, I go to the cinema with her to see a Russian cartoon. For half an hour we watch a tank drawn by a kid squashing poppies. It is pure propaganda and I am dying to tell her that the American propaganda with Tom and Jerry is a lot more enjoyable. The Communists are exasperated by the success of Coca-Cola and Mickey Mouse: Coca is a poison and Mickey is decadent. However I admire Angela Davis's fight to get black students into white universities.

A little event could make me believe in a new era. We are in class, waiting for the question papers of the last exam on American Literature. I know by heart Faulkner, O'Neill, Hemingway and Henry James. We have a question on Faulkner but not on the right book, one on Sinclair Lewis, studied the year before, and one on Norman Mailer which is not on the syllabus. I can just about write something on Lewis. Faulkner's The Sound and the Fury was on the syllabus but we get Light in August instead. I've read it too but haven't studied it. We look at each other. Resigned, I decide to try my luck with Light in August when a voice is raised. We all turn round. It's Philippe's voice, a tall, skinny and shy student with long blond hair in a ponytail. He forms a nice and funny couple with the smallest girl in the uni. He's standing up and calmly he repeats what he has just said because the invigilator has not understood yet: "Sir, we refuse to take this exam because the questions are not from our syllabus."

After a few seconds of amazement, everybody is speaking at the same time to support him. The teacher is embarrassed and during this agitated time, one has to be cautious.

"I.. I must speak to the Dean about it."

We wait for an hour for the Dean to come and when he arrives, he cowardly asks: "Do you want easier questions?"

He has to confront a strong wave of indignation.

"Sir, it's not a question of easy or difficult. All we ask is questions on the books of the syllabus. We have never done Norman Mailer, Sinclair Lewis was last year and the Faulkner's book is the wrong one."

The Dean is perplexed. We are too. We are not used having a visit from a man who lives in an ivory tower. Lots of us have never seen him before. He asks us to come back tomorrow and we will have new questions!

Once in the street, we all surround Philippe to thank him. He smiles shyly. We wonder what was eating him. He's the last person to rebel, he's not even a Communist but a hippy. The next day, we have three questions from the syllabus.

Unlike the others, I never use the word 'reactionary' because I don't understand it. I thought it mean to react, i.e. to rebel but it is always used as an insult next to the word 'bourgeois'. In fact, reactionary means to refuse progress or change.

The excitement spreads all over the country. Everywhere you can hear people talking about barricades and occupation of premises. Even young pupils seem concerned. We can see them in animated conversations, in groups. The two communist tutors are going from one group to the other. I send Cadabra to buy some croissants for some of us and I pay for a 'pain au chocolat' for him. He's coming back taking all his time and stopping at one group. If he doesn't hurry, I'll give him two hours' detention. Thought transfer must function, as he walks towards me.

"Well, Cadabra, you made your tutor wait!"

It was a good job the croissants were wrapped because his fingers with bitten nails were stained with the dirty oil from his moped.

"It's not my fault, Miss, it's Miss Pasaglia who's talking about Trotsky. Who's he?"

"A bloke from the Russian Revolution."

"She told me off because I went to get your croissants, she said it's exploitation."

"Did you tell her I paid you with a 'pain au chocolat'?'"

"Yeah, she said it's corruption."

"Do you agree?"

"Dunno Miss, I don't understand what she's on about."

Within a few days, the lycée goes on strike and the pupils wear armbands with "Head of Section," written on them. Among the teachers, there are two categories: those who duck out of it because they can't cope or don't agree and those who run the troubles and kindle them. Cadabra is delighted: he has the right to cause trouble, and to call some teachers by their first name but he quickly get tired of meetings and prefers to play on the pinball machines at the café with his pals from the third year. He tells me that they are a bit disappointed because all day long they are told about the Class Struggle and they are not allowed to fight with the other classes…

The rumour has it that the school will have a room to smoke like at the university. Cadabra asks Roger: "Sir, can we ask for a pinball machine too?"

"Listen," said Roger, "leave that to the First year! Rather ask for a brothel."

Laughing, he repeats Roger's reply to everybody. Consequently, Pasaglia and Auteuil, the two Red tutors, as they are called, give Roger a good telling-off. Auteuil is nicknamed 'Fauteuil' (armchair) because she tends to sleep around in order to recruit new 'members' for the Party. She says it isn't true, it's to show that she is free to do what she wants with her body. She's not that wrong, but it isn't quite the right approach.

The day when the lycée is occupied and paralysed, Roger takes me to Cannes to track the stars of the Films Festival. Unfortunately, the Festival is cancelled. Jean-Luc Godard and François Truffaut deliver improvised talks. How stupid! It would be much better if they had shown their films. It is the ideal time to communicate ideas through the cinema, but instead, they replace the greatness of their visionary messages by little excited and insipid speeches.

The walls of the amphitheatre are covered with political graffiti, Marcuse's quotations and pictures of the Black Panthers. Why is Angela David shown as an example to follow when there are plenty of black students in our university? Perhaps we are supposed to do a re-make of our Revolution for the Americans…or for the Chinese?

I give way to Mum and in September I re-take my oral exam after checking I know everything about the covers of the books. Monsieur Gasquet is the examiner. The English 'lectrice' (assistant) is sitting with him. I don't know him well and strangely enough, he doesn't have any special reputation. He has no little slips to draw, he just shows me a poem to prepare. He is not reading a newspaper, he listens to me and asks me questions to test my opinion instead of my knowledge. I am very much tempted to use the opinion of our lecturer, it would be wiser. But I am contaminated by the bug of the May Rebellion. I feel fed up with conventions. The poem is written by Robert and Elizabeth Browning and their writing bores me. What's more I am not keen on poetry. Too bad! Let's forget my Degree, I'll learn secretarial skills and go to Vietnam… I take a deep breath and tell him that I don't like these poets and the only thing I appreciate is a certain feminism. He smiles, a little surprised.

"Who do you prefer?"

"Coleridge because he went looking for inspiration in the very depths of himself at the risk of never re-emerging on the surface and thus writing Kubla Khan."

"Ah the use of illegal substances?"

"No, no, I'm not for the use of drugs, unless you're already a genius!"

He laughs.

"I also like Keats because of the beautiful sound of his poems."

Why isn't he asking questions on the meaning of each word as usual?

"And Shelley, do you like him?"

Crumbs, I've read a couple of his poems in the second year, but I don't remember anything.

"Shelley is OK," I say, "but I love 'Frankenstein', his wife's book."

He bursts out laughing, then we go deeper into the matter.

In the afternoon, I turn up at the Faculty for the results. The corridor is crowded, then I see a list with just a few names and I am transfixed to see mine. Gosh, that wasn't an oral exam, it was a conversation! Never mind, it is over. No more exams ever!

A girl approaches me.

"Are you Lefranc?" she asks.

"Yes…"

"You're obviously a favourite of Gasquet's."

"What? I never had him as a teacher."

"The lectrice who was sitting with him didn't want you to pass because your English accent wasn't good enough."

"The bitch!"

"Wait! He was the one who insisted on passing you, saying you were the only one who has a personal opinion and then he said for once a student makes him laugh!"

"How do you know all that?"

"I was sitting at the back of the room, waiting for my turn. As a result I took the risk of giving him my personal opinion too! And I passed!"

"Did you get the Brownings?"

"No, Wordsworth."

So be it. I am a graduate and therefore I am not going to Vietnam. Mum wants me to prepare for the competitive exam for teachers. No way. You have to work like mad to get one out of the five posts for three thousand candidates. And if you are selected you are sent to the middle of nowhere, probably in the North, forever. What am I going to do with my life? I can see either an abyss or a tunnel.

42 The War

I am going out a lot with Marilène because Roseline is working full time. Her parents bought her a chemist's shop in town. Her area is full of doctors and she never thought they could be prescribing so much medicine.

"Don't go to doctor Gonthier. He's liable to put you on six months on Valium for a stiff neck"

"I don't go to the doctor for a stiff neck"

"Old people go for less than that. And I can't tell you how many fake sick-leaves working people get!"

"Don't you tell them if they're taking too many drugs?"

"No chance! It's not my business. I'm not going to argue about the prescriptions, it's not in my interest and in any case, I'm here to sell."

"Hey, that's a lovely poster on your door"

"It's from Francis, a friend from Marseilles, who has an exhibition in Saint Paul de Vence."

"That's interesting! I've got a friend, Marilène, who's got a real talent for painting. She needs to meet an art connoisseur who would guide her."

"I'll give you his phone number, tell him you call on my behalf."

*

I have difficulty in understanding the news. The name of Ho Chi Minh keeps coming back with "…north of the 17th parallel,…south of 17th parallel…" What do the Vietnamese want? Independence? They must have it already since, according to my book of History, the French left after the Geneva Agreement. Do they want a Communist regime? I thought they have it since I heard Dad saying that the leaders of the country had studied Communism at the Sorbonne. Then I look at a map of Vietnam at the library and see that the country is divided in two: the north is Communist and the south is not. My uncle and Dad sometimes speak of this war and they are repeating the same all the time. I listen to them talking when in Chatel-Guyon where my uncle is having treatment for his dysentery caused by amoeba from Southeast Asia.

"They (the Americans) don't know where they are putting their feet! Even the Foreign Legion failed!" Dad says.

I still haven't heard from Isabelle. I write to her several times. I'm telling her about de Gaulle's latest gaffe in Quebec and the new pop singers called Jacques Dutronc and Claude François. At last these singers are not singing melancholic songs!

While I am still working as a tutor in a lycée, I am selling more and more jumpers. That money helps me to take my driving test five times. The inspector must have purposely sent me blind cyclists and unexpected walls!

Marilène and I decide to rent a little shop together, in the Old City. I will sell my jumpers and she will sell her paintings. We decorate the shop ourselves. The months drift by like clouds pushed by the Mistral. Nobody misses Isabelle except me. She has no family and the Social Service says she isn't their problem anymore. I ask the secretary: "If she gets killed, how do we find it out?"

She shrugs her shoulders and rolls her eyes.

*

The hippies are demonstrating in Washington because of a blunder by the American Army. They are talking about the massacre of a village in Vietnam. One morning, the postman brings a flat parcel from the US. I recognise Isabelle's handwriting. Phew, she's alive and back in the States. I don't have the time to open it so I take it with me to the shop. We've just found a witty name for it: 'Marilaine[38]'. It isn't easy to walk briskly in a crowd of tourists who are crazy about the Old City. They are in raptures over the narrow cobbled streets where odours are concentrating. In some streets the scent of hot bread just manages to dominate the smell of fish. I can hear in the distance the shout of the fishmongers: "…bella poutina[39], bella, bella." The Market Flowers is too far for their perfumes to reach us. I regret not having bought mimosa to repel the effluvia of the fresh sardines. Marilène is already there when I arrive.

"You're just in time! I was dying for a coffee! Since you're here I'll go and get it, do you want one?"

"Yes, of course, no sugar. Look, I've received a parcel from Isabelle!"

"At last! You must be relieved…. Oh, it's a magazine! I'll get the coffee, be back in a minute. Shall we go and eat ravioli at the restaurant La Trappa at noon?"

"OK."

The Time Magazine is heavy and thick. I find war photos marked with a cross and realize they are signed I. Tchang. There are terrifying pictures of the civilian

---

38 'laine' means wool, thus making a play on the words.

39 Poutina are baby sardines. Only fishermen from Nice are allowed to fish them because of a long standing Italian law.

population running under bombings. Then another one of General Westmorland operating 40km from Saigon and one of the Mekong Delta under fire. I couldn't take my eyes off her signature.

To take such photos, she had to be in the heart of the action. Isabelle! So fragile that a Madame Léger made her cry! And me, I'm in a place where everything is calm, luxurious, serene and, I daresay, boring. Do we get bored when we haven't got troubles? If only I could join her! I have to stop fantasizing about John as Roseline does about LeClézio. They are the stars of another galaxy and their light is not for us. It's easy to advise others but how do you kill a thing as elusive and as persistent as hope?

Marilène arrives with the coffees, I show her the photos. She's impressed and carries on leafing through the magazine...

"Look at that," she says, "it reminds me of the American cemetery in Normandy."

Across a double page, six columns of passport photos are looking at us, with name, age, rank and date of death. We look at them together. They are so young, between nineteen and twenty-five. Marilène points at those she finds attractive; we don't have quite the same taste.

"What a waste!" she exclaims, turning the pages where the rows of photos continue.

We stop at the same time on one page where a photo is circled with pencil. In half a second I wonder 'which one?'

"Do you know him?"

That's it. I hardly recognize him. I see his name, my gaze is riveted to the photo and the name: John Harry Cassidy. I'm getting short of breath.

"Gosh, you really know him!... It's him?... Isn't it?"

His Army hair cut has hardened him a little, his lovely forelock has been cut off. He's staring intensely at the camera… A woman comes into the shop, and Marilène goes to her. I can hear them chatting in the distance. The woman can't make up her mind. She wants the blue jumper with the lace then finds it too big, the red one is too short, the black one, not good enough. When she leaves, I lash out at her. Is that all she's thinking about when a thousand young men are being killed every day! I cry with rage and grief. I suddenly remember the girl from the uni restaurant who called us names because we were not interested in the war.

Mum is touched by John's death. She tells me about a fling she had with a nice boy who was killed in World War II. Well, he was defending his country but overthere, they are fifteen thousand kilometres away! It doesn't make sense. He didn't have to go. She says that he was helping the Vietnamese of the South to push out the Communists of the North. If the Communist regime is so bad, all we need is to do is waiting until it collapses of its own accord! Why bleed a whole generation to death? And we are so short of men on the Riviera!

A letter from Isabelle arrives after the magazine to say she had to go back to the States because of food poisoning. William is staying over there to do shuttle trips between Da-Nang and Saigon where he's serving. She is on sleeping tablets to stop thinking about it all night long. She also says that an anti-war movement is starting to spread across the States and Jane Fonda is one of their speakers. Pam wrote to William to tell him that John's parents received their son's belongings and they found twigs of lavender.

43 Sexual harassment

I drown my sorrow and my despair by reading the Three Musketeers. There are four volumes of five hundred pages. When I read, it's like going down a staircase taking me to a world where I'm floating among the characters. With a book, I am able to isolate myself in the middle of a noisy crowd. Thus, on a Sunday, on the beach, I don't immediately notice that a man is speaking to Marilene. He is on the other side of the fence, on the private part of the beach. Marilene's towel dropped on his side. He is quite mature, at least 35 to 40 year old, distinguished type, with his black shiny hair parted on the side like Disney's Prince in Cinderella. She finds him 'awesome'. I think that a man, who pays to put his bottom on a soft mattress instead of pebbles, must be suspicious or a sissy. She says that he owns a hairdressing salon in Cannes.

One afternoon, he comes to our shop. Marilene, who wasn't expecting him, jumps off her stool.

"I wanted to make it a surprise," he says in a suave voice.

He has put on a ton of aftershave.

"Aren't you working today?"

"When you're the boss, you work when you want to! Won't you introduce me to your friend?"

"Yes, of course! Sophie…François".

His handshake is vigorous but it's a typical false cliché to say it reveals the person. He removes his sunglasses, glances critically around him and catches sight of Marilene's paintings hanging on the walls.

"Where did you find those awful things?"

Having detested the fellow at first sight I saw him, I am delighted to hear him say this. Marilene is horribly embarrassed but I let her deal with it in her way.

"We… we were given them," she stammers.

He laughs.

"If you want, I can send round my decorator, he could make this into a nice quirky place."

I am getting so hot under the collar that I have to get nearer the fan.

"No, no," says Marilene, "We're only a cottage industry, we don't want anything special, do we Sophie?"

"Yeah, that's right, I suppose it's good enough for the Old City."

He gives us a peck and leaves after fixing a date with Marilene, next Sunday on the beach, in Cannes. After a brief silence, I hear her saying with a hollow voice: "I knew my painting was crap."

"Really? And yet you sold some to people who found it imaginative."

"Yes, but he's a man of experience. He knows about Art."

"Let me remind you that van Gogh never sold a painting. So according to monsieur François, you could be a genius."

"You don't like him, do you?"

"Who? Van Gogh?"

"François!"

"No, I don't."

"Why?"

"His arrogance and his after-shave."

"We're not used to men who are so self-confident, who have maturity and experience… All we know are students."

Six o'clock. We close the shop down and we go to Chez Louis to eat a socca. Roseline joins us. The heat releases its grip, the cicadas go silent, and the terraces of the cafés are getting crowded. Roseline who hasn't seen François yet, is on Marilene's side.

"In the end, if you think about it, we don't know many interesting men," Roseline says, "my father is honest and hardworking but I wonder what my Mum found exciting about him!"

"My father's not exciting either," replies Marilene, "but he's so nice that I understand why she married him. She does what she wants with him. I have to tell him not to let her push him around!"

"At home," I say, "my father is the boss and my mother never says a word when he shouts, for fear that the neighbours would hear."

"Why does he shout?"

"For trivial reasons. We're not allowed to switch the TV on without his permission and once he went mad because we were watching a programme without asking him. At the end of the day the only interesting men I know are James in Oxford, Joseph (we laughed) and… John.

Roseline says gloomily that she knows one but she'd rather not recall the experience.

"I told you Sophie," "we don't live enough!"

We hear the jukebox in the café playing 'L'Important c'est la Rose'. That night I understand that song better. I drink my Orangina to release a lump in my throat. The jungle, the napalm and Isabelle are 6000 km east of Chez Louis. "L'important c'est la lavande."

On the following Sunday afternoon, we are all on the beach in Cannes to the annoyance of Marilene who would have preferred to be alone. François has asked us over and we are so pleased to enjoy the sand instead of the pebbles. He arrives in the company of a tall, lean gentleman of about sixty, with white shoulder-length hair gathered in a ponytail and a short beard. The modern prophet's style. He introduces Edouard de Moret to us. Immediately, I find their complicity and their way of scrutinising people rather unpleasant. It looks as if they are pinpointing every last detail in their appearance. And yet, I don't hear them making any critical comment as I would expect, but, from time to time, their eyes meet with an understanding smile. I drag Roseline into the sea. She dislikes swimming because of her hair but she manages not to wet a single strand!

"What do you think of them?"

"Who's the Father Christmas with him?"

We giggle hysterically as in the old days. We return to the beach because the water has started to wet the nape of her neck! Marilene, embarrassed and annoyed, asks us:

"What are you laughing about?"

"Because I said to Roseline that her bathing cap looks like a cauliflower and she should beware of the hungry seagulls."

François shows no affection for Marilene as lovers would do. He's staring shamelessly at the pretty girls on the beach while Edouard de Moret gives him a lecture on the Jean-Luc Godard's films. Dragged along by Godard's followers, I have probably seen all his films but I dropped out after 'Weekend'. I am perfectly conscious that the cinema will never be the same after Godard but I never enjoy his films. I suggest to Roseline that we should go to the big cinema in the new luxurious commercial centre, Cap 3000 in Saint Laurent du Var, to see 'The Graduate'. We leave the beach with a mutual relief and we go to see the most beautiful film of the year with a great score: The Sound of Silence by Simon and Garfunkel.

"Hello darkness my old friend
I come to talk to you again…"

The tune is forever ingrained in our heads.

We have an expresso on the terrace of a café overlooking the river Var. A stupid river that must make life hell for the fish. One minute it overflows and destroys everything in its way, the next, it's a trickle among white and polished stones, not even able to reach the sea. My imagination takes me away again and I see myself visiting all those wonderful little villages the Var crosses, we are lying in the grass of Estenc where it originates…

In our region, after 15th August, the heat becomes bearable. As I am refreshing my dry mouth with a juicy nectarine, Marilene dashes into the shop.

"I've got fantastic news!"

I prepare myself by wiping the juice that is running everywhere.

"Have you heard of the famous pianist Carlo Filippi?"

"Yep, you've got tickets for his concert?"

"Even better! He's a friend of François and we are going to have supper with him in Monte-Carlo, at the Reserve!"

"Ah. Pity. I would have preferred a concert."

"Is that all you can find to say? Oh dear, I've got nothing to wear! What about you?"

"Me?"

"Yes, I told you, you're invited as well! See, François has connections!"

The restaurant La Reserve is very smart and very expensive and Mum very worried. She finds this invitation a bit fishy. Marilene's mother is delighted. Her only fear is that I might cast a shadow over her daughter. Marilene is very pretty. Can't she see that? Far from casting a shadow, my presence will enhance her daughter's beauty!

The fashionable colour, this year, is silver, so Mum has made me a lovely silver acetate mini dress, sleeveless with a square neckline. As I am suntanned, I look like a chocolate bar in its silver wrapping. I try to reassure her.

"Mum! Please, stop! He will have to behave like a gentleman, he has to mind his reputation!"

"And you, mind yours!"

François takes us in his convertible Caravelle. We drive on the Corniche from where we can see the Bay of Villefranche. I feel a pang when I can no longer see the USS Springfield, a destroyer of the Sixth Fleet. No more peanut butter sandwiches. All the American bases have been closed down to many women's great despair.

I begin to worry about how I should eat in this place. Above all, I must not choose complicated food like melon or peaches. To have graduated in English Literature doesn't teach you the good manners of the upper class. We are shown to a table and Carlo Filippi arrives, pale and romantic with sunglasses. He walks a little as if the piano stool was stuck to his bottom. We are introduced. He touches my hand as if I had leprosy. I whisper to Marilene

"Did you notice, he's dressed in black and white like the piano keyboard."

She chuckles and François turns to her and frowns.

"She hasn't had a drink yet and she's already laughing!"

"It's Sophie..."

The hors d'oeuvre arrives: half a melon filled with port and a spoon. I have never eaten melon that way. At home, Mum cuts the melon in slices and we have it for dessert. I cautiously wait for someone to start. I could wait a long time since the men are waiting for the ladies to start. Eventually I see Marilene taking her spoon and spooning the melon delicately. Phew! Later, full of admiration, I ask Marilene how did she know how to do it.

"I looked at the next table. And you, how did you know so much about music?"

"I read a few digests on music."

Thank God, the dessert isn't a problem because I play safe by choosing the sorbet. The atmosphere is more relaxed thanks to the wine but I have great difficulty in refusing it. I hate wine but the men insist on filling my glass. While Carlo and François are speaking of Jacques Fath's parties in Cannes, I empty my glass in the mini palm tree pot next to me but Marilene drinks it all and starts to act a little tipsy.

"Did you really think about what you said yesterday?"

"Hush! Don't speak so loudly! Yes, I've got my cheque book."

We get up and apologize to go to the Ladies.

"Honestly, you're mad!" says Marilene, "He seems nice and correct. It's a dinner with honourable intentions and you're taking the risk of provoking a scandal!"

"You told me that Carlo asked François to find him a bird for the evening."

"Yes but François knows very well that you don't sleep with just anybody."

"Precisely, he's not just anybody! He must be thinking that he'll do me a favour!"

"No, no, he invited you because I said you were very funny."

"I don't mind playing the clown but not the whore!"

"Sophie! How can you speak like that! Don't you think that if he just wanted to sleep with a girl, he would have chosen a really beautiful girl like some model?"

"You've got a point. Try to find out how they intend to finish the evening."

We go back to the table and I can see my glass full again. I wonder what effect alcohol can have on plants. I pretend to be a little tipsy and I hear François saying: "Let's have the last drink at Carlo's hotel."

"Oh no," I say, "I had too much to drink and I'm dying to go to sleep."

"Out of question to go home so early, Champagne is waiting for us!"

Marilene who didn't give anything to the mini palm tree exclaims: "I forgot my nightie!"

The two men burst out laughing.

I slip off to the toilet but in fact it is to speak to the manager. I tell him that I want to pay my bill beforehand. He looks at me, puzzled. I begin to lose confidence but the idea of Carlo Filippini slipping his hand under my dress, gives me the courage I need. I repeat my demand.

"But really, mademoiselle, it's unthinkable! You're Monsieur Filippini's guest and he's our customer, we are the 'Reserve' and we have our reputation to think of… we can't allow it."

"It's not illegal."

"Monsieur Filippi will object strongly, he may provoke a scandal. You should not have accepted the invitation to begin with."

"There you have a point but one can make a mistake."

"I am sorry but I can't take your cheque."

"I can be sick to order."

"Don't be so childish!"

"I have to. If I pay my part, he won't even notice it. He's not going to scan the bill, whereas if I'm sick, it will have a sorry effect."

He hesitates,

"Alright, I hope he won't notice it. I don't understand you. Usually ladies are proud to be Monsieur Filippi's guest, they even stay for breakfast."

He writes my bill and I pay him with a cheque that he holds with contempt. I feel lighter despite the hole in my account. I come back to the table and I lighten the atmosphere with a few jokes. They find me irresistible when I imitate Joseph's French Algerian accent. Then Carlo indulges us by telling a few dirty jokes. I find it unexpected and disappointing coming from an artist playing Chopin with such romantic panache.

"The night is young," as the English say. François lights a cigar, Marilene smokes to please François, while Carlo and I are finishing our coffee. As Carlo keeps his eyes on me, the dwarf palm has to do without Cognac. The waiter arrives with the bill. It is necessary to attract Carlo's attention away. I ask him to show me how to smoke. I swallow a massive dose of smoke and I launch into a fit of coughing that would make someone with the whooping cough jealous. Carlo signs his cheque without thinking and pours me a glass of water.

"I think you'd better give up smoking, at least finish your Cognac."

"No, no, my head is spinning fast enough already!"

"She's charming!"

"I told you it would make a change!" says François with a wink.

What does that mean? We all get into François's car and he drives silently between the cypress rows leading to the majestic Hotel du Cap. I feel terrible when I see Marilene taking her vanity case out. If they all stay, I have no means of going back home. The manager of the restaurant is right, I should have thought of it before. François informs me that we are going to have a last glass of Champagne in the suite, it's a whole apartment with a Louis XV entrance. From an open double door, I catch sight of a huge four-posted bed with white net-curtains and red brocade hangings. Funny, they have done it out in the colours of the A.S. Monaco[40]. In a corner, there is a baby grand piano. I touch a key.

"Can you play?" Carlo asks.

"Very little…"

"Play something for me… I insist!"

Under the effect of the Cognac, I sit on the stool and I play the beginning of Beethoven's 'Fur Elise.' He looks very impressed.

"It's the first time I've heard Fur Elise played like a military march."

---

40 Monaco Football Association.

"Well, music is not the way I express myself best."

He put one arm round my waist then on my bottom.

"And what is your best way of expressing yourself?"

"Certainly not with my bottom!" I say, removing his hand.

"Don't tell me, it's knitting!"

"Yes, it is and for Marilene, it's painting!"

"Oh, Marilene has better ways! I heard painting is not her best."

I turn round and I realize that there's nobody on the sofa. I ask stupidly where they've gone.

"I expect they've gone to express themselves," says Carlo with a sarcastic smile

He goes to put a record on. I no longer know what to do. Oh no, no, not this beautiful record by the Moody Blues:

> Nights in white satin
> Never reaching the end,
> Letters I've written
> Never meaning to send…

I have to go, quick, before the song reaches the chorus: "…'cause I love you, Yes, I love…" While we are dancing, he drags me toward the bed draped in the Monaco Football colours. I push him away.

"I can understand you want to play hard to get but don't exaggerate, it's one in the morning!"

"Oh my God! My Mum must be worried stiff, I never intended to finish the evening like this!"

"So why did you accept my invitation?"

"To please Marilene."

"And above all, to tell your girl-friends you were given a posh dinner by Carlo Filippi."

"Oh no, you gave me nothing, I paid my part."

"Excuse me?"

I explain. He tightens his jaws, takes a cigarette and go to the window. There is a superb moonlight on the sea. I have everything except the right man.

"Aren't we a bit frigid by any chance?"

Here we are. I thought only teenagers would make this type of remark.

"What do you want to do now?"

"Go back home."

"You should have planned it as you did for the meal!"

"That's true, I didn't think of it. Could you call a taxi for me please?

"Alright, here, the money for the taxi."

He puts the money on a pedestal table and calls the reception to get a taxi. While we are waiting for the taxi he asks me questions about my life as if suddenly I interested him in a different way from the one-night stand. I am touched and I feel some kind of remorse. The taxi arrives and we part courteously. I leave the money for the taxi behind. As I am passing the reception, the butler is chatting with the night porter, I smile to them. Just before I reach the revolving door, I hear Carlo's voice calling me, he rushes toward me and shouts: "Sophie! You're forgetting your money!"

The butler and the night porter's wry smile stings like salt on a wound and lingers for a long time.

44 Dreams and Marilene

Two years go by and I waste them waiting for... I don't know what! I receive a letter from James. He has graduated from Oxford and is working in the City in London. He is writing about what nearly got the better of British self-control: decimal money! He is also enquiring about Isabelle. Unfortunately, I haven't heard any more from Isabelle. On the radio, the news never stops talking about bombing raids. Five hundred thousand tons of bombs have been dropped in the South Vietnam; more than in the Pacific War. Despite this, I would go there if it wasn't for Mum. Isabelle has risked her life to inform the world and has made her dreams come true. As for me, I create jumpers, go to nightclubs and get bored. Marilene is not in a better position. She could be a female Dali or Magritte. She chose François. What's the point of having such a talent and a Degree? And Roseline, the pharmacy shop. Both of them have given up on their dreams. At least I have done one useful thing in my life: I have helped Isabelle to make her dream come true, even if she gets killed.

I do try to do the same with Marilene but she remains blind and deaf to anything which is not François and her Mum approves of him. When she introduces him, her mother is enraptured by the flowers, his kiss on her hand, his impeccable clothes and the hairdressing salon with four employees, in the centre of Cannes. She even advises her daughter to keep me at bay because "one never knows with one's best friend..." She thinks that my hostility toward François is a strategy to get them separated and then I'll try to have him! She knows what she's talking about for she had to fight hard to marry Marilene's father. He was not a Don Juan but he was one of the very rare decent men left after the war. An invisible war followed the World War: women fighting to find a man of the right age when most of them were dead or handicapped. In those days, you could not find this 'product' even on the black market. It reinforced the male chauvinist attitude.

It's six, we close the shop. Marilene is feverish and impatient.

"I'll let you lock up, I'm going to be late, I've got to meet François in ten minutes, in the Place Massena."

"Why doesn't he come to pick you up here?"

"It's too difficult to park in the Old City."

"Really? I didn't know that it was easy on the Place Massena! Marilene, are you following your Mum's advice?"

"What advice? What are you talking about?"

"You're afraid I'll take François away from you!"

"No! I'm not. I'm afraid you'll make unpleasant remarks and… and I don't wish to expose him to temptation… He said you had nice legs."

"So? He can see nice legs all day long in his hairdressing salon!"

I sroke a chord. She lowers her head.

"I'll give you a lift and drop you just before the Place. Is that OK?"

We remain silent during the trip. I am thinking "Nice legs, me? I must check in the mirror tonight!"

Marilene doesn't come back to the shop for a few days. Her mother rings to say she isn't feeling well. A week later, when she comes back, she looks terrible. She is pale under a heavy makeup.

"Listen Sophie, I've got things to tell you but swear to me not to get cross…"

I do and I think, that's it, she's pregnant!

"I've caught an infection and the antibiotic makes me feel very tired."

"Don't worry, take all the rest you need! Is it serious?"

"No… what is serious is that I had a row with François and he doesn't want to see me while I'm sick."

"It's nice of him, he wants you to rest."

"You know that's not it."

"What kind of infection have you got?"

She looks down at the floor.

"No!"

"Yes! François says that it's me who infected him whereas it is the opposite. He has the clap so I went to the doctor then, Roseline's pharmacy to buy the antibiotics, and she said that if I didn't sleep with anybody else, it has to be him who contaminated me."

"Did you tell him?"

"That's why we had a row."

Her face contracts, her lips are tight and she can't stop her tears. I notice how damaged her nice blond hair is. It used to be short and shiny. Now it's like long dry strings, reddened by all sorts of coloration. He must use her as a guinea pig. After making her ugly, he has infected her. I watch her crying, sitting on her stool. I take care to avoid the I-told-you-so and ask her if François gave her an explanation. She clings to her Hermes handbag and sniffs.

"He says that all the chicks have a nest full of bugs, that we are all filthy with…with.," (huge sobs).

"With what?"

"Our holes full of litter…"

"I don't believe it! He didn't say that did
he? …Marilene, you don't believe him, do you? Let me
tell him what I think… at least when you're not together
anymore!"

"I'll never leave him!"

One evening she rings me at home to say that she
isn't coming back to the shop. François has demanded it
because now they are engaged. He says I have a negative
influence on her. He speaks like the nuns and like Dumalle.
Marilene proudly tells me that she goes to Church with her
mother-in-law to be. I suggest coming back to the shop
from time to time, just to paint if she wants to. Roger has
a friend who is an art critic and he says that her painting
needs to mature and he has offered to help her with a short
exhibition in St Paul de Vence. She replies that she doesn't
feel like it anymore.

"Marilene, I can't believe you! You said it was your
passion."

"It was."

"How can you…?"

"He loves me and I succeeded where all the other
girls failed. Have you seen the ruby in my engagement ring?
It comes from his grandmother. I know that he is a bit of
a womaniser, but what can I do? He has so many
opportunities but I know they don't count…can you
understand?"

"No, I can't but it doesn't matter, it's your life. I wish
I could buy your talent."

45 The Season of the Floury Peaches

R oger takes advantage of the political meetings and the chaos that replace the lessons by taking me to the Cannes Festival. We park on the Croisette and we watch starlets, photographers and passers-by for a while. I am hoping to recognize someone when suddenly my expectations are fulfilled. No, it is not a star, it is Edouard de Moret and François. I quickly slide down in my seat.

"What are you doing? Why are you hiding?"

"There, the two men, I know them, the younger one's engaged to my friend Marilene."

"Shit! I don't believe it!"

"Do you know them?"

"Yes, I do!"

Roger slides down as well.

"Are you sure they're engaged?"

"I saw her engagement ring. A superb ruby!"

"Is she rich?"

"Not that I know of. Her father works at the airport and her mum stays at home. Is he a dowry hunter?"

"No, it's not that…"

"He's already married?"

"No but he lives with Edouard de Moret."

"Noooo!"

"If you were living in Cannes, you would know about it."

"But you don't live in Cannes, how do you know?"

"I sometimes go to Jacques Fath's parties, … a bit special."

"So?"

"So they are a notorious couple of queers."

"But... Marilene...?"

"He can do both. I suppose Edouard took a fancy to him and they have been together for years now. François calls him his adopted father. I wonder how a distinguished chap like de Moret can stay with him. You ought to see what he gets up to at parties! One day François dunked his dick in a girl's gin and tonic! If he sleeps with your friend, it's typical of him but the fact that he wants to marry her is another kettle of fish!

"That man is appalling! What about that Edouard, doesn't he mind the other women?"

"No, he considers François to be a spoiled child. All these women are like toys."

"I can't wait to tell Marilene!"

"If you do, you will lose her."

"If I don't say anything, I shall be betraying her."

"Choose!"

"One day she'll be grateful to me!"

"She'll never forgive you."

"I wonder if I ought to tell her Mum... no, it's not a good idea."

"Would she be pregnant?" Roger asks.

"No, she would have told me... Maybe he loves her after all!"

"That's not possible, I know the man. There must be a special reason, I'll find out. Shall we go for a swim now?"

"I haven't got my swimming costume."

"Let's buy one at Prisunic."

"What about towels?"

"Let's buy a large one for two!"

"The water must still be cold and I ate not long ago!"

"You've got your period?"

"No, no, I didn't plan on…"

"Don't be so 'bourgeoise!' Come on, I'll help you to chose an 'itsi, bitsi, teenie, weenie, yellow, polka dots bikini'"

"I can't wear a bikini, I'm too skinny!"

For the first time in my life, I show myself in a bikini on a beach. And it is even more ridiculous than the one in the song: yellow with large orange flowers, but in the sale.

"People are looking at me, I'm as thin as a rake!"

"You've got Twiggy's body. Girls must envy you!"

It will take a long time for me to wear it again.

I tell Roseline about the Marilene-François affair. She rolls her eyes.

"If she's stupid enough to deny it all or to accept it all, that's too bad."

They get married at St Paul de Vence where she should have had her painting exhibition. I am not invited. Exit Marilene.

In the meanwhile, in Paris, they are still running riots with paving stones and barricades, de Gaulle disappears to Germany and a heat wave sends the South of France militants and rioters to bathe in the sea and suntan on the beach. Mum, trained by the German Occupation, stocks sugar, flour and oil in case of a siege. In fact, it's the ants that besiege us. As for Dad, he's livid that the strikes prevent the broadcast of the European Football Cup, Manchester v Lisbon.

No news from Vietnam. We've just heard that Robert Kennedy, who criticized Johnson's policy in Vietnam, has been murdered. To stop worrying about Isabelle, I go to the cinema with Roseline. For the first time we see a western where a child is murdered in cold blood. The mesmerizing music of the film enhances every scene. 'Once Upon The Time in the West' was a formidable film that bowls us over. On a big screen, we watch a wild and desolate landscape turning into towns, Shakespearian characters building them with guns, sweat and blood and the unforgettable sound of Enio Moricone's harmonica.

"I don't know any drug that has the same effect as that film!" says Roseline.

I agree even though I never took any drugs. Roseline buys the record of the film and I buy the Magnificent Seven's.

Maybe Isabelle is living the same experience as Claudia Cardinale in the film. She is among men fighting for a better civilization. Of course, the film critics, confined in their offices, laugh at these spaghetti westerns. The following week we go to see the Kubrick's "2001, A Space Odyssey". Again, we remain silent for a while, struck by the cosmic grandeur of the film, even if we don't understand everything. After those films, I find the New Wave slightly anaemic compared to the American cinema, but the New Wave is meant to change filming.

I often go out with Roger and Roseline. The three of us are suffering of the loneliness of the bachelor but I don't understand Roger's loneliness. If he really is gay, he tries hard to hide it. We always see him alone but he talks about girls as if he likes them very much. One evening, we are in a nightclub and Roger disappears while Roseline and I wriggle with frenzy, in the heat of the strobe light, hammered by the decibels. We are all shaking our bodies as if we wanted to get rid of leeches sticking on our skin.

When Ray Charles informs us that The Sun Died, - we knew that already-, we sit down and watch couples embracing. Roger is sitting at the bar, talking with some men. He could introduce us to them; they are rather good looking and one of them has the rough look of the rogue in Buñuel's film Belle de Jour. But Roger would not. At two in the morning we leave, with humming eardrums, dazed eyes and empty minds.

"Come on girls, let's sit on the beach, I've got news for you," Roger says.

Sitting on the pebbles, we cool our feet in the foam of the little waves. The Mediterranean Sea moves so little that the coming and going of the water sounds like someone breathing. The darkness broken by the lighthouse from Antibes brings us some soothing feelings.

"You could have introduced us to your friends," Roseline complains.

"Oh certainly not! They're not for you!"

"Too good for us?"

"No, no...Probably the opposite" says Roger with a smile.

"The one dressed all in black is bloody handsome," Roseline insists.

"Yeah, he's a splendid venomous mushroom! Seriously, girls, I've heard about your friend Marilene. She's expecting a baby…"

"No!"

"Wait! The hairdressing salon and François's flat are in his mother's name. If he doesn't get married and stays heirless, his mother will disinherit him by selling everything. So he has fulfilled her conditions but keeps his liaison with

Edouard de Moret and he's still after anything in a skirt or… in trousers."

It's the end of summer. The sea is very warm now and the last peaches of the season become flour tasting. I have to leave my job as a tutor at the lycée because I am running the shop. However, without Marilene, I lose my enthusiasm. I need a job with colleagues. Thanks to Roger, who has a friend, director of a language school, I get a post to teach French to foreign students. I love my new job. My classes are like the United Nations: Americans, Chinese, Swedish, English, etc…

I get friendly with an English student called Fiona. She is what the English call an eccentric and the French a nutcase. She is a punk before the fashion hits France, which means that the colour of her hair goes through all the colours of the rainbow. Her black and tartan skirts are very mini and she wears the heavy Dr Martens' boots. In Nice, she can't find any boys or girls to go out with her… except me. She is making a revolution that I would never dare to start. She is relaxed in all circumstances and she reminds me of Vivian sometimes because of her fierce independence. Sometimes, I have to take her defence when, in the street, some dickheads feeling superior and virile, would call her an ugly cow or a clown but she remains as cool as a cucumber and I am the one who's cross.

At night, in bed, I listen to the international programme of the BBC in order to be familiar with the language and the accent. The Viet Cong has just attacked Saigon and Hue by surprise and many helicopters were destroyed in Hue. My heart jumps! It is where William and probably Isabelle are staying. They call this attack the

Tet Offensive. They found an underground town and they are talking about ten thousand killed and twenty thousand wounded.

I feel uncomfortable and restless as if I was not in the right place. Sometimes I go and eat at the cafeteria of the airport, just to see the planes taking off or landing. I love the extra-terrestrial voice announcing the departures. Somehow, I feel that my life should be elsewhere, but where? I stop going to nightclubs where the decibels and the lights isolate me even more. Most of my colleagues, at the language school, are married. The others have a boy or a girlfriend. They invite me to their parties or to dinner but I don't stay very long because I feel like an outsider. Roseline has met a very nice man. He has an antique shop near the harbour and no family. He is kind, reasonably good looking, quite intelligent and he seems to be keen on Roseline.

"How did you meet him?"

"He came to buy a bronchodilator for asthma and then he came back to ask me to explain about the side effects... You know, an excuse."

"Ha! Ha! You're the side effect! He's quite cute and you won't even be bothered by the in-laws!"

Roseline puts an end to this relationship a few months later. She thinks that the income from an antique shop is not reliable enough and she's afraid she'll end up with a larger financial participation than him in running the household! That reminds me of the time when we were together at school and she wouldn't share her croissants or brioches made by her father. I could tell her that a husband and wife ought to help each other, but she has decided to marry the God of Money, like the nuns marry Jesus.

"Roseline, one day, you'll regret it... (She shrugs) Do you want to come with me to a barbecue on Sunday? It's at one of the language teachers' place."

"Are they all in couples?"

"They also invite single people. I'm not keen to go on my own and you could meet someone with a regular income!"

"Are they nice?"

"Yes, on the whole. But there's a girl, Regine, who keeps making unpleasant remarks to me. She's an Italian teacher from another private school and she comes for a few lessons at our school."

"She's got someone?"

"Yeah. An older bloke with dosh. He buys her expensive stuff but you never see him."

"What remarks does she make?"

"Always about the way I dress. I don't know why. The others are very nice, we laugh a lot together but she always looks down at me."

"Is she ugly?"

"Not at all! Quite beautiful, she looks like Grace Kelly but with a very thin face, like a blade. Perhaps she's jealous because the foreign students like me a lot. Apparently she scares them and she bores them. Anyway, other teachers are very popular and she doesn't make any remarks to them, it's just to me...I don't understand!"

46 The Sword of Damocles

Another barbecue invitation! I enjoy more being in my class, explaining the rules of the past participle to bemused students. I tell them that if the direct object is before the avoir verb, it has time to warn the verb and to shout, "I am feminine and plural!" If the direct object is after the verb, it's too late to warn it, and you can't match the gender or the number. The Chinese and the Japanese students look at each other wondering whether I was serious or joking. Nevertheless they understand it now. Sometimes I happen to be ashamed of my own language, especially when I have to explain some of the rules with all their exceptions like the agreement of the plural for the days of the week. Even the foreign IT specialists from Sophia Antipolis are struggling, so to make French more attractive, I look for original texts like "The Djinns" by Victor Hugo where the words perform in a gothic concert. Or else "How to Teach French to American Students" by Ionesco, which makes them laugh every time. The Japanese appreciate Prevert's poems because they remind them of their own poems, the 'Haiku'.

Jean-Paul and his wife Chantal run the language school. While having my coffee in the staff room, I suggest that we invite the students to our parties. Most of them are our age, some older and all have difficulty meeting natives, especially if they are not working. They keep themselves to themselves as I used to when I was an au-pair. "One must not confuse wheat with chaff!" says one teacher. I am livid and protest. Has nothing changed since May 68? The teachers are still eating among themselves. And yet, they are all left wing! Their excuse is that we can't invite just a few, it has to be all or nobody. After long negotiations, they decide to invite one class at a time. We draw lots and it's my class that's the first one to be invited. There are only ten of them. Regine can't help saying that it would be a change for me not to come alone. She always comes alone but says it's because her boyfriend is a busy businessman.

Even if some can't make it, the students are pleasantly surprised to be invited. When I tell Fiona that it's taking place on the heights of Cagnes-sur-Mer, she asks me if she can take her brother because he is her chauffeur. Jean-Paul agrees and says he's delighted to receive Dr Hemingway. I am taken aback. I never knew that Fiona had a brother in France who was a doctor.

"He's not a Doctor of Medicine," says Jean-Paul, "he's a doctor in International Law, he's the British Consul. I met him when he came to register his sister in our school. Because of the way she looks, he was afraid we'd turn her down."

"Would you have done it?"

"Maybe, they turned her down at the secretarial college"

What a mentality! I make up my mind: I must go away. I will take the opportunity of meeting the Consul to ask him for some good tips about finding a job in England. I would prefer New York but it is too far and Isabelle is not there anymore. I am suffocating in my town where the hierarchy and the prejudices were not affected by May 68, where my friends go adrift without me and where I am living stuck between the sea and the mountain; two horizons that hide the world. Whenever I hear a plane, I follow it with my eyes and my heart beats faster.

Jean-Paul winks at me.

"He's not married."

"Who's that?"

"Fiona's brother, Dr Hemingway!"

"Handsome and intelligent! If he's not married, there must be a problem," Chantal comments.

"Yeah," replies Jean-Paul, "he's English,.. a queer probably!"

"Oh yeah, we're not like that in France," I say sarcastically, Oscar Wilde came to die in France because there are so many of them and we don't mind!"

"Yeah, if you like. About the party, it's not a barbecue, it's a mechoui[41].

I will go alone because Roseline wants to 'hunt' in the land of the 'Club Mediterranée'. I would love to go with her but she prefers to go alone. Jean-Paul invites Roger and his friends from the Faculty of Law. Mum has just made me a new white cotton outfit she copied from Courrèges. It's a mini tunic with hot pants. I roll up my Louis XIV curls in a short hair wig.

While I am held up on the 'voie rapide' -the new dual carriageway- by a traffic jam, some drivers take advantage of the situation to chat me up. It should give me confidence but their appearance depresses me even more. A Mercedes tank stops alongside me. Its driver is vulgar looking, full of himself with a skin dried by the sun. A Rolex watch is around his hairy wrist. He compliments me

---

41 Mechoui: a whole sheep spit-roasted. In the fashion after the arrival of the French from Algeria.

on my nail polish! Regine would say: "Sod off, dickhead," but life has taught me not to humiliate people.

When I arrive, a nice whiff of grilled meat comes to my nostrils. Jean-Paul comes over to me.

"Have you got the records?"

"Here they are."

I give him the Simon and Garfunkel albums. As usual Fiona is dressed up as a punk. Her shapeless hair is orange, she is wearing a mini black dress and psychedelic stickers on her legs.

"Aah Sophie j'adore your hot pants."

"Thanks… the mechoui smells nice."

"Oh yes. The meat is ready and je suis très faim."

"J'ai faim, Fiona. Did you come alone? I didn't see a car with CD plates[42]."

"We came in a side-car. James adore, come, je vais introduire lui à toi."

"Présenter, not introduire! Did he come with his wife?"

"He's not married anymore. They got married too early, too young, too quickly."

I thought sidecars were in museums only. No doubt that the brother's means of transport matches the sister's clothing. I quite like eccentricity. I catch sight of a tall man with a gangly figure, holding a glass at the end of his dangling arm. He's talking to Roger. As I approach him, he turns round and smiles at Fiona and me. James. I understand Chantal. Why is he alone? He's gorgeous. Distinguished but with the look of a spaghetti western cowboy. He says he's delighted to meet me as Fiona has

---

42 CD: Corps Diplomatique.

been talking about me for a long time. The conversation is easy.

I mention Oxford, he says he prefers Cambridge and my imitation of the Yorkshire accent makes him laugh. All of a sudden, I know for a fact that he is the one I want and the one who's not for me. At last, I understand Roseline's despair outside LeClezio's door. I quickly take control of myself, I am resigned, I get colder. I am determined to treat him as a pal and try to develop a feeling of virile friendship as I have with Roger.

It must be working because, instead of being interested in my bosom or my legs, he looks in my eyes.

Regine has just arrived. I can see her Grace Kelly silhouette in the distance with her stilettos and her Chanel bag on her shoulder. I almost find her too smart for a 'mechoui'. I know what's going to happen, so I anticipate and cut off the thread of the Damocles' sword hanging over me. I call her to introduce her to Dr Hemingway. She gives him a devastating smile and talks to him about the Italian Consul whose wife is her friend.

Their conversation is animated and therefore I withdraw. Chantal rushes to me to drag me to a group of her friends and she introduces me to one of them called Bernard. He was at the Faculty of Law when I was in Letters. We have a few common acquaintances. He's not bad but his eyes immediately scan my body. He says he's an Inspector of the Customs Office. He finds it very funny when I ask him on which border. He is in an office of a Ministry in Paris. He quickly asks me which beach I go to because he knows one with sand and few people.

The sun is ready. The sheep is setting on the Mediterranean... Hey, what am I saying? My eyes met Dr

Hemingway's. He is sharing a large cardboard plate with Regine. Everybody is eating with their fingers.

"You see, it's even better without mint sauce," I shout across to him.

He bursts out laughing and Regine exclaims: "Sophie, what's that outfit? You look about twelve like that!"

"Do you think I'm more elegant than Sophie?" asks Fiona.

Regine is stuck. She can't criticize or laugh at a student in public and, worse, in front of her brother. In a way, she's not wrong, whatever I wear, I look like a child and I am often asked to show my ID to prove my age. Regine is so much a woman.

Jean-Paul puts on the record of El Condor Passa and people start to dance. Bernard takes my waist without inviting me and we dance. Regine invites Dr Hemingway; I would never have dared. It hurts, even though I've prepared myself for a sad party. The next record is the marvellous Simon and Garfunkel's Scarborough Fair. I excuse myself and leave Bernard to get some Sangria drink. James puts his glass on the table and asks me to dance since Scarborough is in Yorkshire… I speak English to him and my accent makes him smile.

Despite myself, I feel again that emotion I had with John, a century ago, and we carry on dancing to the Sound of Silence.

> …In restless dreams I walked alone
> Narrow streets of cobblestone…

All the words of this song concern me and its poetry is far more beautiful than the Ne Me Quitte Pas[43] These are not Jacques Brel's desperate and servile words, just a little sweet and sour sadness about the loneliness of a city and the difficulty of communicating.

He doesn't hold me tight, he only holds my hand against his shoulder.

> ...Take my arms that I might reach you..

Regine is dancing with a Chinese student who's a businessman. She should have removed her stilettos, as the Chinese man just about reaches her neck. At about midnight, when she starts to dance a close dance with James to the music of Ray Charles's The Sun Died, I leave. Fiona is a bit drunk and half asleep on the sofa. Chantal sees me out.

"So, what about Bernard?"

"We've got a date on the beach."

"Fantastic!"

I follow the road along the sea front. While driving, I still can hear the Sound of the Silence in my head:

> Hello darkness, my old friend
> I've come to talk to you again..

In the darkness of the night, my daydreams bring me back the picture of a little blonde tennis player who stole my freckled boyfriend... In the vast black mirror of the Med, I can see John and William bringing me back to the beach. I stop the car, the beach is deserted, there is no one

---

43 'Ne me Quitte Pas' is Brel's classic song where a woman humiliates herself by asking her lover to stay with her. Nina Simone sings it in English.

now to take me back. Joyce's words about the sea come back to me "..the great sweet mother." All I have to do is to slip into its amniotic fluid... No, one must not do this kind of foolish thing when one has parents. I will leave, but not like that.

47 Knowing the Other

Another Christmas coming, heavy with sadness and solitude. I read, once, in a magazine, that Marilyn Monroe ate sometimes in a Hollywood canteen at Christmas on her own.

While Dad is on the sofa digesting his turkey while snoring, I take Mum to the Mercury cinema to see the Angelique, Marquise des Anges IV[44] with a box of 'petits fours'. The music of the film is as beautiful as the music of 'Gone With the Wind'. The Angelic films have a soothing effect; they lift me up like a fairy tale and don't make me think.

Fiona leaves with her brother to spend Christmas in London. Those two are weird. They only have one relative left, an uncle. Fiona tells me that their parents had put them in a boarding school at the age of seven. Then they died in a small plane crash. James was ten years older than his sister, so he took her out of the boarding school to send her to a college near him as a day girl. He said he had always suffered from being separated from his mother and didn't want Fiona to feel abandoned. She went to a strict and chic college that put her off wearing uniform or normal clothes 'for the rest of her life', as she puts it.

*

I haven't heard from Isabelle for three years now. I don't even know if she has disappeared in America or in

---

44 *Angelique, Marquise des Anges* IV: a swashbuckling historical romance. Was a best selling book, then a film.

Vietnam. Perhaps, I shouldn't have influenced the course of her life. We are hearing about peace negotiations taking place in Paris, with Kissinger and Le Duc Tho. And yet the B52s are dropping bombs non-stop. I take the opportunity of the regular Christmas card to Pam, one of the American teachers, to ask her if she has any news from William at least. She replies quite quickly to say that Isabelle has become friendly with the people of a village near Saigon. She helps them the best she can. She is happy to practise their language, the 'quoc ngu'. She is free to go anywhere and to take lots of photos. She is seeing William from time to time but the American authorities are concerned because she dresses like the women of the village. One day, she had to go aboard a helicopter with journalists and soldiers. When they returned to the base, William found her particularly dejected and one morning, she disappeared. All her belongings were left at the camp except her camera.

*

It's twelve, the end of the lessons. After lunch, I go to the staff room to have my coffee. I find Chantal all excited.

"Guess who's coming to see you? ... Bernaaaaaard!"

"Hello! How are you? I came from Paris for the weekend."

He invites me to the swimming pool in Monaco, on Saturday. It's smarter than the beach. I'm not that keen but I must go out and after all, he isn't bad. In the end, I should be lucky that a man like him can be interested in me. I ought to learn about him and to appreciate him. One of these days, I might have to go on the pill.

Despite the April sun on the Med, I am trembling. I don't know whether it's the cold or my terror on the Grande Corniche[45]. Bernard has a small convertible Volkswagen Beetle but he's convinced he has a Gordini turbo and that he's on the circuit of the Grand Prix de Monaco. He doesn't have time to change gear at the bends. At that speed, I'm not going to the swimming pool but straight to the cemetery. I try to think of something else but it's impossible because I can see the ravine that follows the road. If I say I'm scared, he will accelerate so I tell him I am feeling sick. It works and he slows down.

I feel silly with my one-piece smocked swimming suit. All the other girls are beautiful and already suntanned in bikinis. Bernard doesn't know which way to look. As for me, I am horrified to discover that his back, his chest and his shoulders are covered with hair. He also wears a chain with a kind of identification, probably a souvenir of military service. Well, it's time to go for a swim but above all, I don't want to get my hair wet!

"What's that?"

"My bathing cap."

"You're not going to swim with that, are you?"

"Yes I am, why?"

"That cap is ridiculous and you're the only one wearing one! This is not a beach for bumpkins, this is the Sporting Club[46]."

I realise that he must have paid a lot to get in there. Eventually I fix my hair on top of my head and I slip into the water cautiously. When I come out, he is lying on his

---

45 Winding road between Nice and Monaco.

46 A very selective place in Monte-Carlo.

330

towel, his hands under his head. Oh dear, what has he got under his arms? It looks as if his perspiration made a kind of yellow jelly coagulating on his armpit hairs. Like the pollen on the legs of bees. Is that possible? He sits up and removes his sunglasses.

"Why don't you shave your thighs?"

"I… and you, why don't you shave your armpits?"

"Since when do men shave under their arms?"

" Well, since perspiration makes wax."

The return is silent and horribly long. He takes the road along the sea because there are no bends but the traffic jams force him to drive slowly.

The next day, in the staff room, Chantal asks me why Bernard is pulling such a long face.

"Let's say we both lacked tact. By the way, why hasn't he got a girl friend?"

"Oh, it's an old story. He used to go out with a girl in the first year of Law. She is cute but above all, she's the Brunetti's daughter from the Brunetti Building Company that builds all the council housing in the town and built the Grand Hotel. He thought he had made it but, for her, he was only a flirt. She said a hors-d'œuvre!"

Apparently, they stayed good friends.

"Did she get married?"

"No. She's a solicitor's assistant. She tours all the nightclubs along the coast and goes boating with the Mayor's daughter - see what I mean? So, it didn't work with Bernard… It's a pity." Chantal insists:

"Still, you could see each other again perhaps… He comes every two weeks to see his mother and to go skiing, he loves it…"

"I don't!"

48 The Return

I thought she was missing or perhaps dead. She rings me from Paris.

"Hello! It's me!"

I am so happy that I keep talking about her to everybody: my friend, the war photographer and reporter in Vietnam.

I go to the airport. Again, the sight of planes taking off or landing makes my heart beat more quickly. A mellow voice announces the arrival of her plane. What happened? She hadn't wanted to say anything on the phone, just some trivial statements. Her calm voice didn't sound stressed at all. Here she comes. She is so…different. She walks with the style of a film adventurer. Her hair is short, she is wearing sunglasses, a multi-pockets waistcoat, khaki trousers and, on her fragile shoulder, a big camouflage-coloured bag. She used to rarely look happy but now she has a melancholic smile, almost happy. We hug.

"How are you? Going back to the Hostel?"

She smiles.

"I didn't think of asking you to book me a room in a hotel."

"Don't be silly, you're coming to my bedsit in the Old City. If you want to have a rest, I'll go to my parents and let you have the bedsit for yourself."

"Now, you're the silly one! Life is too short to have a rest. And you're not going away now we're together."

We hugged again. She laughs, I cry. Or is it the other way round?

There are, in the Nice countryside, lots of picturesque and lovely little villages, especially if you don't live in them. Peira-Cava is one of them. There are not many people and the view of the Turini Forest is like a Christmas card. Luckily the road is well maintained and despite a temperature of minus 5° at 1500m high, the coach doesn't need chains. We get to a little quaint hotel. Between Christmas and the New Year's Eve, the customers are scarce; they are all skiing in Auron. We take a minimum of stuff for three or four days.

We don't want to see anyone, just talking, "far from the madding crowd". A saw would be necessary to cut the mountain bread but it's the only bread in the world that tastes really like bread, concentrated bread. Like the taste of wild strawberries. We walk together in the forest. Without Isabelle, I would never find my way back. It takes her a whole day to start to speak about her life over there, so that when I tell her about my life but there's little to say.

We are sitting on the bed with the remains of our supper on a tray.

"Why did you stay so long without giving me any news?"

She explains how she had been so well accepted in this village near Saigon. She took hundreds of photos and gave a lot of them away to the village people. They all wanted to have their family portrait. Then, two teenagers from families she knew offered to take her further into the jungle to take photos. Curiosity killed the cat, she found herself among the Viets.

They were living in an underground village and also wanted photos. They had managed to get magazines and had read reports on Vietnam with Isabelle's photos in them.

They were very critical of the articles that they found to be stupid and naïve, far from all reality. Isabelle told them that she was responsible only for the photos. So they undertook to keep her as a prisoner to educate her.

She lived with them on the other side of the war, with the non-stop bombing and the hope of some negotiation but she kept thinking of William all the time.

" Thinking of William keeps me sane. When you share intense hunger, fear and fatigue, day after day, you start to doubt everything, but the people I was with never doubted. I did. I was hanging onto the time we had in Breil. "

I thought that she could have thought of me too.

"Eventually, we had to evacuate the village because the tunnels collapsed under the bombing. I ran away, taking advantage of the chaos. To my great surprise we were next to an American camp. I was taken to a hospital because of my burns, look –that's where I had my eczema! In the general panic, I left my camera behind but I kept some films. I should have done the opposite!.. Those films are burning me more than fire! If I give them to the Americans, I will be betraying the Vietnamese; if I give them to the Vietnamese, I betray the Americans. I'll give them to you and one day, you can give them to some journalist or historian."

"When?"

"Now if I disappear or in a few years. They are safer with you."

Two o'clock in the morning. We switch the light off. The room has cooled down and we sleep close to each other to keep warm. I am thinking of twins floating in their mum's womb.

The next evening, the hotelkeeper tells us about a local liquor, particularly strong, stronger than brandy and called 'Genepi'. It's made with various plants from the Alps. I buy a bottle because he insists and I think it would make an original gift.

We haven't bothered to wash for three days. I don't use tweezers and I haven't shaved my legs. Just talking, talking and digging into each other's mind. In the hotel, there's no bathroom but a basin in the bedroom and the WC is at the end of the corridor. That night we talk about men, about our past and our future, about life... I have a vague feeling that a night like this won't happen again, as if we were burying our youth...

"If I hadn't met John, I would have had no hope at all in men."

"Be patient. In a war, you quickly see the best and the worse. In time of peace, it takes you years."

"What about William?"

"He's great but I'm not sure any more of what I feel... The time we spent in Breil was so beautiful!"

"So beautiful and so far away."

"Don't you want to taste that Genepi?" Isabelle suggests.

"Have some if you like but not for me! Just to look at it makes my head spin."

She chuckles.

"What makes you laugh?"

"What you said earlier about Bernard the Hairy!" she says pouring two cups of Genepi.

"Yeah but he's a good man, I should have made an effort but I hurt him."

"To force yourself? Is that your idea of love?"

"No, of course but... (I look at myself in the mirror above the washbasin). Who would want that? Look, I've got bushy eyebrows, hairy legs like a yeti, frizzy hair and flannel pyjamas."

She laughs.

"Yes but that's temporary!"

"How do you manage to be naturally pretty all the time? I have to work at it all the time!"

Without thinking, I swallow the cup of Genepi. It burns my inside, making me cough and cry.

"All I need now is a cigarette to finish me off!"

Isabelle remains cool despite the alcohol.

"I'll have to leave again in a few days."

"Isabelle, please, let me go with you!"

"To America? You wouldn't dare. I'm going to get a contract, but what would you do?"

"I'll teach English and I'll cook for us,...oh dear, that stuff is strong..."

"Teach English?"

"I meant French, ... oh, la la, my head is spinning."

"What about Dr Hemingway?"

"Who?"

"The consulate... James!"

"Ha! You're joking! Let me drink à sa santé."

"Let's drink to the American Dream..."

"And the... British Dream," I say, emptying another cup.

"Sophie, someone is knocking on the door."

"So? Open the door then!"

The hotelkeeper's wife tells us that there's a gentleman downstairs who would like to know if it was too late to say hello.

"Oooh nooo! That's Bernard! He loves skiing… don't want to see that dickhead!"

"Did he tell you his name?" Isabelle asks the hotelkeeper.

"James something, he asked for mademoiselle Sophie."

"Ha! Ha! The bastard, he's playing a trick on me!"

"Does Bernard know him?"

"Er…, no, oooh nooo! That's not possible, not possible…"

I swallow another sip of the firewater.

"Alright, tell him to wait a minute, I'll come down," says Isabelle.

I go zigzagging along the corridor to the toilets and I vomit my meal and my despair. I hear Isabelle's voice behind me.

"Listen to me, stay here, you stink, I'll tell him that you are sick."

"Why now? Why, why? He's mad!"

Isabelle puts a jumper on top of her pyjamas and goes downstairs. What if I go down as well? After all, he's just a pal…that's right, I'll tell him… I'll say… James, I love you but I prefer the Gen,… the Genene…pi… we'll have a laugh. I manage to get up and to make it to the door with some hesitation. My pyjamas smells. Everything's spinning. On top of the stairs, I have vertigo and step back until I touch the wall and slip down on the floor…

The next morning, I wake up with a dry mouth. Isabelle brings me some mineral water.

"You must drink lots of water. The Americans taught me that we never drink enough water."

"Tell me, did I dream last night?"

"Do you remember anything?"

"I wasn't drunk, just tipsy. Did you talk about Dr Hemingway?"

"I had to take you back to bed and you fell asleep straight away."

"So, what about Dr Hemingway?"

"He was downstairs. A bit stern but charming! I told him you were sick and I asked him if he was staying in the area. He said he was only passing by."

"You're joking! At eleven at night! How did he know I'm here? What was eating him?"

"He might have come back from skiing."

"I can't believe it! What do I look like now?"

"You should apologize to him."

"How did he know I was here?"

"Dunno. Let's get dressed, I can smell coffee."

At that very minute, someone knocks on the door. I freeze in my pyjamas. It's the hotelkeeper's daughter this time. She says that a gentleman is asking for me downstairs.

"No, no, no! I can't believe it! It can't be him again! Did he sleep here? I can't go downstairs like that, no, no, no!"

"Come down! I'll talk to him."

"What are you going to say?"

"Don't know, I'll find something, get dressed."

She goes out. I don't know what to do, completely panicked. She comes back.

"You're still in your pyjamas! Don't worry, it's not him, it's your friend Bernard the Hairy."

"What? What does that bloke want now?"

"You are very much in demand," Isabelle says laughing, "he's come from Auron where he's been skiing, and he'd stop over on his way down to say hello."

"That's the best one!"

"No, the best one is that he offered me a lift back to town!

"He didn't! He drives like a nutcase! Winding roads are his speciality! And he doesn't even know you!"

"I know, you told me. I said I wasn't going to let you go back alone. He also asked me if we were going to Jean-Paul's party for New Years' Eve."

"What did you say?"

"Probably."

"Where is he now?"

"Gone. I said you were still asleep."

As the coach driver is going into the fourth bend, I stop cogitating on the why and the how of Dr Hemingway's visit. I thought he was in England. Still, nobody takes a mountain road by night! On the other hand, some English people do go into the Med for Christmas! After a pause, Isabelle advises me to go to the American Consulate to ask for a visa if I really intend to go with her. We start to make plans for the future: we will rent a small flat in New York, it will be like our au-pair year but more exciting. Ah girlfriends! They are like rocks when one is swimming in rapids. I send for my visa. It'll take three months. That's what I need to prepare my parents.

49 The Beginning of the End

It is D day when I have to go to the Consulate to apologize. Apologizing to the Consulate appears as the most important and necessary duty of my life. However beforehand, I have to be presentable. I go to the beautician who puts a camphor mask on my face to refine the texture of my skin. She leaves it too long and I find myself with a swollen and scarlet face. Embarrassed, she lets me go without paying. I run to Roseline's pharmacy, in a total panic, to beg her to give me something for my burning face. She cracks up.

"That's nice of you to laugh!"

"Don't worry, it'll disappear in a day or two. Put cold compresses on it."

Fortunately, it goes the next day. Then I want to have a sweet smelling bath but I put in too much of the stuff. When I hear Dad saying: "What's that disinfectant smell?" I go back in the shower to get rid of it.

When in town, I take my time to walk to the Consulate. I'm so scared. As I am passing the Delrieu's record shop, I hear Petula Clarke telling me:

When you're alone and life is making you lonely

You can always go, downtown….
The lights are much brighter there
You can forget all your trouble

Downtown…downtown…

The music and the words cheer me up. It's true, the lights of the shops and the murmur of the town carry me along. Deschannel, if you were here now, I would tell you that, despite their talent, your Jean Ferrat and Yves Montand[47] would have not pushed me forward to the Consulate.

I catch sight of the stone building with the Union Jack waving in the sea breeze. And what if I were to make a U turn? If I go in, what would be the difference? Aren't I getting into trouble, grief, and the torment of frustration again? On the other hand, it would be a pity if he didn't see my new knitted mini dress… I stand a long minute outside, then enter.

I ask the secretary if I could see Doctor Hemingway.

No, I haven't got an appointment, but I tell her that it's a private visit, I'm his sister's French teacher.

She takes the phone and tells him I'm there.

"Please sit down, he's going to see you in a moment."

I've just time to wipe my moist hands on my dress when a door opens.

"Ha, ha, Sophie, you're better today! Please, come in."

"Good afternoon Doctor Hemingway, I…"

"Please call me James!"

"Yes… I came because… for the other day…I wanted to apologize."

" Why? No need to! Your friend Isabelle explained it all to me. You took her to the mountain to cheer her up and you drowned her problems in Genepi! It's very kind of you. By the way I don't know that drink, you'll have to introduce me to it."

"But… I wasn't drunk, just sick… not really, but tipsy and… and…"

---

47 Communist melancholic song writers and poets.

He suddenly takes me in his arms and I dissolve. That's the day when I move to live on cloud nine.

Fiona had rung Mum who thought I was alone in Peira Cava; I didn't tell her I was with Isabelle. James was back from England. He was invited to a cocktail party in Auron and then he could not get away before eleven so he decided to visit me on the way down, just like that, without thinking. I decide not to think anymore, not to torture myself with questions, but to live day by day. If I am happy for sixth months at least, that is already something. In any case it's never for ever.

I always find it easy to describe misery but when it's happiness, that state of bliss making you goofy and light, I am confronted with a grammatical vacuum and an embarrassing lack of vocabulary. Living on a cloud deprives you of action and reflection. You only pay attention to your senses; your mind is floating, your body exulting and metamorphosing as if in adolescence. At last I put on weight. My fried-egg boobs turn into apples. I even get an appetite and eat more. This is a proof that love can have biological side effects.

It's only the beginning. We speak a lot about our lives, about films, music and… crêpes Suzette. I hold his hand like a life buoy, he holds mine like a connecting thread. When he kisses me, the cloud accelerates and I don't know any longer if the cloud is above, under or inside us.

His kindness and his attention are so new to me that I'm on my guard. Perhaps, he has a homosexual tendency as Jean-Paul says but Roseline reassures me: "Those must be indispensable qualities in the world of diplomacy!"

Jean-Paul and Chantal invite Isabelle and me for the New Year's Eve party. I am dreading it.

Fiona goes back to London to celebrate the New Year with her pals. Chantal tells me that Bernard is coming and bringing Cécile Brunetti but as a friend.

"He asked me to invite your friend Isabelle" says Chantal.

"Ah! So, he doesn't like me anymore then"

"I didn't want to tell you but he may fancy her."

"He's got no chance, she's going to America, she's got a contract with a magazine."

"Well, then, it's up to you to cheer him up!"

"Chantal…no, please."

"You don't like him anymore?"

"I'm in love with someone else."

"Oh really, who's that?"

"Doctor Hemingway."

"From the Consulate?"

"Yes."

She takes a pause and stares at me as if I've committed an irreversible crime.

"How come? Does he know?"

"Of course, I'm going out with him."

"I can't believe it! Why didn't you say anything? Has it been going on long?"

"A few days."

"Jesus! How did you manage?"

"Don't know. Just happened. Didn't do anything special. I didn't expect it."

"Me neither. It must be because his sister likes you. How is he? Nice?"

"No."

She looks relieved.

"Not nice, wonderful."

"Ah… Oh you know, it's always like that to begin with… Regine's going to make a funny face!"

"Why? She's got someone!"

"Yeah, but she fancied Hemingway a lot. She went to the Consulate a few times with an excuse to meet him."

"Really?"

"He didn't tell you? See, he's already hiding things from you!"

We go to the party as late as possible. We take Isabelle with us. We are both wearing a Chinese dress. Mine is blue velvet and Isabelle's red silk with black dragons. I attach a hairpiece to the nape of her neck with a silk orchid. She has her camera on her shoulder. Jean-Paul teases her and asks if it was her evening bag. Bernard walks towards us with a calculated nonchalance, I can see he's dying to run to her. He asks her if she wants to drink something and takes her to pour a glass of sangria. He just says a brief hello to me. There are quite a few people I don't know. James knows hardly anybody and yet he is feeling at ease. He introduces himself to groups and leads me with him in conversation. He introduces me as his girlfriend. I am amazed, I thought he would want to hide our relationship. I have the impression I'm at the house of his friends. Chantal asks me to give her a hand in the kitchen. I am a bit annoyed but don't dare to say no. She speaks non-stop as if to keep my attention and I have to avoid answering questions that are too personal. Strange of her, she has never showed a particular interest in me. When I have finished arranging the canapés on the trays, I leave the kitchen briskly and I see James talking to a very smart young lady. She looks like a heroine from an

American series. Bernard calls my name while he's dancing with Isabelle.

"Sophie! Go and try this new sangria. Isabelle and I invented a new recipe."

"You'll see how nice it is" Jean-Paul says.

"I'd rather not. I can't take alcohol and I don't like it!"

"It's not as strong as Genepi," he says with a smile and he invites me for a dance.

Oh no! I don't want to dance with anybody. In the distance I see James bowing before Cécile the starlet before coming towards me. I let go of Jean-Paul immediately with an apology.

At midnight we go on the terrace of the villa to see the fireworks shot out over the sea and to drink Champagne. I think I notice a brief absence of mind from James but he holds me tight and wishes me a tender Happy New Year. He dances with nobody but me, and yet without over demonstrating his feelings in public. I notice Cécile looking at him several times. I ask Chantal who she is.

"Oh I forgot to tell you! This is Cécile Brunetti. Bernard introduced her to Dr Hemingway."

A moment later, when James and I are talking to a couple of British students, Chantal comes again to fetch me; now she wants me to help her to find her ear-ring that dropped in the corridor. Again, in the distance, I see Cécile joining the group where James is talking to the students. After a few minutes, I firmly say to Chantal that I can't find her ear-ring and go back to James. He puts his arm round my shoulders and asks: "OK?" I say yes and Cécile introduces herself to me with a forced smile.

At about two, we leave. In the car, James asks me to come round for tea the next day at the Consulate.

For the New Year's Day, Isabelle comes to eat at my parents' and Mum tries her best to be amicable. Then in the late afternoon, I walk with her to the bedsit and I make my way to the Consulate. When I get there, everything is closed. I ring at the back door but nobody answers. I wait for an hour and I go back to the bedsit and find Isabelle slumped in front of the TV. She tries to cheer me up. She is convinced that there must have been an unexpected problem.

A few days later, I see her to the airport.

"I'm not happy to leave you behind but if he didn't want to see you again, he would not do it that way. I told you, he must have had a problem."

"What do we know about him? It's been three days that the secretary has said he's not available... you're going away and he's disappearing..."

"Stay at your parents' so that I can ring you and... if things don't get better, just join me. Your visa is on its way. It's going to be my turn to pick you up at the airport."

"Yeah, I don't have anything to lose."

"Like me. That's freedom."

Taking Isabelle to the airport is painfully sad. While I was driving her, Isabelle was telling me about this flat in New York where we might start a new life together. It sounds unrealistic.

"At least, come for a year, then you'll see better what you want to do."

Yeah, I do need to know what I want to do. The soft voice announces Isabelle's plane departure.

"I don't think you will come."

"Yes, I will. What have I got to lose? I'll tell Mum it's for a year only."

"Drive back carefully, the rain is bad."

"I wish I could tell the same to the pilot of your plane!"

We hug a long minute. The wretched little girl from Prisunic. Frail and strong.

"Take care."

On the way back, I drive along the Promenade. An icing wind blowing from the sea is bringing in a salty rain. I am amazed to see huge stones, almost rocks, littering the road and the pavement. The beach has completely disappeared, swallowed up. By the light of the street lamps, I can see gigantic waves emerging from the darkness. They rear their heads, roll in towards the Promenade wall and break on the road in a thunderous mass of foam, only ten metres away from me. On this side of the road there is safety, calm, lights from the blocks of flats and shops. Only a few paces away, there is a liquid chaos, a cold, black and mortal danger. You only have to cross the road to be dragged off into eternity. How can it be the same sea, peaceful, cobalt blue and so soothing when the July sun beats down on you? When you lie on its edge, it comes and caresses you with the tip of its insignificant foam, just a few bubbles burst and the water retreats six inches to catch its breath. For me, today, only the sea can show how close death and life are.

The next day, I resist the temptation to go back to the Consulate until three in the afternoon, then I try again, a last time. It's open. My heart misses a beat. I go in. The secretary gives me a big diplomatic smile and wishes me a Happy New Year.

"Is James here?" I ask with great embarrassment.

"Ah, you didn't know! He had to leave suddenly for London because his sister Fiona had a problem."

She rolls her eyes. I am greatly relieved despite my anxiety for Fiona.

"He will talk to you about it himself. He arrived this morning and had to go to a business drink at the Brunetti's. Their villa is in Saint Jean-Cap-Ferrat. He said that the Mayor and an advisor from the Monaco government are there. I'll tell him you dropped in."

I feel myself tipping off the edge again but put a detached look on and say goodbye. Then the angst overcomes me. No, it's over… no more grief. Nobody is going to destroy me. I sit down on a bench in the 'Albert Premier' Garden. Bernard knew what he was doing by introducing Cécile to James. I will not go back to the Consulate, I will not go to my parents' place to wait for a phone call. In fact I'm going to start preparing my departure to join Isabelle. I go to the Galeries Lafayette to choose a suitcase and a bag.

James comes back in the evening, to the bedsit. He has a large box of Marquise de Sévigné chocolates and the latest Beatle's single, Let It Be. We look at each other intensely. I don't make any movement towards him. He steps in and shut the door behind him. I hear that he had to rush away because Fiona took an overdose but she will come back here and try to resume a normal life. Cecile Brunetti told him that I intended to go to America with Isabelle How did she know? James checked with the US Consulate and was told that it was true. He went to the Brunetti's because the invitation was professional and he was feeling dejected. The meeting was about discussing the conditions of establishing an office in London for building entrepreneurs. Eventually, he realised he was of no use to this project and that Cecile had other intentions. She didn't behave like a lady and James left abruptly, exasperated by her bold manners. With a mocking smile he says he avoided a diplomatic incident. I immediately thought of Lady de Winter seducing the Puritan Felton in the Three Musketeers. But James was smarter than Felton.

That night, we climb back on to our cloud nine, taking us far away in an unexplored space of the galaxy of the senses. Where magnetic storms weld bodies, the lightning annihilates them and the summer rains bring them back to life.

50 A Letter

London, 14th July 2028

Dear M. Bianchi,

Thanks for your email. I was a bit surprised you wanted to know what happened to Mum after she married Dad, since we don't intend to publish her manuscript for the moment. My brother John insisted I send it to you because you were one of Dad's best friends before he worked at the Consulate in the South of France. I didn't know you were also a publisher.

I had to ask my aunt Fiona for some details. They got married in the Anglican Church and Mum was disappointed that only a few of her girlfriends turned up. Still there were lots of people.

She used to say it was too good to last and yet they stayed happily together for 49 years. Mum, John and I followed Dad in his posts abroad, then he changed his career to work in Whitehall, so that we would have an uninterrupted education. Dad died from a stroke and it didn't take long for Mum to follow him. She had lost sight of most of her friends. She never recovered from Isabelle's disappearance. She had some of her photos covering riots in Salvador. Dad did everything he could to get people to find her body among the murdered nuns. All that was found was her camera with the film.

Mum always thought that one day she would knock at the door! I've also got some videos taken in the Vietnam war.

During my last holidays in Nice, I heard that Roseline had remained single and was in a nursing home for Alzheimer sufferers. Did you hear that Le Clezio, the love of her life, got the Nobel Prize for Literature in 2008? The most shocking thing was to find out that Marilene and her husband, both died of AIDs. They had a son.

My brother John is an international lawyer and he's just got married. As for me, I am a social worker and single.

Kind Regards,

Isabelle Hemingway

22392715R00215

Printed in Great Britain
by Amazon